Conspiracy

Also by De'nesha Diamond

The Diva Series
Hustlin' Divas
Street Divas
Gangsta Divas
Boss Divas
King Divas
Queen Divas

Anthologies
Heartbreaker (with Erick S. Gray and Nichelle Walker)
Heist (with Kiki Swinson)
Heist 2 (with Kiki Swinson)
A Gangster and a Gentleman (with Kiki Swinson)
Fistful of Benjamins (with Kiki Swinson)

Published by Kensington Publishing Corp.

Conspiracy

WITHDRAWN

DE'NESHA
DIAMOND

KENSINGTON PUBLISHING CORP.
www.kensingtonbooks.com

DAFINA BOOKS are published by

Kensington Publishing Corp.
119 West 40th Street
New York, NY 10018

All Kensington titles, imprints, and distributed lines are available at special quantity discounts for bulk purchases for sales promotion, premiums, fund-raising, and educational or institutional use.

Special book excerpts or customized printings can also be created to fit specific needs. For details, write or phone the office of the Kensington Sales Manager: Kensington Publishing Corp., 119 West 40th Street, New York, NY 10018. Attn. Sales Department. Phone: 1-800-221-2647.

Dafina and the Dafina logo Reg. U.S. Pat. & TM Off.

ISBN-13: 978-1-4967-0582-2
ISBN-10: 1-4967-0582-3
First Kensington Trade Paperback Printing: January 2017

eISBN-13: 978-1-4967-0584-6
eISBN-10: 1-4967-0584-X
First Kensington Electronic Edition: January 2017

10 9 8 7 6 5 4 3 2 1

Printed in the United States of America

This novel is dedicated to my sister, Channon Kennedy.
I would be lost without you.

Author's Note

Most of the action in the novel takes place in Washington, D.C., but certain liberties have been taken in portraying the city itself and its institutions. This is wholly intentional. The world presented here is a fictitious one, as are its characters and events.

PART ONE

Monsters All Around . . .

1

Washington, D.C
Winter

A scared and hungry fourteen-year-old Abrianna Parker stepped out of Union Station and into the dead of night. The exhilaration she'd felt a mere hour ago evaporated the second D.C.'s blistering wind sliced through her thin leather jacket and settled somewhere in her bones' marrow. A new reality slammed into her with the force of a ton of bricks—and left her reeling.

"Where is he?" she whispered as she scanned the growing crowd. Abrianna was more than an hour late to meet Shawn, but it couldn't have been helped. Leaving her home had proved to be much harder than she'd originally realized. After several close calls, she'd managed to escape the house of horrors with a steel determination to never look back. Nothing could ever make her return.

Now it appeared that she'd missed her chance to link up with her best friend from school, or rather they used to go the same high school, before Shawn's father discovered that he was gay, beat the hell out of him, and then threw him out of the house. Miraculously, Shawn had said that it was the best thing to have ever happened to him. Over the past year, he'd found other teenagers like him living out on the streets of D.C. His eclectic group of friends was better than any blood family, he'd boasted often during their frequent text messages.

In fact, Shawn's emancipation from his parent had planted the seeds in Abrianna's head that she could do the same thing. Gathering the courage, however, was a different story. The prospect of punishment, if she was caught, had paralyzed her on her first two attempts and had left Shawn waiting for her arrival in vain. Maybe he thought she'd lost her nerve tonight as well. Had she thought to charge her battery before leaving the house, she would be able to text him now to find out where he was.

Abrianna's gaze skimmed through the hustle and bustle of the crowd, the taxis and cars. Everyone, it seemed, was in a hurry. Likely, they wanted to meet up with family and friends. It was an hour before midnight. There was a certain kind of excitement that only New Year's Eve could bring: the tangible *hope* that, at the stroke of midnight, everyone *magically* changed into better people and entered into better circumstances than the previous year.

Tonight, Abrianna was no different.

With no sight of Shawn, tears splashed over Abrianna's lashes but froze on her cheeks. Despite a leather coat lined with faux fur, a wool cap, and leather gloves, Abrianna may as well have been butt-ass naked for all the protection it provided. "Goddamn it," she hissed, creating thick frost clouds in front of her face. "Now what?"

The question looped in her head a few times, but the voice that had compelled her to climb out her bedroom window had no answer. She was on her own.

Someone slammed into her from behind—hard.

"Hey," she shouted, tumbling forward. After righting herself on frozen legs, she spun around to curse at the rude asshole—

but the assailant was gone. She was stuck looking around, mean-mugging people until they looked at her suspect.

A sudden gust of wind plunged the temperature lower and numbed her face. She pulled her coat collar up, but it didn't help.

The crowd ebbed and flowed, but she stood in one spot like she'd grown roots, still not knowing what to do. And after another twenty minutes, she felt stupid—and cold. Mostly cold.

Go back into the station—thaw out and think. However, when she looked at the large and imposing station, she couldn't get herself to put one foot in front of the other. She had the overwhelming sense that her returning inside would be a sign of defeat, because, once she was inside, it wouldn't be too hard to convince herself to get back on the train, go home and let *him* win . . . again.

Icy tears skipped down her face. *I can't go back.* Forcing her head down, she walked. She passed commuters yelling for cabs, huddled friends laughing—some singing, with no destination in mind. East of the station was bathed in complete darkness. She could barely make out anything in front of her. The only way she could deal with her growing fear was to ignore it. Ignore how its large, skeletal fingers wrapped around her throat. Ignore how it twisted her stomach into knots. Ignore how it scraped her spine raw.

Just keep walking.

"Help me," a feeble voice called out. "Help!"

Abrianna glanced around, not sure from which direction the voice had come. *Am I losing my mind now?*

"Help. I'm not drunk!"

It came from her right, in the middle of the road, where cars and taxis crept.

"I'm not drunk!" the voice yelled.

Finally, she made out a body lying next to a concrete divider—the kind work crews used to block off construction areas.

"Help. Please!"

Again, Abrianna looked around the crowds of people streaming past. Didn't anyone else hear this guy? Even though that side of the building was dark, it was still heavily populated. Why was no one else responding to this guy's cry for help?

"Help. I'm not drunk!"

Timidly, she stepped off the sidewalk and skulked into the street. As vehicles headed toward her, she held up her hand to stop some and weaved in between others. Finally, Abrianna stood above a crumpled old man, in the middle of the road, and was at a loss as to what to do.

"I'm not drunk. I'm a diabetic. Can you help me up?" the man asked.

"Uh, sure." She knelt, despite fear, and asked, *What if it's a trap?*

It *could* be a trap, Abrianna reasoned even as she wrapped one of the guy's arms around her neck. Then, using all of her strength, she tried to help him to his feet, but couldn't. A Good Samaritan materialized out of nowhere to help her out.

"Whoa, man. Are you okay?" the stranger asked.

Abrianna caught glimpse of the Good Samaritan's shoulder-length stringy blond hair as a passing cab's headlights rolled by. He was ghost white with ugly pockmarks.

"Yes. Yes," the fallen guy assured. "It's my blood sugar. If you could just help me back over to the sidewalk that would be great."

"Sure. No problem," the blond stranger said.

Together, they helped the old black man back across the street.

"Thank you. I really appreciate this."

"No problem," the white guy said, his teeth briefly illuminated by another passing car as a smoker's yellow.

Once back on the sidewalk, he released the old man. "You two have a happy New Year!" As quick as the blond savior had appeared, he disappeared back into the moving crowd.

The old guy, huffing and puffing thick frost clouds, wrapped his hand around a NO PARKING sign and leaned against it.

"Are you sure you're all right?" Abrianna asked. It seemed wrong to leave him like this.

He nodded. "I'm a little dizzy, but it will pass. Thank you now."

That should be that. She had done what she could for the man. It was best that she was on her way. But she didn't move— probably because he didn't *look* okay.

As she suspected, he started sliding down the pole, his legs giving out. Abrianna wrapped his arm back around her neck to hold him up. "I got you," she said. But the question was: for how long?

"Thank you, child. Thank you."

Again, she didn't know what to do next. Maybe she should take him up to the station. At least, inside, she could get him to a bench or chair to sit down. "Can you walk?"

"Yes. I—I think so."

"No. No. Not back there," he said, refusing to move in the direction of the station. "They done already kicked me out tonight and threatened to lock me up if I return."

His words hit her strange. "What do you mean?"

He sighed. "Let's just go the other way."

With little choice, she did as he asked. It took a while, but the man's stench finally drifted under her nose. It was a strange, sour body odor that fucked with her gag reflexes. "Where do you want me to take you?" she asked, growing tired as he placed more and more of his weight on her shoulders.

When the old man didn't answer, she assumed he hadn't heard her. "Where are you trying to go?"

"Well . . . to be honest. Nowhere in particular," he said. "Just somewhere I can rest this old body and stay warm tonight. I read in one of the papers that it's supposed to dip down to nine degrees."

It hit her. "You don't have anywhere to sleep?"

"Well—of course I do. These here streets are my home. I got a big open sky as my roof, some good, hard concrete or soft grass as my floor. The rest usually takes care of itself." He chuckled—a mistake, judging by the way it set off the most go-dawful cough she'd ever heard.

They stopped when the coughing continued. Abrianna swore something rattled inside of his chest.

"Are you all right?" she asked. "Do you need a doctor?"

More coughing. *Are his lungs trying to come up?*

After what seemed like forever, he stopped, wheezed for air, and then wiped his face. "Sorry about that," he said, sounding embarrassed.

"It's okay," she said, resuming their walk.

"I really appreciate you for helping me out like this. I know I must be keeping you from wherever it is you're trying to get to. It's New Year's Eve and all."

"No. It's all right. I don't mind."

He twisted his head toward her and, despite the growing dark, she could make out his eyes scrutinizing her. "You're awfully *young* to be out here by yourself."

Abrianna ignored the comment and kept walking.

"How old are you?" he asked.

"Why?" she snapped, ready to drop him right there on the sidewalk and take off.

"Because you look like my grandbaby the last time I saw her. 'Bout sixteen, I'd say she was."

Abrianna jutted up her chin.

"She had a beautiful heart, too." He smiled. "Never could see any person or animal hurting."

The unexpected praise made her smile.

"Ah, yeah. A beautiful smile to boot."

They crossed the street to Second Avenue. She'd gotten used to his weight already, appreciated the extra body heat—but the *stench* still made her eyes water. *Did he say that it was going to get down to nine degrees tonight?* Abrianna had stolen cash from her house before she'd left, but hadn't had time to count all of it. Maybe she could get a hotel room—just for the night. After that, she would have to be careful about her finances. Once the money was gone—it was gone. She had no idea on how she and Shawn were going to get more.

Still walking, Abrianna pulled herself out of her troubled thoughts to realize that she and the old man had entered a park—a dark park—away from the streaming holiday crowd.

"Where are we going?" she asked, trying not to sound alarmed.

"Oh, just over there on that bench is fine." The old man pointed a shaky finger to their right. When they reached it, he dropped onto the iron bench like a sack of bricks and panted out more frosted air. "Whew," he exclaimed.

"That walk is getting harder and harder every day."

"You come here often?" Abrianna glanced around, catching a few figures, strolling. "Is it safe?"

"That depends," he said, patting the empty space next to him. She took the hint and plopped down. "Depends on what?"

"On your definition of safe," he chuckled and set off another series of hard-to-listen-to coughs.

Abrianna wished that he'd stop trying to be a jokester. His lungs couldn't handle it. She watched him go through another painful episode.

At the end, he swore, "Goddamn it." Then he was contrite. "Oh. Sorry about that, sweetheart."

Smiling, she clued him in, "I've heard worse."

He nodded. "I reckon you have. Kids nowadays have heard and seen it all long *before* puberty hits. That's the problem: The world don't got no innocence anymore."

"Doesn't have any," she corrected him.

He chuckled. "Beauty and brains. You're a hell of a combination, kid."

Abrianna warmed toward the old man.

"Trouble at home?" he asked, his black gaze steady on her.

"No," she lied without really selling it. Why should she care if he believed her? In a few minutes, she'd probably never see him again.

"Nah. I didn't think so," he played along. "You don't look like the type who would needlessly worry her parents."

Abrianna sprung to her feet. "Looks like you're cool here. I gotta get going and find my friend."

"So the parents are off limits, huh?" He nodded. "Got it."

She stared at him, figuring out whether he was working an angle. Probably. Older people always did.

"It's tough out here, kid." His eyes turned sad before he added, "Dangerous too."

"I'm not looking for a speech."

"Fair enough." He pulled in a deep breath. "It's hypothermia season. Do you know what this is?"

"Yeah," Abrianna lied again.

"It means that folks can freeze to death out here—and often do. If you got somewhere safe to go, then I suggest you go there tonight. I'd hate to see someone as pretty as you wind up down at the morgue."

"I can take care of myself."

"Yeah? Have you ever done it before?"

"You sure do ask a lot of questions," she said.

"Believe it or not, you're not the first person to tell me that—bad habit, I suppose. But I've gotten too old to change now."

"What about you?" Abrianna challenged. "Aren't you afraid of freezing to death?"

He laughed, this time managing not to choke over his lungs. "Oh, I *wish*—but the devil don't want nothing to do with me these days. I keep expecting to see him, but he never comes."

"You talk like you want to die."

"It's not about what I want, little girl. It's just time, that's all," he said quietly.

Abrianna didn't know what to say to that—but she did know that she could no longer feel her face. "Well, I gotta go."

He nodded. "I understand. You take care of yourself—and if you decide to stay out here—trust *no one*."

She nodded and backpedaled away. It still felt wrong to leave the old guy there—especially if that whole freezing-to-death stuff was true. At that moment, it felt true.

The hotels were packed—or wanted nearly three hundred dollars for *one* night. That was more than half of Abrianna's money, she found out. At the last hotel, she agreed to the figure, but then they wanted to see some sort of ID. The front desk woman suggested she try a *motel* in another district—or a shelter.

An hour later, Abrianna was lost. Walking and crying through a row of creepy-looking houses, she had no idea where she was or where she was going.

Suddenly, gunshots were fired.

Abrianna ran and ducked down a dark alley.

Tires squealed.

Seconds later, a car roared past her.

More gunshots fired.

The back window of the fleeing muscle car exploded. The driver swerved and flew up onto a curb, and rammed headlong into a utility pole.

Bam!

The ground shook and the entire row of streetlights went out.

No way the driver survived that shit. Extending her neck around the corner of a house, Abrianna attempted to get a better look at what was going on, but at the sound of rushing feet pounding the concrete, she ducked back so that she could peep the scene. She counted seven guys running up to the car. When they reached the driver's side, a rumble of angry voices filled the night before they released another round of gunfire.

Holy shit. Abrianna backed away, spun around, and ran smack into a solid body.

The pockmarked Good Samaritan materialized out of the shadow. "Hey there, little girl. Remember me?"

Abrianna screamed. . . .

2

Spring

Abrianna begged for death.

She had long stopped counting the days and nights. There really wasn't a point. Each tick of the clock made it clear that she would die in this dark, dank dungeon of a basement. The only question was, when?

The door creaked open, emitting only a sliver of light into the room before the pasty, skeletal figure of a man entered. Another night of torture was about to begin.

"How are my ladies doing tonight?" he asked. The voice alone sent fear goosing across everyone's body.

Chains rattled.

Three women manacled to the walls squirmed to get away. Not Abrianna.

Her gaze followed the man's flickering candlelight attentively. She was weary—and afraid. But for some unknown reason, she refused to let that fear show. The simple act of defiance gave her power. Not much—but it was there.

Her refusal to cry out or beg for mercy often got under her captor's skin. In the first few weeks of her kidnapping, he'd marveled at the number of lashes or electric shocks she could take before passing out cold.

The man thought himself a scientist. Almost daily, he concocted some crazy mix of poison and got off injecting them with it as if they were a group of test animals.

Two girls had died since Abrianna's abduction.

Maybe tonight, she would be next.

"Which of you wants to be my little guinea pig tonight?" He stopped before one girl. A white girl—blond. "How about you?" He moved the candle in close to her face and smiled when she attempted to twist away. Her chains didn't let her go far.

"Aww. My pet. Don't you want to play with me?"

"Oh, God! Please don't," she begged.

The skeletal man shifted the candle and leaned forward to roll his tongue up the side of her face.

The girl quivered and cried.

Abrianna looked on in disgust, her empty belly flopping.

"No. I don't think that I'll play with you tonight," he informed the blonde, as if he'd been disappointed by her taste.

He moved to the next girl and repeated the same sick performance before the candle. Then his attention focused on Abrianna.

"Noooo. I think I'd rather play with *you* tonight," he announced, creeping in her direction.

Inwardly, Abrianna screeched in horror. Outwardly, she watched his approach with something akin to cool indifference.

"My tough little black angel," he cooed, placing the flickering flame so close that it burned her right cheek.

Abrianna winced, but said nothing.

He laughed. "Oh, I like you," he praised. "And I got something that I think you're going to like." He held something else up but she was unable to make it out. At this point, she didn't have to. It was a syringe—filled with his latest creation.

Despite the prayers for death, Abrianna was terrified.

But she was ready.

Her life had been nothing but one vast cosmic joke. Why not end it? Once she ascended, maybe she'd see her baby brother again—since she hadn't been able to save him.

A key rattled in Abrianna's locks, and minutes later, she went from being chained to the wall to being locked down on a metal table. Tears streamed, but the candle wasn't near her face so her captor didn't see. However, Abrianna could still hear and *smell* him.

Finally, the lone light in the room clicked on, but the grime and dust bunnies clinging to the exposed bulb dimmed the wattage it emitted.

"This little baby should drive you wild," their captor bragged, holding up the syringe again. "Dr. Z helped me make this beauty."

Abrianna stared at the pink liquid.

"Now this may pinch a little—or hurt an *awful* lot," he laughed. Without bothering to look for a vein, he stabbed the side of Abrianna's shoulder and jabbed the plunger, emptying the entire syringe.

The drug was like a fireball blazing through her veins.

Abrianna gasped—but her lungs seemed incapable of processing the oxygen that she desperately needed. Within seconds, she thrashed and convulsed—violently.

The man's maniacal laughter filled her head. Soon, the arm and feet shackles bit into her skin, threatening to break bones. In her mind's eye, the light above her went from a dull yellow to a blinding bright light. She looked away, but it was everywhere—even when she was sure she'd closed her eyes.

The all-consuming pain wrenched her body mercilessly.

She didn't know if her abductor had finally succeeded in breaking her. She heard nothing. Saw nothing.

For an eternity.

3

Washington, D.C.
Summer

Darkness descended over the quiet streets of Benning Heights, approximately twenty miles outside downtown Washington, D.C. A Seventh District police van turned the corner onto Benning Road and braked in front of a pale yellow vinyl 1930s colonial house. A second later, the back doors burst open. "Move it! Move it!" Lieutenant Gizella Castillo barked, ushering the ten-man crew out of the van. Geared up, they fell into position. Four of them, carrying a battering ram, rushed up the residence's stone stairs first.

Lieutenant Castillo's heart hammered in triple time while the hairs on the back of her neck stood at attention. A lot rode on this shit—mainly her career. Hours from a suspension, she committed to this ultimate Hail Mary to bring down Craig Avery—a creepy ex-scientist turned drug dealer, who not only had powerful political friends. For the past six months, as Castillo's missing teenager cases piled up, she'd habitually stepped on toes and pissed off her own police chief by refusing to eliminate Avery from the list of suspects. There were just too many damn coincidences and holes in the man's story to add up. Avery had a history of stalking schools and harassing minors. However, none of it had landed the man behind bars. Castillo believed that was only because Avery had selected the perfect victims. Lost girls. Runaways.

Girls who had no one to look out for them. Girls who had no power or hope. The few they had found had been broken, tortured, and dead.

Avery dumped their bodies in various places around D.C. whenever he finished with them. The bastard.

But there were a few girls still missing.

The smug bastard was so sure that no one cared what happened to these girls. But he was wrong about that. Castillo cared. She'd spent the past two years vowing that she would not only find them, but also take down the man who preyed upon the nation's capital. So what if she'd forged a judge's signature on a search warrant? The missing girls were in this house. She was certain of it.

With a few hard strikes of the battering ram, the front door to the colonial house blasted off of its hinges. "Police!" the officers yelled into the dark house.

Everyone reeled from the horrible smell. It was an awful combination of funk and rot.

Jackpot!

But was anyone still alive?

Elated but scared of what was actually rotting in the house, they moved in.

Three officers climbed the staircase to the second level, three searched the main floor, and three kicked open the door leading to the basement.

Castillo made the split-second decision to go upstairs behind the first set of officers. She got no more than halfway up when bullets rang out. Two slammed into the plaster wall, inches from her head.

All hell broke loose as her team returned fire.

It was hard to see what was happening since the staircase was dark. Castillo finally got a lock on a figure darting across the landing and recognized the man instantly as Craig Avery. The muthafucka wore only a pair of yellow-stained tighty-whities, but fired with a *Dirty Harry* silver revolver. Castillo and her team returned fire, splintering the banister and puncturing various walls. She fired and was certain that one of her bullets nailed his left shoulder. Avery retaliated. His aim was random, but he managed to hit Officer Clemmons. He tumbled back down the stairs, swiping her legs from underneath her like a bowling ball. She fired off a shot, but she had no idea where the bullet actually went because she was tossed back down the stairs with the other fallen officer. The three officers from the main floor redirected and jumped over her to rush up the staircase and join the action.

It seemed like she was down forever, but in truth it was likely no more than a few seconds. Lieutenant Castillo glanced at Clemmons and knew before placing her fingers against the side of his neck that he was dead.

"Fuck." His death was on her. A door slammed somewhere as more bullets were fired. Castillo jumped to her feet and started up the staircase again. Once again, halfway up . . .

BOOM!

Lifted off of her feet and blasted back over Officer Clemmons's body, she slammed into a wall and sank like a stone to the floor.

Five more officers—gone.

For a second time, she climbed back onto her feet, but her ears rang like Gabriel's trumpet. This colossal fuck-up would no doubt cost her her badge.

Castillo swiped away dust and debris that was doing a bang-up job of clogging her lungs. She shook her head several times to stop her ears from ringing, but it didn't work. As a result, she struggled for equilibrium.

Wrapping a hand around the railing, Castillo leaned her weight against it and pulled up two steps. A hand gripped her arm. She jumped and turned, wide-eyed.

Officer Dennis Holder mouthed something. She hadn't even heard him or officers Moore and Stevens rush back up from the basement.

"WHAT?" Panic hit her at the realization that she couldn't hear herself speak either.

Holder shouted again.

Lieutenant Castillo shook her head, wiggled a finger into her right ear as if it would jimmy something loose.

It didn't.

Impatient, the other officers, Moore and Stevens, jetted past them and up the staircase to check on the rest of their team.

"Are you all right?" Holder shouted, but sounded like it was from the bottom of a deep well. He touched the side of her face.

Castillo flinched, the pain shocking. When Holder drew back his hand, her blood painted his fingers. *I've been hit?*

Incredulous, she touched her face, but whatever it was—either a bullet or shrapnel—had only grazed her head. "I'm okay," she shouted back, giving him the thumbs-up.

"You need to come down to the . . ."

"WHAT?" She jabbed her finger inside of her ear again.

Holder grabbed her and pulled her in the opposite direction of the staircase.

"Wait! My men!"

Holder's steel grip led her in the opposite direction. She stopped resisting and followed. The house's foul smell grew stronger the closer they edged toward the door leading to the basement.

At the top of the stairs, there was a pale orange glow that gave the basement a more dungeon-like ambience. Castillo's heart skipped while the hackles rose on the back of her neck.

The remaining missing girls rushed to the front of her mind, but she was unable to voice the dreaded question to Holder. *Are they dead?* Instead, she silently followed him down the steep staircase.

The gray cement floor was splattered with what was unmistakably dried blood. The flickering light bulb couldn't be giving out more than forty watts, which forced her to widen her eyes so that she could see more than just shadows.

Foreign torture apparatuses and metal chains hung from both the ceiling and the walls. Moving around the smelly and claustrophobic basement made Castillo's stomach roll with nauseous acidic waves, but she kept it together. When Holder touched her shoulder again, though, she jumped ten feet into the air.

"Over there," he said, his voice almost normal as the ringing finally faded.

Castillo's gaze followed his pointed finger toward the right corner, where three young girls sat huddled naked with their bony knees shielding half their faces and with metal collars locked around their necks.

Relieved, Castillo felt her knees nearly collapse. "Thank God. We found them."

4

Judgment day. Once again, the courtroom was packed. Kadir Kahlifa wasn't surprised at the media he was getting. It was his intent to get the world's attention so he could expose the corruption that was so plainly going on in the highest levels of government—only no one ever had the guts to do anything about it. They lived in a land of talkers, not doers. For decades, people had talked about a revolution, talked about returning power to the people. The country was no longer a democracy but an oligarchy. He was far from being the only one who felt that way. There was a whole underground movement dedicated to unraveling the farce.

Kadir had grown up in Washington, D.C., in one of the Victorian row houses off Logan Circle. He'd started programming games in QBasic at nine and building databases by the time he was a teenager. In high school, he'd placed first in a statewide competition for a computer program that he'd designed. He had then been offered full scholarships to MIT and Stanford, but he'd elected to take the one from Georgetown University. However, his scholarship had been revoked when he'd exploited a security flaw in their computer science department. It made no difference that he'd gone to the administration to tell them about the issue and offered to fix it. They'd been either too angry or too embarrassed about him inserting a backdoor into the program. They'd made a huge deal out of the matter, and he'd been called before the department chair and then prohibited from returning for his sophomore year.

Kadir had taken his talents to the military. There, he'd transformed into a lean, mean fighting machine and an expert shooter. However, it had also been a grave time that had tested his Muslim faith. Sometime during his three tours in the Middle East, it had no longer felt like he was fighting for America's freedom and protection.

Something far uglier lay beneath the surface.

That had been confirmed when his military stint ended and his work for a private security firm started. The money had been better, but his conscience had continued to nag.

Once stateside, he'd gotten involved with an electronic civil disobedience group concerned with the National Security Agency's surveillance program that was supposed to have ended years ago. But the program went right on collecting Internet communications from major U.S. companies. Its shady activity had been leaked by whistleblowers, who'd warned that the collection was far greater than the public knew. Kadir's friend Ghost was a true believer in the right to privacy and had soon turned Kadir into a believer as well.

Now twenty-five years old, Kadir sat next to his firebrand defense attorney with his guts twisted into knots and his hands slick with sweat, on trial for hacking into the private security firm T4S.

T4S provided for a variety of intelligence agencies, from the Marine Corps to the Pentagon and Department of Defense—as well as major corporations. Kadir's hack had netted over three million emails, which he'd turned over to *Rolling Stone* and WikiLeaks and other syndicates. What most claimed his hacking had exposed was that there was no division between government and corporate spying. Also exposed was a government hatchet job falsely linking nonviolent activist groups to known terrorist groups so that they could be prosecuted under terrorism laws.

Though this was his first arrest, he'd originally pleaded not guilty to all charges alleged in the government complaint, but then he had been denied bail and held eight months without trial by iron-fisted Judge Katherine Sanders.

Kahlifa's hotshot attorney, Bridget Hodges, had filed a motion three months ago asking the judge to recuse herself from the case on the basis that her father had business ties to T4S clients that had been affected by the hack. Kadir's legal team had attempted to prove that the link to the victims created an appearance of partiality. Judge Sanders had failed to disclose her relationship to T4S and, in doing so, denied him the opportunity for a fair trial.

Supporters had come out of the woodwork and rallied behind him.

The Anonymous collective had issued a press release hammering the judge's impartiality and clear prejudice. The judge, by proxy, was a victim of the very crime she intended to judge. Her refusal to recuse herself set her in violation of multiple sections of Title 28 of the United States Code.

The activism had just pissed Judge Sanders off.

After denying bail, she'd ordered Kadir's continued incarceration, stating that he was a danger to the community and, because he had family in Yemen, that he was also a flight risk.

When pressed in the media, the judge had cleaned up her decision by stating that Kadir's computer savvy placed him in a different class of criminality—whatever the hell that shit was supposed to mean.

It didn't matter that his hack had exposed how major companies were hiring T4S to spy on victims and activist groups that were speaking out about their negligence, which had cost powerless people their lives.

How sick does a company have to be to spend millions to spy on its victims? But the truth was that, in this increasingly authoritarian culture, the law was far too often used to protect those in power rather than to hold them accountable. It was up to people like him to fight for transparency in the shadowy world of national security.

Judge Sanders shut down Kahlifa's legal team and denied the requested recusal, stating that her father's link was tenuous at best. It was laughable, but her word was final.

Once that Einstein maneuver crashed and burned, Kahlifa's attorney got to work on a plea deal. Now they wanted him to go from pleading not guilty on all counts to pleading to one count of violating the Computer Fraud and Abuse Act, which carried a maximum of ten years in prison.

Ten years.

"It could be less than that," Hodges said, as if the time were nothing.

He didn't share her optimism—and neither did his family sitting directly behind him in the courtroom.

Ten years would still be among the longest in U.S. history for hacking and, in his opinion, disproportionate to the crime—an act of nonviolent civil disobedience that championed the public good by exposing abuses of power by government and the corporate state.

Ten years. It was a draconian sentence.

Kadir couldn't help but believe that his religion had played a strong part of the hammer coming down. There had been a definite shift in climate for Muslims in the country. At every turn, he felt as if he was being made an example. The sheer numbers in the courtroom were another testament to that. After all, it wasn't like he'd hacked into a *federal* government agency.

But no matter how much he pretended to be calm, cool, and collected, he was dying inside.

The judge's door opened and a barrel-chested white deputy marshal, who was really more pink than white, bellowed, "All rise."

The entire courtroom launched to their feet.

"United States District Court for the District of Columbia, the Honorable Judge Sanders presiding, is now in session. Please be seated and come to order."

Judge Sanders floated toward her bench with her black robe billowing behind her. Honestly, the only thing that she was missing was a hood and a scythe. The few times that she'd even looked at Kadir in court, he was certain that she was mentally castrating him and tossing him into a fiery pit.

Kadir glanced over his shoulder to his father's stony expression. Raising him and his twin brother, Baasim, had turned his black hair gray long ago. His and Kadir's mother's migration to this country was supposed to have been a restart button for the family. They had bought into that American dream bullshit from half a world away, only to find different kinds of corruption, racism, and authoritarianism that were just as deadly and dangerous as the ones at home.

Kadir's mother had stopped coming to the courthouse, but wrote nearly every day. Militant Baasim had announced to the family yesterday that he was returning to Yemen right after the trial. He'd had enough of this country.

Sitting next to Kadir's family was his girlfriend since high school, Malala Jafari. He loved her, but her constant weeping in the court grew harder to bear each day. He kept wishing that she'd follow his mother's example and stop coming. Once Malala heard about the plea deal, she completely fell apart.

Now the only question was whether she'd wait for him until he got out.

The judge stopped rustling paper. "United States against Kadir Kahlifa. Is the government ready?"

Mr. Kellerman, from the prosecution, stood. "Yes. Good morning, Your Honor. Melvin Kellerman for the government. With me at counsel table is Timothy Brown of the U.S. Attorney's Office and Special Agent Quincy Bell of the FBI."

"Good morning," the judge greeted them with a saccharin smile, but it soured when she glanced toward the defense table.

Special Agent Quincy Bell and Kadir exchanged heated looks.

"Is the defense ready?" the judge asked.

Hodges sprang up. "We are, Your Honor. Good morning. Bridget Hodges for Kadir Kahlifa. Your Honor, my client is seated to my right, and I'm assisted at counsel table by Lei Kwon and Emily McGraw."

"Good morning. Be seated."

The knots in Kadir's stomach tightened. For the first twenty minutes, his attorneys and the prosecution fussed over the redacted portions of the sentencing memorandum—mind-numbing stuff.

"All right, Ms. Hodges. Have you and your client had adequate time to review the presentence report?" the judge asked.

"We have, Your Honor."

"Ms. Hodges, would you like to speak on behalf of Mr. Kahlifa?"

"I would, Your Honor." She stood again. "Would you mind if I took the podium? It might be easier for me."

"Of course." Sanders settled back in her chair. "If you actually want to remain seated, that's fine too."

Ms. Hodges smiled, but then made her way up to the podium so that she could speak into the microphone.

All eyes fell on her. This was to be her great sell of Kadir's actions being heroic and not criminal, but surely she knew that at this point it was an exercise in futility.

"There is a saying," Hodges began, "that nothing is certain in life except for death and taxes. But I'd like to add change to this list. Social change. Change is inevitable and it is happening every second and every moment of the day. Some are so small that we hardly ever notice them. And some changes start off small and grow to be a huge movement. Mr. Kahlifa believes in such a movement. He, and many others like him, question the growing overreach of the government and private security firms acting in concert to encroach on everyday civilians' civil liberties. Mr. Kahlifa believes that the people have the right to know what governments and corporations are doing behind closed doors.

"There are great heroes in our history who were not always understood in the moment. Some were at first called criminals. Their actions violated established law. Sometimes it takes time—days, months, a century for the context and meaning of those actions to be properly understood. The development and use of surveillance technologies will be one of the defining issues of our time. The reach of these capabilities is astonishingly broad. Governments can listen in on cell phone calls, use voice recognition to scan mobile networks, read emails and text messages, sensor web pages, track a citizen's every movement using GPS, and can even remotely turn on webcams built into personal computers and microphones in cell phones that are not being used. And all of this information can be filtered and organized on such a massive scale that it can be used to spy on every person in an entire country.

"Kadir Kahlifa, a talented computer programmer, decided to use his skills to break the law. He did so out of a concern that these technologies were enabling governments and corporations to gather information on individuals and organizations without oversight or scrutiny. He did so as an act of protest. And as a result of his action and the actions of others similarly committed to open government, the public has become increasingly aware and increasingly concerned. I know that there are many, like our adversaries in the U.S. Attorney's Office, who do not accept Kadir's actions as acts of civil disobedience. Many who see what he did as one-dimensional, criminal, and malicious. In its sentencing submission, the government argues that Kadir Kahlifa was motivated by a malicious and callous contempt for those with whom he disagreed and that this goal, demonstrated by statements that he made in chat rooms, was to cause mass mayhem by destroying websites and entities he disliked.

"Contrary to the government's representation, this wasn't a malicious and unfocused act against an entity with whom Kadir had a disagreement. It was an act of protest against the private intelligence industry and its ability to do what the United States, in theory, is prohibited from doing: targeting American citizens and other populations worldwide. In a footnote buried deep in its submission, the government argues that Kadir's contributions to the public good are not worthy of this court's consideration because they are substantially outweighed by the harm he caused. The government ignores the letters of support we received. People who know Kadir for his positive work in the community. People who have firsthand knowledge of the countless hours he spent volunteering, teaching, tutoring, creating a community space so groups could meet and organize.

"Kadir Kahlifa broke the law. He knew that he was breaking the law, and he acted at his peril. He accepts the consequences of his actions. He does not—and we do not—minimize his actions by addressing his motivation, but his motivation matters. When Kadir sat down at his computer and broke the law, he did so with the same set of values and principles that he applied to every other aspect of his life. Nothing that Kadir did in this case was for personal gain. In these times of secrecy and abuse of power, when whistleblowers come forward, we need to fight for them so others will be encouraged. When they are gagged, we must be their voice. When they are hunted, we must be their shields. When they are locked away, we must free them. Giving us the truth is not a crime. This is our data, our information, and our history. We must fight to own it. The government has a one-dimensional view of this case. Part of the challenge may be that Kadir Kahlifa's actions are a new form of protest, using tactics that are, concededly, violations of our federal criminal law. But our world is changing quickly, as evidenced by the hundreds of letters of support and thousands of people who signed on to the petitions that we submitted to the court.

"Your Honor, Kadir understands that you must sentence him today and that you must apply the laws in force at this moment. None of us has the benefit of hindsight or knows the changes that will no doubt take place as our thinking and our laws evolve to address the seemingly boundless use of surveillance by corporations and governments and the actions of people like Kadir Kahlifa, who step forward to grasp truths that are hidden from us. This country is at a crossroads for people like Mr. Kahlifa, who go to extraordinary lengths to bring the truth to the light. And we have to make a decision on whether we're going to have a transparent government and corporations that are transparent or continue this war on whistleblowers. The dirty tactics, hypocrisy, and secrecy. That, at its heart, is what this case is all about. What we saw revealed before this court is a travesty of justice. My client believes what every American believes: in democracy—a transparent government, not a government that goes to unbelievable lengths to suppress the truth and its own criminality. Thank you."

Ms. Hodges returned to her seat and flashed Kadir a quick, encouraging smile that didn't reach her eyes. And though he'd liked her statement, Kadir's gut remained twisted in knots.

"Thank you, Ms. Hodges." Judge Sanders said, as though she were sucking a lemon. "Does the government wish to be heard?"

"We do, Your Honor." Mr. Kellerman took the podium.

"Kadir Kahlifa is no whistleblower. The government says that not simply because we don't like what he did. The reason we say that is because of the evidence. And when we sit here today, when the court sits here today to judge, to sentence him based on his offenses, you have to look at all of the factors, the nature and circumstances of the offense and, in particular, with regard to this defendant, I think the nature and the characteristics of the defendant. Based on what we know, we can say for sure that Kadir Kahlifa was an experienced hacker who used his skills through a variety of different entities, from police retirement systems to the FTC's consumer protection websites to DC's public safety website, releasing thousands' credit card information, home addresses, talking about releasing pictures of police officers' girlfriends, personal emails. Personal information about private citizens.

"There is nothing about any of that that is relevant to political protest. There is nothing about any of that that is altruistic. There is nothing about any of that that is related to the injustices that Mr. Kahlifa sees in this world. There is no altruism in any of that conduct. Now, when Mr. Kahlifa and his counsel stand up before this court and refer to all of the letters of support for him, we don't have any doubt that Mr. Kahlifa has done some good things in his life. The court sentences people all the time who do good, who have also committed crimes.

"It is certainly unfortunate, that he obviously has a skill that he has chosen to use to hurt thousands of people that he's never met, who did nothing to him. He claimed that he didn't do it for personal gain, but that doesn't mean that these crimes weren't harmful. Mr. Kahlifa has made an effort to try to deflect responsibility for his role in the T4S hack."

Special Agent Bell and Kadir exchanged looks again. Bell was smug as shit.

Kellerman continued. "Based on all of the harm that this defendant has done, the people submit that one hundred and twenty months is sufficient and warranted in this case. Thank you."

The judge was glowing after Kellerman's speech. "I guess that makes it my turn," she began. "Counsel, as you've heard, I have calculated the guidelines and taken them into account. In my view, the guidelines accurately reflect the nature and circumstances of the offense, but probably more needs to be said on that. In Mr. Kahlifa's *written* plea to the court, he stated that he committed this crime with the best of intentions and sought only to disclose information the public deserved to know and to steal from the rich and give to the poor. But this ignores Mr. Kahlifa 's own words concerning his true motivations—and I do agree with counsel that motivations count—and it ignores the widespread harm suffered by countless individuals and organizations as a result of Mr. Kahlifa's hacks.

"It is, in fact, clear that his aim was to break into critical computer systems, steal data, deface websites, destroy files, and dump online the sensitive personal and financial information of thousands of individuals, all with the objective of creating—in Mr. Kahlifa's words—'maximum mayhem.' These are not the actions of Martin Luther King, Nelson Mandela, John Adams, or even Daniel Ellsberg. With respect to the history and characteristics of this defendant, I do take into account what Ms. Hodges has said about Mr. Kahlifa's charitable acts. He certainly did many charitable acts in his community, including working in food kitchens, tutoring, and the like.

"The most striking fact, however, about Mr. Kahlifa's history is his unrepentant recidivism. He has an almost-unbroken record of criminal offenses that demonstrates a total lack of respect for the law. There is no information in his record that would suggest that he will not continue to reoffend." She sighed dramatically before her big finish.

"Mr. Kahlifa, you are sentenced, sir, to a period of seventy-two months in a federal facility. Following that time, you'll spend a period of three years on supervised release. During the period of supervised release, you'll comply with all of the standard terms and conditions of supervised release. Among them are that you not commit another federal, state, or local crime; you not illegally possess a controlled substance; and you not possess a firearm or other destructive device. You may not own or possess a computer.

"It's also my duty to inform you that unless you've waived it, you have the right to appeal this sentence." She smiled blithely. "Thank you, ladies and gentlemen. You've been very helpful. We are adjourned."

Kadir Kahlifa's heart sank while Malala wailed uncontrollably behind him.

5

After a thorough ass-chewing from the police chief, the mayor, and Judge Berry, Gizella Castillo was effectively suspended for heaven knows how long—but she did have reason to suspect that it wouldn't be for too long. After all, her big Hail Mary had paid off.

Many of Craig Avery's close political connections and ties were likely at this moment crafting carefully worded press releases, changing their earlier position accusing Lieutenant Castillo's dogged investigation of being a politically motivated witch hunt. Some might have been planning apologies and even tendering their resignations. As for the department, Castillo's gamble would make heroes out of a number of department heads, who wouldn't want her illegal tactics sullying the story. And Lieutenant Castillo owed it all to the insistence of one scrawny kid.

The moment her thoughts shifted to the lanky, blond teenaged boy, Shawn No Last Name, he stood up in the center of BridgePoint Hospital's waiting room. As Castillo approached, she noticed his bright powder-blue eyes were glassy and his smudged black mascara. He couldn't be more than fourteen—fifteen, max. Teenage homelessness was a Washington nightmare, especially among the LGBT community, which she assumed the teenager belonged to.

"They won't let us see her," Shawn said, his anxiety evident.

"It's okay," Castillo comforted. "I'm sure that when the doctors clear your friend—"

"Do you know when that will be? How is she? Is she going to be all right?"

"Whoa. Whoa." Castillo held up a hand to stop the rapid-fire questions. But her desire to comfort the young boy lingered—both him and his band of . . . misfits? They were an interesting lot now that she truly looked at them—an eclectic group of goths, transgender kids, and even gangbanger hoods. How these kids had met up was probably an interesting story.

"I'm going to go in and check on her, talk to her, and then I'll see about getting you in to see her for a few minutes. Is that all right?"

Shawn No Last Name, because he steadfastly refused to give her one, glanced around at his friends, and once they nodded their consent, he said, "All right."

"Good." She smiled. "Now did you bring some clothes like I asked?"

"Yeah." Shawn turned, and the goth chick with diamond studs for dimples handed him a black book bag, another staple of a runaway's uniform. He handed the bag to Castillo.

"Thanks."

He nodded. "Just . . ." He hesitated. "Just tell her that we're out here. Okay?"

"Of course."

"I mean—it's important for her to know that we never gave up looking for her." He swiped at his raccoon eyes and struggled to pull it together.

Castillo smiled again, stretched out her hand to touch his shoulder, but the kid flinched and moved back. His reaction surprised her. Had he been abused in the past too? Her gaze darted to the others. Had they? The thread bonding the group slowly materialized before her eyes.

"I'll be back," the lieutenant said.

Three doors down from the waiting room, she rapped on a closed hospital room door and then stuck her head inside before receiving an invitation to enter. "May I come in?"

An older African American gentleman with a head full of salt-and-pepper hair swiveled in her direction. "Sure. Come on in." He pushed up his thick, black-rimmed glasses, and looked relieved that she'd arrived. One glance over to his new patient hinted that the young girl wasn't cooperating. If she was anything like her friend Shawn, Castillo sympathized. He wasn't too big on providing personal information either.

Perched on the edge of the examination table, dressed in an open-back hospital gown, was one of Avery's last living survivors, Bree No Last Name.

"How's it going?" Castillo asked, attempting eye contact and failing.

The doctor sighed and then answered for his mute patient. "All right—considering. She's definitely a fighter. With the right care, I have no doubts that she'll pull through all of this—in time."

Castillo smiled at his words—but Bree didn't.

"Do you mind if I have a few words alone with her?" the lieutenant asked. "I just need to give her this and ask her a few questions."

The doctor hesitated. "Sure. I'll be back in a few minutes."

Lieutenant Castillo nodded, but kept her gaze locked on Bree while the doctor exited.

The young girl lifted her guarded gaze to Castillo's, though she kept her face expressionless.

Castillo's smile grew heavy. "Hello. Do you remember me? I'm Gizella Castillo. We met—I mean, I know that a lot has happened in the last few hours. You may not . . ." At the girl's blank expression, Castillo stopped and searched for another way to engage. "Your friends brought you a change of clothes." She stepped toward Bree with the book bag outstretched.

A light lit within the girl's dark eyes. "Shawn? He's here?" The girl's deep, raspy voice surprised the lieutenant. She sounded older than her estimated fifteen years.

"Yeah." Castillo nodded and pushed up a smile. "He wanted me to tell you that they never gave up looking for you. And it's true. He and his friends were a godsend on this case. They worked the streets better than anyone on my team."

The corners of Bree's lips lifted, completely transforming her stony face into one of beauty. *Bree No Last Name will be a knockout when she's older. Her mental state will likely be up in the air*, Castillo thought. Bree took the book bag from Castillo's hand.

"Do you mind answering a few questions for me?" Castillo asked.

The girl's smile fell.

"I know that this is hard for you—but it's very important."

"Why? He's dead, isn't he?"

"Avery? Yes. But—"

"Isn't that house of horrors enough evidence of what kind of a sick fuck he was?"

"It goes a long way in proving that. Yes."

"Then I fail to see what else I can possibly add."

Castillo took a deep breath and countered, "You can tell me about *you*. What's your full name? How old are you? How did you get in Craig Avery's clutches?"

The teenager's gaze dropped and skittered away.

"Why don't you want to tell me who you are?" Castillo challenged. "Do you have a record or something?"

Silence.

"Are you—and your friends—runaways? You *still* running away from something?"

Castillo knew she'd hit a nerve when the teenager's jawline clenched and hardened. "Surely . . . whatever you're running from isn't any worse than what you just went through. Your parents have to be worried sick."

"You don't know shit about me—about my parents, and frankly it's none of your goddamned business," the teenager snapped.

"Piss and vinegar," Castillo noted, eyeballing the girl and struggling to come up with another way to reach her. A rap on the door interrupted her.

Shawn poked his head inside. "Doctor said that it was all right for us to come in for a few minutes."

Bree lit up and jumped off the exam table. "Shawn!"

Shawn rushed in and zoomed past the lieutenant to embrace his friend. The moment he did, the tough girl act collapsed and she broke down crying.

"I'll just give you guys a few minutes alone," Castillo said.

The friends either didn't hear or purposely ignored her. She supposed that it didn't really matter. She backpedaled out of the room until she bumped into a couple of the other teenagers.

"Sorry. Excuse me."

They poured in and rushed to embrace Bree back into their eclectic group. There were plenty of tears to go around. Castillo, generally a tough cookie herself, felt her eyes moisten. After completing her escape, Castillo went in search of Bree's attending doctor. She'd hoped to get a brief rundown of Bree's injuries. Unable to spot him in the hallway, she instead checked on the other two girls that had been found in Avery's homemade dungeon.

Tomi Lehane, a seventeen-year old girl who had gone missing after partying at a teen hotspot one night, broke down into tears of gratitude the moment the lieutenant entered the room. She had no trouble or hesitancy in describing the hell she'd endured with Avery. His sick fetishes and his often fatal cruelty. Tomi had been with Avery the longest and had feared, before Castillo's team showed up, that her days were numbered. Eventually, Castillo's line of questioning worked its way to Bree. That was the first time that Tomi drew a blank.

"You know. Black girl. Tall, long-hair—"

"Oh. Her." Tomi licked her lips. "There's not much to tell about her. She'd only been there I guess for like five—maybe six months? I don't know. It was hard keeping up with time. But she's . . . a strange one. She rarely ever spoke—which got under Avery's skin."

"What do you mean?"

Tomi shrugged. "I mean no matter what Avery did to her, he couldn't break her. She never begged, she never screamed. Shalisa, the other girl, and I had often whispered between ourselves that . . ."

Lieutenant Castillo cocked her head. "That what?"

"That something just wasn't right with her. You know . . . mentally."

"How do you mean?"

Tomi shrugged. "I don't know. It was like she was there physically but not mentally. Avery could do almost anything and she never gave in—except for one night. I definitely heard sniffling—crying. Real soft like. But it was *just* the one time. Like I said, Shalisa and I thought it was strange—but it wasn't long before we were jealous."

"Jealous?" Castillo asked.

"Yeah. The ability to mentally check out like that? I would have given anything to be able to do that."

Castillo nodded and then thanked Tomi for her time.

Shalisa Young pretty much told the same story. Craig Avery had grabbed her out of the parking lot of a busy shopping center in broad daylight. Her memory of the initial incident was fuzzy. She was sure that Avery had snuck up behind her and placed something over her mouth and nose to knock her out. The next thing that she remembered was waking inside that basement.

"Shalisa!" A frantic woman raced through the door.

"Momma!" Shalisa hopped off the examination table, and mother and child ran toward each other, full throttle.

"My baby!"

Their bodies crashed in the center of the room, and then their arms wrapped tight around each other before the real waterworks flowed.

Lieutenant Castillo made her exit.

Upon returning to the hallway, Castillo caught a glimpse of the attending doctor back at the nurses' station.

"Doctor!" She rushed forward.

"Lieutenant," he greeted her. "What can I do for you?"

"I want to talk to you about the survivors—about their status."

"Health-wise?" He lifted a brow. "Their medical records are private. You know that."

"Of course but—"

"But I can tell you that each of the girls will physically pull through. A lot of cuts and bruises, but nothing life threatening."

"And mentally?"

"Likely a lot of counseling will be needed—probably for a *long* time."

Castillo nodded, but she had more questions about one girl in particular. "About Bree . . . did you ever get a last name out of her?"

The doctor heaved a long, frustrated sigh. "I didn't get *anything* out of her. Bree, huh? That's more than I got. We marked her down as Jane Doe."

"She didn't speak to you?"

"Not a peep. She barely made a sound during the entire examination."

"Huh. I guess I got lucky there for a few minutes."

"I'd say. I'm concerned about her the most. Not just mentally but . . ." His voice trailed off before he looked around and then pulled her aside. "How long was she with this maniac, do you know?"

"About six months."

The doctor shook his head.

"Why?"

"She has a lot of old scars. A lot of old fractures and breaks. Bones that hadn't healed properly."

"So she has been abused long before now?"

"We're talking about *years*," he said, looking over the top of his glasses.

Lieutenant Castillo nodded while more pieces of the puzzle came together, but the number of pieces quadrupled.

"I guess I better go back in there and give this another shot."

"Good luck," the doctor said. "I have a feeling that you're going to need it."

"Thanks." She drew a deep breath and marched back toward the mysterious Bree's room. After her customary quick rap on the door, she entered without invitation—but this time, the examination room was empty. Bree and her band of misfits were long gone.

6

Six years later

*J*ust do it. Jump.

Abrianna pulled her gaze from the September blood moon glowing over the city of Washington, D.C. and allowed it to drift to the streets below. The vertigo was instant. She wobbled on her feet and inched closer to the edge. It was cold for this time of year. The angry wind whipped the hem of her short dress. The temptation to step off and fly down into sweet oblivion was not new. In fact, it came every year at this time. Could she do it tonight? Or would she punk out like she always did? Her curiosity about whether she'd *feel* anything when she hit concrete was disturbing and morbid—morbid because the hope was that she would.

She desperately needed to feel something. Something *real*. Old voices that she'd spent years running away from became a crescendo inside and punched through the thick, drug-induced fog in her head, rattling every brain cell until a sob bubbled up in her throat and tears splashed her face.

The vertigo worsened, and another inch of the building's ledge disappeared. Through her silver pumps, she felt one toe cross over the line to freedom. The rest of her body clung to life. If she could just tilt forward, she could . . .

"Bree!"

Gasping, Abrianna startled. One silver pump caught. Her ankle twisted beneath her, and her balance disappeared.

She fell. At last: *freedom.*

The drop was shortened by a sudden painful grip on her right arm.

"I got you," Shawn cried.

She looked up, without relief or gratitude, at her savior.

Shawn, her best friend, wasn't a big guy. He wasn't particularly strong either. But he was determined, grunting and struggling to hold on to her. "Give me your other hand!"

Shaking her head, Abrianna willed him to let her go, but she couldn't push the words out her mouth.

"Give. Me. Your. Hand!" Veins bulged along the sides of his red face, while fear brightened his blue eyes. "Please," he added, eyes pleading.

I'm being a selfish bitch again.

It was *his* fear that Abrianna responded to. The thought of hurting *him* moved her more than the impending harm to herself. That was her Kryptonite. She couldn't stand the idea of hurting others, especially the few that she called friends. At last, she gave him her other hand.

The next minute was pure agony—for both of them. The rough stone building did a number on her thighs and legs, and Shawn almost dropped her three times. When she was finally up on the roof, they collapsed, huffing and chugging in huge gulps of air. After several seconds, Shawn sat up and looked her over.

"What the *fuck*, Bree?"

With no answer, Abrianna turned away, where the wind transformed her tears into icicles.

"Every fucking year," Shawn complained, frustrated. "I thought things were getting better?"

Silence.

"Is it the buzzing?" he inquired.

Abrianna groaned. She didn't like talking about the constant buzzing inside her head. A buzzing that had lingered since the night she'd been led out of that maniac's basement. She didn't like talking about *any* of the changes in her body from Avery's drug cocktails.

"Maybe . . . we should really look into getting you some help," he suggested gently. "Professionally, I mean—"

"I wasn't going to jump," she lied. "You startled me."

"You shitting me?" Shawn asked, incredulous. "You blaming me now?"

"No." Her gaze dropped to the asphalt roof.

Shawn backhanded his own tears and smudged his mascara-coated lashes. *He's too pretty to be a boy, and too loyal for his own damn good.* "They say it gets better. We'll get through this together—like always." His pink lips curled into a smile as he swung his arm around her shoulders. "You believe that, don't you?"

"You know damn well that I don't believe shit that nobody tells me." She smiled.

He chuckled, mainly to lighten the mood. "Seriously. Are you good?"

She nodded, though they knew she was still lying.

"Are you still saving money to leave me?" he asked.

"Yeah, but I keep telling you that you can come *with* me."

He shook his head.

"Aren't you sick of D.C.?"

"No. Not really. It's home."

"I've never felt like I've ever had a real home. But I'd love to find one in some place like the French Riviera."

"Then you better start taking French lessons, too," he joked.

The roof's door exploded open, and their motley crew of friends stumbled out, giggling and laughing.

"There's the birthday girl." Draya pointed. "Bree!"

One look and Abrianna knew that Draya was as high as she was—only happy.

"What are you guys doing up here? The party is downstairs!" Draya staggered over, grinning as wide as a Cheshire cat, and she didn't spill a drop from her red cup. Then she forced Shawn and Abrianna apart by throwing her arms around them for the hundredth bear hug of the night. "Oh, my best friend is *finally* twenty-one. No more fake IDs. You're legal now. You're a grown woman," Draya bragged.

Abrianna carved out a big smile, but struggled to absorb her girl's happy vibes.

Draya slurred, "How does it feel?"

"Good," Abrianna said, wanting her girl to ease up on her neck. "I can't breathe, Draya."

"Oops." She stumbled backwards, still smiling, eyes twinkling. "Come on, girl. Tamera's late ass has finally showed up with that damn lopsided cake. Everybody is waiting on you." Draya looped her arm through Abrianna's and tugged.

Abrianna stepped on a hard pebble and jerked back. "Ouch! Wait."

"Hey! Where the hell is your other shoe?" Julian's loud ass gestured his plastic cup toward her feet and splashed his drink all over Abrianna's leg.

"Damn it, Jules!"

"My bad." Giggling, he threw his arms around her too. "But a little vodka has never hurt nobody."

They pulled her forward. Abrianna hobbled until she was given enough room to pull off her other pump. As they stumbled down the stairs, their laughter amplified.

Submitting to the moment, Abrianna laughed along with

everyone else. They heard the music from Abrianna's apartment long before they arrived on her floor. And as they approached, bursts of laughter and raucous chatter told her just how much fun the guests were still having without her.

"We found the birthday girl," Draya shouted, shoving the door open.

The crowd cheered, tossed confetti, and blew party whistles and kazoos loud enough to wake the dead.

Abrianna struck a pose and threw up her arms as an invitation to celebrate her presence. Feeding her ego, the cheers and applause continued until the crowd broke out into an off-key rendition of "Happy Birthday to You."

The crowd parted as Tamera, holding a not-quite-square-shaped sheet cake with burning candles and the number twenty-one in the center, waltzed down the center toward the birthday girl.

Abrianna's tears were automatic—despite the fact that it wasn't *really* her birthday. It was her deceased brother's that she'd claimed as her own.

The tune-challenged choir wrapped up their song and demanded, "Make a wish!"

A wish? Abrianna's mind went blank. Not because she didn't need anything. She did. She needed everything. But she wasn't on speaking terms with everyone's favorite make-believe friend in the sky. At the moment, they had the perfect understanding that he didn't like her and she certainly wasn't too thrilled with him.

"C'mon, girl. We ain't got all night," shouted Tivonte, still in full Beyoncé drag—all three hundred and fifty pounds of him. "We came to party and bullshit, bullshit and party!"

The crowd co-signed with a cheer. Abrianna caught Shawn staring. Crease lines were stacked on his forehead.

Fuck it. Smiling, she took a deep breath and blew out the candles.

"YEA!"

An obscene amount of confetti was tossed, party horns were blown, and someone cranked up the music.

Abrianna knew that her cranky-ass landlord, Mr. Gordon, was probably already on the phone with the cops. But after another line of coke hit her system and silenced the buzzing, she really didn't give a fuck.

Moses and Abrianna had only been living up in that piece for four months, and were already on a first-name basis with the beat cops. They were usually up in there three times a week. The first time, their asses kicked the door open and broke it off the hinges. Of course, by that time, Moses and Abrianna had finished whatever the fuck it was they had been arguing about and had been in the middle of fucking each other's brains out.

Those days were over. She and Moses had broken up two weeks ago, but he was taking his sweet time getting all his shit out of the apartment.

Officers James Miller and Bubba (yes, that's the asshole's real name) Bolton had harassed the shit out of them and refused to let her put any damn clothes on while they interrogated them. But most cops were usually dicks and you just learned to deal.

Abrianna didn't remember how long the party went on for or when the last muthafuckas took their asses home. But she believed Officers Miller and Bolton had paid at least three visits during the night. The last time, a couple of her dick-starved girlfriends had hooked the cops up in the stairwell in order to persuade them to take back their threats of arresting everyone.

There were remnants of a memory of Shawn and Tivonte putting her to bed, but she couldn't swear by it. It might have been shortly after they'd held her hair back while she'd thrown up in the bathroom—or was that a memory from another party? It was hard being unable to trust one's memory sometimes. The things Abrianna wanted to forget took root and the things she needed to remember, she forgot.

But she did recall Shawn stroking her hair and whispering something about her seeking help again. Something told her that an intervention was likely in her future.

"You're my best friend, and I don't know what I'd do if something happened to you," Abrianna vaguely recalled Shawn saying.

"I'll get help," she said.

"You promise?"

"Promise." She really did hate lying to him, but what was wrong with her likely had no cure.

7

Just do it. Jump.

Shalisa Young stood on top of the St. Elizabeths Hospital building, in the dead of night, while the rain plastered her thin gown to her body. Numb, she felt neither the rain's growing velocity nor the icy wind. All she cared about was ending it.

The needles.

The buzzing voices.

The pain.

Life.

The moon glimmered off the Potomac, transforming it into black glass. It was beautiful. The view of the city was also beautiful. Maybe she'd miss it.

"Ms. Young," a nurse screamed from behind her. "You don't want to do this!"

Shalisa let the words wash over her. The woman didn't know what the hell Shalisa wanted. *They* just wanted to keep pumping her with drugs. Drugs that made it difficult for her to think.

"Shalisa, sweetheart. Talk to me. You don't want to do this. Please." The nurse crept forward. She wasn't alone. Shalisa heard the soft shoes of the orderlies steadily approaching. No doubt they thought that they could snatch her back from the edge before she leapt.

Like the last time.

But last time she'd been weak. A small part of her had still believed that there had been a mistake, believed that she hadn't done what everyone said she had. She hoped—prayed—for the day when her mother would walk into her bedroom and say that it had been a horrible nightmare.

Shalisa now understood that day was never going to come. She'd *killed* her mother.

Tears splashed her face and mingled with the rain. She hadn't meant to do it. She had been angry with people constantly hounding her about when she was going to get better. The doctors. The pills. The disappointment.

No one understood why she couldn't get better like Tomi Lehane. She'd breezed through college and now worked at the *Washington Post*. How come she was able to put everything behind her? How was it that she was happy and successful?

"Shalisa, please," the nurse pleaded. "Back away, and let's go inside!"

My mother. My sweet mother. The one who'd turned the city upside down looking for her when Craig Avery kidnapped her. The one who'd held prayer vigils and tacked posters in every neighborhood. Shalisa couldn't understand how she could've done such a thing. She'd just wanted her mother to leave her alone for a little while.

She hadn't wanted to hurt her.

She hadn't wanted to kill her.

But somehow she had—just by *thinking* about it one night.

The orderlies closed in.

Shalisa tugged in a deep breath and stepped off the ledge.

8

Capitol Hill

"We're going to be late, Jayson," Tomi Lehane complained to her photographer, as they charged up the stone steps leading into the Longworth House Office Building, south of the Capitol. The word she'd left out was *again*. At this point in her life, she'd conceded her mother's assessment that running late was programmed in her DNA—on her father's side of the family, of course. Over the granite base, past the ionic columns, the reporter and cameraman entered through the first portico and rushed to security check. Once there, the guards moved like molasses and were indifferent to all the obvious signs of her and Jayson's impatience.

When it was Tomi's turn to step up, she flashed Roosevelt her brightest smile and fumbled around for her press badge. "Shit. I know I have it. Just a sec." Trembling, she checked her jacket pockets a second and then a third time. "I *know* I grabbed it this morning," she lied. The truth was that she didn't remember a damn thing after realizing her alarm clock hadn't gone off that morning—other than tripping over Rocky again since he liked to park his large Doberman butt where she rounded the corner of her bed. After so many years, one would think that she'd remember that he slept right there. *But . . . noooo.* In the mornings, her brain struggled through a fog so thick, it was a wonder she could get out of bed at all.

"Where the hell is it?" Her panic crept up when Roosevelt reached out and lifted the press badge draped around her neck.

"Looking for this?"

Tomi imploded with relief, but embarrassment colored her face. "If my head wasn't attached . . ."

Roosevelt, or Rosie, as he was affectionately called, smiled and shook his head before waving a metal wand around her.

Jayson breezed through the checkpoint with his camera in tow, because he always had his shit together. They took off to find the Committee on Homeland Security and Government Affairs. Today, Secret Service Director Donald Davidson was in the congressional hot seat for the latest scandal involving his agents during a presidential trip to Brazil. It wasn't the first time that the agency had been embroiled in a scandal, but it had been thought that the agency had long since cleaned up its act. Instead, it appeared that they'd simply got better at hiding their shenanigans—sort of. And if that wasn't enough, the intermittent security breaches at the White House and reports of drunken off-duty agents had many in the country wondering what the hell was going on with the agency.

The scandals were bad enough on their own, but the extra spice in today's hearing centered on the committee chairman, and the now *likely* speaker-in-waiting Kenneth Reynolds. *Likely,* because the House still had to hold a vote, but the buzz on the Hill was that Reynolds was the only one who could get the 218 votes needed for the leadership role. Everyone in the conservative wing of his party liked and trusted Reynolds—that, and no one else really wanted the job. The party was completely comfortable being the loyal opposition party to Democratic President Daniel Walker, but no one was actually interested in governing or being held accountable for anything.

While conservatives lavished their praises on Reynolds, they paid little attention to the fact that the man actually had very few accomplishments. And "very few" meant literally three. Three post offices renamed in his district, to be exact. Then again, maybe they did pay attention, but figured that it was par for the course for a party that no longer believed in small government, but in no government at all.

"Here we go," Jayson said, pushing open the door to room 1100. The place was jam-packed with reporters, bloggers, and baby-faced interns.

Tomi wasn't at all surprised to find that it was a packed house, but she was disappointed that the opening statements had already started. Her watch read 9:35 AM. A hearing that started on time was as rare as a real federal budget balancing.

Jayson crept to the front of the room and crawled around on the floor with the other photographers, elbowing to get tight shots of the Secret Service director and Chairman Reynolds.

Miracle of all miracles, Tomi found a seat, three rows behind the director.

One look at Reynolds's stern, almost marble-like face and it was clear that he knew that he was the big draw and was ready to become second in the line of presidential succession—not bad for a man of forty-two.

"Lucky bastard." There was no other way to explain it. As the Republican Party ate its own, the old guard of establishment politicians had disappeared and a new crop of uncompromising SOBs had emerged. Their leader was days away from becoming the third most powerful man in the country. Tomi wanted to know how a man that close to so much power had managed to survive in this town for nearly fifteen years and *no one* had any dirt on him. Nada. Zero. Zilch. In the land of the corrupt and crooked, that shit was unheard of. Everyone had a secret in D.C. Right now, Tomi would give anything to know Reynolds's.

Chairman Reynolds's ebony gaze lasered in on the Secret Service director as he accused the agency of having a "culture of incompetency" and "demoralizing decay." Reynolds's harsh words landed on his target, and from Tomi's seat three rows back, she watched as the back of the man's head and ears turned bright pink. Of course the director remained stoic as the chairman proceeded to go into detail about the scandalous behavior of the agents in Brazil.

Reynolds raised his voice for effect. "Despite your previous testimony before this committee that your agents never left sensitive government documents unprotected in their hotel rooms, we now know this to be false, and we have to start questioning your leadership abilities. Don't you agree, Mr. Davidson?"

The director lifted his chin a few inches in subtle defiance, but he kept his cool.

Reynolds remained on a roll. He brought up other deficiencies in the agency. The more he talked with righteous indignation, the more Tomi was convinced that the man was full of shit. For her, the real story wasn't that Reynolds was on the verge of making history as the first African American speaker of the House, but whatever damn secrets the man had nailed up in his closet.

The hearing broke for lunch at exactly 11:45, and everyone sprang out of their seats like toasted Pop-Tarts and filed out of the sweltering room. Tomi too, because she wanted to be in a good position to lob questions at the speaker-in-waiting when he exited from the congressional side doors. But her bad luck continued as a throng of reporters prevented her from getting anything other than a bird's-eye view when Reynolds finally emerged. None of the questions shouted at the congressman had anything to do with today's hearing. They only wanted to know whether he'd secured enough votes for the speakership.

Reynolds flashed a smile that belonged in Hollywood and proceeded to charm the pants off the mainstream media with his well-rehearsed modesty.

"Well, you guys know that this was not a job that I ever sought. I never wanted or aimed to be speaker."

"Does that mean that you really are thinking about *not* running for the speakership?" an alarmed female reporter asked while nearly tripping out of her pumps.

"Well," Reynolds hedged, his smile widening. "There would definitely need to be some changes to the House rules in order for me to be a more effective leader."

"But the current speaker, Hartman, is going to be stepping down *soon*. When will you make your decision?"

"Look. I'm considering this with a great deal of reluctance, and I mean that in terms of sacrifices. My wife, Valerie, and I have been discussing this the last few days. I'm not willing to give up our family time. And I promise that you guys will be the first—no, make that the third—to know our decision when we make it."

Give me a fuckin' break. How she managed to stop her eyes from rolling to the back of her head was beyond her.

"What about your threats to impeach the president?" another reporter asked, catching Tomi's attention.

Reynolds stopped, turned off his charm for his prosecutorial voice. "I, of course, take the proposition of impeachment *very* seriously. The president's rumored . . . *behavior* along with his Secret Service team deserves to be looked at *very* seriously."

"Are charges of impeachment off of the table?" Tomi shouted over everyone's heads.

Reynolds looked up and met Tomi's steady gaze. "Oh no, ma'am. Impeachment is definitely *not* off the table."

"So what do you think?" Jayson said, coming up from behind.

"I think he's full of shit," Tomi admitted.

"Well. At least that explains the smell," Jayson joked.

They stopped and watched as the congressman and the reporters flanking his sides inched their way down the hall.

"No. I mean it." Tomi turned toward Jayson. "Most politicians are full of it. But *this guy* is particularly odious. Nobody is as clean as he's pretending to be."

"Uh-oh. I know that look." Jayson groaned. "You're going to go digging in his closet, aren't you?"

"With a jackhammer and a crowbar. And I know just the private dick that could help me out too."

9

The White House

President Daniel Walker paced as the potential new speaker of the House dropped the bomb of a possible impeachment hearing live on cable news.

"Calm down, Mr. President," Sean Haverty, the president's chief of staff, urged.

"Listen to that ignorant asshole! Do you hear him?" Daniel raked his hands through his thick silver hair while his dark green eyes lit with outrage.

"Fuck staying calm! Impeachment? Me?"

Vice President Kate Washington took a stab at lowering the temperature. "They wouldn't be the Republican Party if they weren't threatening to impeach a Democratic president."

The president railed, "We can't hire enough staff to keep up with the utter nonsense that floats out of the Conservative Industrial Complex. Their twenty-four-hours-a-day, seven-days-a-week propaganda machine never quits or breaks down!"

"Then we're just going to have to ride the tide like everything else," Kate said with what she hoped was a bright smile. "It's not like they have anything to tie you to all that foolishness that went down in Rio."

The president cut a quick glance at his chief of staff.

An alarm went off at the back of Kate's head. "What?"

The men shared another look before the president shrugged and shook his head. "Nothing."

But the one-word answer fell like a lead balloon.

Kate groaned and took a seat across from Haverty's desk. "You've got to be kidding me."

"No. Nothing happened," President Walker insisted.

"Nothing happened, or you don't think that they can *prove* anything happened?" she challenged.

The men shared another look, and Kate's head threatened to explode. "Enough with the damn silent eyeball conversation and just spit it out. Were you or were you not involved in the cover up down in Brazil?"

The president's hesitation was all she needed to lose it. "Damnit!"

Haverty raced and made sure that his office's door was indeed locked. It was. But to add more security, he closed the shades on the two glass panels that framed the door.

"Katie, calm down," the president said, lifting both hands as if that shit really called a time-out.

"Don't you fucking *Katie* me—or tell me to calm down! Ever! What were you thinking? Really? How in the hell did you think that you could get away with this?"

"I . . . I . . . wasn't really thinking," President Walker admitted.

"No shit, Sherlock." She dropped her head into her hands, but then fought the urge to pull her fucking hair out. "It's over. It's over. My career is over."

"Katie—"

"Don't," she warned, squeezing her eyes shut, to block his presence out of her mind. She wanted to block out *everything* she'd just heard.

"How about I give you two a couple of minutes alone so you

can talk?" Haverty suggested. He went back to the door. Neither the president nor the vice president stopped him.

Alone, Daniel leaned against a corner of Haverty's desk. "Say something."

"What would you like me to say?" Kate asked, bolting back out of her seat. "Way to go? How about '*Good job?*' You not only screwed up *your* legacy, but you're taking me down with you."

"Okay. Don't get hysterical."

"Hysterical?" Kate snapped and then in the next second whipped her hand soundly across his face. *Slap!*

Stunned, Daniel stepped back.

"How's *that* for hysterical?" she hissed.

President Walker reined in his temper. "You're angry. I—" *Slap!*

Pissed, he grabbed her hands. "Enough!"

"How could you do this to me?" Kate questioned, feeling that she was indeed growing hysterical. "Huh? All these years I've stuck by your side. I knew that you would be just another Bill Clinton!"

"C'mon. Let's not get carried away."

"It was nothing. Nothing."

"No one risks his entire political career over nothing, Daniel!" She raked her hair some more. "I gotta get out of here. I need some air." She turned for the door.

"Katie . . ."

"Look. It's not *my* forgiveness that you should worry about. It's the entire country's! When Reynolds gets gaveled in and he starts compiling impeachment charges right before an election year, I'm finished."

"If I'm impeached, then you'll get my job." Daniel joked. "Isn't that what you always wanted anyway?"

"Not funny. My name will get dragged down in the mud with

you, killing any chance of my succeeding you in the next election.

"I'm telling you. You're blowing everything out of proportion. Reynolds has nothing. He can't prove anything."

"Famous last words," Kate mumbled.

"Katie, I'll handle it," he said.

"How? This place leaks like a sieve. You make any kind of move to cover up whatever the hell happened in Brazil and the Republicans will fry you, and you fucking know it. They'll open congressional hearings to investigate every damn time you go to the bathroom!"

"I know. I know. I know."

"So what's *your* plan?"

"Right now there is no need for a plan. Reynolds isn't going to find anything."

Kate's patience thinned. "Every man who has ever taken his pants down outside the privacy of his own bedroom thinks that he'll never be caught."

"Katie, I'll fix this," the president said to her retreating back as she opened the office door.

"Sure you will, Daniel. Sure you will."

10

"What the hell happened in here?" a voice thundered through the apartment, waking Abrianna.

Shit. Moses was back.

"THE FUCK?" he barked, slamming the front door.

Groggy as shit, Abrianna rolled over, grabbed a pillow, and jammed it over her head. She wished that for once he knew how to come in the apartment *quietly.* Four months wasn't a long time to live with someone, but it was the longest *intimate* relationship she'd ever had. Now it was over.

Shawn said that it was because she was dick dumb. He was probably right. Moses's dick game was the dream of every woman and porno director worldwide. His shit was for serious riders only, and once upon a time, Abrianna had been there for it.

Not anymore. Moses's temper was another matter completely.

"Look at this shit," Moses roared, kicking something.

"Keep it down," Abrianna groaned. She was not a morning person.

Moses stomped through the apartment. Instead of coming into her bedroom, he went into the spare room—where he made an even louder racket.

"Where the fuck is it?!"

She grabbed another pillow to cover her ringing head.

Moses stomped out of the spare room and exploded into her bedroom.

"Bree! Wake your ass up!" The covers were snatched off and she was manhandled and hauled up by her arm.

"What the fuck?" She barely got her feet under her before he jerked her ass out of the bedroom.

"Where's my shit?" he shouted, dragging Abrianna through the party-wrecked hallway in just her bra and panties, past his buddy Duane in the living room, before dumping her into the spare bedroom.

"Where is it?"

"Where is what?"

"Zeke's coke, you stupid bitch! I'm supposed to be delivering those damn pink bricks this morning. Ain't shit in here!" As proof, he gestured to the panels in the roof of the closet. "The bag is gone. Where the fuck is it?" His grip on her arm tightened as he jostled her around.

"I don't know where the fuck that shit is." Abrianna attempted to jerk free but was instead slammed against a wall.

"I ain't hearing that shit," he growled. "You know what the fuck I got on the line. How the fuck you got niggas partying all up in here last night, wrecking our shit, when you know those packages were up in here?"

"*Our* shit? You don't even fucking live here anymore, remember?"

"I ain't forgot shit," Moses roared. "I left that bag here for safekeeping. So what did you do with it?"

"Ain't did shit with it," she shouted and then flinched when her own voice echoed inside of her head.

"If you don't un-ass my shit . . ."

"Fuck you," she snapped.

"Who the fuck did you have all up in here?" he thundered.

"I didn't plan it. . . . It was a surprise party."

"Well, SURPRISE! My shit is gone. Now what the fuck am I supposed to do? Huh?"

"Let go of my arm," she demanded.

"Oh. Does that hurt? How about this?" Moses slammed her against the wall in three quick sessions. Pain exploded in Abrianna's head, shutting off all communication to her legs, so when he released her she dropped like a stone to the floor.

"Tell me, goddamn it!" Moses punched the wall.

Plaster rained around Abrianna.

"You know *something,*" he insisted. "How the fuck you gonna get jacked in your own crib? Weren't you watching those muthafuckas?"

The buzzing escalated inside her head. Moses grabbed her, but without a second thought, she caught his arm and twisted.

Moses roared until she kicked him in the groin, knocking the wind out of him and forcing him to double over.

He had her twisted.

Moses recovered and grabbed the back of her head and spun her around. A black rage clicked on inside of her head, and Abrianna delivered a jab punch to his throat. Those free karate classes at the YMCA came in handy.

Duane busted up the scene, looking frightened. "Yo, man. Zeke is here."

Moses and Abrianna froze.

"What?" Moses wheezed.

"Yeah, man. I'm going to head on out and let you handle your business." Duane's wide-eyed fear spread like a contagion.

Moses shoved Abrianna away and grabbed Duane before he backpedaled out of the room. "Yo, man, wait. Where are you going? We're in this shit together."

"The fuck we are." Duane attempted to break free. "You put your name on this. Zeke gave those bricks to *you*—not me."

"You put in twenty K."

"Yeah . . . and by the way, I'm gonna need that grip back, seeing how you done lost our shit."

"Now it's *ours?* Make up your fucking mind."

"Half the *money* was mine, but you were in charge of holding the product. Where's the product?" Duane hissed, his own anger overriding his fear.

Abrianna's heart sank. Zeke was an OG kingpin in Washington D.C. In the streets, most referred to him as the *Teflon Don.* His hands were in most of the criminal enterprises in these streets, but the muthafucka had never gotten so much as a traffic ticket. On the flipside, there were also whole cemeteries filled with the bodies of folks who'd crossed *or* tried to cross him.

"Well, I wish you the best of luck, bruh," Duane said. "Call me when you're through and let me know how it all pans out." Duane tried to pry himself loose from Moses.

Moses's grip held. "Duane, if you take one step out of this crib, I'll shoot your ass my damn self."

Duane looked crestfallen.

Finally, Zeke's gravelly baritone rumbled from the living room. "Is this how you muthafuckas treat company?"

Three sets of eyes shifted around the room. None of them knew what to say or do.

When no one answered, Zeke spoke up, "Should I invite myself to the private party back there?"

Moses found his voice. "Nah, Zeke. We're coming up." He glared at Duane and stabbed a pointed finger into his chest. "One move for that fucking door . . ."

Slowly, Duane nodded.

"What do you want me to do?" Abrianna asked.

Moses glanced back, but his anger toward her remained visible. "Put some fucking clothes on, and then I want your ass to write a *list.*"

"A list?"

"Fuck, Bree. I can't take an eighty-thousand-dollar hit." He shook his head. "I was already in for forty K with Zeke *before* this shit. I needed those bricks to break even. I'm a fucking dead man if I don't get that shit back. Times are hard. Niggas ain't hearing no fuckin' excuses. Now I got to go up there with my dick in my hand and tell him I lost his shit? We'll be lucky if the cops aren't white-chalking our asses within the hour."

"Ok. A list." She nodded, eagerly.

"I need to know the name of *every* muthafucka that was up in here last night. It shouldn't be too hard to find the nigga that's suddenly on the come-up. It ain't like you hang out with the smartest muthafuckas out here."

"Fuck, Moses. I don't remember *everybody* that was here. It was a fuckin' surprise birthday party."

"Birthday?" His face twisted. "How come you didn't tell *me* that it was your birthday?"

"It's no big deal," she said, swiping her hand across her throbbing bottom lip. "I don't even like celebrating it."

"So they just showed up?"

"They were here when I got off work."

"See? This is why the fuck you don't hang with criminals and shit."

She buttoned her lip, opting not to remind him that they were a couple of criminals too.

"Write *everyone* that you *do* remember. I got to get that coke back. I already know that bitch Shawn was up in here. That muthafucka was at the *top* of my list."

Abrianna sighed. "I told you. Shawn has been clean for two years."

"Bullshit." He grabbed her swollen and aching chin and forced her to look at him. "What about *you*? Your eyes are still dilated. You snort up my shit?"

"I didn't snort up no damn two keys," she told him, pulling away.

"No. But you might've pulled them out as party favors for your damn friends."

"I wouldn't do no shit like that."

Moses's eyes hardened. "You wouldn't do no shit like that?"

"I AIN'T GOT ALL DAY," Zeke barked.

Moses's gaze raked Abrianna before he hissed, "Put some fucking clothes on." With his grip still locked around Duane's puny right bicep, Moses shoved his boy in front of him to take the lead back into the living room.

Abrianna rushed behind them so that she could dart back into the bedroom and put on some clothes. The whole time she jerked open drawers and tossed out shit that didn't match, the voices rose in the living room. Her gaze fell to the butt of a .45 tucked beneath a stack of panties in her drawer. Without hesitation, she grabbed it and checked the ammunition.

Full clip.

Duane screamed, hitting a note reserved for operatic sopranos. Loud crashing and thumping followed. Abrianna rounded the corner, still not completely dressed. Three suppressed staccato gunshots flew toward Moses's head—and missed.

"Stop!" Abrianna aimed the .45 at Zeke's large head.

His two goons spun with their weapons leveled.

"Hold up." Zeke put out his arms, stopping his boys. He removed his expensive black shades and stared Abrianna up and down. "Well, if it isn't sexy-ass Abrianna Parker. I should've known that you were hiding somewhere back there." His thick lips expanded to showcase his unnaturally white teeth. "I really don't know what you see in this broke muthafucka right here when you could've had a made brutha like me at your beck and call."

Abrianna held her tongue. There was no reason for his ass to know that she and Moses weren't a couple anymore. She would never get rid of Zeke's ass then.

Moses's jaw twitched. Zeke mused aloud, "Maybe I put a hole in your skull and just take Bree here off your hands?"

Abrianna clicked off the safety.

Zeke's two goons twitched, but Zeke's hands went back up to stop any itchy trigger fingers.

"Feisty." Zeke's smile expanded. "I *love* a feisty bitch."

"Let him go," she ordered evenly.

"Ah. Well. You see. I can't do that. Sorry. Not even for someone as fine as yourself." Zeke's eyes roamed over Abrianna again. "Business. You understand."

"We'll get you your money."

"We?" His eyebrows climbed to the top of his forehead. "*You're* taking on some of this debt too?"

Abrianna's gaze drifted to the small puddle around Duane's butt.

Chin up, Moses refused to look at Abrianna.

"We just need a little more time," she told Zeke, her aim steady.

Zeke frowned. "See now. Time is the one muthafuckin' thing that you *don't* have."

Their eyes locked. "You really are fine as fuck. You know that, don't you?"

The comment hung in the air.

When he finished raping her with his eyes, he returned his attention to Moses. "Looks like this one must really care for you, man."

A long silence trailed his open flirtation, but when Moses didn't bite, Zeke sighed in disappointment. "All right. Now that Ms. Abrianna here has ruined my whole homicidal vibe this morning, I may as well be a little generous. I'm going to give you two a little more time on that . . . money—*only* because *you're* vouching for this cockroach muthafucka. *And* you know how I feel about you. Let's say . . . seventy-two hours?"

Abrianna swung her gaze back over to Moses, but again he left her hanging. "All right. Seventy-two hours," she agreed.

"Then we got ourselves a deal." Laughter exploded from Zeke's chest while he signaled for his goons to head out. "Seventy-two hours," he repeated, following them. At the door, he stopped—turned. "But if you *don't* have my bricks or my eight stacks—I'll come see you *personally*, Ms. Abrianna, on how you can repay the debt."

11

At TyKon Tech, Kadir Kahlifa sat iron straight in the only interview suit that he owned. He reminded himself not to fidget every five minutes, but after waiting for nearly an hour, the task became impossible. He also kept telling himself to stop glancing over at the receptionist, a petite white woman with a serious staring problem. The behavior was typical whenever he came in for these interviews.

Finally, a short, squat man rushed into the lobby.

Relief swept over the receptionist's face. The man whispered something to the woman and she pointed a pen in Kadir's direction.

He took this as his cue to stand and offer out his hand, but the gesture was ignored.

"I'm sorry, Mister . . . Mister?" The man scrunched up his face while reading the name printed on the resume.

"Kahlifa," Kadir filled in for him, sounding much cooler than he felt. "Kadir Kahlifa. It's nice to meet you."

"Yes, Mr. Kahlifa. I'm Davy Jones," he said, pushing up his glasses. "I'm sorry to have kept you waiting."

"Not a problem," Kadir lied, ready to follow the man to his office.

"Yes, well. There has been some kind of screw-up with your temp agency."

Kadir tensed. "A screw-up?"

"Yes," Jones said, pushing up his glasses again. "The position has already been filled. I hate that you traveled all the way down here, but we informed them of this last week. My apologies . . . but we most certainly can validate your parking. Do you have your ticket?"

Lying piece of shit. "Uh, yeah. Sure." Kadir clamped his jaw tight and fumbled inside his suit pockets until he found the parking stub. "Here we go."

"Ah." Mr. Jones's flat lips stretched damn near from ear to ear as he took the stub and marched it back to the receptionist for a stamp.

Kadir fought off a wave of humiliation as best as he could, but failed. The receptionist, forever branded in his mind as a Nazi Barbie, smirked when Mr. Jones returned the parking stub to him.

"Again. Please accept my apologies for this . . . uh."

"Screw-up," Kadir filled in for him, still smiling.

"Right." Jones chuckled. "Well, good day."

Tucking his tail in between his legs, Kadir turned and headed toward the building's glass doors. The entire way across the stone floor, he felt the weight of Jones and the Nazi's judgmental stares. Even outside, strolling down Shaw, Kadir knew he hadn't escaped them because the whole damn building was made out of glass. *I'm never going to find a decent job.* Kadir normally batted away negative thoughts, but after months of trying, his optimism was dying a slow death.

The fall breeze also failed to cool him down during the long walk to and through the office's parking deck. Six years later and Kadir could still hear Judge Sanders rapping that damn gavel while the marshals slapped him back into cuffs and hauled him off. Now he was starting his life over, and his name, race, and record held him back. Rent was due in a few days, and he wasn't looking forward to calling his parents to ask them to wire money—again. The loan would come with a lecture about how he needed to leave the United States and return to Yemen with the rest of the family.

Kadir wasn't ready for that step. And his probation wouldn't allow it.

With his mind on his problems, Kadir nearly walked past his black GMC Acadia. It was a good, solid car that he used for the one job that he'd managed to get since he'd been released from prison: Uber. On one hand, it was great because it allowed him to set his own schedule. On the other hand, it was awful because he had to put up with a lot of bullshit from riders, who always found a reason to bitch and complain. It was a hard job for someone who wasn't a people person, but any time he thought about quitting, the lint in his pockets reminded him that he couldn't. Sighing, he started up the car to head home. Then his cell phone rang. He glanced at the screen but didn't recognize the number—so he knew exactly who it was.

"Ghost, my man. What's up?"

"The sun, man. Just the sun." Ghost chuckled at his own bad joke. "You got time for a drink tonight?"

Kadir laughed. "You know I don't drink."

"Right. I meant that you can come and watch *me* drink while I lay out a proposition to you."

"Is it legal?"

"Of course not. Who the hell do you think that you're talking to?"

Kadir's laughter deepened. "Tonight?"

"Tonight."

Kadir shook his head. Ghost was exactly who he needed to stay away from while on probation. "All right. Where do you want to meet?"

12

Shawn and Draya entered Abrianna's apartment with their mouths open.

"What the hell?" Shawn asked, handing Abrianna her usual coffee order.

Abrianna removed the frozen pack of peas from her swollen jaw. "Trust me, *he* looks a lot worse."

Draya marveled at the destruction. There were at least a dozen human-sized holes in the walls. "Did you kill him?"

"No," Abrianna said. "But I thought about it."

Shawn, dressed head-to-toe in hipster Gucci, tsked under his breath. "You *have* to watch your temper. You practically have the strength of ten men."

"Ha. Ha."

"No bullshit." Shawn walked away, frowning. "You know that serial killer fucked you up. Who knows what the hell all that shit he injected y'all with was. It's probably what's behind all those fucking headaches."

"You're making a big deal out of nothing," she said.

Shawn walked away. "Draya, talk to your girl."

Draya sighed. "He's right, you know. You should at least go to the doctor and get yourself checked out."

"No doctors," Abrianna said.

"What about checking on those other girls that were kid-napped with you? Maybe see how they're doing?" Draya suggested.

"No."

"You're self-medicating with street drugs to stop that buzzing in your head, and all it's doing is turning you into a junkie."

Abrianna sprang to her feet. "I'm not a damn junkie. I can quit at any time."

"Really? How about now?" Draya challenged.

Abrianna set her coffee down. "What is this—some kind of intervention?"

"Does it need to be?"

Abrianna swung her gaze between her friends. "I don't believe this."

"We can call the whole gang down here if you'd like," Shawn said.

"Look. I get it. You guys are concerned."

"Concerned?" Shawn blinked his long lashes. "You jumped off the roof!"

Abrianna glanced to Draya.

"Yeah. He told me about it when I sobered up this morning." Abrianna rolled her eyes. "I didn't *jump*. . . . I was startled."

"So we're back to blaming me again?" he asked.

"No. God." She tossed up her hands. "I'm not blaming you. I'm just saying . . ."

"Were you thinking about jumping?" Shawn asked.

Abrianna opened her mouth, but couldn't force a lie out of it. "It *crossed* my mind."

"See, Draya?" Shawn shouted, gesturing to Abrianna. "Did you hear that?"

"Briefly," Abrianna added, to soften the blow.

"Oh—briefly? Well, I guess that means there's no reason for us to worry then, is there?"

Abrianna sighed. "I don't know what you want me to tell

you. I'm fucked up. There. I admit it. But I'm dealing with it the best way I can."

"You can deal with it by getting help," Shawn countered. "I lost you once. I don't want to go through that again."

"You won't have to," Abrianna assured him. "Not if you come with me."

He and Draya frowned.

"Today is the big day," she informed him. "I'm blowing this taco stand. I'm taking the money that I've been saving up and I'm out."

"Wait. What?" they chimed.

"You heard me." Abrianna stood from the sofa and marched to her bedroom. "Thanks for the coffee."

"Where in the hell do you think that you're going? We're not finished talking to you." Shawn and Draya followed her to her bedroom to see that she was already in the middle of packing.

"All right," Draya drawled. "Clearly, we've skipped a few steps. What's going on?"

"Moses. That's what's going on," Abrianna mumbled. "He's always what's going on."

"I thought you kicked him out," Shawn said.

"I did, but the bastard came back this morning because he stored Zeke's drugs here. Apparently one of my *good* friends from the party last night jacked his shit."

"What? No way," Shawn said, shaking his head. "None of us would ever do anything like that." He glanced to Draya. "Right?"

"Of course not!"

"Well, it's sure as shit gone. And when Zeke showed up, he almost whacked Moses in my fucking living room!"

Draya and Shawn gasped. "What did you do?"

"Something stupid. I pulled a gun on Zeke to stop him."

"Holy shit," Shawn said. "And you lived to tell the tale?"

"I need to sit down," Draya said, finding a spot on the bed.

"Zeke," Shawn repeated. "Teflon Don?"

Abrianna nodded.

"I better sit down, too." He joined Draya on the edge of the bed.

"Yeah, well. *Now* my name is on the missing drugs. Zeke gave us seventy-two hours to come up with it or his eighty thousand. *I* don't have his drugs and Zeke isn't taking *my* hard-earned money. So I'm out of here."

"You're running?"

"You're damn right I am. It's now or never."

"Today?" Shawn asked.

Abrianna set her coffee aside and tried to approach this with a little more sensitivity. "I know it's sudden and all, but it can't be helped."

"Shit. You're serious."

"Of course I'm serious. It's time. I want to get out of this city and just . . . just start over. Maybe I'll go back to school or something. If I stay here, I'll just continue to be a victim—always scared that there's another boogeyman waiting to jump out from behind every corner. Clean break. Fresh start. That's what I need."

"Will I ever see you again?" Shawn asked, his frown deepening.

"Of course you will. One day—I'll mail you a ticket to wherever I land."

"I'm going to hold you to that."

"Deal." She walked over to him and kissed his forehead. "No matter where I go or what happens, you'll always be my best friend."

"Damn right."

Shawn and Draya stayed a couple of hours to help clean up the mess from the birthday party and the dust-up between Abrianna and Moses. No doubt the landlord was probably going to throw a fit when he saw the damage to the walls.

Before leaving, Shawn elicited a promise from Abrianna that she would see him before she actually left town. Zeke had given her seventy-two hours, but she'd planned to be gone within the first twenty-four.

Abrianna stopped packing long enough to make it to the National Capital Bank before it closed. In her actual checking account, she rarely kept a balance of more than two hundred dollars. She'd only got the account so it wouldn't look suspicious for her to own the safe deposit box that came with it. Entering the bank, Abrianna presented a key and the proper identification.

However, after she was led to the box, it was what was *missing* inside of it that set her blood on fire.

"Where the hell is my money?" She jammed her hand inside the box and felt around as if she didn't trust her eyes.

Where in the fuck? Abrianna pulled it together long enough to demand answers from the bank clerk and then again with the bank manager. After she endured their stupefied expressions, they produced logbooks showing that she'd last visited the box two weeks ago. When Abrianna had done *no* such thing. Mentally, she snapped the pieces of the puzzle together and knew that Moses's thieving ass was behind this shit.

Storming out of the bank, Abrianna set out to do one thing: kill Moses.

13

"Yo, yo. Kadir! Wait up, man!"

Wrenching his thoughts from his growing money problems, Kadir jerked around in a one-eighty and caught Mook rushing up to him. Automatically, he took a step back and braced for anything.

A nervous Mook smiled. "I got that package you wanted." He opened his black jacket far enough for Kadir to see the brown paper bag folded and clutched next to his stomach. "Nontraceable."

The gun. Kadir's eyes widened while he looked around, paranoid. "What the fuck, man?" Grabbing Mook by his elbow, Kadir pulled him to the corner of his apartment building. "What the hell, man? Don't you know how to keep things on the down low?"

Kadir noted Mook's pink, dilated eyes and his inability to stand still. Rules of the streets were to avoid tweakers—but after four near carjackings, his part-time Uber driving was turning into a dangerous occupation. He needed something for protection, despite being an ex-con. Judge Sanders may as well have just branded EASY TARGET on his forehead.

"C'mon, man. You still want this shit or not? It's two hundred dollars." Mook's large, red, swollen nose dripped despite the constant sniffing.

"What you got?"

"High Standard forty-five with a military hardwood grip," he boasted.

Kadir frowned at the droplets of blood oozing from Mook's right nostril. "You're bleeding."

"Huh?" Mook brushed the back of his hand across his nose, but didn't flinch when he saw the swath of blood arched across his knuckles. "Quit wasting time. Are we doing this shit or not?"

The shaking. The sniffing. The red eyes.

Kadir flipped up his hands and backed away. "Nah. We good."

"What?" Mook rushed behind him. "Yo, man. You came to *me*."

Kadir instantly went to a boxer's stance. "Whoa. Whoa. Back up off me."

Mook took two steps back while his awkward laughter bounced off the brick building. "My bad. My bad. But you put out the request, man. I've been out here doing *you* a favor."

"Wait," Kadir barked, stopping Mook before he took off. Who knew when he would get another chance? "How about one-fifty?"

Mook eyed Kadir. "One seventy-five."

Kadir stepped back.

"One-seventy?" Mook countered.

"Uh—" Kadir stroked his chin.

"Okay. Okay." Mook laughed. "You sure do know how to drive a hard bargain. "One sixty-five!"

Kadir scrunched his nose.

"Shit, man. Cut me a fucking break. You got my ass out here wide open. You tryna punk me or some shit? Muthafuckas pay five hundred for this shit. I'm giving you a major-ass discount as it is."

"All right. Calm the fuck down." Kadir looked around. "Let me see it."

Mook's dark mood swung back into the light, but he took another paranoid look around before he opened his jacket and pulled out a paper bag and then withdrew the gun.

Kadir assessed the weapon and calculated how much time he'd get if he were busted with it.

"Well? Are you going to keep me out here all day or what?"

"One-sixty."

Mook rolled his eyes. "Fine. Fine. Show me the money."

Kadir scooped out his money and peeled off eight twenties.

A jubilant Mook shoved the paper-bag-wrapped package into Kadir's jacket. "What about bullets?"

"In the bag." Mook grinned. "One complimentary box of bullets. I'm better than Wal-Mart out here. I've been telling you."

"Cool. Whatever. Thanks." Kadir zipped up his jacket.

Mook jogged backwards. "If you need anything else, holler at your boy. I'm always around."

That's what bothers me. "Catch you later." Kadir watched and waved until Mook was out of sight before turning and heading to his apartment. Hyper aware of the paper bag crinkling in his jacket, he took the stairs two at a time to the third floor. However, he stopped cold when he spotted his front door cracked open.

The fuck? Fearing the worst, Kadir bolted into the apartment, expecting to find the place empty. Instead, he found two federal agents.

FBI Special Agent Quincy Bell threw up his hands. "Oh, Roland. Look who's finally home. It's our favorite freedom fighter: Kadir Kahlifa." Bell's slick grin appeared ten miles wide, and he looked entirely too comfortable in Kadir's crib.

"What are you doing here?" he asked, remaining in the doorway.

"Oh." Bell looked around the studio apartment. "I guess you could say that I was just in the neighborhood and decided to pay a visit to an old *friend*." Bell's gaze zoomed in on him. "We are still friends, aren't we?"

"Friends?" Kadir leaned against the doorjamb, careful not to rustle the bag inside his jacket. "Is that what people who set people up for federal crimes call themselves nowadays? *Friends?* Boy. *A lot* really has changed since I've been locked up."

"Don't tell me that you're sore about that," Bell said. "I figured that we would let bygones be bygones."

"Hardly."

"Tsk. Too bad. I really hate hearing that. It breaks my heart. Truly." He poked out his bottom lip.

Kadir was not amused.

"Whelp. Let's move on, shall we?" Bell tossed a throw pillow back onto the sofa and took a seat.

This wasn't going to be a short visit.

"C'mon in. Stop being a stranger. This is your place, after all."

"I'm glad you remembered that." Kadir moved away from the door and entered the apartment. Once inside, he caught sight of a huge black agent perusing his IKEA bookshelf.

"You must be Roland?" Kadir said.

"That's Federal Special Agent Hendrickson to you."

"Got it."

"Interesting collection you got here," Roland complimented him. "You sure do like a bunch of code and technology books."

Bell sucked his teeth. "I hope that doesn't mean that you have a computer up in here somewhere. That's a big no-no."

"I'm well aware of that. I'm sure if there were a computer in here you and your new buddy here would've found it."

Bell's gaze intensified. "I don't know. You strike me as someone who thinks that he's clever. Maybe you have some very creative hiding places in this matchbox setup?"

"No."

"No computer?" Hendrickson double-checked.

"No," Kadir insisted. The gun shifted, and for a moment his heart stopped. What the hell was he going to do if he dropped a gun in front of two trespassing federal agents itching for a reason to throw his ass back in jail? Suddenly, Mook's twitchy ass got him thinking that his dumb ass got set up again.

"What about your friend Douglas Jenkins? I think his buddies call him *Ghost?*"

The question threw Kadir. "What about him?"

"Seen him lately? Talked to him?"

"No. Why?"

"Oh." Bell rolled his hand. "There are just some rumors going around about him leading some sort of hacking group. Heard about that?"

Kadir shook his head. "No. Actually I haven't spoken to him since I got out."

"Huh. I thought you two were tight?"

"A lot can change in six years."

"If you say so." Bell cocked his head and studied Kadir. "Are you all right?" Bell asked, eyeing him suspiciously.

"Why?"

"Well. You look a bit off," Hendrickson observed.

"And you look like crude oil," Kadir countered, annoyed.

Bell released an unexpected belly laugh that had his partner shifting his side-eye to him.

"What?" Bell shrugged. "You do kind of look like crude oil."

"Fuck both of you muthafuckas."

Impatient, Kadir hung by the door. "Now as much as I'm enjoying this . . ."

"Reunion," Bell filled in.

"Yeah. Reunion. But I only have a few minutes to shower and get ready for my shift."

"Ah. That's right. You're one of those Uber drivers that zip around town."

"Keeping tabs on me?"

"Damn right," Bell said, finally dropping the friendly charade. "You see—I don't think that fucking hacktards like you ever lose the itch, you know? There is always the call or challenge to hack some new system or play hide-and-seek with confidential information. Guys like you don't retire. You just bide your time and wait for the heat to die down." He stood from the sofa and erased the space between them in two long strides. "Isn't that right?"

Kadir maintained eye contact while mentally willing the paper bag not to rustle.

"Let me put your mind at ease," Bell said, leaning into his personal space. "The heat is *never* going to die down on you, my friend. I'm personally going to see to it."

"How did you pass a background check?" Roland asked.

"I didn't—I got a buddy to vouch for me," Kadir said.

"A buddy?" Bell placed his hands on his hips. "Now which buddy was this?"

"Look. I already have a parole officer I answer to. There's nothing in the paperwork about the feds breaking into my place anytime they want to harass me."

"Then maybe you should take another look at the fine print because I'm sure it's in there."

"Look, Agent Bell. I'm clean. I don't have anything to hide." The bag shifted.

Bell and his buddy laughed.

"That's funny, *Kahlifa*. And if I had a dollar for every time I heard that bullshit, I'd be the one retired."

Their gazes dueled until Bell tired of the game. "I'll be

watching you." He slid on his shades. "C'mon, Roland. I think we've made ourselves clear."

Roland sighed, as if disappointed that no violence had occurred, and erased the space to the front door in a few strides. "Nice meeting you."

Kadir kept his mouth zipped.

"Cheer up." Bell grinned. "I'll make it so that you'd never notice me." He thumped Kadir on the chest. The paper bag crinkled. "Whatcha got there?"

"Lunch," Kadir lied with a straight face.

The men stared at each other.

"Well. Bon appetit." Bell gave Kadir a two-finger salute and waltzed out of the apartment.

Kadir slammed and locked the door before removing the gun from his jacket. *When will I fucking ever learn?*

14

"Where the fuck are you?" Abrianna blasted into Moses's voice mail. "And where in fuck do you get off stealing my money? This is not how the fuck this shit is going down. You got me all the way fucked up if you think that . . . THE FUCK?" Abrianna slammed on her brakes when an asshole came out from nowhere and braked.

"Watch where the fuck you're going!" Abrianna threw up her middle finger. "Learn how to fucking drive!"

The driver whipped off his shades and laid on his horn.

She ignored him and kept her finger up while she completed her turn out of the bank's parking lot.

Abrianna's attention returned to the cell phone tucked under her ear, but the call had disconnected. "Shit." Her acrylic nail stabbed in Moses's number again, but this time she received a fast busy signal. "This muthafucka here." She tossed the cell over into the passenger-side seat and gripped the steering wheel at ten and two. She needed to slow down and clear her head.

Mr. Bad Driver pulled up next to her at a red light and shook his head.

"Fuck you," she mumbled and then jumped when her cell phone rang.

The car's Bluetooth speakers kicked in and the speaker's feminine robotic voice announced, *"Call from Alexei. Say answer or ignore."*

Abrianna rolled her eyes and debated briefly whether to take her boss's call. "Answer," she huffed. "Hello."

"Bree, where in fuck are you? You begged me to schedule you for a double today. Did you forget that shit?"

"Yo, Alexei. Sorry. Can't do it today. Something has come up. I got some shit I gotta take care."

"Fuck that," he shouted, his Russian accent thickening. "I'm running a business. You handle your bullshit on your own time. Get in here, Bree. I joke not. I—"

"All right. I'll see you tonight." She disconnected the call. Minutes later, she swung onto the street corners Moses and his boys held on lock, but couldn't catch hide or tail of them anywhere. But she crept her car through every spot that she could think of, hunting for him. Finally, she picked up her cell phone and called Tivonte—who, by day, was Tyrone and worked as a sous chef at Plume.

"Pick up. Pick up," Abrianna begged over the ringing line.

"Hello."

"Oh, thank God. Tivonte, where does Moses's new girl stay? I know you know."

"Well, good afternoon to you, too, Ms. Girl. I'm doing good. Thanks for asking."

Abrianna caught her breath. "I'm sorry. You're right. Hello, Tivonte. How are you?"

"If you wanna know the truth, I'm still dealing with a hangover from that bomb-ass birthday party you had last night. Did you have fun?"

"Yea. I enjoyed myself immensely. Thank you."

"Enough so that you wanted to kill your damn self," Tivonte charged.

Abrianna sighed. "Shawn told you."

"You're damn right he told me. You damn near gave him a heart attack."

"I'm sorry. I'm fine. It won't happen again."

"Uh-huh. Now what's this I hear about you leaving town?"

"Damn. You already know about that, too?"

"Oh. We stay *all* up in your business, girlfriend. You're the only one of us who got any."

They laughed.

"*Now*," Tivonte said. "What can I do for you?"

"Moses. Where the hell can I find him? I know that he's walled up with some trick. Just point me to where."

Tivonte sighed. "Well, I heard through the grapevine the other day that he's been laying the pipe to Simone Fredds. You know that lopsided-titties heifer who dances down at the Pearls? She stays off one of those townhouses off Volta Place."

"All right, thanks. I owe you one," Abrianna said.

"You owe me *several,* but who's counting? Now you make sure that you see me before you blow this joint. I'll never forgive you if you don't."

"All right. Deal."

Abrianna disconnected the phone and sped her way to Volta but found herself caught up in rush-hour traffic. She damn near crawled out of her skin sitting through the bumper-to-bumper madness. When she arrived on Volta, she immediately spotted Moses's piece-of-shit Durango. The only space available on the whole street was right behind his vehicle. Abrianna whipped her Honda in and jumped out of the car in one fluid motion.

"Stay calm. Don't lose your shit," she coached herself as she bounded up the stairs.

"Moses! I know you're in there!"

She rapped on the door again—harder. "Open this goddamn door and give me back my money!"

Another pound and the door flew open. Abrianna stormed inside.

"What the hell did you do to my door?" Simone screamed as she backpedaled away.

"Where is he?" Abrianna thundered.

"He's not here," she screeched.

"You're a goddamn liar." Abrianna shoved her aside. "Moses! Where the hell are you?!"

"I told you that he's not here," Simone lied, clutching her peach robe closed.

Abrianna cocked her head. "Not dressed in the middle of the day?" She looked up and knew exactly where Moses was hiding.

"No. No." Simone blocked her path to the staircase.

Abrianna sent her headfirst into a wall and then charged up the staircase.

"You crazy bitch," Simone yelled.

Abrianna burst through the first door on the second level. Moses was in the middle of climbing his naked ass out of the bed. His right arm was in a sling. "Asshole! Where in the hell is my money?"

"Bree! Bree! Calm down." He approached with his good arm out in an attempt to ward her off.

"Don't fucking tell me to calm down. Give me back my shit!"

"I was trying to. That was what the dope was for. I was going to flip it and put the money back. I swear."

"You stole my money!"

"*Borrowed*. I borrowed it," he corrected—with a straight face.

"Borrowed, my ass!" She shoved him back a few steps.

"I was going to pay you back."

"Liar!" Another shove and he went straight into the wall,

knocking shit to the floor. "There was more than eighty thousand dollars in there. Where is the rest?"

He pressed his busted lips together and she knew.

"It's *all* gone?"

"Look. I had some debt I had to clean up. I was going to pay you back."

"Stop saying that shit. Thieves don't pay people back! And when they're caught, they do time or get fucked up."

"What about *my* shit?" he challenged. "Where the fuck are my bricks?"

"At this point, I don't even know if there ever were any damn bricks. I never saw them."

"Yeah. Right."

Abrianna grew angrier the more she thought about it. "You robbed Zeke *and* me. You knew that I didn't have any money when Zeke gave us the seventy-two-hour deadline and you didn't say shit. Now my name is on that debt."

"Who the fuck are you kidding?" Moses asked, changing up. "You weren't about to go and pay that shit. Your ass was about to run, and you damn well know it."

"So? It was *my* fucking money! I can do whatever the hell I feel like with it!"

"Well . . . it's gone. All of it. I—"

"You son of a bitch!" Abrianna sprung forward and whooped his ass.

15

Ray's Sports Bar off Fourteenth Street was a dimly lit place with a traditional bar feel. Not everyone knew each other's name, but to former lieutenant Castillo, it still felt like home. She liked washing her troubles away with a few brewskies at the end of the day. Today was particularly troubling, since she'd read about Shalisa Young's plunge off the roof of St. Elizabeths. Castillo had been shocked when the girl was arrested for murdering her mother—and shocked when she was found not competent to stand trial. Now she was gone. Maybe she'd never left Dr. Craig Avery's basement.

When Tomi Lehane breezed through the door, Castillo smiled and waved her over. "Glad that you could make it."

"Whew! I almost didn't," Tomi exclaimed, removing her jacket.

Castillo signaled for the bartender. "What'll you have?"

"A beer is fine." She settled into the booth and looked around the place. "Interesting place."

"Yeah. I like it." Castillo glanced around her second home and pushed up a smile when the waitress arrived. "Two beers and new bowl of peanuts, if you don't mind."

"You got it, Gigi."

Tomi's brows lifted. "Gigi?"

"One has no control over nicknames."

Smiling, Tomi glanced over Castillo's shoulder.

Castillo turned to see Tomi's attention was drawn to one of the flat-screens tuned in to CNN. The newly elected speaker of the House, Kenneth Reynolds, accepted the gravel from the retiring speaker, Miles Hartman, and then addressed the assembled representatives on the House floor.

"Thank you." Deep breath. *"I never thought that I'd be speaker. You have done me a great honor. Before I begin, I want to thank my family and friends who flew in from Illinois to be here today: in the gallery, my mom, Joan. My brother, Lawrence, and my sister, Shannon. I want to recognize my wife, Valerie, and our four kids . . ."*

"Whelp." Tomi pulled her gaze from the screen. "The smug son of a bitch did it. He pulled it off."

"I take it you don't care for the man?"

Tomi laughed. "I don't know him—but no. There's just something about him."

"Is that the reason you want me to dig around in his background? Are you working a story angle?"

"I'm covering a congressional investigation that he's chairing, but that was before this whole hoopla of him being drafted to the speakership. Now add in his boast that he could impeach the president, and I'd say that Speaker Reynolds is going to be in my headlines for a while."

"Are you looking for something in particular?"

"I'm looking for *everything.* On paper, he's the last Boy Scout and I don't buy it."

"Who doesn't like a Boy Scout?"

"What can I say? I'm a cynic."

"Not jaded?"

"Call it a mixed bag." She smiled. "So how are you?"

"Good. I could complain—but why bother?"

"I hear you."

Castillo assessed Tomi again. She really had blossomed into a beautiful woman, but Castillo knew that there were still scars just below the surface. Tomi's jet-black hair reached the center of her back. And her large doe eyes made it clear that she never missed a single thing. She was beautiful without trying. Castillo liked that about her.

Despite Tomi's easy smile, Castillo was certain that Avery had also left his mark on her. *And what about Bree?*

Their beers arrived and Castillo quickly took a deep swig. There hadn't been a day since Bree—or rather Abrianna Parker, as Castillo had later found out when Bree's parents came looking for her—disappeared out of that hospital that Castillo hadn't thought about her, wondered where she was and how she was doing. And sometimes wondered whether she was still alive.

"So what do you say?" Tomi asked. "Do you think you can help me out and see what you can dig up?"

"Really got a feeling about this one, huh?"

"A pretty strong one," Tomi said, drinking.

Castillo looked back at the screen. Speaker Reynolds was still rambling. She stared while his words fell on deaf ears. The veneered smile was politician perfect, but there *was* an . . . oiliness that seeped into the man's delivery. Castillo spotted all the deliberate, well-rehearsed stagecraft in his performance. "The thing is, I already know that Reynolds isn't what he appears to be," she admitted.

Tomi perked. "Oh?"

"Years ago, I'm not sure how many, I had a situation with Reynolds and his wife. Apparently, Mr. Reynolds had a problem keeping his hands to himself. His record is clean because his wife refused to press charges and Reynolds had the political pull to make my incident report disappear before I'd finished typing it up. The shit was pretty bad. I remember thinking that he had gone at his wife, who was barely five-two and one hundred pounds, like they were two dudes in a prison yard. She was a sobbing mess and he was a self-confident, arrogant prick. I'm actually looking forward to digging around his closet."

"So you'll do it?"

"Of course. You know I'd do anything I can to help you."

"Great! Just invoice me your expenditures. And turn over every rock you can find. There's something there. I know it." Tomi beamed. "I *knew* that I could count on you." She tapped their bottlenecks together and they guzzled down their drinks. For the next hour, they caught each other up on what was going on in their lives.

"Oh. *Chief* Holder wanted me to tell you hi." Tomi grinned.

Castillo dropped her gaze. "Oh?"

Tomi cocked her head, smiling. "Are you two still acting like you don't have the hots for each other?"

"It's not an act. There's nothing between us."

"Are you sure about that?"

"Waitress," Castillo called. "Another round."

Tomi laughed. "All right. I can take a hint. But actually, I have to go." She climbed out of the booth.

"What? You're going?"

"Deadline. Sorry. We'll play catch up next time. I promise." She pulled her jacket back on.

Castillo reluctantly climbed out of the booth as well.

As they leaned in for a hug, Tomi knocked over her beer bottle.

"No!"

The bottle stopped and Tomi quickly grabbed it.

Castillo froze. The whole thing happened so fast that Castillo wondered if her eyes were playing tricks on her. "What the fuck did I just see?"

"Huh?" Tomi's face darkened. "Oh. Nothing. That was close, huh?" She fidgeted. "Well, I better get going." She turned, but before she could take a step, Castillo's hand locked on her arm.

"Oh no you don't," she said, eyes bugged. "Tell me I'm not crazy. Did that bottle just stop in midair?"

"What?" Tomi laughed, but sounded like a broken tailpipe. "No. That's crazy."

"Sit down," Castillo ordered and shoved Tomi back into the booth. However, when Castillo returned to her seat, she could only stare at the girl across from her.

Tomi caved, but started the conversation in a lower voice. "All right. You're freaked out."

"That's one emotion," Castillo said cautiously.

"Well, don't be. I mean . . . well . . . I freaked out the first time I did something like that, too. But . . . it's really no big deal."

"No big deal?"

"What I mean is . . ." Tomi struggled for the right words. "I don't want it *turned* into a big deal. I don't want to wind up in a hospital where they poke and prod me like a lab rat. I don't know *how* I can do these things. I just . . . can. But not all the time. I have to really be focused on something. But definitely at heightened states."

"Heightened states?"

"Yeah, like when I'm angry, frightened, and now apparently startled."

"You can stop objects from falling? What else can you do?"

"I can move things, but not large things."

"Like what?"

Tomi huffed. "Oh, I don't know." She looked around and then focused on her beer bottle again.

Castillo followed her gaze. When the bottle moved toward her, she fell back against the booth, stunned.

Tomi stopped it. "See? Just small things like that."

Castillo's gaze swung between Tomi and the beer bottle. "But how?"

"I don't know how. I just . . . can."

"All right. All right. Just give me a minute. This is some freaky *X-Files* shit or something." She pulled a couple of deep breaths to settle her nerves. "How long have you been able to do this?"

Tomi hedged and nibbled on her bottom lip. "The first time I did it, about a month after you rescued us from that basement."

"What? That long?"

"Yeah. And there's other things . . . small things."

"I'm all ears."

Tomi grabbed what was left of her beer and chugged it down. "I've never told anybody about this. But, uh . . . I've been in a few intimate relationships in the past, and the guys often complained that when I'm asleep that I . . . appear dead."

Castillo's facial expressions were getting quite the workout. "Explain."

"They claim that I stop breathing at night—that I lay there like a corpse or something." Tomi chuckled at a memory. "When me and my first boyfriend spent the night together, I woke to him sobbing like a baby. The paramedics were coming into the room with a gurney. I completely freaked everyone out when I woke up. Needless to say, that relationship ended rather suddenly."

The waitress finally brought more beer to the table. Tomi and Castillo reached for the additional alcohol like it was a lifeline.

"The best that I can figure," Tomi said, "Craig Avery might have been a mad scientist after all."

16

Stallion Gentlemen's Club

Abrianna strolled to the front door of the Stallion dressed in black Jackie O sunglasses and with her head hung low. Crusher, in his customary suit and tie at the front door, took one look and shook his bald head.

"Don't say anything," Abrianna warned when he opened the door.

"Not even that you could do better than that loser Moses?" He lowered his own shades so that she could see his sincerity.

"No. Not even that. Besides, you should see him."

Crusher sighed. "I'll never understand you girls. Always flocking to the bad boys who treat you like shit."

A smile ghosted her lips as Abrianna conceded, "We accept the level of love that we believe we deserve."

Crusher cocked his head. "That's profound . . . and sad as fuck."

Abrianna shrugged. "It is what it is. The story of my life."

Moving through the half-filled club, she kept her head down until she reached the girls' changing room in the back. Inside, she dropped her bag and plopped into the chair in front of the corner vanity.

For a long time, she stared at her reflection through the large shades. *Be glad you broke up with that thieving bastard.* Tears leaked beneath her sunglasses. *Pathetic.* Her life was a sad stereotype.

Abrianna removed the sunglasses just as Missy and Cashmere waltzed into the changing room, laughing. Their laughter stopped the moment they took one look at her.

"Goddamn, Bree!" Cashmere leapt back as if a killer in a horror flick had jumped out. "What the hell happened to your face?"

Missy, equally horrified, crept closer to Abrianna's chair for a better look. "Did your man do that to you?"

"Of course not," she lied, flinching. "Things got a little wild at the party last night, and I had a little accident and tripped."

The eye-rolling Olympics started immediately. The excuse was hardly original.

Cashmere strutted to her favorite chair before the wall-length vanity. "Whatever, girl. I warned you that Moses had a bad temper. The last girl he fucked with used to have a whole lot of 'accidents' too."

"Cash—"

"I'm just saying." She tossed up her hands, surrendering. "You and ol' girl sho' do have a lot of shit in common. A bitch can make an observation, can't she? I just wonder how long it will be before we find *your* ass dead in a ditch somewhere."

"That's not fair. Mercedes OD'd," Abrianna reminded her.

Cashmere lifted one of her pencil-thin eyebrows. "Is *that* what your nigga told you?" She laughed. "Then you're stupider than I thought."

"Whatever." Abrianna leaned over and dug her makeup out of her gym bag. There was absolutely nothing that stage makeup couldn't cover up. She wasn't about to tell those girls that she and Moses had broken up. Because then they would want to know why and what happened, and it was none of their business.

By the time more of the evening dancers filtered into the dressing room, Abrianna was right as rain and ready for her close-up. However, she needed a pick-me-up before hitting the stage. At least the coke stopped all the buzzing inside of her head. It was the only thing that did. But then she argued with herself that she didn't need it and she had to work on cleaning up her act like she'd promised Shawn. She kept telling herself that she wasn't going to take the hit even while she prepped the needle and spread her toes.

Within seconds, the cocaine hit her bloodstream. Her problems and exhaustion melted away and bathed the world in a golden, shimmery light. But Shawn's voice floated out to her. *You need help.*

"I know. I know," she mumbled.

Missy and Cashmere twisted their faces.

"What? What the hell are you two looking at?" Abrianna snapped.

"Not much," Cashmere snarled, moving past her. "Alexei has gotta do something about hiring all these damn junkies. It's bad for business."

"For real," Missy co-signed.

Fuck you bitches. Abrianna tossed the disposable needle toward a small wastebasket near the pink lockers, not concerned with whether she made the shot. *It's showtime.*

She took to the stage as Autumn Breeze. The cheers, hoots, and catcalls when she hit the stage exploded her ego. After all, it wasn't too long ago that she had been through a chubby, acne-prone phase. She'd shoved candy bars down her throat rather than deal with the nightmare that she'd lived through. Now there weren't any traces of that ugly duckling. Her skin was smooth milk chocolate, and no one could pinch more than an inch off of her Coke-bottle curves. Celebrity bitches paid a fortune for an ass like hers. And she was young, so her thirty-eight C cups defied gravity. But, in a lot of ways, she was still that same preteen, only she preferred drugs to candy bars. Heaven knew that she carried the same baggage, the same pain, and the same ghosts around everywhere she went.

After her first set, she headed to the champagne room to give private dances. Invisible. That was what most of the girls grinding on golden poles inside that room were. Invisible. The johns didn't see them, not the real women. They never did . . . or even tried. Abrianna was a little girl lost. A barely legal sex kitten, winding her baby-oiled hips and sliding around while a thousand lights from a cheap disco ball turned her into their wildest fantasies. She was what they couldn't get at home. A perfect body, a constant smile, and no judgment about their base desires.

It wasn't much of a life, but it was hers. She wasn't looking for a fucking pity party. She had a plan. At least, she *used* to. Now she didn't know what the fuck she was going to do. The Stallion had been good to her. It wasn't so bad—better than working the seedy streets of the nation's capital. The few times her path had crossed with politicians in expensive suits and unnaturally white veneers, she'd wanted to scrub her body with bleach.

"Marry me," Father Sherwyn panted above a nasty Rihanna beat.

She rolled her hips and teased him with quick flashes of her pussy. "You ask me that every week," she said, smiling.

"That's because you keep saying no," he whined, playfully.

Abrianna turned around, bent over, and grabbed her ankles.

"Oh sweet baby Jesus." Sweat broke out across the good father's forehead.

Wiggling her ass, she dared him to take a bite. "Catholic priests allowed to get married?"

"No, but I'd give it all up for you."

"Really? You'd give up your God just for lil' ol' me?" She sat, spun and spread her legs in a perfect V. Her pussy was an open banquet.

Love, lust, and desire visibly battled across his face.

"Yes. Yes. I'd give you whatever you want," he promised, caressing her inner thighs.

Hulk, the champagne room's watch dog, caught the slick move. "Hands off," he bellowed.

Father Sherwyn jerked back. "Sorry," he apologized, but then refocused on her body.

Abrianna pretended to be sorry that their fun had been interrupted by silly clubhouse rules. Her eyes said, *If only we could be alone. I would rock your world.*

Father Sherwyn tugged on his white collar, and his greedy gaze followed her as her legs lowered to the floor and she pushed away from the table and invaded his personal space.

"Oh, Father, forgive me for I have sinned," the priest whispered.

She placed her hands on the sides of his head and lovingly nestled it between her breasts.

He sighed and wept.

Abrianna sliced a bored look at Hulk. When she let the good father up, his face sparkled with body glitter while fat tears rolled down his face. Nirvana.

Hulk shook his head as if to say, *Pitiful.*

Father Cory Sherwyn was harmless. He'd been a weekly regular for a while. The first time he'd requested a private dance, she'd turned him down. She may have played with a lot of things in her life, but she didn't play with God—just in case he was real. She was an atheist, but she figured, from time to time, she should err on the side of caution. Management disagreed. When word reached Alexei's ears about how she'd caught the good father's eye but had steadfastly turned him down, she had been snatched away to a corner so fast that it had made her head spin. Alexei had given her an ultimatum: dance or take her ass back to the street corners.

No fucking way was she going back on the street corners.

No. Fucking. Way.

⟶•⟵

"The Stallion Gentleman's Club," Kadir grumbled and wondered how he'd let Ghost talk him into meeting here. He personally wasn't a strip club kind of guy but he'd never knock his friends who frequented such places—often blowing through whole paychecks. He parked, stared at the building, and searched for the energy to go inside.

"Just a few minutes. No drinking," he promised himself before climbing out of the car.

An enormous man at the door greeted him, "Welcome to the Stallion Gentlemen's Club. Have a good time."

"Thank you."

Inside, the music was loud, the women were sexy, and the customers all looked happy. It took a few minutes to spot his friend Ghost, waiting in a booth.

"Welcome back to the revolution, brother." Ghost and Kadir slapped palms and drifted into a special handshake. "I can't believe that you're really out."

"*Alhamdulillah*," Kadir said.

"Amen, brother. Praise God." Ghost's smile blanketed his face. "Please. Please. Have a seat." He gestured to the leather U-shaped booth he'd just vacated. A double shot of whiskey awaited his return.

"What's your poison?" Ghost asked, signaling the waitress.

"I'll have a ginger ale," Kadir said, looking around the place. The scantily clad women were definitely hard to ignore.

"Ginger ale? For real?"

"For real." Kadir chuckled and resumed scanning the place.

"Are you expecting someone?"

"No. Why?" He glanced over his shoulder again.

"Oh. I don't know," Ghost mused. "Maybe because you keep looking around."

A bubbly waitress with breasts bigger than her petite frame arrived. "Afternoon, gentlemen. Drinks?" The pretty blonde ignored Ghost and zeroed in on Kadir.

Kadir returned the smile, but not her open interest.

"Two whiskeys," Ghost ordered.

Blondie squeaked a perky, "You got it!"

When she spun away, Ghost's gaze zoomed in on her tight ass. "God, I love this place."

"I see you haven't changed," Kadir chuckled.

"What can I say? Once an ass man, always an ass man."

"Duly noted."

"What about you?" Ghost centered his attention to his old friend. "Any action since you've been out?"

"A gentleman never fucks and tells," Kadir said.

"Ha! I'll keep that in mind when I meet one. But what about *you*? Are you fucking anyone yet?"

"No."

Ghost cocked his head. "Would you tell me?"

"No."

"Asshole." He swigged his drink. "You got to get Malala out of your system, bro. It's fucked up what happened and all, but it's time. Time to move on. You know what I mean?"

"If this is going to be the conversation, then maybe I *will* need that drink."

"Look. We go way back, right?"

Kadir nodded, shrugged.

"As boys, I know that . . . the touchy-feely stuff is off limits but . . ." Ghost leaned over the table and lowered his voice. "I'm worried about you. Men aren't built to go so long without pussy. Six years?" He whistled and fell back against his seat. "Ain't natural."

Kadir managed a half smile while his thoughts drifted to what might have been. While he was locked up, Malala *had* waited for him—for four whole years—then she had been killed in a car crash. Before then, she'd never missed a visit, letters had arrived like clockwork, and she'd planned their wedding with such lavish detail that he saw it each night in his dreams. Then she was gone.

And the world kept spinning.

"Yeah. Sure. Time to move on," Kadir mumbled and checked over his shoulder.

"Seriously, man." Ghost dropped the smile. "What is it? You're making me nervous now. Are you hot?"

"No. Nothing like that."

"Then what?"

Their waitress returned. "Here you go, fellas. Two whiskeys." The wattage on her smile boosted. "Is there anything else I can get you? Wings, nachos—my phone number?"

"No. I think—"

"He'd love your number," Ghost interrupted.

She hesitated.

"He is *shy*," he added.

"Is that right?" Eyes twinkling, she grabbed Kadir's hand and wrote her info on his palm. "My name is Crystal. I get off at midnight," she said, winked, and sauntered off.

The men watched her ass bounce and jiggle away

"You think it's real?" Ghost asked.

Kadir frowned.

"A lot has changed since you've been gone," Ghost picked up his drink and evaluated Kadir. "The revolution really could use you, man. You're tech savvy *and* ex-military."

"What does my military service got to do with anything?"

Ghost shrugged. "Honestly? I was thinking about starting my own little paramilitary security firm. For the people. Truth. Justice. Revolution. The usual shit."

"*Another* revolution? So did you invite me here to recruit me back into doing the same shit that landed my ass in jail or to get me laid?"

"Yes. To both."

Kadir laughed.

"C'mon. Taking down The Man is a lifelong commitment. Deep down, you *know* that you're still a true believer. The shit has gotten worse out here, bro. Everything that you railed against back in the day has come to pass. The American people are asleep, man. They can't see what's right in front of them. The NSA, global corporations—both national *and* international."

Ghost stopped suddenly. "You don't have a cell phone on you, do you?"

"Just a burner, charging outside in the car."

Ghost relaxed. "Well . . . you make sure that you toss it every three days."

"Why three days?"

"I don't trust even numbers."

"Makes sense." Kadir reached for his glass.

"Look. All of this sounds crazy, but the government ain't playing with whistleblowers anymore. They got the whole damn country convinced that *we're* domestic terrorists instead of truth seekers."

"Preaching to the choir." Kadir laughed.

"You were among the first and second wavers, man. Now the government isn't bothering to run us through the courts. Muthafuckas. The government declared war on its own citizens, and the people haven't even noticed the prison bars. The country is one big fucking police state."

Kadir looked around. "This is a prison?"

"I'm telling you, people are disappearing. And that crooked judge that threw you in the clink, she's nominated to be the damn chief justice on the United States Supreme Court now."

"That doesn't surprise me in the least."

"Remember my man Stevie Jay? He was a savant with security walls. There wasn't anything that brother couldn't hack into. Trust and believe that he'd amassed a hell of an enemies list. China, Russia, and the good ol' U.S.A. were all looking for his ass."

"So what happened?"

"Don't know." Ghost went for another sip of his drink. "He just poofed into thin air."

"That doesn't prove anything." Kadir shrugged. "Maybe he just decided to get out of the game. Retire."

Ghost dismissed the comment. "Dude was set to marry the girl of his dreams. *I* was his best man. No way Stevie would've left Felicia crying on her bridesmaids' shoulders, five months pregnant like that. No way."

Kadir digested the information but still couldn't see how it was proof of anything.

"That firm you hacked into six years back that landed you in the clink?"

"Yeah?"

"They are the worst of them all. Part security firm, part paramilitary, and they aren't only operating overseas. It's all fucking scary as shit, man. Sheep. The whole damn country."

Kadir set down his drink. "Not to criticize, but this is a pathetic recruitment speech."

Ghost's smile resurfaced. "The cause is righteous."

Kadir hedged.

"Am I wrong?" Ghost prodded.

Kadir smiled, but only one corner of his lips shifted upward. "Six years was a long time to sit and think."

"Yeah, man, but—"

"And for what?" Kadir challenged. "What have any of our *sacrifices* really ever done? We get one or two laws passed that no one ever follows? Laws are just words on a piece of paper."

"Wow." Ghost stared as if Kadir had sprouted a second head. "You're *really* tossing in the towel? You're like . . . a legend. A lot of guys on the team look up to you—to what you accomplished."

"I accomplished losing years of my life, my fiancée, and my family. I'm not proud of any of that."

Ghost insisted, "The truth still matters."

"To whom?" Kadir finished off his drink. "The truth and a nickel will get me exactly where I am right now: broke and unemployable. Now you're telling me that people are disappearing? Nah. I'm good."

"C'mon, man. I told my guys that you were a shoo-in."

"Sorry. You'll have to disappoint them—but I wish you well, man. Really." Kadir eased out of the booth and stood. "It was good seeing you again." Digging into his front pockets, he pulled out a twenty and tossed it down onto the table.

Sighing, Ghost climbed out. "I can't tell you how disappointed I am . . . but I understand."

"Do you?"

"No. But it sounded like the right thing to say." Ghost offered his hand.

Kadir debated and then shook it. When he looked back up, Ghost smiled. "What?"

"You're tempted."

"No. I'm not," he lied.

"Yeah. Yeah. Keep telling yourself that." Ghost's smile spread wider. "How about you sleep on it? You know how to find me."

The club's DJ boomed over the club. "Gentlemen, the moment that you all have been waiting for. Please welcome her return to the stage: the sexy Autumn Breeze!"

An enthusiastic applause thundered in the place as men gathered around the main stage. Kadir wound his way through the club, and when the most beautiful woman he'd ever laid eyes on took to the stage, he couldn't look away.

Not paying attention to where he was walking, he crashed into bubbly Crystal.

She gasped as her tray of drinks splashed all over her.

Kadir blanched. "I'm so sorry."

Gasping again, Crystal's spunky veneer fell away as she spat out a string of curses and stormed off.

On the stage, Autumn Breeze rolled her hips and Kadir was hypnotized. Her long legs, steep curves, and perfect breasts were definitely real. It didn't hurt that she also had the face of an angel. A tough angel, but an angel all the same.

He was unaware of walking to the stage, but when she moved in close, he slipped his last twenty-dollar bill into the hip string of her thong.

"Thank you, baby," she cooed.

Kadir responded, "You're welcome." In awe, he watched her slink toward the next man dying to place money anywhere on her body. Jealousy curled in his gut.

All too soon, she was gone. The men encircling the stage snapped out of their trances. Kadir wondered if the woman he'd seen had even been real. A heavy hand landed on his shoulder. He jumped and spun around.

Ghost smiled. "If I didn't know any better, I'd say that your ass is sprung."

———✦———

Exhausted by the end of the second set, Abrianna returned to the dressing room and plopped into her vanity chair. A quick count of the night's earnings plunged her deeper into an angry depression. Eighteen hundred dollars was a far cry from the eighty thousand dollars she needed by tomorrow night.

Cashmere pranced back into the dressing room, waving a

card. "Ooooh. Somebody's gotta hot one out there requesting a private dance in the champagne room."

Abrianna glanced back at her in the mirror, hoping that Cashmere was referring to someone else. But the Cheshire cat grin said otherwise. "Now?"

Cashmere nodded, but at Abrianna's eye roll, she added, "Oh, honey. Wait until you see him. Tall, tan, and absolutely fine as hell. I'm not going to lie, I offered him my services, but he wasn't having it. He wants you and *only* you."

Abrianna considered refusing the request to head home, but she wasn't in any position to turn down a single dollar. "I'll be right out."

Cashmere laughed. "You got the long face now, but you'll see. Dude could make a girl change her religion."

At the religion reference, Abrianna's mind zoomed back to the handsome Arab guy by the stage during her last number. Tall, tan, and fine did describe him perfectly. Dark wavy hair, intense brown eyes, and he looked more than fit. She'd bet money she didn't have that he had washboard abs under that black shirt. She glanced at herself in the mirror and smiled. She may as well have some fun before Zeke murdered her. She quickly freshened up and went to stack a little more paper.

Kadir dismissed Ghost's sprung assessment, and hit his boy up. "Look, man. You know I'm good for it."

Ghost grinned and slid his toothpick to the corner of his mouth while he pulled out his wallet. "All right, bro. How much do you need?"

"I don't know. How much does a private dance usually go for?"

"You're shitting me. You've never done this before?"

"What? Are you going to make me fill out a loan application, too?"

Ghost laughed, risking swallowing his toothpick. "Whatever, man. Here. That's two hundred. Tease it out to her, she'll love you for it."

"Right. Got it." He headed off feeling like a nervous schoolboy going to ask the prettiest cheerleader out to the prom.

In the champagne room, a Hulk-looking bouncer stared as Kadir slid into a purple velveteen chair and waited for the beautiful Autumn Breeze.

And waited.

A new waitress introduced herself as Cinnamon and asked whether he'd like bottle service or a drink. He turned down the offer, but minutes later wondered whether Autumn Breeze had received his dance request. *This is a sign that I have no business being in here.*

When Cinnamon glided by a fourth time, he crooked a finger to get her attention.

"Hey, are you ready to place an order?" she asked.

"Actually no. I, uh . . . ." His attention drifted when his private dancer finally arrived. "Never mind."

Following his gaze, Cinnamon glanced behind her. "Oh. Looks like you're in for a special treat." She patted his shoulder. "Enjoy."

Autumn Breeze spoke to the large bouncer, and he pointed her in Kadir's direction. Her walk was something to behold.

"Well . . . hello there, handsome. A little birdie told me that you'd like a private dance."

Kadir heard the words, but he couldn't respond. Luckily, she seemed amused by his inability to talk.

"What's the matter, baby? Cat got your tongue?" She smiled.

"I have money." He jammed a hand into his pants pocket and pulled out the bundle of twenties that Ghost gave him.

"How much do you have here, sweetheart?"

He had no idea. The concept of numbers suddenly seemed

foreign. He glanced at the money, but the bills couldn't count themselves.

She laughed. "Okay, handsome. I get it. Let momma just take this for you." She pried the money from his hand and seductively planted the folded bills in between her breasts.

Kadir's mouth watered. Then his greedy gaze drank in the rest of her. She was tall, an inch or two shy of six feet, but man, she curved in all the right places. She had a way of looking like she could melt in his arms or kick his ass if he stepped a toe out of line. Sugar and spice. He liked that.

"You just sit right there and let me entertain you, sweetheart."

He didn't dare open his mouth and risk sounding like a pubescent teenager. It was embarrassing enough that he lost cool points with himself.

Rufus's psychedelic funk groove "Tell Me Something Good" played, and his private dancer winded her hips and became one with the bass.

"Oh, I loooovve this song," she cooed. "How about you?"

"Love it," he mumbled, entranced by how her hips, abs, and breasts twisted and bounced. Hard, Kadir's cock stretched down the inseam of his pants.

She moved in close. *Real* close.

The sweet musk of her perfume clung to her glitter-dusted skin, but her hair smelled like a field of strawberries.

Autumn Breeze seduced his senses while the room temperature spiked.

Kadir pulled at his collar even though he wore a T-shirt that wasn't choking him.

"First time?" she asked breezily.

"It's *that* obvious?"

"I'm afraid so."

They laughed, and Kadir congratulated himself for keeping his shit together and relaxed.

"Don't worry. I'll make sure that you get the full show, baby."
She turned, dropped into his lap, and grinded him into delirium.

"Nice, baby. Nice," she cooed. "I bet you and junior here keep the girls coming back for more."

Kadir chuckled, but didn't dispel her assumption.

"So what's your name, handsome?"

"My name?"

"You *do* have one, don't you?" Her smile expanded.

"Name? Oh! Yeah. It's Kadir."

"Kadir? Huh. That's an interesting name. Arabic?"

"Very good."

"Does it mean anything?"

He laughed. "It means green."

Autumn Breeze chuckled. "Green. That's not as poetic as I thought. But it's still a lovely name." She leaned back, laying her head on his shoulder and giving him the perfect view of her breasts.

He knew then, in his soul, that he'd died and gone to heaven. "W-what about you?"

"What about me, handsome?"

"Your name. Is it really Autumn Breeze?"

"It is while I'm working."

All too soon, the song ended. Out of cash, Kadir regretted not teasing the money out like Ghost had instructed.

"Did you like your dance, handsome?"

"Yeah, you're very talented."

"Aren't you sweet?" She leaned back down and kissed his cheek. "Would you like another dance? Maybe even order us a bottle?"

Embarrassed, Kadir's cool waned. He shoved his hands into his pockets even though he *knew* he had no money. "Sorry. I'm all tapped out."

She pouted her lips. "Oh. I was just starting to have fun."

Kadir's heart sank.

"Well, you make sure that you come back and see me, handsome. You know where I work." She caressed the side of his face and sauntered off. "Bye, now."

"Bye." He watched her leave the champagne room. The bouncer gave Kadir a knowing smirk and then left to monitor another dancer and her customer.

Kadir stayed seated. However, after five minutes, his boner was still hard against his leg due to that magical dance replaying in his head. When he left the champagne room, he wasn't surprised to see Ghost waiting.

"My *man*! How did it go?"

"You're right. I think I'm in love."

17

Every once in a while, Abrianna enjoyed being a tease. And tonight's dance with the sexy Kadir had ended up turning a bad day into a pleasant night. During her drive home at two o'clock in the morning, through the icy rain, her thoughts kept shifting between nervousness to having to talk to Zeke in the morning and what it would be like to spend the night with the hunky Arab. She liked his wavy black hair, pencil-thin mustache, and those intense chocolate-brown eyes that at times seared into her soul.

The body wasn't too bad either. She could feel how rock-solid he was while breaking a few of the Stallion's house rules in their private rooms. But damn if she could help it. She imagined nothing but hard muscles and a washboard stomach beneath his clothes. Hell. It made her hot just thinking about it now.

Shaking herself out of her stupor, she focused back on the road and her Zeke problem. She raced through a litany of people whom she could still ask for some cash. But birds of a feather flocked together.

She was broke.

And all of her friends were, too.

Upon arriving at her apartment, she found a notice on the

door from the landlord. The rent check Moses had written for the month of September had bounced, and October's was due in a few days. Lately it seemed as if she just couldn't catch a break.

After entering the apartment, she took one look at the holes in the walls that she still had to plaster and just felt defeated. She took a long, hot shower and tumbled into bed. Loneliness crept in some time later while staring at the empty space next to her in the bed. Then a cycle began circulating in her head. Money, drugs, Zeke, loneliness, Kadir. Round and round it went until she closed her eyes. The vivid dream that materialized was all about a different private show for the handsome Kadir.

For this one, she helped him strip down so that she could run her hands along his taut muscles and even sample a kiss from his lips. She imagined he tasted something like peaches and honey.

Abrianna moaned in her sleep. She could almost feel his hand roam over her body and then stop to expertly unhook the back of her bra and then slowly peel it off. She watched his eyes go wide at first sight of a pecan-brown nipple.

"You're so beautiful," he praised, leaning forward and taking her nipple into his warm mouth.

Abrianna moaned while dropping her head back to pleasure herself. Using all of her concentration, she imagined Kadir kissing her in all of her favorite spots before grabbing her hips and taking her roughly from behind. It was quite possibly the hottest sex dream that she'd had in years. She moaned, writhing among her pillows. She envisioned her strong thighs around his waist, anchoring him while he sank deeper.

She was in heaven.

There was some dirty sex talk, but not too much. He had the right amount of swag while working her body like a boss. He feasted like a starved man—greedy for every inch of her. She tightened her vaginal muscles until she milked his very essence from him. She took her time with him, cherishing the moment when she climbed to new orgasmic heights. If it was timed just right, they would come together When her breathing grew choppy, she knew that moment was going to happen in the next three, two, one—

—————

Riiinnng! Riiinnng!

Kadir sprung up in bed. His body was drenched in sweat as he looked wildly around the room. It took too long for him to realize that it had been his cell phone on his nightstand that had wrenched him from the most exotic and most *real* dream he'd ever had. Panting, he glanced down into his lap and saw the wet sheets. He was stunned and embarrassed, even though he was the only one in the bedroom. "The hell?" He couldn't even remember the last time he'd had a wet dream like that. He must've been like thirteen or something. He peeled himself out of bed and stripped the bedding before heading for another quick shower. The whole way, he couldn't get out of his head how real Autumn Breeze had seemed just a few minutes ago.

"I must be losing my mind," he concluded. That had it be it. Right?

PART TWO

Trouble Lasts Always . . .

18

The White House

Newly elected Speaker Reynolds strolled confidently into the Oval Office and accepted the president's offered hand. "Mr. President," he said, beaming. "Thank you for taking the time to meet with me today."

"It's my pleasure, Kenneth," Daniel said, slapping a heavy hand on his shoulder. "Plus, it's customary for the president to meet a newly elected speaker. Congratulations."

"Thank you." Kenneth held his fake smile. "I have to tell you that the whole thing has come as a total shock to me and Valerie."

"I can only imagine. Would you care to sit down?" He gestured to the sitting area of the office.

"Don't mind if I do."

The men walked across the presidential seal carpet and sat opposing each other on separate couches. Reynolds leaned over and plucked an apple from the fruit bowl on the coffee table between them.

Daniel kick-started the conversation. "So how are Valerie and the kids?"

"Fine. Just fine. We are all trying to adjust."

Daniel waved off his concern. "Aw. You'll get used to it."

"I think we will manage all right. It's certainly more attention than we're used to."

"Well, it *is* a historic moment. The first African-American House speaker. You have a lot to be proud of."

"I have a lot to deliver on, of course." His words hung with the hidden meaning.

Daniel, a season politician, picked up on it right away, but pretended he hadn't. "We all have a lot to deliver to the American people. That's why I'm looking forward to working with you and your party to actually get some important legislation passed instead of our parties descending further into the gutter."

"Politics was never meant to be a game of beanbag."

"No. But it was never meant to be a game of gladiators at the Coliseum either."

Reynolds laughed. "Maybe not, but I like that imagery."

Daniel forced himself to laugh along.

There was a rap on the door before it opened and the vice president entered the room.

"Ah, Kate." Daniel stood. "Please join us."

Kate strolled over with a bright smile. "Sorry I'm late. A videoconference ran over. Hello, Speaker Reynolds."

"Madam Vice President." Reynolds accepted her hand. "I'm pleased that you'll be joining us."

"I had to take the time and come congratulate you," she said, pumping his hand. "It was quite a shock when Speaker Hartman announced his retirement. We had so hoped to gain his support of the president's tax reform package. But the administration certainly hopes that it will be at the top of *your* to-do list."

Daniel smiled. Kate always knew how to get straight to the matter at hand.

Reynolds beamed while his gaze briefly drank in Kate's entire frame.

Daniel dropped the smile.

Reynolds responded, "Unfortunately, I can't say that it *is* at the top of my list. My caucus and I share the belief that the Brazil scandal hasn't drawn to a conclusion. Who knows where this troubling path will wind up? The buck could stop at the director of the Secret Service's desk or it could lead somewhere *higher*." He locked gazes with the president. "You know how these things go."

The president stiffened his spine. "From here, it appears that they go in the direction that you *want* them to go, Kenny."

"Please." Reynolds chuckled. "Call me *Speaker* Reynolds. I want to get the hang of it."

Kate lifted a brow while she erased her smile. "Well, someone is certainly smelling themselves."

"Or smelling *blood* in the water," Reynolds corrected, unfazed by Kate's indignation.

"So you really are going to go on an elaborate witch hunt?"

"I consider it more like a hunt for the *truth*. After all, the American people deserve nothing less."

"Cut me a damn break," the president snapped. "This has nothing to do with the American people, and you damn well know it. If it were, your party would actually do their damn job and pass legislation—*any* legislation."

Reynolds remained cool. "I'm not going to help you wag this dog, Mr. President. Your sudden interest in tax reform is a refreshing change of pace, but my party is more interested in removing you than helping you with your sinking poll numbers."

Daniel and Kate glared at Reynolds.

He broke open another smile. "Come on. Don't take your pending impeachment personally. It's just *politics*—or gladiators at the Coliseum, as you so aptly said."

"Impeachment?" Daniel repeated. "On what grounds?"

"Certainly for obstruction of justice, for engaging in a cover-up with the Secret Service. You and the director were room-mates in college, weren't you?"

"Oh, now you're really stretching," the president said.

"Am I?" Reynolds smirked. "I believe that the majority of the American people would see that we're simply doing our due diligence."

"You won't get the votes," Kate said.

"Won't I? A little birdie told me that you didn't think that I'd get the votes for the speakership either."

The president clamped his jaw tight, while Kate cut a quick angry look his way.

Reynolds reveled in his newfound power. "If I were you, Mr. President, I would stop underestimating me."

19

Abrianna always entered Stanton Park with vivid memories of the first night she'd arrived in D.C. Sometimes it seemed like it was either a lifetime ago or yesterday.

"There you are," the voice called out to her.

"Hey, Charlie," Abrianna greeted him, holding up her usual club sandwich.

"All right." He clapped and rubbed his hands to together. "I was getting worried that something might've happened to you when you didn't show up yesterday for lunch."

"Sorry about that. Something came up."

"Don't worry about it. No worries. I hustle around these parts real good. Enough to eat anyway." He laughed. "All that matters is that you're here now."

She sat down on the bench next to him. "Well. I do worry about you out here. I wish that you would let me find you an apartment or something."

"I won't hear of it. You keep saving for that big dream of yours—living on the French Riviera. It will do my heart good to see you off like that."

Abrianna broke down.

"Oh my goodness," Charlie gasped. "What's the matter, sweetheart? Did I say something wrong?"

"No." She removed her shades so that she could wipe her eyes. "It's just . . . that dream may never come true."

"Why not? You have been saving like you told me, haven't you?"

"Yes. But a hell of a lot that's done for me. Moses stole it."

"What? That rat bastard!" Seeing her devastation, Charlie inched closer. "I'm so sorry, sweetheart. I don't know what to say."

"There isn't anything to say. It's gone. All of it." She removed her shades.

"My God. Did he do that?"

Abrianna pulled away and shoved her shades back on. "I'm fine. It's no big deal."

"No big deal? No man should ever put his hands on a woman. I thought you said that he moved out of your apartment?"

"He did. But . . . it's a long story. One I really don't want to get into. Not now. I cried all night. I don't want to do it all day too." She swiped underneath her eyes again. "I have to be about solutions. Crying has never solved anything."

Charlie took her right hand and squeezed it. "You're a strong woman," he encouraged her. "You always have been."

Abrianna chuckled weakly. "I'm a good actress. Nothing more. Nothing less."

"You're also a survivor," he reminded her.

"We're all temporary survivors of life, but we all know it's going to kill us in the end."

"I don't know about that."

"Don't tell me you still hang out here waiting for death to find you."

"You see he still hasn't come for me yet," he boasted

Her chuckling grew into a laugh. "You got a point there. In fact, since I've met you, you appear to have grown younger with each passing day. That horrible cough you used to have is gone. Your diabetes is gone. Hell, you don't even walk with a limp anymore. I'm likely to come here one afternoon to see you jogging around the place."

"Ah. That's what I love about you, Bree. You dream big."

"Yeah. I'm good at that, too." Abrianna studied him. She wasn't being glib about his improving health. He really did look great.

"Want to know my secret?" Charlie asked.

"I'm dying to know."

Charlie held up his wrapped lunch. "One club sandwich a day *and* the company of a beautiful woman." He squeezed her hand again.

She flushed. "Charlie, you've always been so sweet to me."

He lowered his head to hide his own blush. "Well. It's not so hard. You can be with any man you want to, but you choose to spend lunch with me every weekday."

"You still sneak to see your granddaughter on the weekends?"

"Everyone needs a guardian angel around."

"Ain't that the truth? I need one with about eighty thousand dollars in his bank account."

Charlie whistled. "Eighty thousand? What for?"

She sighed. "That's the same long story that I don't want to get into right now, but thanks for offering to listen. I really appreciate that." She placed her left hand on top of his to sandwich it. "If I never told you before: I love you—and our friendship."

"I love you too, kid."

She leaned forward and kissed his cheek. When she pulled away, her gaze swept across the newspaper on his lap.

CRAIG AVERY'S LATEST VICTIM

"What the hell?" She picked up the paper.

"Oh. I—"

Abrianna shushed him and read the article. " 'Shalisa Young, twenty-four, died after jumping off the roof of St. Elizabeths Hospital.' What?"

"Ah. Don't read that." Charlie attempted to take the paper away from her, but she twisted away from him to keep reading. The story that unfolded stunned her. "Wait. Shalisa was placed in a mental hospital after she killed her mother?" Abrianna kept blinking and shaking her head. "The court found her mentally unfit to stand trial two years ago. I hadn't heard anything about this."

Charlie sighed. "It's not like you kept in touch—with good reason."

Abrianna reread the article and was hit with a wave of shame that she hadn't reached out to the other survivors, but the sensation of their rescue would have brought the attention of her parents and that would have brought them to the hospital to take her back home. She didn't want that. She'd had a little taste of fame when the TV movie came out. But media attention had died down soon enough and Abrianna had just tried her best to put the whole thing behind her.

It had been a struggle, and now she was reading proof that it had been a struggle for Shalisa as well—more than a struggle. Clearly, her life had been destroyed.

"Look. I have to go," she said suddenly.

"But you haven't eaten your sandwich."

Abrianna handed back his paper. "It's all right. I'm not hungry. And I have to get down to the club." She stood and slid her purse strap over her shoulder. "You be careful out here—and I'll see you next week."

"Okay," Charlie said, looking and sounding disappointed. "You be careful too, and stay away from that Moses fellah. Love hurts—but not like that."

"I get it. But I never said I loved him."

"Good to know."

20

The Stallion Gentlemen's Club

"Good show out there, Breezy," Alexei praised her. He dropped his heavy arm around her shoulders and pulled her closer.

"Thanks," she mumbled, wiggling to get away. However, Alexei's arm locked around her shoulder.

"Heard you were in a jam," he said.

"What?" Her head jerked up. "Where did you hear that?"

"Where haven't I heard it? In for eighty grand with Zeke, huh? That's tough."

Heat scorched her face. She hated it when random muthafuckas were up in her business.

"I *told* you that fucking with Moses was gonna get you swept up in his bullshit—and there is plenty of it to bury the whole city."

Abrianna groaned. "Do you feel better now that you've got that off your chest?"

"Hey. Just stating facts." He sighed. "Anyway. Someone is here to see you."

Her hackles rose. "Who?"

Alexei's grin widened. "Why don't we step into my *private* office?"

Alexei's private office was just his favorite booth at the back of one of the bars. When they drew near, he signaled to the bartender for a bottle of his beloved Yamskaya vodka.

There was someone already sitting in his booth. A woman.

Now the hairs on Abrianna's arms rose. She attempted to slow down, but Alexei shoved her forward.

"Here she is," Alexei announced, his grin expanding. "As you requested: our Autumn Breeze."

The striking woman lifted her mesmerizing hazel eyes from her cocktail and eased on a red-lipped smile. "Autumn Breeze—a charming stage name."

"I'm glad you approve. I aim to please."

"Please, please. Have a seat." She gestured to the opposite side of the booth.

Hesitating, Abrianna scrambled for an excuse not to sit.

"I promise you that I only bite those who pay for the privilege," the woman joked. "Call me Angel, by the way. I work for a very important woman who is very pleased to be working with you in the near future."

Alexei laughed and hip-bumped her into the booth. Once he was in, she had to keep scooting over so that he could squeeze his six-foot-four frame into the booth too.

Annoyed, Abrianna flashed Alexei a dirty look, but he was too busy flashing his monster-sized grin at Angel.

"Actually, Alexei. I was hoping that I could talk to Abrianna *alone*," she said with the right amount of sugar in her voice.

A server set Alexei's vodka on the table while he blushed a shade of red that Abrianna had never seen before. "Uh, of course. Of course." He worked his way back out with that ridiculous grin on his face "If you need anything, I'll, uh, be at the bar."

"Thanks, sugar." Angel winked.

His blush deepened. "Of course. Just let me know if you

need anything." He took Angel's hand and kissed it before strolling off.

"No sense in letting a good bottle of vodka go to waste." Abrianna poured a shot, hoping it would do something about the buzzing in her head. She'd hadn't done a morning hit in an attempt to quit, as Shawn had begged, but already her body was rebelling.

After tossing back a shot, Angel dropped the smile and studied Abrianna. "You like the hard stuff, don't you?"

Taking it as a double entendre, Abrianna chuckled. "You could say that."

"And how bad is your drug habit?"

"Excuse you?" Her amusement gone, Abrianna set the shot glass down.

Angel eased back "I'm trying to assess if you're a liability. Recreational use isn't a problem, but *junkies* aren't worth the trouble. They don't last long, they're unprofessional, and they usually cost more than they make."

"Maybe I missed something." Abrianna folded her arms. "I don't recall submitting a job application to Madam Nevaeh. That is who you work for, isn't it?"

Angel's smile twitched. "Yes. And Madam Nevaeh works for *Zeke*. I believe that you're indebted for eighty grand, and if you don't have the money by the end of the night, you'll be working for him too."

Abrianna's smugness melted. "What?"

Angel's gaze raked her again. "Two years," she said. "Two years Madam Nevaeh has rolled out the red carpet for you to come and work with her, and you refused. She doesn't offer just anyone the opportunity."

"Because I'm not a hooker."

"It's male entertainment."

Abrianna laughed. "Dancing and fucking are two *different* things—at least they were the last time I checked a dictionary."

"They are both very good *exercises*," Angel countered, still smiling. However, when Abrianna refused to be amused, she came direct. "C'mon, Abrianna. Let's not play the modesty game. You've been on ho patrol on a number of D.C. corners before you landed the job here. Am I right?"

Abrianna refused to answer.

Angel turned sympathetic. "I heard about that unfortunate situation with that one sick bastard. What was his name that was all over the news a few years back? Avery? I heard about how he kept you all down in that basement and did weird experiments with you guys. It was just awful." Her hand crept across the table.

Abrianna jerked back and settled her hands in her lap. "Keep your sympathy."

"I understand you're touchy, but look at how you've bounced back. You're absolutely stunning. I don't think that you realize how much you stick out here. You're a diamond in a coal mine. Everyone knows it but you. Why not capitalize off of it?"

"Because I'm not a whore," Abrianna insisted.

"Anymore," she corrected.

"Right. I'm not a whore *anymore.*"

"All right." Angel sipped her cocktail, before wrapping up the conversation. "Madam Nevaeh's girls make *good* money. Her top earner pulls in a cool twenty thousand a booking. With the right training, you could beat her."

"I'm not interested."

She sighed. "All right then. I'll just take that *eighty* thousand dollars you owe and I'll get out of your hair."

"I don't owe you eighty thousand dollars. Zeke is not my pimp. He can't pimp me out for Moses's debt."

"How you define your relationship is of little interest to me. But I do know that one of three things *will* happen. One, you or Moses is going to pay Zeke back or, two, you'll work for

Madam Nevaeh until the debt is paid or, three, those gorgeous long legs of yours will be busted and your pretty face will be scrubbed clean with acid. Your choice."

Angel slid a black business card across the table, but Abrianna couldn't force herself to pick it up.

"You don't remember me, do you?" Angel said, suddenly.

Her gaze shoots back up. "Remember you?"

"The Sasha Bruce House for homeless teens. I stayed there when you and your friend Shawn used to crash there."

A chill settled in Abrianna's bones. "Oh, yeah?"

Angel nodded. "Look. I only brought it up to stress that we have a lot in common. We both hustled and did what we had to do to survive. I've worked the corners, muled drugs—stripped. I get the hesitance, but this is different. Madam Nevaeh takes care of her girls. She provides a service to some of the most powerful men in the country—the world even. Four of her girls are living like royalty with some sultan in Saudi Arabia right now. We're talking best of the best. You can make that petty little eighty grand in a snap. If you're smart, like some of the other girls, you'll work the circuit for a couple of years— your prime years, stack your cash, and then retire well before you hit the big three-oh."

"Really? You're pitching retirement plans?"

Angel sighed. "In the morning, call that number and a driver will pick you up." Before she walked off, she added, "Cheer up. At least Zeke decided not to kill you."

21

D<small>r.</small> Z arrived at the city morgue clutching a black lion head walking cane. The chief medical examiner, Paul Mitchell, had been roused out of bed to meet the doctor and his assistant there personally. Security cameras monitoring the property outside and inside the facility had been shut down. The doctor signed no visiting logbook and moved about the place as if he owned it. Other than the customary greeting of, "Good evening," Mitchell and the mysterious doctor sidelined small talk.

Upon entering the sterile room, Mitchell led Dr. Z and his assistant to the morgue's cold chamber. There, he pulled out a center drawer to display Shalisa Young's dead body.

Dr. Z sighed wearily.

"You are, of course, welcome to take all the time that you need," Mitchell said.

"Thank you."

Mitchell turned and strolled out. Once alone with his assistant, Ned, Dr. Z spoke. "It's a damn shame, isn't it?"

"Yes, sir," the assistant responded robotically.

"When I think of how close Dr. Avery came to a breakthrough, it just breaks my heart." He shook his gray head. "Sure, he lost his mind toward the end, but he was still brilliant in a lot of ways. A man ahead of his time, really. While he was given free rein with his experiments, even the government gets a little nervous when the body count gets too high. So he was fired, but he kept claiming that he was just on the verge of success.

"But the government's loss was to be T4S's gain. The new arms race is in creating the perfect soldier—or rather, super soldier. Drones are great. You can kill the enemy from great distances without putting boots on the ground. But it's a messy business. High civilian casualties. And, unfortunately, killing the innocent tends to create more pissed-off terrorists. So what has become clear is that even a great superpower country like the United States can never fully eliminate the option of boots on the ground. In these times, Uncle Sam would rather turn to security firms like ours than risk the political backlash of sending more soldiers to die in hostile territory.

"It's better to run a war off the books and preferably with an army of elite super soldiers. Ones who are stronger than the average man or woman. Soldiers who won't need to rely on . . . robotics, for example. Which is a great concept, but what happens when the enemy can hack into the system or its parts break down on the battlefield? You'd need an army of repairmen on the field as well then."

Dr. Z leaned in closer, marveling how both serene and amazingly preserved the body looked for someone who had plunged to her death. In fact, Shalisa didn't look broken at all. One could easily believe that the young woman had simply died in her sleep.

"Extraordinary." The doctor's curious gaze swept the entire length of the deceased's body several times, and his fascination grew.

"Dr. Avery had no problem delivering enhanced strength, but he wanted to go after the great golden goose."

"I'm sorry, sir. But what is that?"

Dr. Z turned a wide smile toward Ned. "Psychokinesis."

"Sir?"

"The psychic ability to influence a physical system *without* physical interaction."

Ned frowned. "Is that real, sir?"

"Depends on who you ask. There has never been any really convincing evidence, but the theory persists even among the naysayers."

"Do *you* believe it exists?"

Dr. Z chuckled. "My working scientific philosophy is: *anything* is possible. One thing's for sure, it's a compelling theory. There are some who believe the ability was once very common in ancient civilizations. They believe it as a working theory of how things like Stonehenge or the Egyptian pyramids were built. The ability to read minds, move objects just by thinking of it? Who wouldn't want to be able to do all of that?"

Ned nodded.

"Unfortunately, most of Avery's subjects died excruciating deaths during his home experiments. Except the three women—now two—the police rescued from his basement. Even I had thought that Dr. Avery died a complete failure until Ms. Young here killed her mother. She kept repeating that she'd only *thought* about it. Of course, the courts found her insane and then we were free to experiment with her at St. Elizabeths. I believe the tests aggravated her state of mind and things went very wrong. Now here we stand."

"What will happen to her now?" Ned inquired.

"Now we'll have her transferred to our lab for a more extensive examination." He sighed and rubbed his tired eyes. "Fortunately for us, she has no living relatives to claim her body, so instead of being buried in a potter's field, she will be donated to science."

Ned absorbed the doctor's words. "But what about the other two?"

"Ah. *That* is the trillion-dollar question."

22

Abrianna had pulled off a miracle. Shawn had agreed to meet her at their favorite Starbucks for coffee well before noon. He wasn't a happy camper since he'd only been asleep for a couple hours when she'd called. And he was none too pleased when she told him her plan.

"Have you lost your goddamn mind?" Shawn thundered, snatching off his shades to hit her with his bright blue gaze. "You're actually going to let those two muscle heads play you?"

"Lower your voice," Abrianna hissed when half the coffee shop crowd swiveled their necks in their direction.

"Nah. Uh-uh. This is what the fuck you get when you drop bombs like this in public. You get a scene."

"Well. I'm not in the mood for a scene, okay?"

Shawn's withering stare nailed her to her chair.

She pretended that her coffee wasn't scalding her tongue.

"I don't get it," Shawn said. "This shit sounds like you got set up for the okey-doke. Why the fuck are *you* stuck with the whole fucking tab? What is Moses doing to come up with the money?"

"I don't know. We haven't talked since I kicked his ass the other day—the second time."

"Uh-huh." Shawn uncrossed and then re-crossed his legs

while simultaneously flipping his blond hair over his shoulders. "I know that the dick was good, Bree. But ain't no way you're telling me that the shit is eighty-thousand-dollars good."

"The bricks were stolen the night of the surprise birthday party, so it's my fault. The tab is on me. I wasn't looking out."

"Bullshit. None of our people would've copped shit out of your crib. You know that."

"I thought I knew that, but the bricks were gone and Zeke was seconds away from putting a bullet in Moses's head."

"And how the hell did Zeke miss that big-ass head of his?"

"Shawn!"

"What? It's no secret that I don't like that muthafucka. Why are you surprised I'm going in? I don't like him, and he sure as hell doesn't like me either."

Her gaze drifted, which she realized was a mistake because it was confirmation.

Shawn pulled a long breath. "Okay. On to another subject: When are you coming to a meeting with me?"

Abrianna groaned. "Can't you give it a rest?"

"How can I when you meet me for coffee at eight in the morning and your eyes are already dilated and your nose is bleeding?"

Gasping, she swiped a knuckle under her nose. "Fuck. Why didn't you say something sooner?"

He watched her as she snatched up the few napkins on their small table. "How about now? Did I get it all?" Before he answered, she dug through her cross-body purse for a compact.

"You have a problem," Shawn insisted.

"At the moment, I have eighty thousand problems." The joke bombed as she checked out her swollen nose in the mirror. "That is, unless you want to make a donation." She snapped the compact shut.

"Shit. Bank of America is blowing my cell up every other hour about my overdrawn account now. Maybe you should go start a GoFundMe page. I'm sure there are plenty of bleeding hearts out there who'd love to help out a stripper with a heart of gold."

"Nothing wrong with your sense of humor at this hour, I see."

"Look, Bree. I love you—and we need to address this. If I can get clean, you can too."

"The only difference is that you *want* to be clean," she said. "I tried yesterday, honestly. But you just don't understand what happens to me when I'm clean. The buzzing, the headaches—the mood swings. It's too much. I can try to cut back, but . . . I can't quit. I think I'd go insane if I did." Her thoughts drifted back to Shalisa Young, living in a federal mental hospital.

"So what? You're giving up on me? Is that what you're trying to tell me? You don't think that I've lost enough friends to drugs. Is that it?"

"So my drug habits are all about *you*?"

"No. Of course not."

"That's what it sounds like you're saying."

"It's not *all* about me, but it affects me. You're my best friend. And . . . I always feel guilty because . . ."

"Because you were the one who introduced me to drugs?"

Their eyes locked, and Abrianna hated that she'd taken the dig.

Shawn lowered his gaze to his cooling coffee. "Yes. I hate that *I'm* the one that got you hooked because I'm scared that it's going to kill you one day."

His voice trembled with more emotion than she was prepared to deal with at that early hour. "I don't have much out here," Shawn continued. "We both don't. But *you* . . . I honestly don't know what I'd do if something ever happened to you. I mean that."

A warm glow spread throughout her. Just knowing that *somebody* gave a real fuck touched her.

"Oh God. I gave you a big head now," he joked, and the mood lightened considerably at their table.

Somehow she'd managed to get out of the conversation without having to promise that she'd go to rehab—something that she was definitely not interested in doing. "So you'll go with me out to Madam Nevaeh's crib?"

"I don't know about *that*."

"C'mon. Please? What if I roll out there and it's a fucking trap, and the next damn thing I know I'm being shipped to some sex-slave operation down in some crazy, dangerous border town?"

"And what the fuck am I supposed to do? I'm a lover, not a fighter. Besides, I'm a pretty bitch too. They'll just be getting two for the price of one."

She laughed.

He didn't.

"Please." Abrianna gave her best sad puppy-dog eyes.

"I don't know. I have another show tonight. When are you doing this?" He picked up his coffee.

"I'm waiting for her car now."

Shawn choked. "What?"

"May as well get the shit over with. Angel said that I can make the money back in no time."

Shawn sighed. "Since when do you believe shit that random bitches be saying?"

"That's why I want you to come with me."

He said nothing for a long time.

"Please?"

"Are you *really* all right with doing this? I thought that after . . ."

"Craig Avery," she filled in for him. "It's all right. You can say his name. I'm not going to fall apart."

"There's got to be another way to come up with the money."

"I'm all ears."

Shawn cocked his head. "You *really* can't think of another way?"

Understanding set in. "You're shitting me, right? You're not seriously suggesting my *parents*, are you?"

He shrugged. "They are an option."

"No. They're not." The grip on her coffee cup tightened, but before she knew it, the old screaming voices from her childhood filled her head. A familiar helplessness covered her like an old blanket.

Outside the coffee shop's glass window, an eye-catching midnight-blue Bentley rolled up to the curb. Seconds later, Abrianna's cell phone trilled.

Shawn lifted an eyebrow while she answered the call.

"Hello." She turned and waved to the driver. "Yes. I see you. I'm on my way out." She disconnected the call.

"You're shitting me. *That's* your ride?"

Abrianna sprang to her feet. "You coming?"

Shawn's gaze swiveled between her and the car, and then back again. "Fuck yeah."

23

Zeke had always considered himself to be a reasonable businessman. He'd learned at an early age what it took to be a real boss in Washington, D.C. Money was power. Fear was respect. And mercy should be doled out, but rarely. It was important for his people to see that he was a strong but reasonable leader. The way Zeke saw it, he had been more than reasonable with his old high school friend Moses Darrough.

Back in the day, Moses had been the big man on campus. He'd been the school's football superstar. That meant that he'd won all the hot chicks and bragged endlessly about the number of college football scholarships that had been offered to him. But then there had been the injury and the scholarship money had dried up and the gold-diggers-in-training had dropped his ass like a hot potato. Since Moses hadn't bothered to actually learn anything other than how to throw a ball around, he'd become a shadow of his former self. He'd gone from hood superstar to the neighborhood hustler.

Zeke, on the other hand, had always had a good head for business. But as big of a name as he'd made for himself as the Teflon Don, Zeke knew that the real men of power wore thousand-dollar suits and worked for the government. To get with those people, the lobbyists on K Street needed men like him to provide certain services and products to bribe the G-men to get the legislation that they wanted. It was a very intricate and profitable system—for *all* involved.

One could take a man out of the streets, but could never take the street out of the man. Zeke provided everything from drugs to pussy for numerous parties and galas.

Such bribes also extended to *all* the branches of the government. When political affiliation failed and expensive trips and vacations didn't work, companies and K Street would once again come to his door—and in return they offered protection. For pussy, there was no one better than Madam Nevaeh. Only the best women worked for her, and she knew how to keep her girls in line *and* how to keep all their mouths shut. She threw the best parties and blended effortlessly in with the political elites. Primarily because her mother had once lived the life before marrying her sugar daddy and becoming a senator's wife.

Zeke had doubts that the undeniably sexy Abrianna Parker would be a nice fit in her stable. Of course, he had given serious consideration to making Abrianna his mistress, but with Nevaeh hosting her annual masquerade party this weekend, he figured it was as good a time as any to see the kind of money she could make them. He could always sample the product himself later. And as far as those *other* services, his hottest product on the market right now was a crazy synthetic party drug called Cotton Candy. Its pink coloring was popular with the kids as well as the affluent urbanites. Its number-one selling point was not only could it get your ass like supernova high, but a single dose could last up to three days. With the price point of a hundred and twenty dollars a gram compared to the five dollars a gram for regular cocaine, Zeke was well on his way to becoming the Bill Gates of the streets.

In the past six months, he'd had other crime bosses from

surrounding states begging to do business, all trying to work out the recipe. When that hadn't worked, they'd conspired to find out who ran his labs.

Zeke vowed that he would die before he let that information hit the streets. However, the dude he'd swiped up claimed to have worked with some crazy fucker some years back. Said the man used to do all these wild experiments for the government. That shit didn't surprise Zeke one bit, not with historic shit like Agent Orange and the annual *new* virus always breaking out in Africa after American doctors arrived with *vaccinations.*

Eventually, the lab rat claimed, his old boss had gone bat-shit crazy after years of using some of his experiments on himself. Zeke knew then that the scientist couldn't have been a brother. The number-one rule of the streets was to never get high on your own supply. Regardless, Zeke had a unique and hot product that stacked paper in his offshore accounts. Life should be good, but instead he had to deal with Moses's messy ass.

It was hardly fair to make his girl Bree pay off Moses's debt while he roamed the streets free as a bird. That shit wouldn't look right. Homies on the street would think that he'd gone soft, and then the next thing he knew, other street punks would think that they could get over too.

A lesson needed to be taught.

The sound of two car doors slamming caught Zeke's attention. Sighing, he reached for his glass of brandy and waited for his men to lead his old high school buddy into his study.

"Get off of me! Get off of me, muthafucka," Moses barked, but he was still dragged into Zeke's office against his will.

Zeke remained calm and forced himself to put aside their history together.

"Yo, Zeke, man. What . . . what is this all about? This shit ain't even necessary, man. You know all you had to do was text me, homie. I would've came without all of this static," Moses said, still wrestling with the two heavies, Roach and Gunner.

Leaning back in his leather chair, Zeke asked, "Would I be texting the burner that you tossed, or was there some other number that you failed to tell me about?"

"What? Ooooh," Moses said. "I forgot that I haven't given you the new digits yet. See what had happened was I broke my old shit and had to get a new number. But I was going to tell you about it."

Zeke stared straight through Moses.

Moses started squirming again. "Really, man. This is all just some misunderstanding.

"Were you going to tell me that you moved too?"

"Well, that couldn't be helped. Bree and I . . . had a little lover's spat and . . ."

"Yeah. I heard she broke your shit," he said, gesturing to the cast on Moses's arm.

"What? That's bullshit." He lifted the cast. "I broke this, uh, while moving my shit in my new girl's crib. That's all."

Zeke chuckled. "Yeah. That would be my story too if a girl whooped my ass."

Moses dug in, "I don't know where you're getting your information, but that's *not* what the fuck happened."

"Really. I don't have the energy to pretend to care," Zeke said, bored. "But I do want to discuss my missing bricks, i.e. my money."

Moses's eyes grew wider by the second. "Man, I'm sorry about that shit. The best I can figure is my ex must've flipped that shit on her own as payback when we broke up."

Zeke looked to his boy Roach.

Roach released one of Moses's arms and walked across the plastic on the floor to set a large satchel on Zeke's desk. When he opened it, everyone could clearly see the hundred-dollar bills piled high inside.

"So how do you explain this?"

Moses's tall ass looked faint. "Now, see. That ain't what it looks like."

"It looks like a bag of money to me. How about you, boys?" Roach and Gunner nodded.

"That's what it looks like to us too, boss," Gunner said.

Moses's childhood stutter roared back to life. "B-b-but . . . that isn't mine," Moses said.

Zeke let that lie hang in the air between them.

"I mean . . . I know what you're thinking," Moses said.

"Really? Do tell. What the fuck am I thinking?"

"Y-y-you . . . think that I sold your bricks and kept the money. But I didn't. I got that from the bank."

"What? You're a bank robber now?"

"No! I . . . I . . ." The man's eyes moistened. "C'mon, man. Cut me a break. You know me. I would *never* steal or cheat you."

"And yet, here we are." He opened a drawer on his desk and removed his precious baby: a .44 caliber revolver.

Moses lost his shit and the waterworks came fast and furious. "Yo, man. Don't do this. Please. I know I fucked up. I swear. I was going to do right by you. See?" He gestured to the bag. "There is more than what I owe you there. Take it, and let's call it square."

"So now this *is* your money?"

Moses worked his mouth, but didn't seem to know what to say.

"You know what? I'm going to cut you a break."

Moses slumped in relief.

"I mean . . . I'm still going to kill you—but I do believe you when you say that this money doesn't belong to you. You stole it—from the bank, but it belongs to your girl Bree, doesn't it? You just emptied all the money that she'd stashed away for years in her safe deposit box."

"How did you . . . ?"

"I have eyes and ears everywhere. You taking the money

prevented her from skipping town and from simply paying your debt. So you stole my shit, stole her shit, left her to pay your debt on her back, and plotted to start making your own king moves. With this kind of kick-starter money, you thought that could set up shop in my muthafuckin' city under my nose. How am I doing?"

Moses's voice failed him.

Disappointed, Zeke sighed. "What happened to you, man? In high school, you had the whole world at your feet. Now look at you. You're sad, man. Just a pathetic waste of space. I'm embarrassed for you."

Moses's tears and nose ran fast and furious.

Zeke winced at the pathetic mess standing in front of him. "Honestly," he said, standing from his chair, weapon in hand, "you should be thanking me. I'm clearly about to do you a favor."

Moses nodded, agreeing.

"I'll never understand how you pulled a hot chick like Abrianna. But I guess there's no accounting for taste."

Moses dropped to his knees.

Roach and Gunner released his arms and stood back at Zeke's head nod.

"I know. I know. I'm such a fuck-up. I know." Moses wept.

"Finally. Something we can agree on." Zeke placed the barrel of the gun against Moses's forehead. He experienced a small surprise when Moses leaned into the gun.

"Do it," he sobbed. "Just do it."

Zeke shook his head and pulled the trigger.

24

Abrianna's gut had officially turned into a butterfly conservatory. She couldn't believe that she was going to work as a highly paid escort.

"Holy shit," Shawn gasped as they entered through the private gates of the massive Beaux-Arts estate. It was the type of home that belonged in *Robb Report* and *Architectural Digest*. "Oh my damn. We've died and gone to heaven," he exclaimed, scooting up in his seat and pressing his face against the window. "The house that pussy built," he grumbled.

Abrianna smacked his arm.

"Owww! That hurt."

"Be on your best behavior," Abrianna warned.

"Or what? You're going to put me in the hospital too?"

"I might."

"Whatever, girl." He hand-pressed his vintage Culture Club T-shirt and even raked his fingers through his flat hair. "How do I look?"

"What the hell are *you* nervous for?"

"I'm not." He shrugged. "It's just that you never get a second chance to make a first impression."

She rolled her eyes. The car rolled to a stop, and she looked up at the beautiful home with a chill seeping into her bones.

Abrianna wasn't impressed by the moneyed class. She'd learned early about the kinds of evil that dwelled behind limestone walls, in secret bedrooms. The fact that she was reduced to this gnawed at her.

By the time the driver opened her door, she was well on her way to becoming a human Popsicle from the car's freezing air conditioner. Nonetheless, she accepted the driver's hand and stepped out onto the stone driveway. "Thank you."

"My pleasure, ma'am," he responded with a tip of his hat.

Shawn raced around the Bentley to offer an escort.

Her glacial stare leveled him.

"What? We might as well get into character," Shawn reasoned.

Giving in, she looped her arm through his and they marched to the door. It opened as Shawn lifted his hand to knock, and an expressionless older African-American butler, complete with black tails and gloves, nodded in greeting.

"Ms. Parker, we've been expecting you."

She stiffened and then forced herself to relax.

"Please. Come in," the butler added.

Shawn shifted a look in her direction, clearly asking whether she was sure she wanted to do this.

She wasn't, but she nodded anyway. After crossing the threshold, her hand tightened on Shawn's arm.

"Follow me," the butler instructed after closing the front door.

They fell in line behind him. While Abrianna focused on the coming meeting with Madam Nevaeh, Shawn oohed and ahhed over everything from the marble floors to the twelve-foot ceiling.

"How many rooms are in this place?" Shawn asked.

"Thirteen," the butler answered without breaking his stride.

Shawn repeated the number under his breath and then asked, "So that makes this how many square feet?"

"Ten thousand, three hundred," a female's voice floated out to them, just as they stepped into a sitting room.

Abrianna's gaze swung to the right just as a six-foot, red-headed beauty stood from a gold sofa stuffed to the max with varied throw pillows. She glided toward them in a startlingly white silk robe with feathers fringing each wrist. Nevaeh's red hair was piled with loose curls at the top except for the few tendrils strategically framing her face.

"Hello, Bree," she said, flashing a brilliant smile that actually reached her eyes. "I'm *so* happy you accepted my offer."

Abrianna opened her mouth to respond, but Shawn cut her off. "Whoa. Nobody is accepting anything just yet. We're here to negotiate."

Despite being annoyed, Abrianna snapped her mouth shut and allowed Shawn to lead.

Seeing her reaction, Madam Nevaeh swung her gaze between Abrianna and Shawn. "And you are?" she asked, sizing him up.

"Shawn." He offered his hand. "Pleased to meet you."

The madam was slow to place her hand into his. "You happen to have a last name?"

"Not one that's important for these negotiations," he said.

Her smile shaved off a few inches, but there was clearly a willingness to play this game out. "Would you care to sit down?" She gestured for them to select from a variety of chairs and sofas in her pristine salon.

"Henry," she said, catching the attention of the marble-faced butler. "Would you tell Juanita to bring us some tea?"

"Certainly, madam." He bowed and exited the room almost majestically.

When Madam Nevaeh saw that her guests were still standing, she insisted. "Please, sit."

Finally, Abrianna and Shawn selected two armchairs on opposite sides of a small table while Madam Nevaeh returned to her spot on the sofa. Once she was settled, a golden-haired Yorkie sprang out of nowhere into her lap. It was likely that Abrianna hadn't noticed him since his fur matched the sofa and the throw pillows.

"Now. This is highly unusual," Madam Nevaeh began. "But what exactly is it that you want to negotiate?"

Since Abrianna had no idea, she shifted her gaze over to her friend.

Shawn got straight to the point. "Maybe *you* should lay out exactly what is expected of Ms. Parker and *exactly* how long she'd be required to work for you to clear her debt."

A stout, middle-aged woman entered the salon with a tray of teacups. Shawn and Abrianna took theirs and then went through a two-minute ritual preparing their cups. The whole time, Abrianna felt the weight of the madam's stare.

When everyone's drink had been taken care of, the host resumed the conversation.

"Let me cut to the chase. I already own you. Your debt with Zeke has been paid, and if you try to renege, we already know what the consequence will be, don't we?"

Shawn was unfazed. "Run game on someone else. Bree never owed Zeke a dime, and slavery is illegal in America, at least the last time I checked. If you already paid the man, then he just hustled you out of eighty thousand dollars—but a woman who can live like this, in this town, is no fool. I doubt that you paid that man a dime yet. Now. My friend here heard of a job opportunity to come work for you, and if the terms are to her liking, the person you will be paying is her. Then she, if she chooses to, will pay Zeke." He stopped and sipped his tea.

Abrianna, impressed, swung her gaze to Madam Nevaeh. A rose-colored flush swept up the madam's neck and brightened her cheeks.

"I must say, Shawn, you're as clever as you are pretty."

"Thank you."

"All right." She reached for a scone from the small saucer and handed it to the Yorkie in her lap. "My girls make on aver-

age seven to ten thousand a night. Some have made more."
Nevaeh cocked her head. "Stand up," she ordered. "Let me
have a good look at you."

For some reason, Abrianna looked at Shawn. When he nodded, she stood.

"Don't be shy. Step forward and spin around," she ordered.

With a deep breath, Abrianna tried to stop the amount of
curse words racing through her head. She didn't want to do
this shit, but she pulled herself together and spun around.

"You are a stunningly beautiful woman, Abrianna, but I suspect that you already know that." Nevaeh sighed. "Twenty
years ago, you would have definitely given me a run for my
money. Just stunning."

"She is," Shawn agreed.

Abrianna heard the words, but they didn't penetrate. Such
praise rarely really did. She never saw what they saw anyway.
She certainly never *felt* beautiful. She came from an ugly place
and she'd done ugly things—horrible things. And this wasn't
any different.

"Look, it's no secret that I've wanted you to work for me for
some time. A partnership between us would be *very* beneficial
to *both* of us. But like I was saying, my girls can make ten grand
a night—sometimes more. Hook the right john and there
could be extras in the form of gifts: jewelry, cars—condos."

"This is just temporary. I'm not looking to become a full-
time mistress," Abrianna informed her.

"A lot of my girls have found that they had no idea what
they wanted until it was presented to them. The same could be
true for you."

"I doubt that."

"We'll see."

Returning to her seat, Abrianna gulped down the rest of her
tea while wrestling with shame. During that time, she missed
portions of the conversation exchanged between Madam Nevaeh

and Shawn. Only when they leveled their eyes at her did she look up to their expectant gazes.

"I'm sorry. I didn't catch that," she confessed.

"This weekend," the madam said. "Are you available?"

"I—uh—"

"Because I'm hosting an important event. A lot of rich and powerful men in D.C., especially from the Hill, will be there. I don't see why it can't be your stunning debut."

"*This* weekend?" This train was taking off fast. If she was going to back out, now was the time to do it. Stripping was one thing; being a high-priced prostitute was another. But then how else was she going to make that kind of money quickly? Unbidden, Craig Avery's evil face flashed in her head. Suddenly, the cool room felt like a sweltering sauna. Her heart raced, and her hands went numb and clammy.

"You do . . . investigate all of your clients, right?" Shawn cut in while Abrianna struggled to find her voice. "No weirdoes or sexual deviants."

"I don't deal with riffraff, if that's what you mean. She will only be dealing with the top-of-the-line clientele, I assure you."

The room fell silent while their gazes drifted toward Abrianna again. As much as she wanted to run out screaming, she knew what she had to do.

"Yeah. Sure. This weekend is fine."

"Excellent." The sparkle returned to Madam Nevaeh's eyes as she reached over the Yorkie's head to pick up a small bell that sat next to the plate of scones.

Shawn and Abrianna exchanged glances. She could tell that, even after his hardball negotiation, he hadn't changed his mind about her doing this.

With her morning high crashing her to the ground in epic fashion, her doubts doubled and then tripled within seconds. In that short time, Angel entered the salon, beaming.

The dog barked excitedly and then leapt out of Madam Nevaeh's arms and raced to Angel.

"Baby!" Madam Nevaeh huffed before tossing an unfinished scone back onto the China saucer. Smiling, Angel bent and scooped the barking dog up in her arms.

"Hey, Baby. How are you? Have you missed me?" Angel made kissy noises while Baby licked her face.

Nevaeh rolled her eyes. "Fine. Whatever." She took a deep breath and returned her attention to the matter at hand. "Another thing: I'd prefer that you use a classier name than Autumn Breeze. Stripper names are . . . *cheap* and unbecoming. Besides, you have such a beautiful name, Abrianna. I'd prefer if you use it."

"No. It's just . . ."

"I insist," she said.

Despite the smile, it was clear she meant business and that her name really wasn't up for discussion. Given that she was completely at Nevaeh's mercy, Abrianna agreed.

"Excellent!"

"Angel, dear. I'm placing Abrianna in your hands. You can pick something out for her from Desiree's closet. They are about the same size, I think."

"Yes, madam. My pleasure." Angel beamed at Abrianna. "Welcome to the family."

25

Kadir wasn't technically violating the terms of his parole by logging on to his neighborhood public library's computer to research his old nemesis, T4S. The public library was one of the exceptions in his probation.

Though he'd been curious about the security firm before his talk with Ghost, he had convinced himself to put the company in his rearview. But he could no longer do that. What unfolded on the screen was his worst nightmare. The size of the company stunned him. It had quadrupled in six years, apparently with the aid of the federal government, and had become a quasi-government entity with far-reaching and terrifying powers. T4S's hand was in everything and was literally *everywhere* in the world.

Its paramilitary expansion concerned him the most. They not only sent elite soldiers into hot zones around the world, but had expanded in the arms development industry by leaps and bounds. The outsourcing of military and security functions signified the country's loss of oversight—and what was worse, the company was almost completely immune to prosecution. The crimes on human rights piled up around the world— unpunished. The lawlessness planted seeds of revolt, or what the U.S. government called terrorism.

Kadir clicked on a few links and discovered that the man leading T4S's research and development was Dr. Charles H. Zacher. While there had been companies like Soldier Nanotechnologies, which worked to develop devices that could help soldiers in the field detect such threats as chemical warfare, T4S's Dr. Zacher was singularly focused on creating soldiers who could better withstand the rigors of war. The sci-fi notion of a super soldier.

Seven years ago, Dr. Zacher had introduced the notion of a thought helmet: military helmets that formed pre-speech thoughts into quantifiable bits of information and beamed them to others. *Silent Talk*, Zacher had called it. It would enable battlefield communication between soldiers without giving anything away to the enemy. A few years later, Dr. Zacher had stated that he, along with two other scientists, was developing a drug that would allow the actual soldier to have this ability *without* the use of a special helmet, since a helmet could always be stolen from a fallen soldier. If the soldier were provided the ability, it would revolutionize the battlefield.

"'Cognitive technology threat warning system'?" Kadir read. "What a whack job."

The hours rolled by as he read article after article with growing anxiety.

Deep down, you know that you're still a true believer. Ghost's voice echoed inside his head.

"Excuse me, sir. But we will be closing in five minutes," the librarian told him.

"Oh, okay. Thanks." Kadir glanced at his watch, surprised by how much time had passed. He printed a couple of the articles and then left the library, his head flooded with disturbing information. Climbing into his car, he failed to convince himself that he no longer cared what these crooks were up to.

Because he did. Only there wasn't anything that he could do about it.

Or could he?

———◦•◦———

Special Agent Bell had to make a decision. Follow Kahlifa to his next destination or flash his credentials at the librarian and find out what the ex-con had been so engrossed with on the computer.

"This is ridiculous," Roland complained. "Dude was probably just looking for a job."

Bell laughed. "You don't know Kahlifa like I do." He climbed out of the car.

Roland groaned and exited the passenger side and followed. "Do you know who you remind me of?"

"I'm afraid to guess." Bell pulled on the library's door and discovered it was already locked. He knocked on the glass.

"That cop in that French book *Les Misérables*," Roland said.

Bell frowned. "What?"

Roland snapped his fingers. "Javert! That was his name."

"Please say that you're kidding."

"Nah. I'm for real, man. Dude really had it in for Jean Valjean, the book's main protagonist. Javert just couldn't believe that a criminal could change, so he basically chased the damn man all over creation to bring him in. That's your same issue with Kahlifa."

"What in the hell are you doing reading French literature?"

Roland shrugged. "You're not going to shame me because I'm cultured."

The librarian reached the door and opened it. "I'm sorry, but we're closed."

Bell flashed his credentials. "I need to see the computer that that last guy who was in here a few minutes ago used."

Surprised, the woman blinked a few times and then stepped back. "Sure. Of course."

The agents entered and followed her to the rows of terminals. "It was this one," she said, pointing.

"Thank you, ma'am. This should just take a few minutes."

"No problem. I'll leave you to it," she said and scampered off.

Roland sighed. "I'm telling you, you're obsessed."

"Hot damn. Take a look at this," Bell gloated, pointing toward the terminal's history cache. "Kahlifa was researching T4S. The same security firm that he hacked that landed him in jail. Now what do you have to say?"

Mild surprise rippled across Roland's otherwise bored expression. "I'd say . . . that it's *not* illegal to read articles in a public library. And that it doesn't prove anything."

"You just can't admit when you're wrong, can you?"

"I don't have to. I'm never wrong."

"You are, and I'm going to prove it!"

———◆◆———

Kadir had planned to go home. However, he drove past his apartment building and didn't stop driving until he arrived at the Stallion Gentlemen's Club. After parking, he sat in his car and contemplated going in. Doing so could do more harm than good.

There was no question that he wanted to see Autumn Breeze again, but he didn't want her to think that he was turning into a stalker. *You are stalking her.*

"No. I'm not," he argued. When he realized what he was doing, he felt even more foolish.

"Just go and get it over with it." He climbed out of the car. As he walked to the door, he continued his inner pep talk, assuring himself that a dancer like Autumn Breeze was surely used to having regular admirers. He imagined that the dancers depended on regulars for their livelihood.

"Welcome to the Stallion Gentlemen's Club. Have a good time," the doorman said.

"Thanks."

However, the moment Kadir walked through the door, his confidence and pep evaporated. The place was packed. It was the weekend, he reminded himself. Of course, there would be *more* patrons. While he searched for a table or spot at one of the bars, Kadir's regret crept around his head, but he stayed because the desire to see the sexy Autumn Breeze again was stronger.

"What can I get you?" a bartender asked once Kadir had settled into a stool.

"I'll, uh, have just a ginger ale."

"Come again?" the man shouted, cupping his ear toward Kadir.

"A ginger ale," Kadir shouted above the music.

The bartender shrugged. "All right. That's what I thought you said. One ginger ale coming up!"

Kadir glanced around. The women on the stages displayed amazing acrobatics and impressive dance moves in the low lighting. But none of them interested Kadir.

"Ooh. Hey!" A bubbly half-dressed woman beamed a smile at him. "You're back! You must've had a really good time last night if you're back for more."

Kadir smiled, but had no idea who the woman was.

"I'm Cashmere, by the way." Her gaze drank him in, making it clear who was the predator and who was the prey. "Can I interest you in a private dance?" She stepped forward and pressed her overflowing breasts against his arm.

"One ginger ale." The bartender set his drink down in front of him. "You want to open a tab?"

"Uh, no. How much?"

"Eight-fifty."

"For a ginger ale?"

The bartender cocked his head. "Buddy, people don't come to a strip club expecting grocery-store prices. You're embarrassing yourself."

Annoyed, Kadir dug through his pocket for the money. Money he shouldn't be spending in a joint like this so close to rent being due. He slapped down a twenty and then returned his attention to Cashmere. "Is Autumn Breeze working tonight?"

Cashmere's sunny smile dimmed, but she answered in the same bubbly voice. "Sorry, lover boy, but she's not."

"Oh." His mood dipped.

Cashmere's smile widened. "I'm not even sure that she's coming back. I heard she got a new job working for an escort service."

"Escort?"

Cashmere beamed. "Yeah. I guess dancing wasn't nearly as exciting as making money on her back."

"Cashmere!" the bartender barked, clearly eavesdropping.

"What?" she asked innocently. "We're just talking."

Kadir plastered on a neutral expression, but inside, his heart sank. Turning from Cashmere, he nursed his ginger ale.

Picking up the hint, she realized that she'd said too much and lost a potential customer. "Your loss," Cashmere said and walked away.

Kadir remained at the bar to finish his expensive soda, after which he left his change on the bar and headed out, vowing never think of Autumn Breeze again.

A half an hour later, he arrived at Ghost's underground bunker. "Tell me more of what you know about T4S."

Ghost's thick lips spread into a big smile. "I thought that you would never ask."

26

Abrianna was a nervous wreck, and the Bentley would be there at any moment. She longed for a quick bump of coke to get her through the evening, but with eagle-eye Shawn around to help her get ready, she didn't dare risk hitting her stash.

"There, girl. You are officially fierce!" Shawn set down her flat iron and stood back and admired his work. "You wanted bone-straight, you got it, baby." He snapped his fingers.

"Thanks," Abrianna said, popping up from the chair to swing her long mane. "You are a life saver." She pecked him on the cheek and then raced to the bedroom to get dressed.

Shawn followed. "You know, I really want to wish you luck tonight like a good best friend should, but . . ."

"Yeah. I know. I get it." Abrianna said. "But I really appreciate you helping me. I know you got your own show tonight at the Bachelor Mill."

"Yes, honey. I'm Queen Madge tonight. So you know I'm going to work the hell out of my old 'Vogue' moves."

"Well, all right, Madonna." They high-fived.

Knock. Knock. Knock.

Abrianna gasped. "Shit."

"I'll get it," Shawn said.

"Thanks. I better go get in this dress," she said, racing to the bedroom.

Seconds later, Shawn entered the room. "Jeeves said that he'll wait for you in the car. Probably doesn't want anything to happen to that pretty little Bentley."

"Okay. Can you help me?" Abrianna asked, presenting her back to him.

Shawn zipped her in, and they turned to face her bedroom mirror. "Wow," they said at the same time.

"You look gorgeous," Shawn added.

For the first time, Abrianna felt pretty. "Thanks."

Staring into the mirror, their silence grew awkward. "All right, girl. I'm out. I can't be late tonight."

"Break a leg."

"I will. And you . . . is there a saying for wishing someone luck in your new profession?"

"I can only imagine."

They laughed as Shawn let himself out.

The moment the door closed, Abrianna raced for her stash of coke only to find it gone.

"Damn it, Shawn!" How in the hell was she going to get through this night now?

———— ◦•◦ ————

"You look lovely this evening, Ms. Parker," George greeted her, opening the door to the Bentley.

"Thank you, George." Abrianna smiled and carefully climbed into the backseat.

George slammed the door shut. The drive back out to Madam Nevaeh's estate was long. The whole time, Abrianna kept telling herself that it wasn't too late to back out. As far as the money, she could pack up it up, catch a flight to Anywhere, USA, and start her life all over again. Provided that Zeke didn't track her down and kill her. There was a high probability he might have better luck than her parents.

"Is everything all right, Ms. Parker?"

Abrianna looked up to catch George's gaze through the rearview mirror. "Yes. Everything is just . . . fine."

His gaze lingered a few more seconds before returning to the road.

When they reached Madam Nevaeh's estate, they had to wait in a small line of cars dropping off other guests. Abrianna grabbed her red and black masquerade mask and slipped it on. Though it fit snugly around her face, it provided a sense of safety that she could hide her true self.

"You have your bracelet, ma'am?"

"Huh? Oh." Abrianna opened her clutch and removed a gold bracelet loaded with charms of angels, harps, and wings. The trinket, as Angel had explained, was how the gentlemen of the evening would be able to identify Madam Nevaeh's high-priced girls. "Do you mind helping me with this?"

"Not at all, ma'am." George turned in his seat while she brought her arm forward. He snapped the bracelet in place and then handed her a card. "Remember to text seven-seven-seven to the number on my card," he said, handing it to her, "when you're ready to leave—that is, unless you, um . . ."

"Secure a date?"

George flushed. "Yes, ma'am."

"Gotcha."

"Here we are." George pulled up to the door. A valet opened her door and offered assistance.

Abrianna chiseled on a smile and climbed out. The moment she stood, the buzzing started and her stomach looped in knots. *Here I go.* Bravely, Abrianna placed one foot in front of the other, sealing her fate.

27

Forty-eight hours into her investigation, private investigator Gizella Castillo found her target to be an incredibly boring man. So far, the case was straightforward. Nothing so far contradicted the bio on the Seventh District of Virginia's cookie-cutter political home page. But she, like Tomi, had a bad vibe from the man. Then again, she got that same vibe from every politician she had ever laid eyes on.

After the night had fallen, Castillo had tailed Speaker Reynolds to an affluent neighborhood across the border in McLean, Virginia. While his car had to wait in a long line for drop-off at the home, Castillo circled around and parked in the drive of a vacant estate a little way from the party house and cut the lights.

She watched as Reynolds climbed out of his chauffeured black Mercedes. Smiling broadly behind a black-and-purple mask, he walked, envelope in hand, toward a genial doorman. He was hard to miss with his broad-shouldered physique and distinctive swagger when he walked.

"So where is *Mrs.* Reynolds?" she wondered.

Turned out he wasn't the only politician she recognized from the Hill. The masquerade party seemed to be a who's who of the establishment elite, mixed in with a few athletes from the Washington Nationals baseball team and even a couple of Hollywood actors. Castillo felt as if she were staking out a red-carpet event.

"Great party," she whispered bitterly. "So this is how the other half lives?"

Absently, Castillo wondered what everyone would think if she crashed the event in her denim jeans and white T-shirt ensemble, which currently had a few Doritos stains at the hem. The thought gave her a wry chuckle. This was definitely not the ordinary political hobnob, and clearly it wasn't something that she could crash.

Reaching over into the passenger seat, she grabbed a steno pad and her night-vision binoculars, which, so far, had proved to be the best investment in her new line of work. The built-in illuminator and camera made sure that she didn't miss a thing.

By the looks of it, this stakeout could last all night. It was a good thing she'd come well-prepared with snacks and the like. Lowering her binoculars, she grabbed her laptop from the passenger seat and searched for the property deed through public records online—only to come up with zilch.

"Well, who in the hell owns this place?"

———◆◆◆———

The moment Abrianna stepped into Madam Nevaeh's estate, she was surrounded by gorgeous people in expensive gowns and smart tuxedos. Twinkling golden lights and large white silk panels high above the merry crowd blocked out the numerous windows from peeping Toms. No one had to tell Abrianna that she was moving through some real movers and shakers in D.C. The power the people surrounding her wielded was palpable. A kernel of doubt that she'd stuffed down in her gut sprouted roots among the butterflies that fluttered like mad. *What am I doing here?*

"Your coat, ma'am."

"Uh, what?" Abrianna jerked out of her reverie to look at a masked man on the other side of the door. It was Henry. His face was still blank and hard as a slate of marble.

"Would you like me to take your coat?" Henry asked.

Her hand flew to Madam Nevaeh's beautiful white chinchilla. "Sure." However, when she took off the coat, she felt as if she'd removed a layer of protection.

Abrianna grew aware that a line was clogging up behind her. "Thank you," she told Henry and moved as quickly as she could away from the door. Not knowing what to do next, she wandered into the thickening crowd in one of the salons in search of a familiar face. Instead, she luckily drifted in the direction of a server carrying a tray of champagne flutes. Despite the need for at least two glasses, she grabbed just one.

Now what? Abrianna scanned the perimeter and sipped champagne. The chatter and laughter were slightly louder than the man tickling the ivories on a beautiful black grand piano in the next room. The atmosphere was gay so she worked hard to plaster on a smile.

After ten minutes, her awkwardness and insecurities grew tenfold. She wasn't sure what the hell she was supposed to do next. The rules Angel had gone over earlier flew right out of her head. Angel had made it seem like everything would be a cinch, but she had the feeling that the night was going to be anything but easy. But surely she couldn't make her money holding up the wall. *It's not too late to turn around and go back home.*

Zeke flashed in her head, and she knew that wasn't true. Even if by some miracle he didn't kill her, he had enough power to make her life a living hell.

"Well, aren't you a vision in red?"

As if merely thinking about his evil ass had conjured him out of the pits of hell, Abrianna turned to find a grinning Zeke. Hooked onto his powerful right arm was a smiling Madam

Nevaeh. They had both donned sparkling white. For the first time, Abrianna wondered if the two were an item.

"Abrianna, you look absolutely stunning! The women are already buzzing about you," she bragged.

Were they? She scanned the crowd again. This time, she noted a number of women tossing curious gazes her way, calculating. Instantly, Abrianna squared her shoulders in a defensive stance.

"Oh. Relax." Nevaeh laughed as she abandoned Zeke's side to take a spot next to Abrianna. "The women here are *not* the ones you've come to impress." She took Abrianna's right hand and lifted it. "Good. You remembered to wear your bracelet."

Repelled by her cold hands, Abrianna pulled her hand free of the woman's touch. "Okay. I'm here. Now what?" She'd meant to rein in her attitude, but failed.

Madam Nevaeh ignored it and kept her smile level. "Now, my darling, we mingle!" She removed Abrianna's empty flute from her hands, set it on another passing waiter's tray, and proceeded to escort Abrianna deeper into the milling crowd.

Abrianna took a brief look back. Zeke had disappeared into thin air.

For the next hour, Abrianna was introduced to too many oil and gas businessmen to keep count. Then there were a number of lobbyists, who appeared shiftier than the oilmen. But hands down the worst were the wall-to-wall politicians. In fact, the later it got, the more alcohol they poured down their throats and the slimier they became. None of them gave their real names. Most were either movie or comic-book characters or just made-up names. It didn't matter if some were standing in front of their wives or girlfriends; when they noticed Abrianna's gold bracelet, they openly flirted and checked her. It didn't take long for her to feel as if she were on an auctioning block.

Eventually, Abrianna hid out in one of the many bathrooms

in the house. However, she was clueless about the angry pack of women who'd come in behind her.

"I swear Madam Nevaeh is scraping the bottom of the barrel with the latest crop of girls," one girl complained.

"Uh-huh. You can say that again," her companion chimed in.

Abrianna rolled her eyes but refused to turn and confront them. *I don't give a shit about these bitches.* She took a few deep breaths, mumbled a couple of *"namastes"* to herself, and kept pushing.

"Oh. Give it a fucking rest," snapped Angel, who had magically appeared. "Don't you girls have something else to do? Neither one of you are pulling in the money you used to make. If anything, Madam needs to retire you old bitches walking around her, looking like Skeletor with those bad face-lifts. Who is your doctor? Stevie Wonder?"

The women literally clutched their pearls and gawked at Angel.

"You got something to say?" she asked.

The women lifted their chins and stalked off in an angry huff.

Abrianna smiled at Angel. "Thanks, girl."

"Oh. They are harmless," she said, waving off Abrianna's gratitude. "They're just scared of the young." Angel looked Abrianna over. "It doesn't help that you're the knockout in the room. I think there's a little bidding war going on over you with Madam Nevaeh."

"You're kidding?" Abrianna said, stunned. "Between who?"

"A couple of lobbyists and a senator, I think. You'll find out the winner soon enough."

Abrianna's heart sank. This still felt like a slave auction.

"So how are you liking it so far?" Angel asked.

"I guess it's okay. Since I don't know what I'm doing."

"You smile and look pretty." Angel smirked, snapping her compact closed.

A woman to her right snuck a sideways look in their direction before mumbling, "Whores," under her breath and waltzing away.

Angel placed a hand on Abrianna's arm to stop her from snapping back at the woman. "Let it go. Clearly, she's someone's clueless wife."

"Why would someone bring his wife here?"

"Not everyone here is on the prowl for a mistress. It's still a fabulous party to network among the elite."

"I guess." Abrianna huffed and resumed touching up her makeup in the vanity mirror.

"What? Don't tell me that you're bored."

"Okay. I won't tell you."

Angel smiled and lowered her voice. "Are you holding?"

Abrianna frowned, surprised.

"You look like you need a pick-me-up." Angel snatched Abrianna by the wrist and dragged her down the hall to an empty bedroom. "C'mon. We have to be quick," Angel warned, producing a vial of coke from her clutch bag.

"I thought you said that Madam Nevaeh frowned on our using while on the job?"

"What Madam doesn't know won't hurt her," Angel countered.

To Abrianna's surprise, one of the charms on Angel's bracelet was a tiny coke spoon. "In this job, one must always be prepared."

"I'll make sure that I remember that."

A few minutes later, they emerged from the bedroom, smiling to themselves. The coke was weaker than the shit Abrianna was used to, but it lowered the level of buzzing in her head considerably. Maybe she'd be able to get through the night, after all.

Almost immediately upon their return from upstairs, Madam

Nevaeh swarmed back to Abrianna's side. Behind her, a strikingly handsome African-American man hovered.

Nevaeh made the introduction to Mr. Lucky, whose wolfish grin unsettled her.

Nevaeh yammered on, but he paid the madam about as much attention as Abrianna did.

"So are you enjoying yourself this evening?" he asked.

"How can I not? It's a fabulous party," Abrianna deflected.

"It is. It's the perfect cap to a great week for me. I'd love nothing more than to end the night with a beautiful woman or two." His black eyes performed a slow drag over Abrianna. "I don't see why one can't be with the most beautiful woman in the room."

Abrianna chuckled, but was convinced that she'd officially met the oiliest man at the party. And it would be just her luck for him to be her first client.

PART THREE

Behind Dark Doors . . .

28

Just do it. Jump.

Trembling, Abrianna leaned over a balcony at the Hay-Adams Hotel. Her gaze locked on to the vast emptiness twenty feet below. She couldn't see the bottom, but it was there. Waiting. Calling her name. Shame and disgust seeped into her bones. How could she ever look herself in the mirror again?

Mr. Lucky, as her john called himself, believed he was a real ladies' man. Sure, he was a handsome black man, and she'd heard plenty of times from Madam Nevaeh throughout the night that he was an important man too. She'd bragged about his money and power and then made it clear when he'd selected Abrianna how important it was that she please him.

Abrianna had put on a brave face, but now it cracked.

The wind picked up and whistled through the manicured trees below. The shaking leaves sounded like angry voices. The buzzing inside her neared a breaking point.

You're losing your shit, girl. If you're going to do it, do it.

Abrianna placed her hand on the rail and leaned forward. Since she was alone, she allowed a tear to leap over her lashes and skip down her face.

She could still feel the bastard's grimy paws all over her and even the stinging ache between her legs. He'd hurt her. He'd meant to—men always meant to. Sick bastards. Abrianna wanted to close her eyes, but she feared that, behind her eyelids, she'd see the long line of abusers she'd had to suffer all her life.

Just do it! Jump!

The rail rattled in her hands, but then that newspaper headline flashed in her head. Did she really want to end up like Shalisa Young?

"There you are," Mr. Lucky boomed from behind. "I wondered where you'd run off to."

Abrianna's heart broke. She missed her chance—again.

"What are you doing out here?"

Straightening her face, she faced him. "Just getting some fresh air."

His wide, veneered smile shone unnaturally beneath the moonlight. "Yeah?" He joined her, wearing a matching robe. "It *is* nice out."

She nodded, but then cringed with every step he took.

"Mind if I join you?"

"Sure. I'd love the company," she lied, smiling.

Lucky stopped before her and untied her belt. When he pulled it open, his eyes rounded as his greedy gaze roamed. "My god. You are exquisite."

"You keep saying that."

"And you keep being coy."

He slid his hands around her hips and glided them over her ass. "Is it really true that tonight is your first night with Madam Nevaeh?"

She nodded.

"So I'm your first?" he boasted, puffing out his chest.

Abrianna dropped her gaze.

"Heeeey. Don't be shy. I'm having a great time. You've been wonderful." He pulled her forward so that his hard-on stabbed her inner thigh. "But you know that I'm not through with you yet, right, sweetheart?" He brushed her hair back from her face. "I hope that you're ready for round two."

Abrianna's gut twisted, but she held her smile. "Whatever you want."

"Good. But first I got us a little something to enhance the mood."

Abrianna cocked a brow. "Oh?"

He grinned and reached into his pocket and pulled out a packet.

Her eyes widened.

"Mmm-hmm. I knew *this* would get your attention." He leaned forward and nuzzled a kiss against her neck.

Abrianna's lips stretched into her first genuine smile.

"C'mon," he whispered. "Let's go back inside." He took her hand and led. "I'll just chop this up, and then we can get this party started. Would you like that?"

"I'm for whatever you like. I'm here for you, remember?" Abrianna licked her lips and eyed his packet of cotton candy.

Mr. Lucky's awful laugh and wolfish gaze wrecked her nerves. "Hot damn. I'm a *lucky* man, the luckiest in Washington. Did you know that?"

"That's what you keep telling me." Playfully, she placed her right index finger against his lips, really wanting him to shut up, and he pretended to bite it off. From there, they moved to the living room part of the suite. He sat on the couch and poured the coke onto the glass table. "Now, fair warning: you have to be careful with this, baby. This here is primo, top-of-the-line shit. I'm gonna get you so high that you're never gonna want to come back down."

Like an eager puppy, Abrianna followed him to the table. *Hurry. Hurry. Hurry.*

Mr. Lucky made his perfect pink lines and leaned over and vacuumed one into each nostril. "WHOO! Wow!" He rubbed his nose. "Goddamn. That's some good shit!" He grinned at her. "C'mon. You got to hit this."

"Yeah?" Abrianna didn't hesitate. Her head was wired to explode. She needed this hit bad.

You have a problem, Shawn said inside of her head.

Abrianna ignored him and got down on her knees. However, she only did half a line before she threw her head back and gasped.

"What did I tell you? That's some strong shit, huh?"

Abrianna grinned as her head cleared and lifted her higher.

Mr. Lucky brushed her hair back lovingly. "Go ahead and finish. I got another surprise for you."

Greedily, she polished off the last two lines. Almost immediately, a kaleidoscope of colors twirled before her dilated eyes and she could hear her own blood rushing through her veins.

He beamed. "Didn't I tell you that I knew how to make you feel good?" He leaned over and nibbled on her neck. "Just ride the wave, sweetheart. Ride the wave."

She enjoyed the thrill of being light as a feather while a cool breeze drifted from an open window.

"That's it," he moaned, sliding his hand down the front of her naked body. "So fucking beautiful."

Abrianna released a long, winding moan. She couldn't help it. The world inside of her mind went soft and hazy. Lucky lowered his head and tugged a dark nipple into his mouth while his left hand wrapped around his cock to jerk himself off.

Abrianna's defenses melted away until the knock at the door.

Mr. Lucky's head sprang up from his late-night meal with a crazed look in his eyes. "That must be the other surprise." He grinned.

Popping up from the couch, Abrianna's mind slowed as she wondered where he was going.

The man strolled toward the door, his dick swinging between his legs. After a look through the peephole, he snatched it open. "Kitty! Welcome to the party."

A tall woman, whose pale skin looked as though it had never spent a day beneath sunlight, strolled into the room wearing a long, black trench coat. "Hey, handsome. I hope I haven't kept you waiting too long."

Abrianna sat up and assessed the woman. She was average: thick, brassy brown hair that was cut into layers but was in serious need of conditioning. Brown eyes, minimal makeup, but the carats sparkling from each ear were definitely real.

Madam Nevaeh employs all types.

"I hope that I haven't missed *all* the fun," Kitty said huskily.

"You're right on time, my love," Mr. Lucky said, closing the door behind her. "Can I take your coat?"

The smiling woman was already untying her belt. "You most certainly can." She took her time with the buttons, turning it into a mini seductive burlesque performance. When she snatched both flaps of the coat open, she revealed a black, leather teddy. It only made her pale skin more blinding, but she had an impressive body.

Mr. Lucky whistled and rubbed his cock again. "Yeah. We're about to have some fun."

Belatedly, Abrianna realized that Kitty's gaze had fixed on her.

"So who do we have here?"

"Our little pet for this evening."

"Really?" She handed Mr. Lucky her coat and strolled toward Abrianna. Lust shone brightly in Kitty's eyes. "Have you tasted her yet?"

"I couldn't help myself," he chuckled, tossing the coat over the back of a chair and following.

Abrianna's skin prickled. *A threesome?* Madam Nevaeh hadn't said anything about that. But she had mentioned how much of a valued customer Lucky was. Not for the first time that night, Abrianna felt like cattle.

Kitty caressed the side of Abrianna's face. "You have a name, sweetheart?"

"Abrianna."

"Lovely. It suits you." Kitty's gaze dragged over Abrianna. "Do you mind if I touch you?" she asked, but didn't wait for an answer.

"Look at the titties on you," Kitty panted, licking her lips.

Lucky moved to a chair across from them to watch and stroke himself.

Abrianna tuned out. Mr. Lucky's Cotton Candy kicked in and mentally drew her away. She couldn't process her emotions. She didn't want to. Her mind committed to divorcing itself from what was happening. It was the safest thing for her sanity, she knew. She was there for one reason and one reason only—to pay a debt. But inwardly, she wept all the same.

Soon the room blurred as tears rushed to her eyes, but even in this state, Abrianna was a pro at not letting anyone see them.

"Goddamn, baby. You taste so fucking good," Kitty moaned.

They were the last words Abrianna heard before she drifted off on a pink cloud. It took her blissfully higher than she'd ever been—where nothing and no one could touch or hurt her.

29

Rise. Morning prayer. Breakfast.

Kadir changed things up and skipped stealing the *Washington Post* from his eighty-year-old neighbor at the end of the hall. He needed a break from the want ads. Jobs that he was never going to be hired to do. The problem right now was that he couldn't stop Ghost's revolution from looping in his mind. It was stupid because he knew exactly where that road would lead him.

And yet, he was tempted.

When he wasn't thinking about the offer, he was thinking about Autumn Breeze. Surely, he wasn't the only man. However, he promised himself that he would return to the Stallion.

This is what my life has come to?

There was a knock at the door.

Who in the hell? The only person who popped into his head was Special Agent Bell—again.

Knock. Knock. Knock.

"I'm coming. I'm coming." He sighed and then pushed his chair back and climbed to his feet. But before he opened the door he shot a cursory glance to the writing desk by the bookshelves and wondered whether he needed to find a better hiding place for the gun. Deciding against it, he opened the door.

"Excuse me, but are you Kadir Kahlifa?" a short Arab man asked, staring intensely.

Hesitating, Kadir raked his gaze over the stranger. "That depends on who wants to know."

"I was told that you are a cab driver?"

"An Uber driver," Kadir corrected.

"Right." The man assessed Kadir again. "My brother and I would like to use your services. We called for a cab some time ago and they haven't shown up. Mook, uh, the guy that—"

"Yeah. Yeah. I know who Mook is," Kadir said, rolling his eyes.

"Well, *he* recommended you. Are you available to take us the airport?"

"Oh." Kadir relaxed and finally eased on a smile. "Sure. I can do that. Give me a few of minutes and I'll meet you downstairs."

A relieved smile broke across the man's face. "Great. We *really* appreciate this."

Kadir closed the door and rushed to clear the table. He shoveled oatmeal into his mouth, made a disgusted face as the slimy texture slid down his throat. "Yuck." He tossed the rest of it in the trash and washed the bowl.

He rounded the corner back into the living room and grabbed his shoes by the door. While he laced up, CNN droned on about the president's possible impeachment. However, the report went in one ear and out the other.

Kadir finished tying his shoes and grabbed his jacket, phone, and then, lastly, the paper-bag-wrapped gun from out of the desk. Quickly, he tucked it inside his jacket and zipped it up.

Still, Kadir was nervous, walking with his illegal weapon through the empty halls of his apartment building. It would serve him right if Agent Bell sprang out of nowhere and busted his ass. Halfway out of the building, he'd all but convinced himself that was exactly what was about to happen. Instead, it was Mook who bum-rushed him the moment he stepped outside the building.

"Kadir, my main man!"

Kadir spun around with the gun pointed through his jacket.

Mook threw up his hand. "Whoa! Whoa! What's up? It's just me, brother. Don't shoot. It's all good." His smile wrapped around his whole head. "We're cool, right?"

Kadir relaxed and looked around. "What the fuck are you doing rolling up on me like that?"

"Heeey! No disrespect intended, my man. I just ain't seen you in a couple of days. You've been walled up in your apartment since those Men in Black paid you a visit."

Kadir side-eyed him. "You knew about that?"

"Yo, man. I hear about everything in these parts. Like, uh, you stealing your neighbor's paper. Brother in three-B got some bad news down at the clinic. That fine bitch that stays in the apartment above you ain't had no dick in two years. The—"

"All right. I got it. You're a nosey fucker. You've made your point." Kadir started to march off, but then pulled up short. "Wait. You mean that you sold me this gun when you *knew* that I had two federal agents in my apartment waiting for me?"

Mook's wide grin grew another couple of inches.

"The fuck, Mook? You trying to get me locked back up?"

"Nah. Never that. I knew that you could handle those two federal cockroaches. And you did. No biggie."

Kadir walked away before he shot the man.

"Aww. Now. Don't be like that," Mook whined before racing up behind Kadir. "We're still cool, right?"

Kadir blocked all the bullshit tumbling out of Mook's mouth.

"You mad, man?"

Silence.

"Yeah, you mad," Mook answered his own question. "All right, then. Check it. I'm going to make it up to you. Next time you need something, Mook is your man. You feel me?"

Kadir removed his car keys and hit the automatic unlock button on the key ring.

"I'm serious, man. Totally one hundred. Whatever it is. Day or night, you're my number-one VIP! Fifty percent off whatever deal I got going. *And* you already know that I got the low-low on everything, right?"

Kadir slid behind the wheel, rolling his eyes. "Give it a rest, Mook. We're straight."

"Yeah?" Mook asked, hopeful.

Kadir slammed the car door in his face.

"All right. Cool. I see you got places to go. Got to make that money. Probably taking the Al-Sahi brothers to the airport. Am I right?" Mook rambled from the other side of the window.

Kadir unzipped his jacket and tucked the gun under the seat.

"That's good. Smart move," Mook continued. "Keep the weapon close, but not too close. Smart."

Kadir started the car and rolled down the window. "Enough with the commentary," he snapped. "I don't need the whole world knowing my business."

"Oh. Right. Gotcha." Mook twisted an invisible key against his lips and mimed throwing it away—but he ruined the performance by talking again. "Trust me, man. My lips are sealed."

Kadir shifted into reverse. Mook shouted and waved as he drove from his parking space to pull up in front of the building.

Minutes later, the Al-Sahi brothers exited, rolling several large luggage bags.

Kadir hopped out of the car, smiling. "Let me help you guys

out with those bags." It was a good thing that he was in good shape—each of the men's bags weighed a ton.

Mook hugged the corner and watched. "All right now. Y'all have a good trip," he shouted after everyone piled into the vehicle. To Kadir, he gave an added thumbs-up.

Annoyed, Kadir waved back and pulled away from the curb, starting the meter on his app. "Reagan National, right?" he double-checked with his silent passengers.

"Yes, sir. If you could hurry, that would be great," the tallest brother informed him.

"Not a problem. I'll get you there in a jiffy," he assured them.

The brothers nodded, then fell silent. True to his word, Kadir made a couple of cuts through some lesser-known roads. In no time, he had them cruising down I-395 South to the George Washington Memorial Parkway and then straight to the airport.

"Who are you flying on this morning?" Kadir asked, glancing back in his rearview to the quiet brothers. The short one who had come to his door kept mopping sweat from his forehead.

"Air France."

"Ah. France. I've always wanted to go there," Kadir said off the cuff as he took the ramp for the Air France terminal of the airport. "You guys going for business or pleasure?"

"Business," the tall brother replied, his face void of expression.

"Business? Huh. As much stuff as you packed, I figured you were moving." Kadir laughed.

The brothers did not.

Kadir ditched his failing comedy act. "All right. Here we are." He pulled up to the curb and parked.

The three men exited the car simultaneously and got their bags from the back of the SUV.

"Here you go. Keep the change," the sweaty brother said, handing Kadir two folded hundred-dollar bills.

Kadir's spirits lifted. "Thanks! I really appreciate it." He shook the man's hand and found it equally sweaty. "Have a great trip." He rushed back to the driver's-side door and hopped in. "Looks like today is going to be a good day."

30

Floating in a drug-induced haze, Abrianna was back in her childhood bedroom again. Scared—no, terrified. Not of the dark. Not of the monsters that sometimes slept under the bed or in her closet. Those weren't real to her anymore. The real monster slept down the hall—lying in wait until the entire house was quiet. Then he crept out of his room and tiptoed to hers—or her baby brother's. The images crystalized. Abrianna's twelve-year-old self slowed her breathing. She strained her ears to detect the slightest sound. The only thing she heard was the sound of her own heartbeat, hammering.

The hinges on the door squeaked as it opened. Abrianna's heart leapt from her chest, clear into the center of her throat. *He's here!*

Eyes wide open, Abrianna sprung upward in a bed, frightened—no, terrified. After a few deep breaths, she stuffed the old ghosts to the back of her mind and took in her surroundings.

The room. The bed.

None of it looked familiar.

Exhaustion failed to describe how tired Abrianna truly was, but somehow she mustered enough strength to put a little more brainpower into the morning riddle of *Where the fuck am I?*

Temples pounding, she now had a migraine that was out of this world. Snapshots from the masquerade flickered into view: the beautiful gowns, the flowing champagne, and the copious amounts of drugs she'd dumped in her system. She fell back against the bed's pillows, ashamed and disgusted.

You are a junkie.

Abrianna's stomach muscles clenched. In the next second, a river of bile rushed up and burned her esophagus. She slapped a hand over her mouth, peeled back the sheets, and raced to the suite's adjoining bathroom. She barely got the lid up on the toilet before emptying the scant contents of her stomach. Unfortunately, her shame and disgust remained.

A quick wash-up at the sink put her face-to-face with her reflection. "Damn. I look a hot-ass mess."

That, actually, was putting it nicely. Her carefully flat-ironed hair was now a kinky mess that could possibly snap a few hairbrushes in half. Her face was swollen, her eyes bloodshot.

"Just great." She leaned in and examined her neck. *Did that muthafucka choke me?*

Images sped behind her eyes. The party. Mr. Lucky. Kitty. She gagged and raced back to dry heave over the toilet bowl. Her entire body became one large cramp. At some point, she laid her head on the cool, porcelain bowl and nodded back off to sleep.

When she woke again, her neck had a severe crick that made it nearly impossible to lift. *I gotta get out here.* However, she discovered that standing was still a challenge so she crawled back into the suite to look for her clothes.

A phone rang somewhere in the suite, rattling what few brain cells she had left around her head.

"Somebody answer that," Abrianna groaned.

Ring. Ring. Ring.

"Hey!" She clutched at her head at the sound of her own voice, but remained annoyed at Mr. Lucky's motionless body.

"What's the matter with you? Are you deaf?" She pushed herself up onto her knees to shake his foot. The moment she touched him, a chill shot down her spine. "Oh shit."

———※———

Castillo listened in stunned silence as news reports of an airport bombing at Reagan National poured in over the car radio. Reporters were already tagging it a terror attack and warning potential fliers that all flights had been grounded. Minutes after, the wild speculations of who was responsible began. But, at this point, she wondered whether Americans really knew one terrorist group from another one. The entire city was at the highest alert.

Castillo glanced at the car's clock and debated whether it was time to throw in the towel on the Reynolds surveillance. She had spent the whole weekend watching the Hay-Adams Hotel, waiting for her target to re-emerge. Maybe Reynolds had somehow gotten by her. It wasn't impossible. She had taken the occasional bathroom break or catnap, but during those times, she'd kept a camera leveled at the door and recording at all times. *Maybe there's a back door?*

Castillo reached for her cell phone, ready to punch in Tomi's number to get her opinion on the matter, when she decided instead to see if she could bribe some information from the check-in desk—again. It hadn't worked the last two nights, but the third time could be the charm.

"Let's get this over with." Sighing, she hopped out of the car and made her way across the street to the hotel. The doorman held open the door.

"Welcome back to the Hay-Adams."

"Good morning," she mumbled. *Great. The doorman now knows me by sight.*

———※———

The White House

"What do we know?" President Walker asked his national security advisor, Scott Wolf, as machine-gun-toting agents ushered him into the White House Situation Room.

"Not much, sir," Wolf said, gravely. "Only that twin bomb blasts went off at zero-nine-eleven hours."

The president stopped halfway across the room and spun around.

"Yes, sir. I know. We caught the sick irony," Haverty cut in, referring to America's most deadly terrorist attack on 9/11/01, the day the country had lost 2,996 souls.

"All hands are on deck. We're waiting to see whether there is a second or third wave coming," Wolf said. "We're establishing a secure teleconference to manage the crisis."

The president and vice president exchanged looks.

"Let's pray that doesn't happen," Kate chimed.

The president shook his head and paced. The television screens built into the walls were tuned to various cable networks. They watched a few minutes of the footage in stunned silence.

Kate knew that what the president really wanted was a stiff drink. Hell. She wanted one too.

"Do we have an idea who is behind this yet?" the president asked.

"All the usual suspects, Mr. President," Wolf said, settling into one of the chairs at the long table in the center of the room. "So far we're already up to twelve terrorist organizations claiming credit."

"Of course," the president said before glancing at his watch.

It was only 9:48 AM. Just the beginning of what would likely be the longest day of their political lives.

The president hit a button and the volume came up on one

of the flat-screens showing CNN. Sure enough, the network already had a reporter on the scene and was giving America a quick rundown on what they knew from the ground. Around the reporter was total chaos. People milled about like swarming bees. Many were crying or were bloody and confused.

"Jesus," Kate said, reverting to an old habit of biting her nails.

The public emergency responders were also on the scene, and those same crying, bloody, and confused travelers were being led toward the right people for aid.

Despite all the powerful people that were assembled in the room, each of them felt utterly helpless waiting for the vital information to trickle in. After being swept up into the story that was unfolding right before their eyes, Kate caught the president looking back down at his watch so she checked hers as well: 10:19 AM.

"It's been more than an hour since the bombing. Do you think we're out of the woods for another attack?" she asked the president.

"Dear, God. I hope so," he answered without sparing a look in her direction.

Secret Service Director Donald Davidson waltzed back into the bunker, which surprised Kate since she hadn't noticed when he'd left. Other top members of the cabinet also migrated inside: the director of the FBI, the secretary of state, and the deputy chief of staff. But it was the look on Davidson's face that caused Kate the most concern.

"What is it?" she asked.

He shook his head as if he were refusing to answer, but he took another look into her "Don't make me ask you again" face and shared the new intel. "Capitol Hill has been evacuated. The top members of House and Senate are accounted for. However . . ."

"However?"

"House Speaker Kenneth Reynolds is MIA. Capitol Police are searching for him."

"Oh." Kate looked away with a shrug. "I'm sure that he'll show up sooner or later."

"We'll find him," Davidson assured her. "If he's still in town, we'll find him."

31

He's dead. Abrianna backed away from the bed, stunned. She took in the whole scene, wondering how in the hell she hadn't noticed so much blood—and that smell? She placed a hand over her mouth and nose. The air in the room seemed stale and hard to process through her lungs. Next, she focused on the blood-stained pillow over his head—and bits of brain splattered on the wall.

Move the pillow.

"I don't want to move the pillow," she argued with herself.

Move the pillow.

"I don't want . . ."

Move the pillow!

Abrianna held her breath and climbed onto her feet. *Just do it.* Slowly, she crept toward the bed, her lungs burning inside of her chest. Finally, she took hold of the pillow and yanked it away.

The gruesome, bloody mess of Mr. Lucky's half-missing face sent a scream shooting up her throat, but Abrianna slapped a hand back over her mouth to prevent it from escaping and alarming others in the hotel. At the same time, she lost all feeling in her legs and stumbled until her ass hit the floor—hard.

Abrianna didn't stay down long. It was definitely time to get the hell out of there now.

My clothes. Where in the fuck are my clothes? There was a slew of shit sprawled across the floor—not much that she recognized, but she plowed through every bit of it. Within seconds, she had everything but her bra and right shoe.

Knock. Knock.

Abrianna froze.

Knock. Knock.

"Room service," a woman with a thick African accent said from the other side of the door. The knob rattled, and Abrianna quickly realized what was about to happen. She flew across the room.

The door opened an inch before Abrianna reached it and slammed it in the woman's face. "Uh—we're not decent," Abrianna shouted. "Come back later."

Silence.

Abrianna placed her ear against the door, but when she couldn't hear anything, she looked through the peephole.

"Um . . . ma'am. Are you checking out today?" the maid asked.

Abrianna watched the woman flip through a clipboard.

"Uh, no! We're going to stay another day," Abrianna lied.

The African maid noted something on the clipboard, returned it to her cart, and then finally moved away from the door.

Abrianna collapsed in relief—until she remembered that she still needed to get the fuck out of there. Racing across the suite, she snatched up her clothes again and dressed as fast as humanly possible. She didn't sweat the zipper because her coat covered it up. The other shoe was still missing, but fuck it. There were plenty of shoeless people on public transportation. She should blend right in.

Wait!

She stopped, certain that she'd forgotten something. *My clutch!* The last thing she needed was to leave her fucking ID up in that bitch. The cops would beat her home. Abrianna searched around again, mumbling and cursing each time she came up empty. When she was seconds from giving up, she found the clutch underneath the nightstand table—next to the dead body. It wasn't *all* she found.

A gun.

The murder weapon?

She stared at it while pieces of a crazy puzzle snapped together in her head. She took in the whole scene. *I'm being set up.* Once that realization hit her, her mind tumbled back to Kitty.

"Fuck!" How could she have been so stupid?

Grab the gun.

Abrianna hesitated. If she got caught with the weapon, it was game over. She'd never be able to convince anyone that she hadn't killed this guy *What if that bitch planted my finger-prints on it?*

That seemed like a possibility.

She grabbed the fucking gun. For a few insane seconds, she tried to cram the weapon into her clutch bag, which was stupid. But it was hard to think straight when trying to avoid a murder rap. Finally, another solution occurred to her and she stuffed the damn thing into her coat and held it closed as she raced for the door. Unfortunately, she raced straight into the housekeeper.

"Uh, no. Sorry." Abrianna blinked and tried to hustle around the woman and her cart.

"Okay to clean the room now?" the housekeeper asked after her.

"No!" Abrianna pivoted. "Uh. My, um, boyfriend is still sleeping. Don't disturb him right now." She walked backwards to the elevator bay. "He's really, really tired—just let him sleep."

The woman nodded, but looked at Abrianna oddly. It was probably the one-shoe thing. So Abrianna laughed and hopped on one foot while she removed the other shoe and stuffed it in the coat with the gun. "Don't you hate it when you break a heel?" Abrianna rambled, feeling the gun shift in her pocket.

Her heart hammering, Abrianna rushed to the elevators and stabbed the down button. It took an eternity for the elevator to arrive. At last, the bell dinged and the doors slid open.

Abrianna froze.

A hotel security man and two Terminator-looking men in suits that screamed government officials attempted to exit the elevator.

"Excuse us, ma'am," the security guy said stiffly while moving around her.

Abrianna wasn't aware of what she said back, but she watched as the men moved past her and headed in the direction she'd just come.

The housekeeper looked up and smiled at the men. They moved around her as well and knocked on the hotel room door from which Abrianna just fled.

Get the fuck out of here!

———◆◆◆———

Entering the Hay-Adams, Castillo once again felt out of place in a pair of old jeans and an '84 PURPLE RAIN vintage concert T-shirt in such a grand lobby. Everything about the hotel screamed money and privilege. It was impossible not to feel small beneath the vaulted archways and the baroque filigree ceilings. Castillo marched to the front desk, where she was greeted with a smile. "Good morning," the woman said. "Will you be checking in with us today?"

"Uh, no. I'm actually looking for someone who is staying here."

"Of course." The woman picked up the phone. "You have the room number?"

"Actually, I don't." Castillo winced. "Would you mind looking to see if you have a Mr. Kenneth Reynolds registered?"

The woman's smile faded. "I'm sorry. We don't have anyone checked in by that name."

"Are you sure?" Castillo pulled a hundred dollars from her pocket and slid it over the counter.

The clerk didn't even bother to look at it. "I'm quite sure."

"You didn't even look in the system," Castillo complained.

"I don't need to look in the system, ma'am. I believe that you were already told that we have no one registered under that name."

Castillo looked across the counter at another check-in girl, who was clearly listening in on the conversation. "I see."

"Is there a problem?" A man materialized from around the corner. His blue eyes settled on Castillo.

She quickly read MR. ERIC ANDERSON—MANAGER from his gold-plated name tag and knew it was time for her to make her exit. "Nope. No problems here," Castillo said, lifting up her hands and backing away from the counter. "Thank you for all your help."

"It's been my pleasure," the front desk clerk said.

A bell dinged behind Castillo. She turned just as a woman bolted out of an elevator and nearly mowed down an older couple who were unlucky enough to be standing in front of the door.

"Excuse me. Pardon me. Excuse me," the woman said, fleeing past the old couple and toward the front door.

Castillo caught the woman's profile and recognized her from her dress as the woman who'd left the masquerade party with

Speaker Reynolds. Operating on automatic pilot, Castillo lifted her smartphone and snapped a picture. While the doorman opened the door for the running woman, Castillo looked down at the photo, and her breath caught in her lungs. *It can't be. Can it?*

She glanced back up at the door. The woman was nowhere in sight.

32

The first time Tomi's phone rang, she groaned and stuffed a pillow over her head, thankful when the call finally went to voice mail. However, the caller hung up and called back. "You got to be kidding me," she grumbled. It was the first Monday she'd scheduled off in years, and she'd really looked forward to sleeping until noon. She ignored the phone as her machine sent the caller to voice mail again.

Then it started ringing a *third* time.

Rocky barked.

"All right. All right. All right," she moaned, tossing off the pillow and grabbing the phone.

"This better be good," she told the caller.

"Are you seeing this shit?" Jayson barked.

"Seeing what shit?" she asked, opening one eye.

"The news reports. There's been a bombing at Reagan Airport," he said, hyped.

"Whaaat?" Tomi snatched back the sheets and tumbled out of bed. "Terrorists?"

"That's what they're saying," Jayson told her as she raced into her livingroom to power on the television. The channel was already on CNN, and she watched wide-eyed as they reported live from the scene. "Do they know who is behind the attack?"

"Nothing definitive, but the usual suspects are all taking credit for it."

"Figures." She watched the journalist talk about the dead bodies and the injured. All numbers were expected to rise.

"This should be setting everyone's hair on fire on the Hill," she said.

"Boss is calling for all hands on deck. You coming in?" he asked.

"Damn straight. Be there in twenty minutes," she told him and then disconnected the line. However, she didn't immediately rush away from the television. Tomi grew increasingly fascinated by the chaotic scene behind the reporter. It had been years since the country had been hit by terrorists on their own soil, let alone near the seat of American power.

Rocky barked and pulled her out of her TV trance.

"Yeah. Yeah. I'm coming, boy." She rushed to let him out the back door so he could handle his business and she could shower and get dressed. But as she turned on the hot water, her cell phone dinged with a text message. Out of habit, she reached for the smartphone and saw a picture from Castillo.

When she tapped the screen, the picture enlarged with Castillo's texted question, **Look familiar?**

Tomi squinted her eyes, and recognition bolted through her skull. She quickly hit the phone icon to call Castillo, who picked up on the first ring.

"Where did you get this picture?" Tomi asked, cutting to the chase.

"Just snapped it a few minutes ago at the Hay-Adams," Castillo answered.

"Do you really think it's her?" Tomi asked. "I mean, it's been a while."

"I'm not one hundred percent sure, but I'm definitely in the high ninety percentile," Castillo said. "And that's not all. Notice the dress?"

Tomi hadn't, but took a moment to do so now. "It looks like . . ." She scrolled back to the previously sent pictures.

"Like the woman from the masquerade party?"

"You don't think . . . Wow," Tomi said. "Small world."

"Tell me about it. Wait. Something's going on."

"What do you mean?"

"I don't know. I'll find out and call you back."

"All right, but I'm headed into the office to . . . hello?" Tomi looked at the phone and saw that Castillo had already hung up. She shrugged and hurried into her shower. She'd deal with Speaker Reynolds's dirt later.

<hr />

Castillo disconnected the call and tried to make sense of the sudden swirl of activity going on in the lobby of the hotel. She wasn't the only one confused as to what was going on. An elevator bell dinged and two obvious government employees filed out of the sliding golden doors with stern faces and an urgency that made Castillo's heartbeat kick up a gear.

Manager Asshole raced to meet the men in the center of the lobby. Hushed and fast words were exchanged between them while Castillo pushed away from the counter and crept boldly forward. Once she made it within three feet of the men, Manager Asshole waved for the government guys to follow him. However, she did manage to hear something about security surveillance as the three filed past her.

Something is definitely up.

"Kasey, call the police," Castillo heard the manager order.

At the girl's puzzled look, he huddled next to her and whispered something.

The color drained from her face. "Yes, sir," she said, picking up the phone.

What the hell?

Manager Asshole disappeared around the corner.

Castillo started back to the front to eavesdrop when another bell dinged from the elevator bay, but this time when the golden doors slid open, an African woman wearing a uniform released a gut-wrenching wail that raised the hairs on the back of Castillo's neck.

A wave of employees rushed toward the short woman to console her.

The other guests entering the hotel glanced around wildly until their focus zoomed in on the hysterical housekeeper.

Castillo's interest in the manager and government guys faded.

"Someone get her some water," someone shouted.

"I'll get it," another woman wearing the exact housekeeper uniform volunteered and took off.

"Elle l'a tué! Elle l'a tué!"

Castillo dusted off her high school French and was fairly confident in her brain's translation. "She killed him! She killed him!"

"It's all right. Calm down," a coworker cooed and patted her back.

Finally, a bottle of cold water was presented to her, but some of it splashed out of the bottle when the housekeeper tried to drink. As soon as she got a couple of gulps down, she wailed, *"Elle l'a tué!"*

"Who killed who?" Castillo shouted to the woman.

Everyone, including the wailing woman, stopped to look up at Castillo.

However, before Castillo received an answer, two pairs of strong hands latched on to her arms. "What the hell?"

"Ma'am, you have to leave," a red-faced security guy said.

"Leave? What for?"

"Come with us," he said.

Castillo was lifted off her feet and carried backwards toward the front door. "Hey! Put me down!"

When she was carried past Manager Asshole, she knew exactly where their orders to have her removed came from.

"All right. All right. I'll go. Just put me down."

Neither guard trusted her at her word and continued to carry her out the front door. Once beneath the portico outside, the men set her back onto her feet.

"Sorry about that, ma'am," the red-faced guard said with an embarrassed nod.

"Yeah. I just bet you are."

"If you don't leave, we've been instructed to call the police," the second security guy warned.

A second later, the wail of police sirens filled the air.

Castillo held up her hands and walked backward. "I'm going. I'm going." She spun around and jogged back across the street. Once in her car, she didn't slip her key back into the ignition. Instead, she reached over to the floor of the passenger seat and pulled out her camera and mounted a long lens. "There's always more than one way to skin a cat."

33

Abrianna looked like a hot ghetto mess when she stepped onto the city bus, but didn't give a damn at that moment. Her mind was still wrapped around what she'd left back at that hotel. In a lot of ways, she felt as if she were sleepwalking. Nothing seemed real. So much so that she questioned whether she was still on a bad trip. There were plenty of stories on the street about how the latest craze, Cotton Candy, made people hallucinate.

You have to go to rehab. Shawn's voice floated inside of her head.

At this point, she would gladly go to rehab if it would erase everything that had happened since she'd agreed to work for Madam Nevaeh.

Her eyes burned as if they swam in battery acid instead of tears. She made a lame attempt to pull herself together. It didn't work, and soon after, she felt the weight of someone staring at her. Abrianna turned and saw a little girl. No more than six probably, just staring.

Abrianna gave her the *"What the hell are you looking at?"* stare, but it had absolutely no effect on the nosey child.

"You're bleeding," a woman said.

Abrianna lifted her gaze from the little girl to a woman sitting and frowning next to her.

"Your nose," she added. "You're bleeding."

"Oh." Abrianna touched her nose and then examined her fingers. "Shit." She dove into her clutch, retrieved a travel-sized Kleenex packet, and cleaned up as fast as she could. In the compact mirror, she noticed her fresh-out-of-bed hair was pointing in all directions. Her eyes were still bloodshot, and her nose was swollen.

When she finished cleaning her face up, she smiled at the woman. "Thanks."

The child's mother just rolled her eyes and shook her head.

Fuck you then. A few transfers later, Abrianna finally reached her block. She pressed a bell, alerting the driver she needed to get off at the next stop. But as she stood to go, the .45 in her coat slipped. Time stopped as she watched the gun fall and hit the floor. She braced for it to fire.

It didn't.

Relieved, Abrianna snatched the gun up. When she looked up, the other passengers darted their gazes away to pretend that they hadn't seen shit. Standard hood protocol: no snitching.

Awkwardly, Abrianna shoved it back into her pocket.

The bus rolled to a stop and Abrianna exited the back door. The barefoot walk to the apartment felt long and humiliating. "Where is this damn key?"

"Ms. Parker!"

Abrianna whipped her head toward the voice and groaned when she saw her landlord rushing toward her.

"I need that rent. You guys are two months behind."

His words didn't compute.

The man was red faced and wagged his finger at her. "I'm not running a damn charity. Rent is due on the first of *each* month."

Abrianna didn't have time for this conversation. "All right. All right. I'll get you a check this afternoon."

"No more checks from you two. Money orders only!"

Finally, Abrianna found her key during her *fourth* frantic search.

"Do you hear me?" Mr. Gordon shouted.

"Got it. Money order only," she shouted, jamming the key into the lock.

"I mean it. I'll put your ass out!"

Abrianna rushed into the apartment, slammed the door, and collapsed against it. After several deep breaths, she rewound everything in her head and played it back—slowly. There were so many images blurring together that she struggled to make out what was and wasn't real. She could still feel some of the Cotton Candy sloshing in her system, causing her hands and legs to tremor.

What about Kitty? Abrianna suddenly wasn't even certain that the woman had even been real. That reality unnerved her. It wouldn't have been her first time hallucinating while high. Abrianna racked her head some more, but remained unsure whether she could trust her memory.

Hot, Abrianna pulled off the chinchilla and then slid the straps of her dress over her shoulders so that it glided off of her curves and pooled at her feet. Once she stepped out of it, she slid down the door and sat with her knees to her chest. *What now?*

Remembering the clutch, she quickly dumped out its contents. Spotting her cell phone, she picked it up. Out of habit, her first call went to Moses.

No answer.

Her second went to Shawn—but it was before noon and her best friend was a notoriously late sleeper. Her call went to his voice mail.

"Shawn. It's Bree. Call me. I'm in some serious shit." She wanted to say more, but knew better to than risk it. She disconnected the call and thought about whether she should call Madam Nevaeh. But how in the hell was she going to explain a dead client? What about her money? Maybe something like this had happened before? Surely, she or Zeke had people who could clean this mess up. Either way, shouldn't she give her a heads-up about what had happened before the police came poking around?

Thinking about the police, Abrianna realized that she was wasting time. She had to bounce. Disappear. Her fingerprints had to be all over that hotel room—not to mention a fancy place like that was bound to have surveillance cameras.

Cameras. She felt sick.

Abrianna's gaze shot toward the television at the other side of the living room. Maybe they were reporting on the murder right now? She rolled onto her knees and crawled across the floor to power it on. However, the mad scramble on all the local channels had nothing to do with a dead body found at a five-star hotel but everything to do with a bombing. It took a few minutes for it to sink into Abrianna's mind that the reports were talking about Reagan National Airport.

"The hell?"

"*A large explosion rocked Regan National Airport earlier this morning at nine eleven a.m. One hundred and twelve people so far have been counted dead and over sixty-two wounded, twelve critically. All numbers are expected to rise much higher. Several of the injured had limbs blown off by the force of the explosion. This was the first terrorist attack in the D.C. area since the attack on the Pentagon on September eleventh, 2001.*"

Abrianna shut off the television and stared at the blank screen. What the hell was going on today? Digging back through the pile of clothes that she'd just pulled off, Abrianna retrieved her cell phone. But once she had it in her hands, she stopped herself from dialing Madam Nevaeh's number. *What the hell am I going to say? What kind of protection can she even offer?*

She lowered the phone. Abrianna needed more time to think about this one, but after another five minutes, she still drew a blank. *Call Madam Nevaeh.* Surely, she would know what the hell to do. How else could she survive in her business and in this town?

Abrianna retrieved her cell phone and punched in the madam's contact number. She coached herself to remain calm, but as the line continued to ring, her anxiety mounted. "C'mon. Pick up the fucking phone!"

Finally, the line transferred to voice mail and she stuttered after the beep, "Uh, yeah. Nevaeh, this is Abrianna Parker. I-I kind of have a situation. I need you to call me back as soon as you get this message. Please. It's an emergency. I'm currently at my apartment, but I have my cell right next to me. Call me back. Bye." Abrianna disconnected the call, and then fretted on what to do next.

Pack.

Quickly, Abrianna stormed out of the living room. In the bedroom, she grabbed a weekender and gym bag and started stuffing them with clothes. She moved like a Tasmanian devil between the bedroom and the bathroom—until she caught her reflection in the mirror again.

"What the hell?" She leaned in and then looked down to see that she had splatters of dried blood all over her. "Fuck!" Immediately, she stripped out of her underwear and turned on the shower.

Once underneath the hot spray, unexpected tears flew down her face, blending with the water. She did nothing to stop them. The shower had always been a safe place to let her real emotions run loose.

Thump!

Someone is here.

Hyper-alert, Abrianna held her breath as her tears dried instantly. "Moses?"

Silence.

Abrianna shut off the water. "Moses, are you out there?"

Silence.

Her heart racing, Abrianna strained her ears to listen.

On the other side of the door, the hardwood floor creaked.

Someone is out there.

Abrianna pulled back the shower curtain and liner and stepped out of the tub. Quickly, she grabbed a towel and wrapped it around herself before she searched the countertops for a weapon. There was nothing, except for a package of razor blades. She took one, knowing that it would only come in handy if the attacker got extremely close.

She tiptoed toward the bathroom door, imagining everything from the Loch Ness Monster to a terror squad of ISIS militants on the other side. At long last, Abrianna placed her hands on the doorknob and twisted.

"Shawn!" Abrianna slumped with relief. "You scared the shit out of me."

"Good. You not calling me all weekend scared the shit out of me too!" He nestled his hands on his hips. "I've been dreaming that you were taken by another serial killer or some shit."

Abrianna rolled her eyes while her heart struggled to find a normal rhythm. "I see that you're in your feelings this morning."

"Damn right I am," Shawn snapped. "Haven't you been paying attention to the news? The damn world has gone crazy. Bombs are going off at the damn airport and shit." He took a deep breath. "So . . . how did it go? I don't want too much graphic detail . . . but . . . you know. Well?"

"I don't even fucking know where to start," she said, exiting the bathroom to head into her bedroom.

"I can't tell if this is going to be good or bad news. You weren't hurt, were you?" Shawn asked, following.

"*I* wasn't hurt, no. Well, other than my fucking pride, but it's pretty much used to the shit at this point."

"So are we talking in riddles today? Is that it?" Shawn asked and then noticed the bags stuffed with clothes on the bed. "What's going on in here?" Shawn asked, gesturing to the bags. "You going somewhere?"

"I . . . I got to leave town for a little while," she said, sliding on a clean black T-shirt. "And I need some money. Do you have any on you?"

"Uh. Slow your roll. Why the hell are you leaving town?"

"It's a long fucking story," she huffed and then searched for a pair of shoes.

"Does it look like my ass got somewhere to go? Spill it."

Abrianna didn't answer while she shoved her feet into a pair of black Timberlands. Hell. She didn't have the words yet.

"Bree . . . you're stalling," Shawn said impatiently.

The buzzing started up in the back of Abrianna's head. She blinked as her double vision kicked in. *Oh God. Not now.*

"Okay. This is clearly serious. You're upset," Shawn said, concerned. When she stood from tying her shoes, he took her by the hand. "C'mon. Let's go into the living room. I'll make you some green tea and you can just tell me what's gotten you so upset. Whatever it is, we can fix it together."

Abrianna allowed him to pull her along, but said, "Shawn, trust me. There's *no* fixing this."

"Don't be silly. Of course there is." He directed her into an armchair and told her, "Sit down. I'll put some water on."

She sat, but soon felt that she was wasting time. Who knew how much time she had before the police came banging down her door. But where in the hell was she even going? Or what she was going to do when she got there? Mexico floated in her head, but she didn't know the language and she was sure that the country extradited fugitives back to the United States all the time.

Shawn returned. "Okay. It'll take a few minutes for the water to heat up and then we'll be in business." He sat catty-corner to her on the sofa. "Now. Tell me. What happened?"

"I got to get out of town," she said slowly.

"Yeah. You covered that part," he said. "You haven't told me why."

"The party . . . was nice. Different. I was, uh . . . chosen by this guy who called himself Mr. Lucky at the party. I'm pretty sure that wasn't his real name."

"I hope not."

Abrianna sighed.

"All right. Go ahead. I'll be quiet. Finish."

"That's just it. I . . ."

Shawn reached over and covered her trembling hands. "Take your time."

"He, uh, took me to the Hay-Adams Hotel downtown."

"Nice."

"Uh, we, uh . . . you know."

Shawn nodded.

"Then uh, another girl showed up."

Shawn frowned. "Another one of Madam Nevaeh's girls showed up?"

"I'm not sure. I don't think so. I think Mr. Lucky and the girl were in some sort of relationship."

"Aw. Hell. Don't tell me this man's *wife* showed up or something."

"No! Please. Let me finish. This shit is hard enough."

"Okay. Okay." Shawn made a show of zipping his lips.

Abrianna confessed. "I don't know what happened at the hotel. I woke up this morning with Mr. Lucky missing half of his head. I don't know if that other bitch—uh, Kitty, I think her name was. I don't know if *she* killed him or he killed himself, to be honest. All I know is that ain't *nobody* going to believe that my ass didn't have shit to do with it. So I gotta split until shit dies down." Abrianna hopped up from the sofa and started pacing.

Shawn stared at her.

After a minute of him staring, she snapped. "Well, say something."

He opened his mouth—and then closed it. Opened it again—and closed it again.

"Great. You don't even fucking believe me." Abrianna threw up her hands. "This shit is sooo fucked up."

Shawn still struggled to come up with the right words.

"Shawn?"

"Uh . . . all right." He took a deep breath. "Now I'm going to ask you a question and I don't want you to get mad, okay?"

Abrianna pulled a deep breath. "Okay. What?"

"Were you high?"

Abrianna's face reddened—in embarrassment. Not anger.

Shawn rubbed his neck. "You said you woke up this morning. What have you been doing all weekend? Do you even remember?"

Abrianna bit her lower lip and shook her head.

"You blacked out?" he said.

She didn't answer.

"What did you take?"

She sighed. "What difference does it make?"

"I'd say a lot since you're telling me you woke up next to a dead body and you have no clue how it happened. I mean, who's to say that you *didn't* kill him?"

"Shawn?"

He tossed up his hands. "Don't kill the messenger. But I've been telling you for a long time that you are a completely different person in the last few years when you get high. If you're not putting people through walls, you're contemplating jumping off buildings."

"Are you serious right now?"

"As a heart attack. Why do you think that I've been hounding you to go to rehab? Even right now, I don't know if this really happened or you were hallucinating. Hell, six months ago you told me that you were talking to your little brother. Your brother who has been dead for seven years."

"Yeah, but that was different."

"Really?" he asked, eyebrows raised. "How?"

She couldn't come up with an answer. And she'd already admitted to herself that she didn't trust her memory.

"Who's to say whether there *really* was another girl in the room?"

Doubt crept around the back of Abrianna's mind again.

"Half the damn time you're trying to kill yourself when you're high. It's not too big of a leap to go from suicidal to homicidal."

"What?"

"I'm just . . . Be honest here, Bree. I love you. But I don't know what to believe."

Abrianna's heart sank. Again, she searched every corner of her mind for fragments of memory. "I don't know what to believe either," she finally admitted softly. The endless black wall in her head made Abrianna's heart race.

The teakettle whistled.

"Sit still. I'll go make the tea." Shawn stood up.

Abrianna's gaze fell onto the gun by her clutch bag on the floor. She hadn't been hallucinating. "Shawn?"

"Yeah?" He stopped and turned to face her.

She started to speak when suddenly the window behind her exploded in a hail of gunfire.

Out of pure instinct, Abrianna dove to the floor. However, Shawn wasn't so lucky. He fell next to her in a pool of blood.

34

Castillo loitered near the coroner's van. Sure, she was back on private property, but hotel security and management were too busy dealing with police and the government-looking officials while she waited for confirmation on the identity of the dead body. While she waited, her mind kept wandering back to Abrianna Parker.

The back doors of the Hay-Adams finally burst open. As two coroner techs approached, Castillo flicked away her cigarette and flashed the men her biggest smile.

"Two hundred for a quick look?" she asked, producing two folded bills from her jacket's breast pocket.

The men glanced at each other, shrugged.

"As long as you make it quick," one said.

"You got it."

They opened the back door of the van and, before loading, allowed Castillo to un-zip the body bag.

"Damn," she muttered. She had her verification. Speaker Kenneth Reynolds was dead. She snapped a quick picture.

"Hey! You didn't say anything about photos."

"Really? For two hundred dollars—what did you think?" Castillo rolled her eyes and re-zipped the bag.

One tech with an attitude huffed, "Is that it?"

"Yeah. Thanks." She handed them the money. "Don't spend it all in one place," she advised, winking.

While the techs rolled their eyes, Castillo rushed back to her vehicle. The entire way, her heart pounded. Behind the wheel, she took several deep breaths. She was sitting on quite a bombshell. And yet there was a sliver of guilt about turning over all this information to Tomi. Bree was one of them. A survivor from hell. Who knew what the girl had been living with and through these past six years?

Lord knew that she had been dealing with her own private hell. Couldn't she have easily gone down a different road? She glanced up at the building and admitted to herself that she still knew only half of the story. She had no idea what had transpired upstairs in that suite.

Maybe Reynolds had attacked Bree?

Maybe he'd had it coming?

Maybe, just maybe.

35

Abrianna screamed and covered her head as glass rained around her on her living room's carpeted floor. But she couldn't take her eyes off Shawn, lying so still across from her. Just as she felt herself slipping into shock, a voice thundered through her inner madness: *Get the hell out of here!*

But she was torn. She couldn't leave her friend. "Shawn," she called, crawling toward him even as the gunfire continued. Before long, she heard the sound of rushing feet. The gunmen were racing to the apartment.

"Shawn, can you hear me?"

At long last, he blinked. But he must have also heard the men because he said, "Get . . . get out of here."

"No. I can't leave you like this."

"Bree, please. Just . . . go. Go!"

The men drew closer.

Shawn closed his eyes and she panicked. "Shawn! Please, Shawn. Wake up!" She shook his shoulder, but his eyes remained closed.

The men were almost at her door. Abrianna looked around, spotted the gun.

A second later, the door burst open just as she reached for the weapon. The next few seconds passed in a blur. She remembered wanting the gun and the next second the gun zipping across the floor and into her hand. Her thumb swept the safety off and she fired. Four bullets flew from the barrel. Three found targets and sent the men reeling back and collapsing outside of her door.

Stunned, Abrianna scrambled in a spider-like scurry toward the kitchen back door. Once she reached it, she lifted her arm up to unlock and open it. In the apartment building's hallway, she glanced left and then right before making the decision to race toward the back of the building.

On her feet, she took off, both elbows and knees up as high as she could get them. Before long, she was flying. A few of her neighbors cracked open their doors just as she zipped past. One or two even called out her name—but she didn't dare stop before she rounded the corner.

In her mind, she kept seeing Shawn falling. She wanted to stop—go back. But in the next second, bullets zinged past her head. "Shit!" Abrianna rounded another corner, exiting her apartment complex.

Seconds later, the shooting continued. *What the fuck?*

Jagging to the right, Abrianna ducked behind another apartment building and then another. She had no idea where in the hell she was going, but eventually, all the zigzagging led her to a crowded street, where she spotted a man climbing out of an SUV with an Uber sticker on the windshield. She sped forward while the man stuffed a money clip back into his pocket. Without a second thought, Abrianna dove into the backseat before the door slammed behind her.

The driver swiveled around in his seat. "What the hell?!"

"Drive!" she ordered.

He pointed. "Hey, Autumn—"

"Drive!"

Suddenly, the back window of the SUV exploded in another wave of bullets.

"Fuck!" Kadir twisted back around in his seat, shifted into drive, and slammed on the accelerator.

They took off like a rocket.

Abrianna sprang from the backseat and into the front passenger seat and then squeezed down into the floorboards just as another window exploded.

"The fuck?" Kadir shouted, ducking and weaving between cars. Horns blared from every direction.

"Whatever you do, don't stop," she warned him.

"Who in the fuck are these people?"

"I have no idea," she panted, still trying to think.

Far too many times, he came dangerously close to clipping one car after another. After running through several red lights, he checked his rearview mirror again. "Okay. I think we lost them," Kadir said. When the woman didn't respond, he glanced down at the floor. "You can climb out now."

She nodded, but didn't make a move. An odd combination of bravery and fear was splayed across her face.

"Are you hurt?" he asked.

She shook her head, but then added, "I don't think so."

Now that the danger seemed to have passed, he eased his foot off the accelerator while looking for a place to pull over. An awkward tension thickened the air. "Look . . . I'm sorry about this, but . . . I don't know what's going on and I don't want to know. I can't get involved."

She didn't respond.

"Hey!"

Her gaze snapped up at him. It was clear that she hadn't heard a word he'd said.

"Are you sure that you're all right?" he checked. "I could take you to the hospital."

"No," she barked. "No doctors. No hospitals."

Kadir's gaze swung between the road and the woman huddled down on the floorboard. "Oookay." Returning to the rules of the road, he hit his turn signal.

"What are you doing?" she asked.

"Pulling over."

"Why?"

"Why? I just told you. I don't want to get involved in whatever it is you're in, lady. Those goons just shot up my car."

At the sudden sound of squealing tires, Kadir's gaze returned to the rearview mirror. A black SUV zigzagged through traffic as it barreled toward them. "Oh, shit!"

"What?" Abrianna crept up from the floorboard to look through the missing back window and spotted the trouble. "Go, go, go!"

"I'm going," Kadir shouted, jamming his foot down on the accelerator.

But the SUV gained ground.

"They're catching up to us," she shouted, panicked.

One of the SUV's tinted windows slid down, and an incredibly large gun appeared.

Abrianna ducked just as the weapon spat out a booming fire that took off the passenger's headrest before shattering the front window.

"Fuck!" A stunned Kadir swerved out of his lane but sped up.

The SUV stayed on his tail while still unloading.

"Shoot them," Kadir barked.

"What?"

"Shoot them!"

Abrianna had totally forgotten about the gun in her hand. She climbed up from the floor, took aim, and fired.

But nothing happened.

"Shit," she swore. "I'm out of bullets!"

Kadir reached underneath the seat, but got only the tips of his fingers on the weapon before he had to swerve to miss a Lexus. "There is a gun underneath my seat. Can't you reach it?"

Ignoring her fear, Bree crawled over the divide to reach in between Kadir's legs. At first, the paper bag confused her, but she quickly felt the outline of the gun.

"You'll have to load it."

"What?"

"Please tell me you know how to load a gun. There's a box of bullets in the bag."

More bullets hit the body of Kadir's vehicle, and he shouted, "Hurry before they turn us into Swiss cheese!"

"I'm going as fast as I can," Abrianna snapped, dropping a few bullets on the floorboard. Her concentration was shot.

"Oh God," Kadir moaned.

Abrianna kept loading. Finally, she snapped the clip back into the gun, chambered the top of the weapon, and came up looking for her target. It was perfect timing, too. The SUV was coming up on the wrong side of the road to the driver's left. She wasted no time aiming and firing.

Clearly she'd caught the shooter off guard as his weapon fired wildly up in the air before falling out of his hand and onto the street. "Got him," she announced.

But one gun was quickly replaced by another—the driver's.

One bullet grazed Kadir.

"Fuck this shit." Kadir gripped the steering wheel with both hands and deliberately swerved into the SUV, crashing into their side door. An oncoming commercial truck blared its horn at the two vehicles playing a dangerous game of bumper cars as they barreled toward a potential head-on collision.

Kadir jerked back into the right lane while the SUV slammed on its brakes.

The truck also slammed on its brakes, but despite it kicking up a shitload of smoke, it slammed into the SUV, turning the front half into an accordion within a blink of an eye.

"Fuuuck," Kadir said after catching the collision in his rearview and finally easing off the accelerator again.

Bree caught her breath against the searing pain in her right shoulder and, abandoning the gun on the floorboard, worked herself back into the passenger seat to see the wreckage they were jetting away from.

At long last, police sirens wailed.

Kadir groaned and slumped in his seat.

When Bree realized that the vehicle was slowing down, her panic returned. "You can't stop!"

"Why? Are the cops looking for you too?"

She didn't answer.

Kadir shook his head. "Lady, I'm not going back to jail over whatever gangster bullshit you're involved in. I'm on probation."

"Gangster shit?"

"What? You're going to deny it? Those guys were trying to blast your head off just for the hell of it, I suppose?"

"I don't know who those guys were or what the hell they wanted!"

"Yeah. Yeah. Right." He pulled the car over. He didn't care how disturbingly beautiful she was or how great she danced. He couldn't get involved. He stopped.

"No, please."

"Sorry, lady. This is where we part ways."

The sirens grew louder.

Abrianna cocked her head. "You said that you were on probation?"

"Yeah, so?"

"So I'm guessing that you're not supposed to have a firearm wrapped in a paper bag under your seat. Am I right? And we just discharged that firearm in the middle of a high-speed chase."

He stared at her.

"Hate to break it to you, but your waiting here for the police to file a report will just end with you being placed in the back-seat."

The sirens grew even louder while Kadir and Abrianna engaged in a staring contest.

"Ticktock," she warned and sweat broke out across her fore-head.

Kadir groaned and shifted the car into drive.

Abrianna smiled. "Thank you so much."

"Yeah. Yeah. Whatever." He pulled away from the curb. "I can't believe this!"

She squeezed her eyes shut as if *he* were working her nerves. "I'll pay for the damage. I just need a second to think."

Kadir shook his head. "Lady, I don't want your money. I just want you gone." He checked his mirrors and started to work his way over.

When Abrianna climbed up from the floorboard, Kadir finally noticed the blood blooming on her right shoulder.

"Holy shit! You've been hit," he said, alarmed. "Why didn't you say something?"

"You were shouting at me," she reminded him, but sounded weak. She leaned her head against the door. "I just need to rest for a few seconds. I-I'll be fine." She closed her eyes.

"Shit." Kadir's panic returned. "Hey, lady. Are you okay? Wake up."

She nodded once and went still.

My God, she's going to die on me. "Goddamn it!" He needed to get her to the hospital. *Hospitals call the police for gunshot victims.*

This was the last thing he needed in his life right now, but what else could he do? "Hey. Stay with me now. I think I know somebody who can help. Just . . . stay with me." He reached a hand over to shake her.

No response.

"Oh shit. Don't die on me."

36

As Tomi rushed through her shower, her mind drifted back to the picture Castillo had sent her by text. It had been six years since she'd seen Abrianna. Suddenly all the horrors that had happened down in Craig Avery's basement replayed in Tomi's mind. All of those sick experiments and that evil, maniacal laughter that rang incessantly in her head. With little effort, Tomi remembered the dank, stale air. The constant screams—especially of the girls who had never walked out of that dungeon alive.

When Bree had disappeared from that hospital, a part of Tomi had envied the teenager. She hadn't had to suffer through the media circus that followed. Everyone wanted to know what it was like being under the control of such a mad man. More than a few had profited off of their misery. Books by pseudo-psychiatrists and crime aficionados had come out of the woodwork, and before a solid year had passed, a made-for-TV movie had been produced.

After a while, their collective nightmare had been replaced by the next horror story in the news. And the public had moved on. Tomi could never figure out what had hurt more—the country's captive attention—or their collective dismissal.

After the shower, Tomi quickly got dressed. She placed some

food down for Rocky, caught a few more seconds of the frantic and chaotic reporting on all the cable news, and raced out of the door. In the car, she listened to the minute-by-minute updates on the National Public Radio station.

Everyone seemed to be on the same page: the airport bombing had indeed been a terrorist attack by Muslim extremists. Numerous groups around the world had taken credit and praised the men who'd carried out the destruction.

Tomi was sickened by what this meant for the country again. More days than not, America sat on the razor's edge of another civil war. This attack would undoubtedly make things worse.

Tomi arrived at the *Washington Post* without any memory of actually driving there. "Shit. I forgot my ID badge," she swore when she got to security.

Roosevelt, the guard, rolled his eyes with a chuckle but waved her through. "I swear, if your head wasn't attached."

"I know. Thanks." Tomi patted his shoulder and then hustled by.

She found Jayson at her desk, but everyone's eyeballs were glued to CNN's coverage of the TERROR IN WASHINGTON, as it had been dubbed, on their computer screens.

"Did I miss anything?" she asked.

"Just everything," Jayson responded, shrugging. "The president scheduled a press conference for two o'clock. I guess that means that they're pretty sure that a second attack isn't imminent."

She tapped him on the shoulder, evicting him from her chair. "Thank God for that."

"Well, I say anything is still possible," he said, dropping his feet from the desk and standing. "Either way, the president is screwed. This when he's already staring down the barrel of an impeachment? Not good." Jayson shook his head. "The Republicans are going to roast him for sure."

Tomi snickered. "Not surprised. Republicans impeaching

Democrats is a rite of passage." She planted her face in front of her computer screen.

The chaos on the cable news station had died down, and there appeared to be more order. But Tomi remained fascinated by the heart-wrenching personal stories of the survivors. Most described a morning of tranquility or excitement for whatever trip they were about to embark on—when out of nowhere there was a loud explosion and dead bodies lying everywhere. Then there were already stories of the missing and the dead.

A pair of retirees who were leaving for their first vacation in years, planned by their adult children—gone.

The children who were leaving on their first international trip abroad away from their parents—gone.

Newlyweds heading out on their honeymoon—gone.

More than once, Tomi reached for a Kleenex from a box on her desk. Then a thought occurred to her. "Has the House speaker or the Senate majority leader announced a press conference to counter the president?" She minimized the CNN site and pulled up another window to check her email.

Jayson simply looked down at his smartphone. "I got nothing."

"Surely there's going to be one." Tomi picked up her phone and dialed the speaker's press office. "Maybe we should get down there and be on standby," she said while waiting for the line to connect.

"I'm down if you are," Jayson said.

Her call was finally picked up on the fourth ring, but she was both surprised and disappointed that nothing had been scheduled thus far by the president's loyal opposition. When she pressed for information, her call was disconnected.

"Hello?" Tomi pulled the head unit away from her ear and stared at it.

"What?" Jayson asked.

Tomi hung up the phone. "How rude."

"Hung up on you again?" He snickered. "I don't know how much longer you're going to make it in this business with such horrible people skills."

Tomi popped him on the arm. "Hey! Not funny!"

"Ow!" Jayson whined, stepping back. "That hurt."

"I barely touched you," she said, rolling her eyes and hanging up the phone.

"I promise you that you have no idea how heavy handed you are."

"Riiiight. It's more likely that you don't know how much of a big baby you are."

Editor Martin Bailey materialized out of thin air. "So what are we working on?"

Tomi and Jayson snapped to attention.

"We just placed a called to the new House speaker's office to see if there is a presser scheduled for this afternoon," Tomi informed him, grateful to have something to report.

"And?"

"And—nothing so far," she added.

Jayson jumped in to have something to contribute to the conversation. "We were thinking about just heading over there for a wait-and-see."

"Just *thinking?*" Bailey shifted a toothpick to the corner of his mouth. "Are you guys waiting for me to chip in for cab fare or something?"

Tomi hopped to her feet. "We're going. He meant that we were just *going.*"

"Uh-huh. How is that piece on the new speaker that you were working on?" Bailey asked.

"It's coming along," she hedged. "Just looking into confirming a few details."

"Great. I look forward to reading it," Bailey said. "Don't forget your ID badge if you're going to the Capitol."

"Yes, sir. Of course."

Grunting, Bailey moved on to terrify the next journalist crunching a deadline.

"He's in a good mood," Jayson deadpanned while still rubbing his arm.

"Come on. I have to swing back by my place for my ID."

"Again?" Jayson asked, stopping at the next cubicle to pick up his camera bag. "What's with you and that damn badge?"

"Keep talking and you'll get another punch."

At the threat, Jayson held his arm and fell back a few steps.

"I knew that would shut you up." Tomi laughed as they marched past the security desk. "Bye, Rosie."

"Leaving so soon?" Roosevelt asked, tipping his hat.

"Well, the world is going to hell in a handbasket and *somebody* has to write about it," she answered with her usual quip.

Roosevelt laughed as always.

"Since you have to run by your crib," Jayson said, "how about I just meet you down there?" Jayson asked.

Tomi laughed. "You're still afraid to get in the car with me?"

"Damn right," Jayson laughed. "You're a horrible driver. I don't know who was crazy enough to give you a license."

"Since that hurt my feelings, I'm going to forget you said that." Tomi waved him off. "See you down at the Capitol."

"You got it."

They parted ways in the parking deck.

Tomi climbed into her vehicle, listened to a few seconds of the Terror in Washington coverage on the radio before instructing the car's phone to call Castillo.

After a few rings, Castillo picked up. "I was just thinking about you."

"Thinking about calling me with some news, I hope."

"Oh. I definitely got some news, all right."

Tomi perked up. "Sounds promising."

"We need to meet."

"What? *Now?*" Tomi started the car. "I have a busy load this morning. I have to get down to the Capitol to see if our guy gives a counter press conference on the airport bombing."

"*Our* guy?" Castillo asked. "You're *not* referring to Reynolds, are you?"

Tomi frowned. "Of course I am. Who else would I be talking about? He *has* left the hotel, hasn't he? I can't imagine that he'd still be there with all this madness going on."

Silence.

"Hello? Castillo, are you still there?"

"Well . . . yes, Reynolds has *definitely* left the hotel—but he won't be holding any press conferences."

"What do you mean? Why not?" Tomi asked, turning out of the parking deck and onto the main road.

"What I mean is . . . he's dead."

37

"Is it done?" Madam Nevaeh snapped across the bedroom toward her lover.

A growling Zeke disconnected the call on his cell phone, snatched back the red silk sheets, and sat up.

Nevaeh shook her head, folded one arm across her body, and pulled a deep drag from her cigarette in a vain attempt to calm down.

"She got away," Zeke spat, hefting himself out of the four-poster bed to strut naked to the adjoining bathroom.

Nevaeh blew out a long stream of smoke while her angry gaze blazed into the back of his head. "That's it? She just fucking got away? How the fuck did that happen? Aren't your guys supposed to be professionals?"

Zeke said nothing as he stormed toward the shower and turned it on. Hot water only. Full blast. Within seconds, steam filled the large bathroom.

His silence got under Nevaeh's skin. She followed him to the bathroom in her red, furry, kitty-heeled house shoes. "This really isn't the time to be giving me the silent treatment," she said, her voice echoing off the bathroom's natural acoustics.

"Calm down, Tanya. There's no reason for you to get hysterical," Zeke said without sparing her a glance.

"Calm down?" she repeated incredulously. "That Amazonian bitch could cost us everything if the cops get to her before we do."

"It's not going to happen," he assured her casually.

Nevaeh's blood simmered. "How can you be so sure?"

"Because I have eyes and ears in every corner of this rat-hole city. She's not going to get far."

Nevaeh wanted to believe him, *wished* that she could believe him, but she'd learned life's number-one lesson a long time ago and that was to depend only on herself in this life. She took another drag off of her cigarette while alternate plans circled in her head. "I should have never let you convince me to bring her on," she mumbled in regret.

Zeke's keen ears heard her from the shower's hard spray. "It didn't take *that* much convincing," he shouted, lathering up in her favorite French soaps. "You know a million-dollar thoroughbred when you see one. You saw how all the men at the masquerade party drooled over her the minute she walked into the room. Every one of them were ready to empty their bank accounts for one night with her."

Unconvinced, Nevaeh took another drag from her cigarette. A long, curving ash dangled from the other end. She sighed and casually walked over to the toilet bowl to flick the ash into the water.

Zeke chuckled from the shower. "Those two idiots have no idea that I'm the one that snatched those bricks from the house. I got my shit, her life savings, and the hottest piece of ass in one swoop."

"Excuse me?"

Zeke poked his head around the glass door. "The hottest ass next to yours, of course."

"I fail to see how her murdering our client is profitable. You said that she had a temper, but you never said anything about her being homicidal."

Zeke considered her words. "You're right. That was a major oversight."

Nevaeh rolled her eyes. "You think? What are we going to do when word gets out about Speaker Reynolds being offed by one of our girls? We probably should go ahead and cancel the party next week. The manager at the Hay-Adams is going ape shit with the cops and federal agents crawling all over the place."

"It won't get out that we had anything to do with it," Zeke countered. "Everything will go as planned. *I* will make sure Ms. Parker is taken care of well before that. Believe that. My men fucked up at her apartment, but I will rectify the problem."

His assurances were met with another eye roll.

Zeke started singing in the shower while scrubbing his genitals.

Madam Nevaeh hadn't intended to watch a peep show, but her anger ebbed as she became fascinated and then completely turned on while he stroked himself. It got to him, too, judging by the soft groans emanating from the stall.

"So what's up?" Zeke asked. "Are you going to stand out there and watch or are you going to get your fine ass in here?"

Madam Nevaeh suppressed her desires and quipped back lazily, "I'm still trying to make up my mind."

"You better hurry up!"

"How about you hurry up and tell me what our next move is with Abrianna Parker? I've worked too hard and too long on my back to let some stripper with homicidal tendencies flush it all down the toilet." Nevaeh flicked the rest of her cigarette into the toilet bowl and flushed.

Immediately, the hot water pelting from the shower turned icy cold.

"Goddamn it!" Zeke thundered, jumping back and then nearly losing his balance.

Nevaeh's lips twitched. "Sorry about that."

"You need to get that damn water heater fixed. Don't make

any damn sense for this shit." Zeke muttered a few more curses. "Now get your ass in here," he ordered.

Rolling her eyes, Madam Nevaeh slid off her nightgown, stepped out of her kitten heels, and strolled to the shower's glass door. She stepped inside just as heat returned to the water.

Zeke's thick lips sloped into a smirk as his gaze slid over her Coke-bottle figure. Sure, a lot of it had been maintained through a few nips and tucks over the years, but her fifty-eight-year-old body could still give a lot of twenty-somethings a run for their money.

"You promise that you're going to take care of this?" she asked, gliding her arms around Zeke's muscular neck.

"My word is bond."

She smiled, not because of the promise, but because of his hardening cock rising up between her inner thighs. "Good. Now fuck me."

38

Special Agent Bell nearly fell out of his seat when airport security's surveillance photos splashed across his computer screen. "Hey! I know that guy!"

His partner, Roland, stood from his chair in the next cubicle and crooked his neck toward Bell's screen. "Yeah?"

"Don't you recognize him?" Bell asked, reaching for his phone to call his supervisor. "I swear. I take my eyes off this man for less than twenty-four hours and look what happened."

"Kahlifa?" Roland waltzed around the cubicle and into his partner's private space to take a better look. "Are you sure?"

"Of course I'm sure."

Roland shrugged as if he didn't quite see it.

"Really, man? You really need to get your eyes examined." Bell's call went straight to his supervisor's voice mail so he hung up and took a screenshot.

"There's nothing wrong with my eyes," Roland shot back defensively. "It's just . . ." He shrugged again.

"It's just what?"

"It's just that all those Middle Eastern dudes look the same to me, you know?"

Bell sent the pictures to the printer and then cut Roland a look.

"What?"

"You do know how racist that sounds right now?" Bell asked, chuckling. "What if I said that about all *black* dudes?"

"It wouldn't bother me—after I punched your teeth in," Roland said with another roll of his shoulders.

Agent Bell rolled his eyes. "Sometime today, you really need to look up the word *hypocrite.*"

Roland beamed as Bell walked past him to head to the printer. "C'mon. We need to see the director about this."

Sighing, Roland fell in line behind his partner. "Are you sure that you aren't willing yourself to see a resemblance, Javert?"

"Don't start that shit," Bell warned. "Besides, I don't remember you being so in love with him when he said that you looked like crude oil."

Roland went silent for a few seconds. "Yeah. The dude was an asshole for that."

"Right." Bell reached the director's office but was told that he and the deputy director were currently briefing the president at the White House. However, Bell was able to talk to Associate Deputy Director Jim Webb, and informed him that he was positive that the man on the surveillance cameras was Kadir Kahlifa. Within a half an hour, Kahlifa's file was pulled and distributed to a team of agents and to a second team with Homeland Security.

It wasn't twenty minutes later that they all descended on the Park Flats apartment building in the Seventh District.

———⊷◈⊷———

"Fancy seeing you here," Chief Holder said, startling Castillo in her car.

After her initial jump, Castillo smiled back. "You know me. I try to go where all the action is."

"Yeah. That does seem vaguely familiar," he said, grinning.

"You look good."

"So do you, *Chief* Holder. Congratulations."

"Thanks. I, uh, wished that you could have come to the swearing-in ceremony."

She nodded and grappled for an excuse, but came up empty. "You're right. I should have gone. It's just . . . hard. You know?"

"Yeah. I get it. Well . . . I miss you," he confessed.

Castillo closed her eyes. "Don't."

Holder backed off. "So I can't even tell you that I miss you?"

"No," she said bluntly. "I told you before, I just want a clean break."

He nodded.

"I—I just think that's what is best for all involved."

"All?" he questioned. "It's just the two of us. Or does what I want even get calculated in this equation?"

"Dennis, why are you doing this?"

"Really? You still don't fucking know?" he asked, hurt.

At her silence, he nodded. "All right. I'll drop the personal shit. What are you really doing here? Are you working a case?"

"I am," she said, sounding relieved at the change of subject.

"For Tomi Lehane?"

She smiled. "I don't like discussing possible clients."

He laughed. "I'm the one who gave her your number, re-member?"

Gizella hedged. "Yes. I'm working a case for Ms. Lehane."

He weighed his next words. "Does your case have anything to do with Abrianna Parker?"

Their gazes locked. "Why do you ask?"

Holder sighed, looked at the folder he held, and handed it over. "Because, if I'm right, she's in a world of trouble."

Stanton Park

Charlie watched the children play. He smiled, listening to the bubbly laughter. He envied their carefree attitudes and boundless energy. It filled his heart with joy. He missed the days of his youth, when he had his whole life in front of him and the possibilities were boundless.

Ned walked over and joined him on the bench. "It doesn't look like she's coming today, sir."

Charlie nodded. "No. I think that's pretty fair to say. What time is it?"

"Three o'clock, sir."

Charlie nodded.

"Maybe that whole thing at the airport threw her off schedule?" Ned suggested.

"Maybe."

Silence drifted between them before Charlie asked Ned, "Do you remember what you wanted to be when you were their age?"

Ned looked at the children. "I think I wanted to be a fireman, sir."

Charlie smiled. "A fireman, eh? That's an admirable profession. What made you decide to pursue science instead?"

Ned shrugged. "Honestly, I don't remember, sir. I was just always good in the subject, I guess. Science fairs were like Christmas to me."

Charlie chuckled.

"What about you, sir?"

"Science," Charlie answered. "It has always been my first love. I desperately wanted to develop something that could change the world—for the better, of course." He stood and tucked his sudoku puzzle beneath his arm. "Let's head out. Maybe Ms. Parker will join me tomorrow."

Ned bobbed his head. "Sir, mind if I ask you how much longer you are going to monitor Ms. Parker? Surely, if Dr. Avery's experiments were working, she would be showing signs by now."

"Who said that there hadn't been any signs?"

Ned stammered. "Well—I, uh. You never mentioned that she was, Dr. Z."

Charlie laughed. "My boy, she shows signs nearly every time we meet. She's failed to realize it though. Almost daily, we sit here on this bench, talking—and she has yet to realize or notice that sometimes I never move my mouth at all."

"Sir?"

"She can hear my thoughts—which is why I'm always careful of what I'm thinking."

Ned's mouth fell open. "You're kidding. Why, that's wonderful."

Dr. Z shook his head. "She's been self-medicating, using street drugs to control the buzzing in her head. She hasn't realized that the buzzing is actual thoughts from the people around her. The more people, the louder the buzzing."

"Fascinating, sir."

"Yes, yes. Only I'm not at all sure that I can help her control it. It would've helped if we had been able to retain Dr. Avery's notes—but they are lost. Possibly forever."

"Did Dr. Avery destroy them?"

"Maybe. I don't know. I have a funny suspicion that his assistant, Alvin, took them, wherever the hell he is." Charlie sighed. "C'mon. Let's get back to the lab." Without the use of his cane, Dr. Charles H. Zacher headed out of the park, perfectly upright—perfectly healthy.

39

"I need your help," Kadir announced to a shocked Ghost as he carried Abrianna into Ghost's underground bunker.

Ghost stared at Kadir and the bloody, unconscious woman. "What the hell happened?"

"Trust me, man. You wouldn't believe me even if I told you." Kadir spun around in the dark and stonewalled room, looking for a place to lay her down. Three other guys, huddled in front of computers and homemade servers, stopped what they were doing to stare wide-eyed at him too.

"Where can I put her?" Kadir asked. "She's been shot."

"Shot?" Ghost bolted out of his shock, closed the metal door, and nervously looked around. "You *shot* her?"

"No. Not me," Kadir snapped, offended.

"Oh."

"Where can I put her?"

"There's the cot room," one of the hackers suggested.

"Where?" Kadir asked, looking around.

"Follow me." Ghost led Kadir through a maze of gadgets, wires, and spare parts to the back of the bunker.

The place was surprisingly larger than it had appeared the first time he was here.

"There," Ghost said, opening a door. "You can put her in here."

Inside a gray, windowless six-by-eight room sat a solitary cot and a flat pillow. The only problem was that someone was already lying on it.

"Yo, Roger. Get up," Ghost barked and kicked the cot.

Roger groaned. "Whaat?"

"Get up. We got an emergency, we need the bed."

Roger had difficulty processing the request so Ghost helped out by physically grabbing him. "I *said* get up!"

"All right. All right. I'm up," Roger said, while Ghost ushered him out the door.

"Whoa, man. What happened to her?" Roger asked, swiping the sleep from his eyes as Kadir moved past him.

"Not your business." Ghost shoved him toward the door.

Roger rubbernecked as long as he could, but eventually was hustled out of sight.

Kadir placed the woman who'd both endangered and saved his life down as gently as he could. After that, he stared at her. Beneath the bruises, swelling, and dry blood, the woman was still an undeniable beauty. Inappropriately, the lower parts of Kadir's body stirred.

"Okay. How can I help?" Ghost asked, hovering at the doorway.

Kadir shook his head and stood. "I have no idea." He pulled his gaze away. "I'm not a doctor."

A blank-faced Ghost stared back. "And I am?"

Kadir rubbed his shaky hands along the legs of his jeans and willed his brain to squeeze out something—anything.

"Is the bullet still in her?" a voice asked.

Ghost and Kadir's necks swiveled toward Roger, who clearly didn't know how to mind his own business.

"I have no idea," Kadir said, helplessly.

"Maybe you should check," Roger suggested.

"Right." Kadir's gaze returned to the unconscious woman, but he didn't move.

"C'mon, man. Surely, you didn't bring her here to watch her die?" Ghost said, not moving toward the woman either.

Kadir closed his eyes, prayed to Allah, and then kneeled next to the bed. As the woman's perfect breasts rose and fell, it took a herculean effort not to look. "I need scissors."

"Scissors?" Ghost repeated and then looked to Roger.

He shook his head.

"We don't have any scissors," Ghost informed Kadir.

Perspiration beaded Kadir's forehead. Time was of the essence. He took hold of her bloody T-shirt and ripped it open with his bare hands. Her perfect, upturned breasts, encased in a black lace bra, captured the room's attention.

"Damn," Ghost and Roger echoed in sync.

Kadir tossed an angry glare over his shoulder, "C'mon, guys. Show some decency."

Contrite, the men mumbled, "Sorry."

Drawing a deep breath, Kadir turned back toward Abrianna and the nasty, pulpy bullet wound in her right shoulder. He leaned forward, trying to eyeball whether it was a clean in-and-out wound.

"Well?" an anxious Ghost asked. "Is it still in there?"

"I can't tell."

"Can you feel around?"

"In the wound?"

"No. In her toe. Of course in the wound!"

Kadir hesitated. *What if I hurt her?* "I should wash my hands."

"Man, quit stalling," Ghost whined.

"I'm not. She could get an infection!"

"The break room is around the corner," Roger said, nodding his head in its direction. "There's plenty of hand sanitizer in there too."

Nodding, Kadir bounded back onto his feet, but when he started to jet out of the room, he saw the men's hungry gazes were still affixed on Abrianna's exposed bra.

"Goddamn it. Do you mind?" He took off his bloody jacket, covered her, and then rushed out. As he squeezed past the two men at the door, Ghost grumbled, "I don't see the harm in looking."

Kadir rolled his eyes. "Just show me where the break room is."

"Do you know how long it's been since we had a female down in here?" Ghost asked, leading the way.

"All the more reason you should spend more time above ground."

"Captain Obvious is in the house," Ghost grumbled. Roger watched the men disappear around the corner. He thought for a second, looked around, and then crept into the room. At the edge of the cot, he noticed the rapid movement behind her closed eyelids. Was she having some sort of seizure? He didn't wonder about it for long because his eyes were drawn back to what lay beneath the jacket. Unable to stop himself, he removed Kadir's jacket.

"Damn." Wide-eyed, Roger reached toward the woman's breasts. His heart pounding, his mouth salivating, he could already feel her luscious mounds. Suddenly, Abrianna's right hand shot up and she jammed a .45 under his chin.

"Whoa." Roger's hands came up in surrender. His eyes flew to her disturbingly black gaze. He would have to check later, but he was *pretty* sure that he'd pissed himself. "I—I was just trying to help."

The gun dug deeper into his chin.

"I didn't mean any harm," he added.

She unclicked the safety.

"You right," he said as if she'd spoken. "I don't know what came over me. I—I shouldn't have disrespected you like that. I'm sorry."

Silence.

"Please, don't shoot me. I'll never look at another pair of breasts again in my life. I *swear*. Just, please, don't kill me." He swallowed so hard that he made a gulping sound.

Kadir and Ghost reappeared at the door.

"What the hell is going on?" Kadir demanded.

"A friend of yours?" Abrianna asked, her voice deadly.

"Uh." Kadir gazed at the disturbing scene. "I guess that depends on what he did."

"Oh, nothing much," she answered. "Just thought that he could cop a feel on a vulnerable woman. Pretty pathetic, really." She sat straight up, forcing Roger to ease back.

"What? Wait. No." Roger spat out a humorless laugh. "This is just . . . a misunderstanding."

"Roger, stop talking and just get out of here," Ghost ordered.

"Right. Right." Roger started to move until Abrianna lifted a brow. "That is, if that's all right with you, miss?"

Gaze unwavering, Abrianna lowered her weapon. "Leave."

"T-thank you." Slowly, he crept away from the cot. There was absolutely no question now. He *had* indeed pissed all over the front of his pants.

Abrianna wrinkled her nose at the pungent stench, but said nothing as the man turned around with his head hung low in shame.

Once he was gone, Kadir moved past Ghost to step into the room. "Are you all right?"

"That depends on your definition," she stated, swinging her legs over the side of the cot.

"Right now, it means: are you in any pain?"

"Life is fucking pain. Surely you're old enough to have

learned that by now." She glanced down at her bloody shoulder and, without hesitation, stuck two fingers in and dug around.

Ghost and Kadir watched and winced as if they were feeling what she clearly wasn't.

A minute later, she successfully pulled out the bullet and stared at it. "Amazing that something so little can cause so much damage." She looked over at the stunned men. "You got something I can patch my shoulder up with?"

Neither man spoke.

"Hello?"

"Uh . . ." Kadir looked at his buddy.

"Alcohol, needle—thread?" she added for clarification.

"I don't think . . . I can send one of the guys out for some," Ghost suggested.

"Why don't you do that, Einstein?"

The men exchanged another look before Ghost sighed. "You owe me," he told Kadir. "Big time."

Kadir nodded and watched his friend scramble off.

Abrianna glanced around. "So where did you find this broom closet?"

"Sorry. I can't answer that."

She shifted her gaze to him. "Why is that?"

"I *could* tell you . . . but then I'd have to kill you."

Only one corner of her lips curled upward. "You might have to get in line for that today." She stood and rotated her neck, making it sound like a handful of candy rocks popping. "So let me guess, this place is off the grid?"

"Hopefully."

"So that makes you and your friends, what? Criminals?"

"Ex-criminal. Well . . . at least I am."

"Believe it or not, that actually makes me feel better."

Kadir crossed his arms and leaned against the wall. "Is that because you're a criminal yourself?"

"I could answer that." She smiled. "But then I'd have to kill you."

His gaze lowered to the gun still in her hand.

She laughed and clicked the safety back on. "Relax. I'm not going to kill you and your perverted friends."

"Thanks for putting my mind at ease," he deadpanned. "Mind if I ask what you plan on doing?"

Abrianna pulled in a breath and thought the question over. "The only thing I can do: figure out who's trying to kill me."

Kadir drank in the woman's statuesque beauty and couldn't imagine who would be crazy enough to want to have her killed. He also noticed how dilated her eyes were. Was she high? She seemed different. Almost robotic. "Well, I wish that I could help, but I have my own set of problems. More so now that I don't have a car to make a living."

"Sorry about that," she said, not looking sorry at all. "Give me a few hours and I'll see about reimbursing you or getting it replaced."

Kadir's laughter filled the room. "No offense, lady, but uh . . . after you're patched up, I'm cool if we *never* see each other again."

"See. Now you're hurting my feelings." She smirked.

"Don't take it personal."

"Trust me. I won't." She took another look around, but the silence grew uncomfortable.

"What's your real name?" he asked. "I mean, if that's not privileged information, too."

She drew in a deep breath. "I'm called a lot of things," she said flippantly. "But it's Abrianna. My friends call me Bree."

"Is that what we are now? Friends?"

"Well . . . you did just save my life. I'd say that puts us on the fast track."

He nodded. "I'd say it was nothing, but that would be a lie."

She smiled.

"Abrianna," he repeated, liking the way it rolled off the tongue. "Nice. It's quite beautiful. It suits you."

She cocked her head. "Are you flirting with me?"

"I—I, uh . . ."

The sound of boots slapping on concrete stole their attention. Ghost reappeared at the door with a brown paper bag.

"Got what you asked for," Ghost said, grinning at Abrianna, who still stood by the cot, shirtless. He approached, googly-eyed, as if he'd be rewarded with a kiss or a pat on the head for his trouble.

Kadir noted her effortless effect on men and frowned. He also experienced a stir of jealousy when she turned her smile toward Ghost.

"Thank you," she said.

"Don't mention it."

She returned to the edge of the bed and dumped out the bag's contents. She went for the bottle of alcohol first, opened it, and doused her entire shoulder without flinching. The men watched in amazement as she sterilized a needle, threaded it, and then proceeded to patch the hole in her shoulder. All without flinching or making a sound.

"She's not fucking human," Ghost mumbled.

"You might be right," Kadir whispered back.

When Abrianna finished, she splashed more alcohol over the stitched wound and then used medical tape to secure a cotton bandage.

"How in the hell do you know how to do all that?" Kadir asked.

"A life on the streets, baby. I've patched plenty of bullet wounds in my time."

"It doesn't hurt?" Ghost asked.

"Like a muthafucka," she answered. "But what are you going to do?"

The sound of more rushing feet grabbed everyone's attention.

"Turn on the TV," ordered Roger, who was now wearing a pair of gray sweats, before rushing toward the small nine-inch television sitting on a stack of plastic crates in the corner of the room.

Bree tensed, suspecting that the murder at the Hay-Adams had hit the news. Instead, a reporter stood in front of the Reagan National Airport with the words BREAKING NEWS and TERRORIST ATTACK emblazoned across the bottom of the screen.

"What is this?" Kadir asked, surprised that it wasn't the insane car chase that he and Abrianna had escaped in the past of hour.

"What? You don't know?" Ghost asked. "Where have you been?"

Kadir raised a brow.

"Oh. Right. Never mind."

"CNN has obtained exclusive video from Reagan National Airport's exterior security cameras. It's one piece of evidence that the authorities are looking at as they search for suspects. So far, the death tally is at three hundred and eighteen people with an additional two hundred wounded. More than six terrorist groups have claimed responsibility, but authorities say that it is too soon to know for sure which group is really behind the twin blasts. These photos released by the police are at the top of federal authority's suspects list. The two men in black are the suspected suicide bombers while this man can be seen leaving after helping the men load the suspected bombs onto airport luggage carts."

Kadir's jaw dropped.

In the next instant, the image was blown up on the screen and there was no doubt to anyone in that cramped room who it was.

Abrianna looked at Kadir and lifted a lone brow.

"The man is considered dangerous," the reporter said. *"Au-*

thorities ask that, if you see him, you not approach him, but call the number at the bottom of your screen."

Kadir shoved Roger out of the way and turned off the television. Afterward, he spun around and faced the small group. "I—I had nothing to do with it."

"Have a twin, do you?" Abrianna asked.

"No!"

Ghost cocked his head.

"I mean, yes. But that's not him. My brother is in Yemen."

Abrianna's confusion was clear from her twisted expression. "So that *was* you with the suicide bombers?"

"Well . . . yes."

"So you're not an *ex*-criminal?" she asked.

Kadir tripped over his tongue. "No. I mean, yes."

Ghost laughed, shaking his head. "Damn, man. Now you even got me confused."

Kadir took a deep breath and combated his rising panic. "I am an *ex*-criminal, but *that* is most certainly not what it looks like."

"It looks like a couple of suicide bombers got out of your car and went inside the airport and blew it up," Abrianna said.

He took a couple of seconds to process that. "Okay. So *technically* it *is* what it looks like."

"I'm glad that you cleared that up," she said, enjoying his fluster.

"Let me start over," Kadir said. "I don't know those guys. They just live in my apartment complex and needed a ride to the airport. That's it."

No one responded.

"You believe me. Don't you, Ghost?"

He shrugged. "Yeah, sure. Why not?"

"I'm an Uber driver. It was just a damn fare."

"Sounds simple enough to clear up." Roger shrugged. "The federal government is filled with open-minded people. It should be no problem to prove that you, a Muslim American with a federal record, didn't collude with two other suicidal Muslims who live in your apartment complex, who you're on surveillance cameras dropping off in your car at the airport and helping them load bombs onto a cart."

"Shit." Kadir raked his hands through his hair. "I'm fucked." He turned the television back on, but this time, a different news reporter, Elly Simpson, stood in front of the Hay-Adams Hotel with the same BREAKING NEWS banner at the bottom.

"It's a gruesome scene down here at the luxury hotel Hay-Adams. A man's body—riddled with bullets, according to some staffers' accounts—was discovered in one of the hotel's federal suites. The name of the victim is yet to be released. However, we have been able to pick up rumblings that the victim is indeed a high-profile member on the Hill."

"Holy shit." Abrianna blinked in utter incredulity when she saw her own image on the television screen.

"The police are on the lookout for this woman seen here on the hotel's security cameras leaving the crime scene. If you have any information, the local authorities would like for you to call the number at the bottom of your screen."

Kadir, Ghost, and Roger turned their shocked eyes toward Abrianna.

She gave them a one-shoulder shrug and a small smirk. "What can I say? It's been a helluva crazy day."

40

Tomi wasn't expecting Chief Holder to join her and Castillo at the Lunchbox café. But when Castillo slid Holder's photographs from the Hay-Adams surveillance cameras across the table, she was faced with a dilemma.

"What are you going to do?" Castillo asked after the young reporter went over everything she'd gathered from the night of the masquerade party.

"What do you mean, what am I going to do? I'm going to write the story," Tomi said matter-of-factly. "What else can I do?"

"The president's administration is trying to bundle what happened at the airport with what happened to Speaker Reynolds. Of course, it makes perfect sense why they would want that. Anyone other than a terrorist would land the conspiracy theories at his feet. Reynolds was going to pursue impeachment, after all."

"Well, nothing there indicts the president," Holder said. "Not unless Abrianna Parker is an assassin working for the federal government."

Tomi laughed. "There is a difference between real-world reality and political reality. Some random girl from a party just happens to go to the Hay-Adams and kill the newly elected speaker? Not flashy enough. The conservative media industry could spin Bree into being a contract killer for the president before the first commercial break. That's just how it is here."

"Do *you* believe that?" Castillo asked, sipping her coffee.

"It's not about what I believe. It's about the facts."

Castillo shook her head. "I know that I'm a cynic, but the facts are kind of murky here. Bree going with him to that hotel doesn't prove a hell of a lot. Was she there? Yes. Did she kill him? We don't know."

"Whoa. Whoa. I'm not trying to convict her of anything. Just stating that she was there is bad enough. Not to mention, she didn't go to the police."

Castillo laughed. "If my memory serves me correctly, Ms. Parker wasn't much of a fan of the police, even though *this* former cop risked everything to rescue her from Avery's basement."

"Wait. Are you suggesting that I *don't* write about this? These pictures are going to be leaked to the press, if they haven't been already. My only advantage is, at this moment, I *know* who she is."

"*We* know who she is," Castillo corrected. "We also know what she's been through."

"You're losing me again."

Castillo sighed.

"I can't *not* write the story. It's my job," Tomi said.

"I'm not saying don't write it," Castillo said.

"Oh. Then I must get my hearing checked because that's exactly what it sounded like you were saying."

"I'm saying . . ." Castillo realized that she didn't know what she was saying. "Just . . . be careful. I think Abrianna Parker is in a very fragile state, and I'd hate to see her end up like Shalisa."

"Shalisa who killed her mother?" Tomi asked.

Holder nodded like he'd come around to Tomi's way of thinking.

"Look. No one is more sympathetic to what Abrianna has gone through, and *is* going through, than me. But maybe it's because of that—a violent streak exists."

"Then you should be worried," Castillo said. "Because, the way I see it, if *they* could snap, then maybe one day *you* will too."

41

"You're wanted for murder?" Kadir thundered. "Why didn't you tell me?"

"I haven't exactly had the opportunity," Abrianna said, defensively. "I don't remember you mentioning that you were a domestic terrorist."

"I'm *not* a damn terrorist," he roared back.

"And I'm not a murderer!"

Their gazes shot over to Ghost, who looked around to see if they were staring at someone else. "Why are you guys looking at me? My face isn't plastered all over the damn news. Thank God. *But* if you want my opinion, I'd say that you guys are in a pretty fucked-up situation."

Kadir pulled in a deep breath. "He's right. We're fucked. Between the two of us, we probably have every government agency in the book scouring the city."

"And some that *aren't* in the book," Ghost tagged on.

"You find this funny?" Kadir challenged his friend.

"If you're riding through hell, you may as well laugh while doing it." Ghost shrugged. "At least that's what my grandmother always said."

A cell phone trilled.

Ghost jumped. "What the fuck is that?"

Abrianna looked around and picked up her jacket off the floor. "Relax. It's just my cell phone."

Ghost exploded. "You brought a cell phone down here?"

Before she could answer the call, Ghost snatched the smartphone out of her hands. "HEY!"

"Number-one rule: no cell phones!" Ghost thundered.

"Give that back," she snapped, lunging for the phone, but then she hissed out in pain. Her drugs were finally wearing off.

"Are you all right?" Kadir asked.

Ghost whipped around and threw the offending gadget down as hard as he could at the concrete floor. It shattered instantly.

Abrianna gasped.

Ghost wasn't done. He stomped his big gorilla-sized Timberlands down on top of the phone several times.

"Have you lost your fucking mind?" she screamed.

Ghost faced her. "No. Have you? These damn things are tracking devices. Are you trying to get caught? Don't you know that Big Brother is *always* watching? The moment they ID you, the first thing they're going to do is look for any device attached to your name. Within seconds, they can lock on to the GPS in your phone, which would get them in here to bust this operation. This place is off the grid, and I'd like to keep it that way."

Abrianna glared at Kadir. "Are you going to *do* something?"

He shook his head, siding with his lunatic friend. "Sorry. But he's right."

Ghost dialed down the anger. "I don't mind helping you guys out, but you're not the only ones who have something to lose."

Abrianna's curiosity finally piqued. "What is this place?"

"See? Now you're worried about the wrong damn thing."

Her gaze shifted back to Kadir. "Are you going to check your boy or what?"

"Check me?" Ghost looked at Kadir. "Are you going to check your girl or what?"

"I'm *not* his girl!"

"Lucky him."

"All right. All right. Enough." Kadir rubbed his throbbing temples. "This isn't getting us anywhere. Squash this shit so we can use our energy to figure out what we need to do next."

Ghost and Abrianna glared at each other.

"I mean it. Are we good?" Kadir asked, his gaze darting between them.

Ghost worked his jaw, chewing on the words that he really wanted to say. "I'm good."

Kadir looked at Abrianna. "You?"

"I'm *more* than good," she said, though her eyes spat fire.

Kadir relaxed, but his gaze lowered to her bandaged shoulder, where dots of blood seeped through. "Here, let me . . ."

Bree jerked away from his touch.

Stunned by her reaction, Kadir blinked. "You're bleeding," he told her.

She glanced down at her bandaged shoulder, but shrugged it and his concern off. "I'm good," she said, lifting her chin.

The woman baffled Kadir, but if she insisted on being stubborn, there was nothing he could really do about it. He turned toward Ghost. "Hey, you got something that she could put on? A T-shirt or something?" The strain of not looking at her incredible body had grown to be too much—for all the men in the room.

"You're in luck." Ghost went to a closet next to the door that neither Abrianna or Kadir had noticed and pulled out a duffel bag.

"Here." He tossed a black T-shirt toward Abrianna. "It might be a little too big for you, but it will do the job."

Bree caught the shirt but, before putting it on, sniffed it.

"It's clean," Ghost told her.

"Just checking." She smirked before lifting the T-shirt over her head. However, getting her sore arm through the short sleeve presented a challenge.

"Here, let me help." Kadir stepped forward. Once he got her arms through and pulled the shirt down over her head, their faces came intimately close. Instantly, Kadir was intoxicated by her vanilla-scented skin and sensuous lips. Images from that incredible dream came flooding back.

Abrianna, on the other hand, was entranced by the flecks of gold in Kadir's dark gaze. The attraction took her back. Maybe it was the combination of his honey-brown skin, intense eyes, and wavy black hair. He was a handsome man—dangerously handsome.

Ghost coughed to clear his throat.

Jolted out of their momentary trance, Kadir and Abrianna cast their gazes toward a weary-looking Ghost.

"Could you give us a few minutes?" Kadir asked his friend.

Ghost lifted a brow. "Are you sure?"

Kadir nodded.

"All right," Ghost grumbled while casting a displeased look toward Abrianna.

She mirrored his expression while tapping her foot impatiently. Once the irritating man left, closing the door behind him, she shifted her attention to Kadir. "Interesting friends you have here."

"They are good guys," Kadir said.

"If you say so."

"Look . . . Bree, was it?"

She affirmed with a simple head nod.

"Look, Bree. Regardless how you feel about Ghost and his team, we *need* them right now."

She laughed. "The hell I do. I don't need *anyone's* help. Thank you very much."

Kadir laughed. It was clear that she didn't hear the irony of her words. "You *are* joking, right?"

Her jawline became marble-hard.

"Well, it sure seemed to me that you needed *my* help when you dove into *my* car with those goons chasing you—and when you were bleeding out in that same car. Who were they?"

Abrianna's face darkened, but she couldn't refute his words. Instead, she said something insane. "That was different."

"Different?" he asked, incredulous. "Different how?"

"I don't know. It just was." She shrugged, avoiding his gaze.

Kadir crossed his arms and waited her out.

"What?" she challenged.

"I think you know what," he said. "Two words. First one starts with a T."

"Oh my God. You've got to be kidding me."

He clammed up and waited.

Bree huffed and shifted around on her feet for another thirty seconds. "All right. So I needed your help earlier."

"And?"

"And . . . you helped."

He laughed. "You really can't say it, can you?"

"Don't be ridiculous. I can say it . . . if I want to."

Kadir lifted one of his brows, still waiting.

"All right." Abrianna took a deep breath. "*Thank* you. There. I said it. Are you happy now?"

"Actually, I am." Kadir's smile revealed two rows of perfect pearl-white teeth.

Abrianna scowled even though her pulse quickened. "Okay. Now that we've gotten that out of the way, any way one of your flunky friends can loan us a car or something? I need to get my hands on some cash so that *I* can get the hell up out of D.C."

"That's it?" Kadir asked.

"Look. I can't make any guarantees, but maybe I can get

enough money from Madam Nevaeh to help your situation, too," she said. "All I know is that I can't stay in . . ." She glanced around. "Whatever this place is."

"That's my whole point. This is the safest place we can be right now." He gestured to the broken smartphone. "Ghost's paranoia about tracking devices is legit. He's a master at cloaking this place from the federal government for years."

Abrianna's body language loosened. "Yeah?"

He nodded. "Yeah. So you might want to *try* and be nice. You'll get more bees with honey, I've been told."

She sucked in a breath. "I'm *not* apologizing to him."

Kadir folded his arms again.

"He broke my phone!"

Silence.

"He should be apologizing to me!"

Silence.

Abrianna locked her jaw tight, determined to win the silent war—but she didn't last a minute. "Fine! Whatever. I'll apologize."

He smiled. "Thank you."

Abrianna pretended that the fluttering in her stomach was just her body still reacting to the fact that she'd actually been shot.

"Hey. Are you sure that you're all right?" he asked, his smile flipping.

"Yeah. I'm fine. Why?"

He nodded like he didn't want to argue, but said, "You're sweating pretty bad. May I?" Without waiting for permission, which likely would have never come, Kadir placed his hand against her forehead. "You're burning up."

"I'm fine," she insisted, unconvincingly.

"Sit down," he ordered, forcing her back to perch on the edge of the bed. "You have a fever."

His words confused her. "No. I feel fine." Abrianna placed

a hand against her forehead and was clearly surprised at how wet it was. "It's nothing. I'm fine."

Kadir remained dubious, but didn't want to push. "Sooo .. . you want to tell me what's going on?" Kadir said, nodding his head toward the turned-off television.

Abrianna pulled another deep breath. "I can't tell you what I don't know."

Kadir waited again.

She squirmed under his stare. "Look. I went to this party and I hung out with this guy . . . and some other chick. I did some drugs and . . . I blacked out. When I came to, the man was dead and the other girl was gone."

Kadir frowned. Remembering what Cashmere had told him. He wanted to ask whether she had been an escort at that "party," but couldn't get himself to ask.

"It's the truth, I swear."

"Then what happened?"

"I got the fuck out of there. I know a setup when I see one."

"So who was the other girl?"

"How the fuck would I know?" Abrianna snapped. "I didn't know either one of them before Friday night."

A strange look fell over Kadir's face.

"I know that look," Abrianna sneered. "You're judging me."

"No, I'm not," he lied.

Sensing his deception, Abrianna inched away from him. She had no intention of explaining her whole damn life to a complete stranger. *Who gives a fuck what he thinks?*

"What about the rest?" he asked.

"The rest?"

"I wasn't anywhere near the Hay-Adams Hotel when you dove into my car. And you hardly explained who the goons were that tried to take us out."

"I don't know who *they* were." She shrugged, defensively. "I was at my apartment explaining what happened to . . ." Her throat tightened.

Kadir's brows lifted.

Abrianna coughed to clear her airway. "Bullets just flew through the window, cutting Shawn down right there in front of me." *Shawn.* Her gaze dropped as it suddenly felt as if a steel vise was harnessed around her heart. She couldn't imagine what her life would be like without him going forward.

"Shawn?"

"He, uhm . . . my best friend."

Kadir placed a hand over her trembling ones to encourage her.

Abrianna continued, "Everything else just happened in a blur. I got the hell out of there as fast as I could. But . . . those assholes chased me out the back of the building. I ran until I saw that guy getting out of your car, and the rest is history." Once she'd finished the story, she assessed Kadir's reaction.

There wasn't one.

Suddenly, she was back on her feet. "Look. Thanks for saving my ass back there. I appreciate it. I'm sorry about your car, too. But I think that I can handle things from here." She headed toward the door.

Kadir waited until she opened it before speaking up. "Hold up."

She didn't wait. She charged ahead, winding her way through the crazy narrow maze of computer servers.

"Abrianna, wait up," Kadir called, but ended up chasing after her.

Ghost and his crew swiveled their attention from the news reports on their screens when Abrianna barged in.

"How do I get out of this hellhole?" she barked.

Kadir caught up and grabbed her good arm. "Excuse her," he said to Ghost and his crew. "She's running a bad fever."

Belligerent, Abrianna tried to wrestle free, surprising Kadir with her strength, but he wasn't a punk either and managed to drag her all the way back to the tiny gray room and slam the door. "Calm the fuck down," he growled. "Where in the hell do you think you're going? We're the most wanted people in D.C. right now. You won't last ten minutes out there!"

"Why do you care?" she snapped.

The question caught him off guard. *Why in the hell do I care?*

"It's my problem," she said as more sweat beaded on her forehead. "I'll handle it. I don't need your help." She moved to step around him, but the moment her hand touched the doorknob again, the floor seemed to tilt beneath her, wreaking havoc on her balance.

Kadir caught her before she hit the floor. "No. You're not going anywhere," he said, and carried her back to the cot and laid her down. "You are going to rest here, whether you like it or not. *Then* we'll think of a plan for you—or us—to get out of D.C."

42

Special Agents Bell and Hendrickson stood outside of an FBI interrogation room in similar wide-leg stances with their arms folded across their chests as they observed the nervous junkie squirm in his chair through a two-way mirror.

"So what do you think?" Bell asked his partner.

"The truth?" Roland asked, assessing the man again.

"Always."

"I think we're wasting valuable time with this dude. I mean, look at him." He gestured toward the glass. "Either he's tweaking or he's in withdrawal."

"So what? You want to cut him loose?" Bell asked.

Roland shrugged. "I don't know, man. It's your call."

"How is it that the other teams get to question the normal neighbors and we get stuck with the local junkie?" Bell asked.

"Luck?"

"Not funny."

Bell assessed Mook again. "Hell. We already got him here. Might as well hear what he's got to say."

Resigned, Roland sighed and fell in step behind his partner into the interrogation room.

"Sorry to have kept you waiting, Mister, uh . . ."

"No need to be formal. Folks call me Mook," the junkie said, smiling.

"I see . . . Mook." Bell shot a look to his partner, whose bored expression was set in granite.

Bell pulled out a metal chair to the left of Mook and stepped over the seat and squatted down like he was settling into a saddle. "All right, let's get started." He produced a pocket recorder and hit record. "Can you state your full name for the record?"

"I told you, folks call me Mook." He twitched and scratched the side of his neck. His dry skin sounded like chafing sandpaper.

"Yeah, well. That may be true, but I'm going to need your full government name, if you don't mind."

A tic twitched at the side of Mook's right temple. Clearly, spitting out his name was a problem.

"What's up? You got a warrant out or something?" Bell asked.

"Nah. Nah. At least, I don't think so." Mook sighed. "Name is Michael."

"Michael what?" Bell asked, already feeling his patience strain.

"Michael Legend," Mook spat and then shifted in his chair uncomfortably.

"Michael *Legend*?" Bell echoed.

"Yeah. Crazy name to live up to, huh?" Mook scratched his neck again and shifted around in his chair.

"It's a good name," Bell acquiesced. "Now, Michael, we've heard that you pretty much know everybody at the Park Flats apartments. Is this true?"

"Yeah. I make a habit of getting to know my neighbors. That's not against the law or anything, is it?"

"No. No. It's not against the law. In fact, it's a mighty neighborly thing to do, if you ask me. I wish more people had a sense of community and got to know their neighbors. It certainly would make our jobs a little easier. Wouldn't it, Roland?"

"Yep," Roland said.

Mook smiled, exposing his butter-yellow teeth. "See? I've been saying the same thing for years. But folks don't be hearing me though. I gets along with everybody, mainly 'cause they know that I can get anything they need on the low-low."

"What? You running a black market, Mr. Legend?"

Mook opened his mouth, thought about it, and then quickly snapped it shut.

Bell grinned. "Well, we're not here to talk about that right now. We're more interested in what you know about one of your neighbors. A Kadir Kahlifa. You know him?"

"Oh. K-Man. Oh yeah. I fucks with him. He's cool." The yellow teeth made another appearance while a gust of halitosis drifted under Bell's nose.

The agent blinked his watering eyes several times. "Good. So what can you tell us about him?"

"About who?"

"About Mr. Kahlifa," Bell stressed. "Say like, when was the last time you saw him?"

"K-man? Oh, well. That's easy. I saw him this morning. I did him a solid and sent some bizness his way."

"Some . . . *bizness?* What kind of bizness?"

Mook shrugged. "He's a cab driver . . . well, one of those uh, whatcha call it?"

"An Uber driver?" Roland filled in from his post by the door.

"Yeah. The Al-Sahi brothers needed a lift to the airport when their cab didn't show up so I sent them his way."

Both Bell and Roland came to attention.

Roland finally moved from the door to lean over the table toward Mook. "Say that shit again."

Mook sensed that he'd said something wrong. "Hey, why do

y'all want to know so much about Kadir anyway? What'd he do?"

"That's *our* bizness," Bell said. "Who are the Al-Sahi brothers? They live in Park Flats, too?"

"Yeah." Mook shrugged. "I don't know too much about them. These are some new cats that moved in over at unit thirty-seven-B a few months back. I think . . . late spring—or sometime around there. They pretty much stay to themselves—late-night workers though. The lights in their apartment are on all hours of the night."

Bell cleared his throat, hinting to get back to the point.

"Anyway, Najjar and Brahim needed a ride to the airport so I gave them K-Man's apartment number and sent them his way." Mook shrugged. "He appreciated the bizness."

"Would you be able to identify the Al-Sahi brothers?"

"Sure. I mean, a lot of those Middle Eastern cats look alike, but yeah."

Roland tossed his partner an *I-told-you-so* look over his shoulder, before asking, "Are you sure?"

"I could point them out in a lineup, if that's what you mean." Then he realized what he'd said. "Wait. They do something? If they did, scratch that. I don't know nothing about nothing. I ain't no snitch."

"Hold tight," Roland said, leaving the table and then the room.

43

The Bunker

Abrianna was burning up. She was unaware of her clothes being stripped from her body or of Kadir's nightlong vigil by her side, placing and replacing ice-cold towels on her forehead and body in an attempt to lower her temperature.

"So is she going to make it or what?" Ghost asked when Kadir finally stepped out of the room.

Kadir shook his head. "I honestly don't have any idea."

Ghost sighed long and hard. Frustration etched deep lines across his forehead. "What if she doesn't?"

Kadir's temples twitched in irritation. "I don't know. I'll cross that bridge when I get to it."

"News flash, buddy, but we're already standing in the middle of that fucking bridge."

Kadir stepped back and eyed his friend. "I'm starting to think that you *want* her to die."

"Honestly?" Ghost asked. "I don't give a shit. I may not have as many problems as Jay Z, but I don't need another one. And neither do you."

Kadir raked his hand through his tufts of wet curls.

"Do you want my opinion?" Ghost asked.

"Do I have a choice?"

"No. Not really," Ghost said. "The question was a courtesy."

"I figured as much." Kadir sighed. "Go ahead. Hit me."

"I don't like this. I don't like her. She is trouble. It's written all over her. Big T on her forehead."

"That's not what you said when you first saw her at the Stallion."

"Oh, she's hot. Don't get me wrong," Ghost said. "There isn't a man in here, I suspect, that wouldn't drink her bath water. But none of that is going to make us feel better when we're behind bars. And if she croaks, I'm not helping you move a dead body. I didn't sign up for that."

"Are you kidding me? The entire country thinks that I'm a homegrown *terrorist* and you're worried about a simple murder case?"

"You can explain your shit. You're a fucking cab driver."

"Uber driver."

"Same difference. My point is that you didn't know those dudes. As long as they can't tie you to those two shitheads, they'll have to cut you loose."

Kadir cocked his head and gave him a flat look.

"Well, sure—they might torture you a bit to make sure. But after a little waterboarding, you'll be out of there."

"Is this supposed to be a pep talk, coach?"

"No. I'm handing your ass a reality check. You don't know anything about this girl." Ghost glanced inside of the room where Abrianna tossed and turned. "And that story you told me about her just waking up next to a dead body is fishy as hell. She could've killed that dude. You don't know."

"She said that she didn't do it."

"What the hell else is she going to say? She needs a sucker like you to help her get out of the city."

Kadir's gaze cast into the room as well. Abrianna's tossing and turning stopped. Her sweat-drenched hair plastered itself against her peaceful face. "And what about those other bruises and scars all over her body? Don't tell me you didn't notice."

Kadir didn't answer.

Ghost snapped his fingers in front of his friend's face.

Kadir jumped.

"Man, you got it *baaad*."

"I don't know what you're talking about."

"Sure you don't." Ghost crossed his arms. "All I know is that I asked you to come aboard this operation and you told me to go to hell."

"I did not."

"In so many words you did. You gave me a big speech about how you were playing shit straight from here on out. Our revolution against our tyrannical government no longer interested you. Then you teased me by coming here, asking about T4S. *But* the minute a hot chick jumps in your car, suddenly you don't value your freedom so much."

"It's not like that."

"Then what's it like?"

Kadir huffed and paced around. There really wasn't a reason for his willingness to stick his neck out for a girl that he didn't know.

"I'm waiting," Ghost said.

"I don't know. I . . . I believe her, all right?"

Disappointed, Ghost hung his head.

"Look, what is it going to hurt to help her get out of town, huh? I'm already neck-deep into this mess anyway. I just need a car or something to get her across town, all right?"

Head back, Ghost closed his eyes and prayed for strength.

"Look, man. I'll owe you big for this one," Kadir asked.

"Oh. You *already* owe me big." The friends' gazes locked,

each willing the other one to come to their senses. But it was Ghost who relented first. "All right," he said, sighing. "Let me see what I can do."

Ghost's lips split into a smile. "Thanks, man."

"Yeah. Yeah. Now what about *your* situation? You get her to where she needs to go and then what?"

Kadir sighed. "The way I see it, I only have one play."

Ghost lifted a brow. "You're going to turn yourself in?"

"You have another suggestion?"

"You could run. You got people in Yemen. You could easily disappear without a trace. All we have to do is get you around a no-fly list, which I'm sure you're on by now, with some fake IDs and a passport."

"You can do that?"

"I know a guy who knows a guy." Ghost shrugged. "The typical way these things go."

Kadir shook his head. "I'm not running. I didn't do anything wrong."

"You don't have to do anything wrong to be locked down for life. The government needs a perp walk for this. You'd be the new face of homegrown terrorism. Any Muslim will do."

"I thought you just said they'd have to cut me loose after a little waterboarding."

"I changed my mind. They'll crucify you."

Kadir shook his head. "I'm not running."

Ghost sighed. "All right. A hard head makes for a soft ass."

"I'm not even going to ask what the hell that's supposed to mean." Kadir laughed, but then lowered his volume when he remembered Abrianna was still resting a few feet away.

"Why don't you at least test the waters?" Ghost suggested. "Call that special agent you said dropped by your crib the other day. State your case to him and gauge the temperature of the shit storm you're about to walk into."

"Agent Bell?" Kadir laughed. "That man hates me—and frankly, the feeling is mutual."

"You're not asking the man out to the prom," Ghost reasoned. "Run your story by him first and judge his reaction. Who knows, maybe the media is hyping the shit up for ratings. It wouldn't be the first time."

Kadir considered the suggestion.

Ghost popped him on the shoulder. "C'mon. What do you have to lose?"

PART FOUR

Only Women Bleed . . .

44

After a long pause hung over the line, Kadir answered, "Hello, Special Agent Bell."

Chuckling, Bell turned his back to the interrogation room to give the caller his undivided attention. "Well, I'll be hot damn. I was just thinking about you."

"I just bet you were," Kadir said.

"What can I say? You're a very popular man right now. It takes a certain amount of talent to go from criminal hacker to domestic terrorist in a single bound."

"You'd like to believe that, now wouldn't you?"

Bell smiled and leaned casually against the door. "I'm just going by what all of America is seeing right now: you dropping off your suicide buddies at the airport. What's the matter? You didn't have the guts to join them for that big virginal orgy in the sky?"

"I had nothing to do with that sick shit."

"Sure you didn't," Bell chuckled. "You were just at the wrong place at the wrong time. Is that the card you're going to play on this?"

"It's not a card. It's the truth."

"Uh-huh. And now this situation with this girl . . . ? Seems you've been busier than I have given you credit for. By the way, what's your girlfriend's name?"

"You got it all wrong. I *told* you the other day that I got a job as an Uber driver. Those guys were nothing more than a fare. I don't know anything else about them."

At the familiar story, Bell faced the interrogation room holding Mook. "Is that right?"

"Yeah. That's right. And there's a neighbor of mine who can back me up on this, too. He's the one who recommended that I take them to the airport when their taxi never showed up. Hell, you could probably call around to the local cab services and verify that shit."

Bell's confidence waned, but his thoughts darkened. His big fish was trying to slip loose. "Tell you what. Why don't you come on in and explain it all personally to me? If it all checks out, you have nothing to worry about."

"That's why I'm calling," Kadir said. "This shit playing on rotation on the news ain't right, man. I want to come in, but I want safe passage. I'm well aware of how trigger-happy law enforcement can be with darker-hue brothers."

Bell grunted. "Is that right?"

"And what about the girl?"

"We're not discussing her. It's not important."

"Not important?" Bell laughed. "Speaking for the whole department, I beg to differ with you on that."

"Yeah, man. I want to clear my name. The sooner, the better."

"Well, I certainly want to see that happen too. Where are you right now?"

"Ah. Ah. Ah. Not so fast," Kadir said. "I need some guarantees. I want to speak with your supervisor."

Bell went silent.

"Hello?" Kadir said. "Are you still there?"

Bell tightened his grip on his cell phone.

"Agent Bell?"

"Yeah. I'm still here," he responded through gritted teeth.

"Good. I need to speak with your supervisor or director first."

"I don't know, Kahlifa. That's a pretty tall order, seeing how—given your circumstances. The higher-ups are in a more 'shoot first and ask questions later' kind of mood."

Silence.

"Believe it or not, I'm the closest thing you have to a friend here at the agency."

"Then I choose not to believe that," Kadir said.

The veins along Bell's temples bulged and pulsed. "It's up to you if you want to come in quietly to rectify this situation—or you can come in a body bag. It really doesn't matter to me. Your choice."

"You're not offering me a whole hell of a lot of assurance. Given how you feel about me."

"Trust me. There are no feelings involved. I'm just doing my job. And I'm damn good at it."

Silence.

Bell's grip hardened. "Kadir?"

"I'll stay in touch."

"Kadir," Bell snapped, feeling his opportunity slip. "Don't be stupid. You *want* to turn yourself *and* the girl in."

Silence.

"Kadir?"

"Here's the thing," Kadir said. "I don't trust you."

"That's unfortunate," Bell said. "Because if you run . . . I'm going to have to put you down." A grin finally returned to his tight mouth.

Another silence lapsed over the line before Kadir responded, "I'll keep that in mind."

Click.

Shawn White opened his eyes at Hadley Memorial Hospital. Weeping, Draya, Tivonte, and Julian all leapt up from the few chairs gathered around and rushed to his bedside.

"Oh my God!" Draya gripped his right hand despite the butterfly needle and tubes springing out of it. "It's a miracle."

Confused, Shawn blinked several times before his vision cleared. "Heeeeeey," he said, forcing on a smile. In the next second, he was swept up into a coughing frenzy that seemed to set his chest on fire.

"It's okay. It's okay," Draya soothed, and then she barked at others, "Water! Somebody get him some water."

At the same time, Julian and Tivonte spun toward the only table in the room—where bundles of flowers, a phone, and pitcher of water sat. Julian held the plastic cup while Tivonte poured.

Once the water was passed to Draya, she pressed the cup to Shawn's parched lips. "Careful. Careful," she coached. "Take your time."

Shawn heeded her words, realizing how the cool water soothed his throat. However, the burning in his chest and gut remained. After draining the cup, he dropped his head back against the pillows and chugged pure oxygen for a full minute.

"How are you feeling?" Draya asked, fretting.

"I'm feeling . . . pretty fucked up—but grateful to be alive," he admitted.

Tivonte edged closer to the bed, his long mink lashes crooked as he batted them. "What is the last thing that you remember?"

Shawn frowned as he struggled to remember. The patchwork images were confusing at first, but then it all flooded back to him. "Bree," he gasped, springing forward.

"Whoa. Whoa. Whoa." The three friends placed a restricting hand against his chest.

"And where do you think you're going?" Draya asked, taking over as mother hen. "Do you have any idea how long it took for the doctors to put Humpty Dumpty back together again? Nuh-uh. You're going to lay right back down here and rest so your body can heal."

"Where's Bree?"

Draya placed a silencing finger against her lips. The friends looked at each other.

Julian rushed to the hospital door and glanced outside. "It's clear," he whispered, but when he crept back toward the bed, he added, "But probably not for long."

Impatient, Shawn attempted to get back out of bed. "You don't understand. She's in trouble."

Draya was having none of it. "Trust me. We *do* understand," she said, pushing Shawn back down. "The entire *country* is looking for Bree."

At Shawn's pinched face, she continued, "She's wanted for murder. They think that she killed a very important political guy."

"I know," Shawn said. "Well—not *who* she killed. Uh. She told me this . . . story about a john from that masquerade party Friday night."

"What did she say?" Julian asked.

Shawn hesitated. He struggled to recall the story—or, to be frank, still grappled with whether he believed her. But at his friends' anxious faces, he repeated Bree's story.

One by one, he saw the same disbelief creep across their faces.

When Shawn finished, Tivonte settled a fist against his right hip. "What the hell was she on this time?"

Shawn groaned, closing his eyes. "I didn't believe her either," he said, regretfully.

"Uh." Tivonte glanced around the small group. "I can't front. The shit sounded suspect to me, too. Especially since we've all seen the pictures from Hay-Adams circulating on the news every hour on the hour."

Julian nodded and added, "You mean, *especially* when the dead dude in question is like second in line to the presidency. Fuck. When the government gets their hands on our girl, they're going to put her and that hottie she's playing Bonnie and Clyde with up under the jail."

At Shawn's look of confusion, they realized it was their turn to fill Shawn in on the video of Abrianna and this suspected terrorist engaged in an epic shootout. It had gone viral around the country.

To Shawn, it seemed as if the whole world had gone crazy. "So they got away?" he asked.

None of them heard Castillo enter the room or witnessed her silently listening by the door. She spooked them when she finally spoke up. "She's gotten away—for now."

Everyone's heads whipped around.

The former lieutenant unfolded her arms and waved to Shawn. "Hello. Remember me?"

Shawn did remember but didn't wave or smile back. "Make a habit of listening to private conversations, do you?"

Castillo smirked and bobbed her head. "Yes. Actually, I do." She casually strolled to the side of the bed. "You'd be surprised how much information one can glean when people think that no one is listening." She smiled. "Regardless, it's good to see you again—still among the living."

"What can I do for you, Lieutenant?"

"Well, actually. I'm not a cop anymore," she informed him. "I'm a private investigator now."

"Really?"

"Yep. And once again, I'm looking for Abrianna."

"Why? So you can turn her over to your old friends?"

"So I can help her," Castillo corrected. "Your friends are right—Abrianna is in a lot of trouble. If you care about her, which I *know* that you do, you'll help me."

Shawn evaluated her sincerity, but in the end he had to break it to her. "Sorry. But I have no idea where she is."

Castillo nodded, waited, then asked, "You said that you didn't believe Abrianna's story . . . about waking up next to a dead guy. How about now?"

Shawn lifted his chin. "I'm lying in this bed—because somebody tried to kill *her*. So yeah. I believe her."

Castillo nodded. "Good. I do too."

That admission received surprised looks.

"I can't say that I understand *everything* that's going on. But my natural conspiracy-theorist mind thinks that whoever *did* murder Speaker Reynolds either didn't know Abrianna was there or . . ."

"Thought she was already dead," Julian said, thinking aloud.

The group looked at him.

"C'mon. Think about it," he said to his friends. "We always have to double-check that she's breathing when she's asleep. The shit is fucking creepy."

Castillo frowned, not understanding.

Julian continued along Castillo's conspiracy theory. "If the killer thought Abrianna was already dead, they must have been damn surprised when she woke and sprinted out of there. That's why they showed up at Abrianna's place, gun blazing. To finish the job."

The rest of the group started nodding along.

"It explains the high-speed chase," Castillo added before reaching into her jacket and pulling out pictures that she'd bribed Holder's forensic team for and now placed on Shawn's lap.

Shawn glanced around and then hit the power button on the bed that elevated his upper body so that he could take a better look.

"These are the men that were killed at Abrianna's apartment—not too far from where you were lying. And these two men were pretty mangled after the car chase across town. Do you recognize any of them?"

Shawn stared at the pictures and then back at Castillo.

Patiently, she waited. The other three friends wreathed around the bed had already given her their answers the day before. The typical: they didn't know anything, see anything, or hear anything. She hoped that Shawn, given their previous history, however brief, would trust her more. "Do you know them?" she asked again.

He swallowed hard, debated. "You're going to help her?"

"I'm going to do all that I can."

The room fell silent. "I've seen that guy," Shawn confessed, pointing to one of the pictures from the apartment.

"Yeah?"

Shawn nodded. "He . . . works for this major street kingpin. He's known as the Teflon Don. Ever heard of him?"

"Zeke Jeffreys?" Castillo questioned.

Shawn nodded, but Castillo's confusion remained. "And why would Zeke's guys try to kill Abrianna? Was she dealing or something?"

Shawn sighed and then said, "Maybe you should pull up a chair. This might take a while."

45

Abrianna tossed and turned throughout her fevered nightmare. Everywhere she turned, she felt evil's razor-sharp claws slash across her body. She screamed, terrified. Visions of her being strapped and tied to a pole and then spun over a fiery pit filled her head. In the distance, she could hear maniacal laughter, but she couldn't make out where it came from.

"Please! Let me go," she shouted and begged. Hot tears scalded while they streaked across her face. The more tears she shed, the louder the laughter grew. Her pain had never meant anything to anyone. Hadn't she learned that lesson already?

The pole turned, spinning her over a growing pit of fire. The closer the flames came toward her face, the louder she screamed and fought to get loose. Somewhere in the recesses of her mind, she knew this torture wasn't real. It couldn't be. If she could just wake up, she would be able to prove it.

But no matter how loud she got, the torture went on forever.

"Wake up! Please!"

The fire singed every hair on her body while her skin blistered and curdled. Surely, she was cooking from the inside out. Her grip on reality waned. Maybe this horror was really happening. She would die roasting on this spit and there was nothing that she could do about it.

"Pleeeaassee. Wake up," she sobbed.

"There. There. Everything is going to be all right," a voice soothed from the great beyond.

For a brief, miraculous moment, something cool pressed against her forehead. She attempted to lean into it, but the coolness disappeared as fast as it came. The fire below resumed its endless torture.

"Noooo. Please," she cried.

The voice and the cool touch returned. "It's all right. It's all right."

She sighed, too exhausted to build up hope. But soon the fire retreated, crackling so far below her that she could no longer see it. The tears blanketing her face cooled. At long last, Abrianna tumbled into a deep sleep where she thought of nothing and no one.

Madam Nevaeh put on a brave face when the cops finally showed up at her door. At this point, she'd been expecting them. Too many guests from her masquerade party had placed Speaker Reynolds at her home Friday night for the department to ignore. Those same guests were calling in droves canceling their RSVPs for her next event. It was no surprise. It would be hard for business to rebound as long as there was a taint of homicide associated with her—just as she'd tried to explain to Zeke.

The police kept the questions light. Yes, Reynolds had attended her party, but she had no idea whom he'd brought or left with. When presented with a picture of Abrianna racing from the hotel, she feigned ignorance.

But when the cops left, the FBI showed up. Handling beetle-eyed Bell and his humongous partner was more difficult. For the first forty minutes, Bell treated her like she'd set up Speaker Reynolds for the hit job and hinted more than a couple of times that he knew *exactly* what and who she was and wasn't buying for a second that she had nothing to do with Abrianna. But he was definitely more interested in the suspected terrorist that Abrianna had been captured on video getting into an SUV with. On that point, Madam Nevaeh was sure that her innocent performance worked because she really didn't have any idea about any of that bombing bullshit.

Finally, when Bell was completely red-faced with veins bulging everywhere, Special Agent Hendrickson stepped up and reeled in his partner. Madam Nevaeh didn't know the dynamics between the two men, but she knew people. And these two didn't like each other. She also held no illusions and knew that the agents hadn't bought all of her story, but she didn't care either. She just wanted them out of her house.

They left.

But then there was a third knock on her door and Henry ushered a private detective into the salon.

"My goodness, who's next?" she asked, unable to contain her annoyance.

"Hello," Castillo greeted her. "Ms. Ellison?"

Nevaeh blinked at the casual use of her government name. "Yes?"

"Hi. I'm Gizella Castillo. I'm a private detective. Mind if I take a few minutes of your time? A mutual friend thought you may be able to help me."

"What mutual friend?"

"Here. Why don't you say hi?" Castillo held out her smartphone so that Nevaeh could see Shawn White, grinning and waving from his hospital bed. "Hey, girl. You've been naughty."

"What's this?" Nevaeh's eyes snapped back to Castillo. "What's going on? Did . . . *Abrianna* send you here?"

Castillo smiled. "So you *do* know Abrianna Parker?"

Nevaeh bristled at her mistake. "Look. I don't have to answer any of your questions. I don't even know who you work for."

Shawn took exception to her trying to dismiss him. "I'm looking for my *friend*. If you want me to come back with the cops . . . or the FBI, I can."

Nevaeh crossed her arms. "What do you want?"

"Who was the other girl?" Shawn asked.

Madam Nevaeh stared at him like he'd grown a second head. "What other girl?"

"Bree said that another woman showed up at the hotel that night, but when she woke up, the woman was gone . . . and that Reynolds dude was dead."

"And you fucking believed that?" Nevaeh laughed. "Then how about you check out this nice little bridge that I'm selling in Brooklyn?"

Castillo cocked her head. "Why would she make up something like that?"

"What the hell do you expect a murderer to do, confess? What? Do you think life is like an episode of *CSI*? Abrianna killed that man, and if she thinks that she can somehow implicate me, then she has another think coming."

"What? You're going to send Zeke to kill me?" Shawn challenged and then jerked up his shirt so she could see his bandaged midriff. "*Again?*"

Madam Nevaeh thrust up her chin.

"Yeah. Your henchman sent his hit squad to Abrianna's house while I was there. Your guys tried to knock her off before the cops got to her, didn't you?"

"No."

"Liar!"

"What damn difference does it make?" the madam snapped, only slowly realizing what she'd said. "I want you to leave my house—*now!*"

Castillo took a seat.

"That's not going to happen."

"Don't think I won't call the police."

"Call them," Castillo dared. "Tell Chief Holder that I'll need to move our dinner date back from seven to eight though when you do."

Nevaeh glared.

Baby yelped, startling Nevaeh. She released the Yorkie, and he rocketed out of the room. "All right. What do you want? I don't know anything about another girl showing up, and I don't have any idea where Abrianna is right now. And I'm sorry that you got shot. Maybe you should reconsider the type of people you call friend?"

"You're lying," Shawn insisted.

"Believe what you want to believe," the madam dismissed him. "I really don't give a damn."

46

For two days, Tomi's front-page article identifying her former basement roommate as the leading suspect in Speaker Reynolds's murder case made her a complete rock star on Capitol Hill. Martin Bailey beamed and strutted like a peacock around the office while the rest of her colleagues congratulated her to death. When the cable networks and talk radio programmers started calling, she realized that she had arrived.

Now, as she sat in the green room, while an intern who doubled as a makeup artist powdered the shine off of her face and Jayson told her how great she was going to be, the first wave of doubt crashed over her like a tidal wave. All platitudes went in one ear and out the other.

As airtime approached, simple things—like her name—became a blank in her mind.

Then: Showtime.

She was quickly escorted onto the set, where a microphone was pinned to her blouse. The host, Greg Wallace, smiled while his makeup was being touched up. His hair, which Tomi inwardly bet wouldn't move an inch in an F5 tornado, was left alone.

Before she knew it, they were being counted down from commercial break and Wallace welcomed everyone to the show.

"Joining us now, after her blockbuster reporting of the House speaker's death, is *Washington Post* reporter Tomi Lehane." He turned toward her. "Thank you for joining us."

"It's my pleasure," Tomi responded.

"Walk me through this," Wallace began. "You were the first to identify the woman seen in all the photographs from the Hay-Adams as being a Ms. Abrianna Parker. Tell our audience how is it that you *personally* know Ms. Parker."

"Uh, certainly." Tomi smiled, but then when she opened her mouth again, she quickly closed it as she suddenly saw the trap— that she had personally laid and walked right into. They were going to make *her* a part of the story. Her *and* Avery.

"Ms. Lehane?"

"Uh, yes. Well." She blinked several times. "Ms. Parker and I unfortunately shared a horrible nightmare. We were both abducted as teenagers by the same madman."

"And that madman was Dr. Craig Avery. Am I right?" Wallace pressed.

Tomi reddened and then belatedly remembered that she needed to speak. "Yes."

"Can you recount some of the horrors you and Ms. Parker endured?"

"Certainly," she said, still smiling but now bouncing her right leg nervously under the table. Quickly, she summarized the experience.

"Did you ladies ever find out what kind of crazy stuff that nut job was injecting you with?"

"No clue," she said, the leg bouncing faster. "All I know is that it . . . made me very sick and that it killed others."

"Let me ask you." Wallace put on his contemplating face and leaned in close. "Did you follow any of the reporting of what happened to another rescued victim, Shalisa Young?"

Tomi's heartbeat jumped off rhythm.

"Did you hear about the tragedy that had befallen her?"

"Yes. Yes. I, uh, read about it the papers."

Wallace nodded. "For our audience, Shalisa Young was charged with murder a few years ago. She allegedly killed her mother and was later found not mentally stable to stand trial. She was sent to St. Elizabeths federal mental hospital, where just last week she committed suicide by jumping off the building."

Tomi nodded.

"Now we have another situation, with another Avery survivor wanted for questioning in Speaker Reynolds's murder case. Coincidence?"

"I'm not sure that I follow you," Tomi lied.

"Well, I guess the plainest way I can put it is: Is there some kind of link between what Avery did to you ladies down in that basement and the madness that at least two of three survivors have exhibited?"

Tomi's temples throbbed.

Wallace's earpiece emitted a piercing sound—so loud that he reflexively snatched it out of his ear. "Whoa!" He laughed, facing the camera. "Sorry about that, folks."

Camera one's red light went out, to the puzzlement of the cameraman.

Wallace quickly turned to camera two. "It looks like we're experiencing camera difficulty. We'll take a break and return with Ms. Lehane right after commercials." He pushed up a plastic smile for the two seconds it took to clear for commercial.

"What the hell was that?" Wallace roared, his television charm gone.

Tomi snatched off her microphone, bounced out of her chair, and rushed off the set.

"Hey, where are you going?" Wallace hollered. "The interview isn't over."

"Oh, yes it," she mumbled under her breath, marching past Jayson.

"What's the matter?" Jayson asked, rushing to keep up. "What happened?"

Tomi kept moving, handing her temporary building pass off to the receptionist before heading out the glass doors. She couldn't explain even to herself why she was on the verge of tears. Castillo had warned her before she'd outed Abrianna, but the stars in her eyes had got in the way.

"Will you slow down?" Jayson asked.

She didn't.

And eventually, he stopped chasing her. But then a black Mercedes rolled up next to her as she raced down the sidewalk.

Tomi glanced over just as the back window rolled down.

"Ms. Lehane?" an older African-American man inquired.

She frowned but kept walking.

"Ms. Lehane, I know that this is rather odd, but I was wondering if I could have a few minutes of your time."

"For what?" she asked, marching.

"Just to talk," he said, smiling.

"Talk about what?"

"Well . . . it's sort of a personal nature. It's not an appropriate topic of conversation to be shouting out of a window."

She stopped and so did the car. "I don't get into strange cars with men I don't know. Tell me what you want or get lost."

The man's smile widened while he spoke without moving his mouth. *I want to talk to you about the powers I believe that you and Abrianna Parker have developed over the past six years.*

She stared at him, heart racing. "Well?" she asked. "Aren't you going to tell me what you want?"

Finally, the man's cocky smile dropped. "Can you not hear me?" he tried again.

"Look, buddy. I don't have all day."

"No. Of course not." His frown deepened. "There must've

been some sort of mistake. I apologize for the inconvenience."
The window rolled up and the Mercedes pulled away.

Tomi watched and didn't relax until the car disappeared around the corner.

"Who the fuck was that?" Jayson asked, finally catching up with her.

"I have no idea," she said, but suspected that it wouldn't be the last time she'd see the man.

⟶•◆•⟵

Abrianna opened her eyes, shocked that she'd been able to do so. The blurred images made it impossible for her to identify any of the images surrounding her. Still, she didn't panic. She didn't have the energy. Suddenly something moved on her left, and Abrianna used all of her willpower to focus on it.

It was a face.

Kadir smiled. "Hey, sleepyhead. Welcome back."

She smiled. "Hey, you."

He chuckled. "Is that your slick way of saying that you don't remember my name?"

Her face heated with embarrassment before she joined him, laughing. "Busted."

"I thought so." His smile stretched wider. "It usually takes people a while to retain my name. It's Kadir, by the way."

"Kadir," she repeated, chuckling. "Now I remember."

"How are you feeling?"

"Like I've been run over by a Mack truck."

"I'm not surprised. You looked like you were really going through it. Even got in an argument with my buddy Ghost on whether or not we should get you to a hospital."

She frowned. "That really would have been a risk for you."

"At the same time, if you had died on me . . ." Kadir shook his head.

"Then lucky for you, I came back," she joked.

Kadir chuckled, nodding. "Extremely lucky."

Abrianna liked his laugh—and found herself taking another look at him. He was handsome—almost beautiful, really. With skin the color of golden honey and eyes a rich brown. Even his lips were full, the way she liked them, and his pearl-white smile was fresh and blinding. Suddenly, she could barely take her eyes off of him. Maybe this was the Nightingale effect in reverse.

It occurred to her that Kadir was gazing at her with the same intensity. His eyes were locked on to her lips with such naked desire that Abrianna's body started tingling.

"Is there anything that I can do for you?" he asked innocently enough.

Abrianna shook her head, but then felt pressure along her bladder. "Um. Is there a bathroom in this place? I really have to go."

"You're in luck. There's one down the hall. Do you think that you can sit up?"

"Yeah. I think . . ." She attempted to sit up, but was stunned by how much effort it took.

"Here. Let me help you." Kadir gently took her by the shoulders and helped sit her up.

When the bed's top sheet fell from her chest, Abrianna was surprised to see that she'd been stripped down to her underwear.

"Sorry," Kadir said, reading her expression. "You sort of sweated through your other clothes. I had them washed though." He gestured to the neatly stacked clothes on top of the small television. When she still didn't say anything, he added, "If it gives you any comfort, I did try my best not to look while undressing you."

She cocked her head. "Your best, huh?"

To her surprise, he blushed.

"Let's just wrap this around you," Kadir said, taking the lead in draping the sheet around her body and knotting it underneath her right arm. Once that was done, they focused on getting Abrianna to her feet.

However, she was embarrassed by how rubbery her legs were and how they threatened to drop her flat on her ass every third step.

"Don't worry. I got you," Kadir assured her.

Taking him at his word, she clung to him. The effort wasn't easy.

Exiting the cot room, Abrianna experienced a low buzzing inside her head.

Kadir caught her pained expression. "Are you all right?"

Ghost rounded out of the break room, holding a mug of coffee. "Well. Sleeping Beauty is finally up."

Kadir nodded. "Yep. Ye of little faith."

Good. Then you can get her out of here.

Abrianna frowned, confused. She could've sworn that she'd clearly heard Ghost's voice inside of her head, but she would also swear on a stack of Bibles that his lips hadn't moved.

Ghost noticed her hard stare. "What?"

She didn't respond, but instead cut her gaze away from him.

Kadir looked up and assumed Ghost was talking to him. "What?"

"Nothing." Ghost shrugged. "I thought your girl had something to say."

"Me?" Abrianna said. "You're the one that seems to have a lot on his mind."

Ghost frowned. *What the hell is this bitch talking about?"*

Her heart skipped. This time, Abrianna was positive she'd heard Ghost without his lips moving. That realization caused her to miss taking the next two steps.

Kadir grunted as he strained to keep her upright while they moved past Ghost. "Don't worry. We're almost there."

The bathroom turned out to be another closet-sized room.

Concrete floors and walls were all painted the same dull gray color. Apparently the bathroom also doubled as some sort of storage room as there were a few industrial-size metal shelves cram packed with cleaning supplies and toiletries. There were also two large yellow mop buckets, completed with drying mops jammed into the corners.

"Sorry," Kadir said, sheepishly looking around. "I know that this isn't the Ritz . . . or even the Hay-Adams . . . but at least it's clean and functional."

"Beggars can't be choosy," she joked.

"Yeah. I guess." He smiled.

Abrianna noticed the lone dimple he had on the right side of his cheek and smiled along with him.

"All right. Here we go," Kadir said when they arrived at the sink that stood next to the toilet. "Should I—"

"I got it," Abrianna said, sliding her arms from around his neck. She quickly propped herself up by grasping the sides of the sink.

Kadir noticed her trembling. "Are you sure? If you want, I can close my eyes again and help you on—"

"No. That won't be necessary," she said, shutting him down. Her embarrassment was shifting into mortification.

"Oookay." He crept backward with his hands still extended. Apparently, he was prepared to dart back to her if she started to fall. Once he was outside the door, he looked reluctant to close it.

"I'll be all right," she assured him, finding his continued concern sort of endearing. A first for her.

"Okay. I'll just be on the other side of the door." Kadir took hold of the doorknob and slowly closed it. "Riiight out here," he repeated.

"Got it."

"Call me if you need me," he added, the door still slowly closing.

"I will." Abrianna hung on to her smile until the door finally snapped shut. Alone, she finally took a look at herself in the mirror. It was difficult to even recognize the woman who stared back at her. From all the intense sweating, her hair's natural curl had returned near the roots of her hair. Her face looked dull, and were those bags under her eyes?

"Oh God." She lowered her gaze to the sink and took time to focus on moving from the sink to the toilet, which was only two feet away, before she made things worse by peeing on herself.

No. What would be worse is to let go and face-plant on this concrete floor. She shrugged. She would lose a couple of teeth that way. *Wouldn't that just complete the picture?* Against her better judgment, she took another look at herself in the mirror.

"Okay. You can do this." Despite saying the words, Abrianna didn't let go of the sink. She locked eyes with her reflection and tried to will strength into the fragile image. "You. Can. Do. This."

As the seconds ticked, her gaze grew more intense and her grip on the sink tightened. "You. Can. Do. This," she growled.

Crack!

Abrianna gasped and then stared in shock at the cracked mirror. At first it was just a single line straight down the center, but as she looked at it, more cracks appeared and spider-webbed across the entire thing. Then, unexplainably, large shards fell off of the wall.

"Abrianna, are you all right in there?"

Jerking her head toward the door, she spotted the knob already twisting. "NO! Don't come in here!"

At her command, the door slammed shut and the lock above the knob engaged.

Kadir rattled the doorknob when it wouldn't open. "Hey, are you sure you're all right?"

She stared at the door, stunned.

"Abrianna?" He knocked.

"I—I'm fine," she finally managed to respond. "Everything is . . . all right. I'll be out in a second."

"What was that noise?"

"Just . . . the mirror," she said. "I guess I scared it."

He didn't laugh, but she knew that he lingered by the door. However, she dismissed him to look at the broken glass strewn around her. *Did I do that?* The rational side of her quickly denied it, explained that it was just some kind of freak accident. *But what about the lock on the door?* She'd clearly seen it lock itself practically at her command.

That's not what happened, the rational side spoke up again, but it didn't offer a logical explanation to what she'd seen. It just denied, denied, denied.

And it didn't work.

47

After a brief but much-needed shower, Abrianna had only one thing on her mind: to get to Madam Nevaeh. Through her connections, she was sure to have some kind of exit plan. Clearly, she knew people in high places. It stood to reason that she could help her.

"Are you sure that you want to go tonight?" Kadir asked, watching her slip her foot back into her Timberland.

She shrugged. "The sooner, the better."

"It's just that . . . well, two hours ago, I wasn't sure that you'd even wake up. And now you're feeling well enough to try and evade every law enforcement agency out there looking for us to get across town to this . . . person."

"Look. I've never been one to try and wear out my welcome." She grabbed her jacket.

"What? Ghost?" He waved off her concern. "His bark is worse than his bite. Trust me."

Abrianna laughed. "I trust no one—but myself."

Kadir sighed.

"Look. If you're afraid of getting caught, you don't have to come. I know that you have your own situation. I don't need you to hold my hand."

Slapped by her words, Kadir reared back. "I'm not *afraid.* I'm concerned. A little while ago you couldn't even stand up on your own. Now . . . now look at you."

"Well—that was then and this is now. As you can see, I'm fine." She looked around. "I could use a weapon though."

Ghost appeared at the door. "Talk any sense into her yet?"

The buzzing returned.

"Not yet. She wants a gun."

"Ah. Of course. Once you get a taste of the Wild Wild West, it's hard going back." He elbowed Kadir. "Why don't you give her your gun? You're not supposed to have one anyway. A violation of your parole."

"Really? *That's* what you're concerned about? Not that the world has been given a carte blanche check to shoot me on sight for being a terrorist?"

"Well—on the off-chance that you're not killed and are able to explain your side of events—it would help not to be packing."

"Yeah—because law enforcement *never* shoots unarmed people of color." Abrianna laughed.

Ghost bobbed his head. "She has a point. Maybe you should keep the gun."

Kadir tucked the gun back into his waistband. "Funny."

"C'mon. If we're going to do this thing, we better get a move on it," Ghost said.

Abrianna stopped. "Wait. Hold up. You're coming too?"

"Damn right. If I give you my van, I may never see it again," Ghost said.

"We could jack another car," Abrianna said.

"Sure. Why not? They're going to throw the book at you anyway, right?" *Crazy broad.*

"Who in the hell are you calling crazy?" she snapped.

"What? I didn't call you crazy." *Not out loud.*

Kadir frowned. "No one used the word crazy."

Abrianna glared at Ghost. "I don't need *your* help."

Ghost tossed up his hands. "Fine. Get caught. Why the fuck should I care?"

Kadir grabbed Ghost's arm. "Wait. We can *definitely* use your help."

"No, *we* can't," Abrianna countered stubbornly.

Ghost's hands went up again. "Fine."

"No. Just . . . give me a few minutes to talk to her," Kadir said, nodding toward the door.

Ghost rolled his eyes and marched out of the room.

When Kadir closed the door behind Ghost, Abrianna noticed that the buzzing stopped. "What's with you?" Kadir asked. "Of course we need his help. The city is damn crawling with every agency of law enforcement. If we jack a car, we risk the owner reporting it stolen before we get to wherever we need to go. On foot or public transport is a certifiable way to get caught too because there are cameras with face-recognition everywhere. Ghost has a van. We hide in the back. Wham bam. Smooth sailing."

"Wham bam?"

"It's . . . it's a saying."

Abrianna sighed, but realized that her ego was just getting in the way. He was right. A carjacking could backfire and alert the cops.

"Well?" Kadir asked, cocking his head and weighing whether or not she was caving.

After another deep breath to let him know that she really didn't like this, she responded, "All right. Fine."

"Thank you." He smiled and then awkwardly patted her on her good arm. "I'll go tell Ghost we're ready." However, when Kadir opened the door, Ghost stood right in the entranceway, arms crossed.

"What? No quickies?" Ghost joked, shaking his head. "You're really turning into a big disappointment."

"Get the van ready," Kadir told him.

"Real disappointment," Ghost insisted before turning away. Kadir shook his head and followed his friend.

Minutes later, Kadir returned to the cot room carrying a black scarf.

"What's that?" Abrianna asked, suspiciously.

"This is for you. I'm sorry—but I'm going to have to blindfold you."

"The hell you are," she said, stepping back and settling both hands onto her waist.

Kadir sighed. The strain of dealing with both her and Ghost was starting to etch thin lines into his face. "This isn't negotiable," he said. "You've already seen too much. The last thing they want you to know is where this place is and how to get back to it."

"Are you kidding me? I'm a criminal too—or is being wanted for murder not enough street cred for your nerdy friends?"

"Nerdy?"

"I'm sorry. Keyboard gangsters. I don't want them to bust a hashtag on me."

"Funny. And you still have to wear the blindfold."

"I didn't wear one when you brought me here."

"You were out cold," he reminded her.

"Was I?" She cocked her head.

Kadir studied her. "I call bullshit. You were out. Now turn around."

Abandoning her bluff, Abrianna turned. "This is ridiculous," she complained.

"For a fugitive, you sure do complain a lot," Kadir said, placing the blindfold over her eyes.

When Kadir moved up behind her, Abrianna picked up the scent of Irish Spring and smiled.

"Can you see anything?"

"No."

Kadir rolled his eyes. "I don't know if anyone has ever told you, but you're a real pain in the ass."

She smiled. "It may have been mentioned once or twice."

He shook his head and took her by the hand. "C'mon. Follow me."

Abrianna raised a brow, surprised not only by his hand's size but its strength and warmth. Once they were out of the cot room, Abrianna's buzzing headache returned. But as Kadir led, Abrianna slowly realized that the buzzing sounded more like voices—about four or five of them. However, it was hard for her to focus on just one. When she tried, the buzzing transformed into a pounding migraine. She stopped and tried to regain her bearings.

"Are you all right?" Kadir asked, stopping.

She nodded, but her knees folded.

Kadir launched into action and caught her. "It's okay. I got you."

She curled and laid her head against his Irish Spring–scented chest.

"Let's go back."

"No," she panted.

Abrianna tuned her ears so that she picked up every sound around her. It wasn't much to go on. Kadir and Ghost's booted feet treaded most of the way on concrete, but the twists and turns and strange echoes left her confused. Before she knew it, she heard hinges creaking and she was being settled onto some thick carpeting. *It must be the van.*

"Can I take this off now?" She reached to remove the blindfold but was stunned and surprised when her hand was swatted away.

"No. Not yet. Lie down," Kadir instructed.

Before she could complain or question the order, she felt the van dip as Kadir climbed in next to her.

"There is a blanket to your right, man," Ghost informed his buddy. "Y'all get under that and stay low."

He slammed the door shut.

"Lie down," Kadir repeated.

Abrianna followed his instructions but was immediately assaulted with the stench of motor oil and cigarettes. The scent clung to the van's carpet fibers. "Oh my God. I think that I'm going to gag."

"Hold it in until we get to where we are going," he warned. Next, he covered her with what had to be the hardest, scratchiest blanket ever made. Up front, Ghost climbed in behind the wheel.

"Are you guys comfortable back there?" he asked.

"We're getting there," Kadir responded, twisting his body so that he lay chest-to-chest with Abrianna.

All thoughts of cigarettes and motor oil flew out of her head. The only thing that surrounded her now was the fresh scent of Irish Spring.

"Are you good?" he asked, whispering.

"Yeah. I'm cool."

Ghost started the van, turned on the radio, and pulled off.

"Now can I take this off?" she asked again.

Kadir hushed her. "Keep your voice down."

Abrianna pulled the blindfold from her eyes, but she still saw nothing.

Ghost drove over what seemed like an endless bed of gravel. Their bodies jostled and rubbed against one another while neither of them spoke.

For Abrianna, it was because she couldn't think of anything to say. Their bodies jostling short-circuited her ability to make small talk.

"Nervous?" Kadir asked.

"No," she lied. "I'm more anxious than anything," she added as a cover. "I just want to put this whole thing behind me.

"Hmmm. That makes two of us."

Finally, the van drove off the gravel and onto smooth pavement.

"Do you have any idea where you want to try to go after all of this?" Kadir asked.

"If I had my way, I would leave the country."

"Oh?"

She nodded, forgetting that he couldn't see her. "I always wanted to go to France. Live on the Riviera."

He chuckled, his chest rubbing hers briefly. "So you *are* a romantic. You had me fooled."

"What is that supposed to mean?"

"Oh. I don't know. Our brief history together, I sort of had you pegged as a wham-bam-thank-you-sir type of chick."

Abrianna wanted to say something slick back but couldn't. "I guess you would think that."

"Look. I'm sorry. That was completely uncalled for."

"It's okay," she said, "I'm used to people judging."

"That's not what—"

"Hey, guys. Keep it down back there," Ghost reprimanded them.

A few minutes later, her eyes made out his outline in the darkness.

Ghost spoke up again. "Hold on, guys. Looks like we have a roadblock up here."

Immediately, Kadir and Abrianna held their breaths and then strained their ears to listen as Ghost lowered the volume on the radio.

"Afternoon, officer," Ghost greeted.

"License and registration," a voice barked into the van.

"Yes, sir."

"Make sure that you keep your hands up where I can see them," the cop instructed.

"Yes, sir." Ghost's voice tightened.

The van went silent.

"Where are you coming from?" the officer inquired.

"Just getting off work," Ghost lied. "Pulled a double down at the hospital."

"Is that right? Are you a doctor or something?"

"Nah. Nothing that glamorous. I'm just the janitor," Ghost informed him.

Abrianna tuned into the conversation and effortlessly picked up Ghost's thoughts.

This muthafucka is working my nerves.

She smiled.

"So where are you headed?"

"Virginia. Going to see the fiancée."

"Is there anyone else in the vehicle with you?"

"No, sir. It's just me."

Silence stretched between the men. But Ghost chanted in his head, *Don't look in the van. Don't look in the van.*

"Well. All right. You have a good night."

"Yes, sir, officer. You do the same."

Ghost shifted the van into drive and they were off.

Kadir huffed out a long breath that warmed Abrianna's face and rustled a few strands of hair.

"Yo, man. It's crazy out here," Ghost said, driving. "I wish that y'all could see this shit out here. The whole damn city is crawling with pigs."

Ghost's commentary did nothing to settle Abrianna's nerves.

Kadir clearly felt the same way because ten minutes later he pulled the blanket down off of his head. "Yo, man. Do you mind? It's nerve-wracking enough back here."

"Sorry, man. But it ain't a picnic up here either. I'm starting to see prison bars in my future. Your ass is going to owe me big time for this."

"You already made that clear—several times." Kadir lay back down and pulled the blanket back over their heads. "Are you still good?"

"Yeah. I'm fine," Abrianna said.

"Shit, man. We got another roadblock," Ghost announced.

Abrianna cursed herself. *This really was a bad idea.* Her hard-headed insistence was likely going to land them all in jail. She could've waited a little longer. What was the rush?

Luckily, the second checkpoint went the same way as the first. A few irritating questions, nervous chanting in Ghost's head, and then they were off again.

"This has to be like the longest car ride of my life," Kadir grumbled.

"That makes for the two of us."

Things didn't play out the same way when Ghost rolled up to the third roadblock.

"License and registration," a cop barked into the van.

"Man, they have they roadblocks all over the place." Ghost complained, attempting humor but sounding annoyed.

"Step out of the vehicle, sir," the cop ordered.

Abrianna's heart stopped. "What's happening?"

A tense Kadir shushed her so that he could listen.

"Why do I need to step out?" Ghost asked.

"Sir, step out of the vehicle," the cop repeated—louder.

What the fuck do I do now? Ghost thought.

Abrianna closed her eyes and thought, *Just step out of the car and play it cool.*

Sighing, Ghost opened the van door and stepped out.

"Oooh. This is not good." Kadir inched away from Abrianna.

"Stay still," she hissed.

Outside the van, an angry Ghost's voice was unmistakable, but they couldn't hear exactly what was going on. Abrianna tried to zero in on Ghost's thoughts—not that she knew exactly how to do that—but even that was impossible.

The wait was excruciating.

Neither she nor Kadir had discussed what to do in this situation. Why was she so damn stubborn? They were all going to be arrested.

"You're arresting me now?" Ghost yelled. "For what?!"

"Shit." Kadir pulled the blanket off of his head and crept toward the front of the van.

"What the hell are you doing?" Abrianna hissed after him.

"Shhh."

Abrianna frowned. The shushing thing wasn't sitting right with her, but she buttoned up anyway and watched Kadir creep forward while some sort of argument went on outside of the van. The fact that he was able to move without rocking the van impressed her. But, with all the lights swirling through the front windshield, she was certain that at any moment he was going to be spotted and all hell would break loose.

Abrianna waited and watched with bated breath.

By the way Ghost carried on outside, she could tell that he was moving away from the van and was apparently putting up a scuffle.

Kadir dropped in behind the driver's wheel, shifted the van into drive, and took off.

"Hey!" a voice yelled.

Stunned yet amused, Abrianna laughed as she crawled her way toward the front of the van.

Shots were fired.

Abrianna ducked but continued toward the front passenger seat. "What the hell?"

"What? You wanted to hang around until they opened the van's doors?" Kadir asked. "I thought that you wanted to get to that madam's house."

Police sirens wailed behind them.

"Yes. But I preferred that we do it *without* the police escort."

"Now you tell me."

Abrianna smiled, but then noted that the sirens were drawing closer. "You're going to have to get on some of the back roads. Cops get nervous for high-speed chases through those—especially here in D.C."

"You're reading my mind," Kadir said.

"No. I wasn't," she snapped.

Frowning, he glanced over at her. "It's just a figure of speech."

Embarrassed, she dropped her gaze and shrugged. "I know."

A police car sped up, nearly pulling even on the driver's side.

"They are going to try a rolling roadblock. We need to get off of this street," Abrianna said, reaching for her seat belt.

"What? Now you're buckling up?" Kadir asked.

"Damn right. Ninety percent of police car chases end in crashes."

"Ninety percent? Where did you get that number from?"

"Made it up," she admitted. "It sounds true. There! Take that right before they can cut us off."

Without questioning the order or even slowing down, Kadir hung a sharp right. So sharp that at least one back tire came up off the road while they rocketed head-on toward an approaching car.

The car's driver laid on his horn while Kadir righted the van and swerved into the correct lane, but not without taking the other car's side-view mirror.

"Shit. That was close." Abrianna panted with a hand placed over her heart.

Kadir said nothing as his hands remained locked on the steering wheel. At the next intersection, he took a sudden left and then left again.

The police fell behind, but they were definitely still in hot pursuit.

"You know, you're getting pretty good at this," Abrianna said, impressed.

"Yeah. It's a lot easier when people aren't shooting at you."

"I see that."

They cornered right at the next intersection, but another roadblock was up ahead.

"Shit," they swore together.

"Hang on." Kadir slammed on his brakes and jerked the wheel.

Abrianna's fingers dug into the dashboard as the van whipped around a hundred and eighty degrees, laying fresh black tire tracks in the road.

He slammed onto the accelerator again and took off, heading back toward the racing policing cars.

"Uh, maybe I shouldn't have complimented you so soon," she said, staring wide-eyed into the oncoming flashing lights. It was an endless sea of blue and white. "Do you know what you're doing?"

"We're about to find out."

Abrianna's heart launched its way into her throat, and their dangerous game of suicidal chicken was in full force. *They'll stop. They'll stop. They'll stop.*

But they weren't stopping.

This is it. We're going to die. Abrianna braced for impact. *Make them stop. Make them stop.* Her entire body grew warm and then hot. The van's radio came on full blast and the interior lights flickered on and off.

Startled, Kadir's foot came off the gas pedal as he looked around.

In the next second, the speeding police car directly in front of them kicked up a shit load of smoke as the tires squealed.

Just when the patrol car got within a few feet of their nonde-script van, it fishtailed and then spun. The cars speeding be-hind it were all slamming on the brakes and kicking up smoke, but still T-boned the first cop car.

Kadir reached the next intersection and made a hard right. The van swung wide and felt as if it was about to flip over, but at the last moment, it righted itself before speeding away from the train of police cars still slamming and piling on top of one another.

"The fuck," Kadir said, startled. "Did you see that?"

Abrianna swallowed hard. "I saw it. I just can't believe it."

48

"Are you sure that this is the right place?" Kadir asked, looking around the humongous but *empty* home. "I mean, it's nice and all . . ."

"No. No. No. This can't be happening," Abrianna said, raking her hands through her thick hair, just barely stopping herself from pulling it all out by the roots. She couldn't reconcile the luxurious and ornate place that she and Shawn had visited just days ago with this vacant shell. It threw everything that she thought she knew into a tailspin. So much so her legs threatened to drop her where she stood. "I need to sit down."

Kadir turned toward her and saw that she was already halfway down before finishing her announcement. He rushed to help before she crashed to the floor. "Careful," he said, succeeding in reaching her and aiding her to a soft landing.

"I don't understand what's happening," she whispered as a series of images and a warped timeline comingled inside of her head. Did this mean that Madam Nevaeh really *did* have something to do with the dead speaker? Had she set her up? How far did all of this go? Zeke? Moses?

"I feel sick," Abrianna confessed, light-headed.

Kadir glanced around. "Do you know where the bathroom is in this place?"

She did know, but shook her head because she didn't have the strength to get back up.

"Oh. Okay," Kadir said. "Usually I'd suggest that you put your head between your legs and take a deep breath."

Abrianna complied. "You mean like this?"

"Yeah. That's it," he said, watching and feeling sorry for her. Then he remembered that he probably should feel sorry for himself, too. Kadir reached over and stroked the back of her head. "It's going to be all right," he assured her. "We'll figure something out."

Abrianna pulled her head from between her legs and cocked it toward him. "Yeah? Like what?"

Maybe it was the way that the moonlight streaming through the large windows illuminated her face that caused his heart to skip. She looked small—vulnerable. The need to protect her flooded his entire system. She was scared and struggling not to let it show. He was late in realizing that she was waiting for an answer—so he kept it real. "I don't know. I really don't."

"Then how do you know that things are going be all right?" she asked, her tone hardening.

"Because hope is all we have right now," he said. "It's our starting point."

She laughed. "You can't be for real."

Now that she said it, Kadir did feel a bit like a cornball.

"Shit don't work out all the time," Abrianna added. "But people keep shoving their heads into the clouds, praying to an invisible God who don't give a shit about none of us. War. Famine. Capitalism on crack. It's all engineered to destroy us all, but people keep dropping to their knees to pray, hoping that He'll swoop in and save the day."

A lone tear leapt over Abrianna's lashes and skipped down her face. "I used to be like you. I was much younger though," she added softly as her gaze drifted away from him. "I used to pray that my father would stop coming into my bedroom at night. God didn't stop that. God was too busy to stop that too. Then I discovered that I wasn't the only one in the house that he was abusing. My little brother . . ."

Kadir's gut tightened.

"He was so small," Abrianna whispered. "He needed someone to protect him. It should have been me . . . but I started praying instead—for him."

Kadir's eyes stung with acidic tears while his throat constricted. "What happened?"

"Exactly what I should've known would happen: nothing—except my father's sickness killed my baby brother."

The empty salon suddenly was like a mausoleum, cold and empty.

"I'm sorry," Kadir said. "I didn't know."

"How could you?" She swiped her eyes. "But my whole point was that, in my life, things never work out. The worst *always* happens."

Kadir let her words drift around the room while he thought about it. His track record of things eventually working out was pretty bad, too. However, he didn't mention it because it wasn't a pissing contest.

"Maybe I should just turn myself in," Abrianna said. "Let them do whatever the hell they're going to do."

"That's an option," he acknowledged slowly. "Not that it's a good one, but it's an option."

Her gaze slid back toward him.

"Have you ever been arrested?" he asked.

"No. But given the country's statistics, it's really just a matter of time."

Kadir chuckled. "You're probably right."

They sighed at the same time and then cut each other sheepish grins.

"Well, take my word for it, the federal government is not an organization one risks their freedom with casually." When he realized what he'd said, he laughed.

"What's so funny?" she asked cautiously.

"Only that I'd thought to turn myself in too."

"So you're one of those 'do as I say, not as I do' people?"

"No. It's just that I think they have far more evidence to lock you up than they do me."

"Except for the part where you're aiding and abetting a wanted criminal."

"Shit."

"Hadn't thought about that one, huh?"

He shook his head and allowed the house's silence to wash over them once again. "Well, I guess that means that we better get busy proving that you didn't kill that guy. Huh?"

"So you believe me?" Shock swept across her upturned face.

He smiled, nodded, but then couldn't pull his gaze away. "You really are beautiful," he said before thinking better of it. But if he hadn't said it, he would've missed the blush that darkened her cheeks.

"Thanks," she whispered.

Kadir didn't plan his next move either. He simply leaned over and kissed her. Surprised and pleased that she hadn't socked him, he deepened the kiss and didn't give a damn that he'd been the first one to moan. Slowly, he curled toward her, leaning her back until she lay flat against the deep-piled carpeting. With the moonlight splashed over her body, she looked like an artist's masterpiece. From that moment on, he couldn't stop kissing and touching her.

Kadir was instantly addicted to the taste and touch of her. He couldn't keep up with the sensations swarming him. For one thing, there were too many to name and he was certain that he hadn't experienced all of them at the same time before. However, he wasn't the only who was eager.

Abrianna ignored the warning bells inside her head and pulled and yanked at his shirt until she'd hauled it up over his head before attacking the button and zipper on his jeans.

He got busy getting her out of her clothes as well, stopping only a few times when he got anywhere near her bandaged shoulder. Once the frenzy of getting naked was over, Kadir stretched his tawny body over her golden-brown one to take his time allowing his hands to roam and his mouth to taste every inch of her. She was sweet and intoxicating.

Lost in the magic Kadir's mouth created, Abrianna shoved the lone voice in her head to the deep recesses of her mind. All she wanted was for Kadir to keep doing what he was doing. Damn the consequences. She needed this—bad.

Kadir's lips abandoned hers, and a pang of disappointment hit the center of her chest. However, his lips didn't stay away for too long, as they soon planted feather-light kisses down the column of her neck and then across her collarbone.

Abrianna's entire body sighed in relief. Mindlessly, she ran her hand through his soft hair and then down his steely shoulders and then along the hard planes of his back. She marveled at his incredible body. However, that pleasure was nothing compared to the pleasure she felt when his mouth honed in on a puckered nipple.

She squirmed beneath him while an ache intensified between her legs. Kadir's slow but exquisite lovemaking had the potential to drive her mad. When she realized that it was his intent to make her ask or even beg for what she wanted right now, Abrianna wasted no time, shoving her pride and ego aside.

"Please . . . fuck me."

She felt his smile against her belly button, since he was in the middle of heading south. "Not yet, baby."

So the torture continued. The weird flopping in her belly stopped, and what felt like a million butterflies lifted off in perfect unison.

Still, it was a sweet torture as he peeled open her legs and praised the beauty of her small nest of curls. A smile glided across his lips as she watched lust fill his eyes. She was wet before, but now she was flooded with her body's clear honey. His next kiss silenced the buzzing inside of her head and nearly melted the pain and tension from her body.

"Oh my God," Abrianna cried as she tossed her head from side to side and naturally arched her body to receive more. She wanted—needed more.

But Kadir moved at his own pace. Lapping her honey and putting the perfect polish on her pink pearl. The kissing continued even as he slid a finger into her pussy and then a second one. When it set a rhythm of pumping and twirling while his mouth worked its magic, Abrianna started inching her body away from the building climax.

Kadir grinned as he followed her inch for inch. When it was clear that he wasn't going to let her escape, her hands returned to his head and hair. She would caress it for a few strokes and then grab huge tufts of it in an attempt to pull him away whenever a tongue stroke caused her to float too high. Even in that, he resisted her.

Soon, her long, silky legs started trembling all around his head. He listened as her breath turned choppy.

"Oh my God," she moaned as her eyes damn near rolled to the back of her head.

Kadir's dedication to the job continued.

Abrianna gasped, her hips lifting off the floor. "I'm coming," she panted, unable to catch her breath. The pressure that was building at her core was huge, and she was a little fearful of the climax—that it could overwhelm her and make her lose control. Control was something that she clung to, what little that remained anyway.

"Wait. Wait," she begged.

Kadir ignored her and continued to drive her closer to the cliff.

She tried to lower her hips, but for each stroke of his fingers, they went back up. The roller-coaster ride kept her dizzy. Tears surfaced and then leaked out of the corners of her eyes as she shuddered in delight.

Approaching delirium, Abrianna's hips surged and rotated while her breathing thinned to the point that she couldn't tell whether she was coming or going into cardiac arrest. Finally, Kadir's tongue hit the lining of her pussy and Bree's entire body vibrated. Whatever self-control she'd held on to was tossed out of the window.

Still, Kadir's tongue refused to relent. She inched up the carpet and tried to push his head away, but with her locked knees, her efforts were rendered useless.

"I—I can't breathe," she gasped, but even that declaration failed to get her any mercy. A second orgasm started building at the base of her clit, and before she could prepare herself, Kadir hit the detonation button and her body gushed more honey.

Satisfied that she was primed and ready, Kadir reached behind his head and pulled her legs open. He climbed up her body and pressed a kiss against her lips so he could share her sweet taste.

But Abrianna had waited long enough and shoved Kadir over onto his back, so the moonlight now painted his nicely sculpted body. *Clearly, prison does a body good.*

Then her gaze swept toward his cock and stopped. Her imagination had failed to do Kadir justice. His smooth, thick cock had to be the prettiest thing she'd ever seen. Its full mushroom head with its cute curve toward his body told her that she was in for the ride of her life.

When she touched him, Kadir sucked in a breath that made his dick jump in her hands. But when her hands wrapped around his thick shaft and began to slide up and down, his body experienced its own spike in temperature. He moved closer, giving her room and an opportunity to glide her hand all the way down to the base of his cock and then up around his purpling head.

When his gaze returned to her face, he loved the way she seemed fascinated by what she was doing. The look of raw desire sparkling in her eyes was what turned him on.

"Come here, you," he whispered. He pulled her over to him, but there was no need. Abrianna saddled up with ease, her body's wet lips parted, and eased his steel rod in with no problem.

She sighed and he moaned when she rolled her hips.

Kadir hissed as his face contorted with pleasure, but as good as she felt, he really got off watching her enraptured face. She was still the most beautiful woman he'd ever seen. Entranced himself, he reached up to caress and squeeze her full breasts. But then he longed for the taste of her again and pulled her upper body down so that her jiggling breasts rocked against his chest while he devoured her lips again.

Their rhythm quickened. Soon, his low, deep moans blended with her whimpering sighs to make their own unique music. Soon after, the inevitable approached.

"Come for me, baby," he pleaded.

Abrianna's lips found his just as they took that final leap and cried out. Her voice echoed throughout the large mansion as she collapsed against his chest.

49

"Wow," Kadir sighed into the dark. "That was . . . wow."

Abrianna giggled and then slapped a hand over her mouth when she realized what she had done. She *never* giggled. Ever.

Kadir laughed.

Listening to his rumbling chest while she still lay on top of him managed to erase her embarrassment and planted a smile on her face. What was wrong with her? She even liked the man's laugh.

"I, uh, hadn't planned on doing that," Kadir confessed. "But, boy, am I sure glad that I did."

"Yeah. It was nice," she admitted.

For the next few minutes, they allowed the house's silence to cloak them.

A list of questions scrolled through Abrianna's head. Of course, she realized that she should have asked them before they screwed each other's brains out. But she was most certainly not the first person to put the cart before the horse.

"You have a girl?" she settled on asking first.

"No," he answered, lazily stroking her back.

Abrianna caught both the brief hesitation and the note of sadness in his voice.

"You?" he countered.

314 / DE'NESHA DIAMOND

"No. I just got out of a long relationship."

"Oh? How long were you guys together?"

"Four months."

Kadir's chest rumbled again. "Four months? That's a long time to you?"

"Oh God, yes." Abrianna lifted her head to look up at him through the moonlight. The man really was gorgeous. "What about you? What was the longest relationship that you've been in?"

"Fifteen years."

"Fifteen?" Her eyes bugged. "How old are you?"

"How old do I look?" he asked.

Abrianna looked at him, cocking her head to one side and then the other. When she couldn't settle on a number, she stroked her chin. "Hmmm."

"C'mon. You're starting to scare me."

"I'm thinking. I'm thinking. Don't rush me."

He chuckled. "All right. Take your time."

"Forty-five?"

"Forty-*what?*" His brows crashed together over his incredulous expression.

"What? Are you older?" she asked innocently.

"Hell no!" He shifted to being indignant. "I'm thirty-one."

"Oooh. I was off, huh?" She could no longer keep a straight face and started laughing.

"Ah. I get it now. You got jokes," Kadir accused before chuckling himself. "Ha. Ha. Very funny." He curled a finger under her chin while he lifted his upper body so that he could press a kiss to the tip of her nose. "You're amazing. You know that?"

"Amazing?" she echoed. "First time I heard that one."

"So you're going to pull my other leg now?" he asked before sharing another laugh. But then it petered out and the silence returned. Abrianna searched for a topic to fill it, and Kadir beat her to it.

"Tell me about yourself," Kadir said.

Abrianna tensed and then tried to climb off of him.

Kadir's arm wrapped around her and held her in place. "There's not much to tell."

"You said you grew up on the streets," he plowed on. "Is that literal or . . ."

Reflexively, Abrianna attempted to climb off again, but Kadir held firm.

"What's with you? Why are you so scared to share just a little more about yourself?"

Tension coursed throughout her body until she finally forced herself to break Kadir's hold so that she could finally roll off of him. "Look. I'm not looking to get into anything really serious. We can just skip the pillow talk."

"Wow." He rolled over onto his side and propped up his head. "You got some pretty thick walls around you, don't you?"

She shook her head. "What do you want from me? I'm just a survivor. I survive one catastrophe after another. That's it. And so far, I'm finding out that I'm pretty good at it."

"With a little help."

Deciding not to dig her heels in, Abrianna relented. "With a little help. Do you want me to thank you again?"

"Nah. The one time is enough." He gazed up at her illuminated face and saw her naked vulnerability. "Look. I'm not going to push you. Clearly, you're not comfortable talking about your past. I can respect that."

Her gaze found his again before she mumbled, "Thank you."

"Besides, it gives me more time to talk about myself. I'm shameless that way."

She smiled and then allowed him to pull her back down so that she could curl up beside him.

"So what do you want to know?"

Abrianna shrugged, not feeling right about asking for anything that she wasn't willing to give herself.

No worries. Kadir chose the topic himself.

"You asked me about my longest relationship," he started off. "I have to say that it was sort of my longest and only real relationship."

"You're shitting me."

"No." He shook his head. "She was the love of my life."

That caught Abrianna's attention. "Really? What happened?"

Kadir pulled a deep sigh and then told her everything.

———————————

At a slight noise, Abrianna's eyes flew open. Moonlight remained pooled around her while she lay against Kadir's chest on the floor of Madam Nevaeh's empty salon. She waited to hear the noise again, but all she could pick up was Kadir's steady heartbeat.

"Go back to sleep," Kadir said, surprising her that he was even awake. "It's nothing."

Abrianna started to respond when she finally heard the noise again. She sat up. "What was that?"

Kadir sat up as well. "Don't know. I'll go check it out."

Quickly, Abrianna scrambled across the floor to gather her clothes.

The only thing that Kadir snatched up was the gun before creeping toward the front door. If it had been any other time, Abrianna would've taken a moment to appreciate how hot and dangerous he looked, but as it stood, the entire United States military could be right outside of the house, ready to take them down, and they had just one gun between them.

Her heart hammered as she hopped into her panties and just grabbed her shirt before rushing on her tiptoes to catch up with Kadir. Halfway up the hallway, it was clear that the noise was someone wiggling a key into the front lock.

Madam Nevaeh?

The front door swung open just as Kadir and Abrianna entered the foyer.

"Don't move," Kadir ordered, his weapon aimed straight at the woman entering the house. She looked up and screamed.

"Angel?" Abrianna said.

Angel stopped screaming to peer over the shoulder of the naked gunman. "Abrianna?"

Kadir lowered the weapon a few inches. "You two know each other?"

"Unfortunately."

Angel swallowed while her head kept swiveling between the two of them. "Wh-what are you two doing here?"

Kadir handed the gun to Abrianna. "I'm going to put some clothes on."

Abrianna rushed around Kadir to get to the door. "Are you alone?" she asked Angel.

"Yeah," Angel said with her gaze glued to the gun. "You haven't answered my question. What are you doing here?"

"Don't tell me you don't watch the news."

"No. I mean . . . I know that you got yourself in . . . some trouble, but why are you here? Shouldn't you be, like, on your way to Mexico or something by now?"

"I would if I could, but I still have what you call a cash flow problem. Where is Madam Nevaeh?"

Angel shook her head. "I don't know."

The girl was a bad liar.

"C'mon. You got to know. You have the keys to her house."

"I was just told to come and make sure the movers grabbed everything. I'm not interested in getting involved in whatever is going on between y'all."

"Too late." Abrianna invaded Angel's personal space to glare into her eyes. "You got me involved, remember? Or were you part of the setup, too?"

"Me? You're the one who killed that guy. No one told you to do that shit."

"I didn't kill him. It was that other trick that Madam Nevaeh sent to the Hay-Adams that night."

"What other trick?"

"Oh, come off of it. Another woman showed up at the hotel to fulfill Mr. Lucky's fantasy of having a threesome."

"Bullshit. That's not how Madam Nevaeh operates. She would've cleared a threesome with you first, and she most certainly wouldn't have sent you out on your first night to perform one. Madam is not a street pimp."

Abrianna shook her head. "Look. I may be a lot of things, but crazy isn't one of them. Another woman showed up at the hotel that night! Kitty," she remembered suddenly. "Her name was Kitty."

Angel laughed and shook her head. "I know all the girls who work for Madam Nevaeh, and there isn't a Kitty."

Abrianna stared, but no matter how much she concentrated, she couldn't tune the buzzing in her head to Angel's thoughts.

Angel eyed her strangely. "Are you okay?"

"No, I'm not okay. I've been set up and I have no way of proving that I didn't do it and I don't have any money to get out of town." Frustrated, Abrianna raked her hand through her hair. "I really needed Nevaeh to pay me."

"Pay you?" Angie barked, incredulous. "For what? Killing a client? You were already eighty grand in debt to her. She was already doing you a favor when Zeke talked her into taking you on."

"Zeke!" Abrianna smacked the palm of her hand against her forehead. "Why didn't I think about him before? *He* could've sent that woman to the hotel."

"Now who is this Zeke guy?" Kadir asked, rejoining the conversation, fully dressed.

"Drug lord," Abrianna said. Her mind raced. Had Zeke set her up to take the fall? Was that really the price of covering Moses's debt?

"Of course. Madams, strippers, and drug lords. What did I expect?" Kadir asked.

Abrianna frowned. "What's that supposed to mean?"

"Nothing. Forget it," he said, but his set jawline made it clear that he was irritated.

Angel backed toward the front door. "Like I said, I don't know what's going on, and I don't care. I'm just going to pretend that I didn't see you guys here tonight and you didn't see me."

Abrianna raised her gun. "That's not for you to decide."

"What? You think I'm going to snitch to the police? Tell them all about my illegal career as a high-priced call girl?"

"No. But you damn well may try to warn Madam Nevaeh that I'm looking for her."

"Oh. I think she got the memo." Angel laughed, glancing around the empty foyer. "I'm the only one who thought you'd be hauling it out of the country." When she saw the argument wasn't working, Angel shifted tactics. "Look. I work for the woman. We're not best friends. C'mon. I'm from the streets, just like you are. I keep my nose out of where it doesn't belong. And right now, it doesn't belong in the middle of whatever the hell y'all got going on. Zeke brought me the keys and asked that I check everything out. That's all I know."

Abrianna cocked her head. "What's the story between Zeke and Madam Nevaeh? Business or is it more than that?"

Angel sighed.

"I'm not letting you out of here until you answer *all* my questions," Abrianna said, leveling the weapon at Angel. "I'm a desperate woman so you better start talking."

"I told you, I don't know anything. I have a strict 'don't ask, don't tell' policy with other people's business. Why don't you ask that friend of yours? He sent that lady cop here—or private detective. I can't remember which. I'm sure he has more answers than I do."

"Who, Shawn? He's dead."

Angel laughed. "Well, you might want to tell the people at the hospital that."

50

Abrianna ignored Kadir's sermon about the risks she was taking by sneaking into Hadley Memorial Hospital to see Shawn. But he could talk until he was blue in the face for all she cared. Shawn was the most important person in her life. And she was going to see with her own eyes that he was still alive. Once Kadir realized that there was no talking her out of what he considered a suicide mission, he found himself agreeing to helping her pull off the impossible.

After a brief trip to the Salvation Army, Kadir produced a mismatching set of nurse's scrubs and a pretty questionable Halloween wig that made her look as if she resided in a dump truck.

"It's homeless chic," Kadir said. "Think Kanye West collection."

Abrianna rolled her eyes. "Whatever. C'mon. Let's get out of here."

Angel coughed. When Abrianna and Kadir's gaze swiveled in her direction, she smiled. "Oh. Great. You do remember that I'm here."

"It's hard to ignore you since you won't stop bitching," Abrianna said.

"Well. If you'd just let me go, then I'll be on my way."

"We've already been over this. We can't let you go yet."

"Ah. Yes. You have to find your imaginary threesome partner, Kitty."

"I didn't imagine her."

"No. Of course not," Angel condescended. "But you do know that holding me against my will is a federal crime?"

Kadir and Abrianna looked at each other and then burst out laughing.

"We're well aware of the *federal* crimes we're stacking up. Thank you."

Angel rolled her eyes and continued to twitch in the chair that Kadir had dragged in from the patio. "C'mon. Can't you at least loosen this rope a bit? It's too tight."

Abrianna marched over, but instead of loosening the rope, she shoved Angel's own scarf into her mouth and wound it around her head. "There. Much better." She stepped back to inspect her work. "Silence is golden."

Angel grunted and grumbled into the scarf.

"See? It works like a charm."

"We better get going," Kadir said before leading the way out of the vastly empty house.

An hour later, Kadir drove to the employee service entrance at the back of the hospital. Luckily the place was incredibly busy and they blended in with the patients and staff effortlessly. It didn't mean that her heart wasn't pounding a mile a minute.

Kadir snuck onto a terminal and found Shawn's room number in less than a minute.

When Abrianna finally entered Shawn's room, a tsunami of emotions swept through her entire body and her rarely seen tears rolled down her face. "Shawn!" She rushed to his side. "Shawn, are you awake?" Abrianna whispered, leaning over him.

When he didn't move, she shook his shoulder. "Shawn!"

He groaned, irritated.

"Shawn, it's Bree. Wake up!"

Shawn pulled open his eyes. "Bree?"

"Oh thank God!" She rained kisses all over his face. "I thought that you were dead. I saw how they . . ." A sob prevented her from completing the sentence. "You were gone. Oh God."

Shawn's face twisted. "God? You believing in God now? Who are you, and what have you done with my best friend?"

"Oh, don't tease me. You have no idea what I've been through these last few days."

"I have a pretty good idea." His gaze drifted over Abrianna's shoulder to spot Kadir. "Hello."

Kadir, manning the door, smiled back. "Hello."

Shawn lowered his voice. "Okay. Who is Mr. Fine and Sexy over there?"

"Long story."

"He's the one that they're looking for on the news though, right?"

"You've been watching the news?"

"Damn right. You're the hottest thing on there lately." He glanced over at the television. "See? You on now."

Abrianna head's swiveled toward the television set and her mouth fell open. "Ohmigod. It's my dad!"

Kadir tossed a glance at the television set and then had to do a double take at the decidedly conservative Caucasian male on the screen. "That's your father?"

Abrianna rolled her eyes away from the screen so she could find the remote. Once she spotted it, she shut off the television.

"I'm so sorry that I didn't believe you," Shawn said. "I shouldn't have doubted you."

"It's okay. Really. I would've doubted the story if it hadn't happened to me."

"So did Castillo find you again?"

"Who?"

"You know. Lieutenant Castillo. Well, she's a private detective now. She came by here yesterday, and I sent her over to talk to Madam Stick Up Her Ass. The bitch refused to talk though."

The words pouring out of his mouth were gibberish. "I don't know anything about that. Why is *Castillo* looking for me? Who hired her?"

Shawn blinked. "She . . . didn't say. At least, I don't recall. Hell, I doubt she's the only private dick looking for you." He shifted his gaze back to Kadir. "For the both of you. You're on the terrorist watch list."

"Great. You hear that, Kadir? We're famous."

"Guess we can head to Disney World now."

Shawn laughed and then groaned in pain.

"Careful," Abrianna warned him, concerned. "Are you all right?"

"Peachy. He's funny," Shawn said, nodding toward Kadir.

"Mind if I take a look?" she asked, pulling back the sheet before he could respond. When she saw his dressing wrapped tight around his abdomen, more tears sprang to her eyes.

"My goodness," Shawn laughed. "You've really sprung a leak today. It's okay. They managed to put Humpty Dumpty back together again."

"I'm sorry. I just . . ."

"Don't. Shh. Shh. It's all right. The doctors say that I'll live, probably right up until I get their bill."

Abrianna chuckled. "That's probably true."

Shawn pushed a few buttons on the side of the bed to sit up and adjust himself. "So what's the plan? Are you blowing this taco stand, or are you going to take your chances with the feds?"

Kadir laughed.

When the best friends looked at him, he quickly apologized. "Didn't mean to butt in."

"With no money, I can't get far," Abrianna said. "I have to find that other chick so I can have some kind of proof that I'm not just lying."

"What? You think you're going to be able to get her to confess?" Shawn asked.

"Or trick her into confessing . . . *before* I'm arrested."

"Speaking of which," Kadir cut in again. "We're going to have to wrap it up and get out of here."

Abrianna nodded but really ignored Kadir. Now that she had Shawn back, she didn't want to leave his side. They had been through too much together.

"Shit," Kadir swore. "Someone's coming!"

"What?" She glanced around the room and realized there was nowhere for them to hide.

"The bathroom," Shawn suggested, pointing to the wooden door across the room.

With no time to debate, she and Kadir raced to the bathroom, but they hadn't even made it halfway there before Tivonte, Julian, and Draya entered.

Everyone froze, before Tivonte belted out a, "Oh my God! Bree!"

"SHHHHHH," Abrianna and Shawn hissed.

But Abrianna rushed to embrace her friends.

Anxiety started webbing its way onto Kadir's face. The more people saw them, the higher chance of them getting caught. "Abrianna," he warned.

She held up a finger and resumed the reunion with her friends. A half hour later, she had them all up to speed with what she and Kadir had done and were working on doing.

Julian jumped in, "That detective chick has already been over to talk to Madam Nevaeh. The woman will not be moved. She's wasn't even interested in giving her name, rank, or serial number. Pretty much told Castillo to fuck off."

"Where did she find her? Because we went out to her crib last night and the place is empty."

Shawn blinked. "She cleared out in one day?"

"Yep. Vanished without a trace."

Tivonte spoke up. "Well, I don't know about Madam Nevaeh. But I know my restaurant is catering a party at her man's crib tonight. Maybe she'll show up there."

"And who is her man?" Abrianna asked.

"Aw, see? Y'all loooove to slay me about my ass being up in everybody's business, but the minute y'all need to know something, where do y'all go?"

"Is this sermon going to be long?" Abrianna asked. "I do have every law enforcement agency looking for my ass right now."

Tivonte huffed. "Fine. The tea brewing in the streets is that she and the Teflon Don bump uglies on the regular and have been since our asses were in grade school."

Abrianna beamed. "Then I guess we have a party to crash."

51

Abrianna had always known that Draya had skills as a costume and makeup artist. Tivonte bragged on her all the time. Her talent was renowned in D.C.'s growing theater and drag-show circuit. But the reflection that stared back at Abrianna now blew her mind. "Damn. I'm a handsome man."

Beaming, Draya stepped next to Bree and admired her handiwork. "I agree."

Behind them, Kadir frowned.

Abrianna spun around. "You don't agree?"

Kadir frowned. "I plead the fifth."

Tivonte smirked. "It's okay to be attracted to men."

The group chuckled.

"You look nice too," Abrianna told Kadir, even though she was still trying to get used to how Draya had aged him thirty years with believable wrinkles around his eyes and mouth. The gray hair spray was a nice touch too.

Kadir kept staring, then asked, "It doesn't hurt having your breasts strapped down like that? I mean, your chest really looks flat." He reached over and touched them for himself.

"It'll take some getting used to," Abrianna admitted, swatting his hand away and facing the mirror again for another look. The low-crop wig. The goatee. Draya had even strapped small pillows around her waist to hide her curves.

"One thing for sure," Julian said. "Zeke and that madam are never going to recognize either of you tonight at that party."

◆

A proud Zeke watched his guests mix and mingle from the second story balcony of his private estate west of Washington. The place was packed with the rich and powerful—from both sides of the law. For his birthday, he made sure he showed out with the best that money could buy.

Today, he was also closer to going from kingpin to full-fledged cartel mode. After a year-long negotiation, he had finalized a distribution deal for his Cotton Candy with King Carlos, a rising kingpin out of Detroit. While everyone partied and had a good time, Carlos's men were loading their first shipment from his warehouse.

Basking in all of it, he signaled to the band playing on the pavilion. The music faded and guests tapped champagne glasses until Zeke had everyone's attention.

"Thank you, everyone," he said. "I promise that I'll keep it short and sweet. First: I thank you all for coming. I truly appreciate the love *and* the gifts. The gifts a little more than the love, actually."

The crowd laughed.

"This past year has been one hell of a ride. I've met new friends and we all made *lots* of money. I have every bit of confidence that this next year will be even better." He lifted his glass. "Cheers, muthafuckas!"

Laughing, the crowd echoed his cheers and then applauded.

Minutes later, Zeke descended the stairs to join his guests out on the back lawn. Sometime later, he sauntered behind Madam Nevaeh and slid his arm around her waist. "Why the long face, Tanya? Aren't you having a good time?"

She rolled her eyes, but kept her plastic smile firmly in place.

He chuckled. "C'mon. It's my birthday. You're supposed to be nice to me."

His reasoning failed to move her.

"So it doesn't matter to you that after tonight I'll be one step closer to making all *our* dreams come true? C'mon. Smile. Who wants to be a king without a queen?"

Smirking, Madam Nevaeh turned around in his arms and faced him. "You're always promising me the world."

"Don't forget the moon and stars," he added.

Her smile strained. "And yet you can't manage to find and kill one measly stripper?"

"Here we go again." Zeke sighed. Nevaeh had finally burst his sunny bubble. How many times do I have to tell you that the *situation* is being handled?"

"Handled how?" she snapped. "You don't even know where that *situation* is right now. She may be in a federal interrogation room right now running her fucking mouth about our whole operation."

"Don't be ridiculous," he chided. "Abrianna Parker is nothing but a junkie street rat with no credibility. She can't prove anything because she doesn't *know* anything. And there's nothing concrete linking her to us, not even a money trail. We've never paid her a dime. She was just a woman who crashed a masquerade party and ended up killing a guest. I have eyes and ears everywhere. If and when she pops up, I'll cut her fucking head off."

"You're wrong," she said. "You forgot about her *friend* who came out to the house with her that day. Shawn."

"He's not a problem."

"For you! He's still alive *and* making threats," she said, heated.

Zeke jerked her closer. "Lower your goddamn voice."

"Let me go." She wrestled but failed to get away.

"If the kid had anything, he would have made a move already. But I'll take care of him, too. Now chill the fuck out, you're fucking up my vibe. We're supposed to be having a good time."

"How about you just have a good time without me?" Nevaeh wrenched herself free. "And don't you ever manhandle me like that again. I'm not your property. We're partners. *Business* partners. Remember that."

"Oh? Only business partners now, huh? It's that serious?"

"Damn right. At least until you learn not to break promises." She marched off.

Zeke watched her go, shaking his head. "If I didn't love that old broad . . ."

⸺◆⸺

After eavesdropping on the lover's spat, Kadir stepped to Zeke. "Care for an hors d'oeuvre, sir?"

"Huh?" Zeke pulled his gaze away from Madam Nevaeh's firm backside. "What? Oh." He looked at the offered tray. "What is it?"

"Snapper Crudo with Chiles and Sesame," Kadir said.

Zeke pulled a face, but then selected one. "Sure. Why the hell not? Thanks."

Kadir smiled.

"Hmm. Not bad." Zeke munched, nodding his head.

"I'm glad you enjoyed it," Kadir responded. "And happy birthday, sir."

Zeke finally looked straight into Kadir's face and returned his smile. "Thanks."

⸺◆⸺

Abrianna and Draya fell in step behind Madam as she stormed away from Zeke. Madam Nevaeh bypassed the crowded downstairs bathroom and instead went to one on the second floor.

However, when she attempted to close the bathroom door behind her, Abrianna and Draya shoved their way inside.

"What in the . . . who are you?!" Nevaeh reeled back. "What are you doing here?"

Abrianna closed the door. "Let's skip the games. Why the hell did you set me up?"

"What?" Nevaeh took another step back. "I don't even know who—Abrianna?"

Abrianna whipped out the gun she'd tucked behind her back and aimed it at Nevaeh. "Lower your voice," Abrianna hissed, moving forward.

Draya fumbled, removing something from her pocket.

"I know it was you behind setting me up. You or your boyfriend, Zeke, out there. Which is it?"

Nevaeh took another step back. "You're talking crazy."

Abrianna inched closer. "That was the real price for those eight stacks, wasn't it? I was to take the rap for killing that politician."

"You're crazy—just like your friend Shawn. I told him that I had nothing to with whatever happened at that hotel."

"Is that why Zeke's goon gunned Shawn down and tried to take my head off?"

She hesitated. "That was to make sure you didn't talk to the police. I didn't want your murdering Reynolds linked back to me."

"Where is she? Where is Kitty?" Abrianna persisted. "I know she was one of your girls."

Nevaeh shook her head. "I swear. I—I don't know who you're talking about. I already told your friend Shawn, I didn't send anyone else to that hotel. Nor would I. It was your first date—with a very important man, may I add. Isn't it more likely that your little drug habit I've heard so much about had something to do with what went on that night?"

"No," Abrianna barked.

"No?" Nevaeh laughed. "Please. Look at you. You're high now. You're not sure what you did that night yourself."

※ ⋯ ※

Wreathed by smiling friends, Zeke looked up to see his new partner, Blade Carlos, approach and offer him one of his trademark cigars.

"Don't mind if I do." He graciously accepted one and took a long whiff of the hand rolled treasure. "Ahh. Divine."

Carlos chuckled and handed Zeke his double guillotine cutter. "Trust. There's more where that came from, partner."

Zeke accepted the cutter and snipped off the tip. "So everything is cool?"

"I'm waiting on word from my men now. They'll call as soon as they finish loading up."

"Good. Good." Before he could ask for a light, one appeared from his right. He turned toward a familiar face.

"Well I'll be damned. If it isn't the old pain-in-ass Lieutenant Castillo. My bad. *Ex*-Lieutenant now, isn't it?" He signaled to the people clustered around him and they instantly drifted away.

"Oh. They don't have to leave on my account," she said, looking around.

"What the hell are you doing here?" he asked.

She smiled. "I couldn't miss a big night like this. Have to admit that I'm stunned by how much you've come up."

"I'm not. I always knew that I'd land on top," he boasted. "And I must say, you clean up well." Zeke took and lifted her hand so she could pirouette under the arch of his arm. "Nice. Now what brings you here, Gizella?"

She blinked, momentarily taken aback by the use of her first name.

He continued, "I assume that you've crashed my party because you wanted *something*?"

"Maybe I was just in the neighborhood and wanted to see how the other half lives?"

Smiling, he shook his head. "You really shouldn't bullshit a bullshitter. Besides, I already heard about you popping up all over the town, sticking your nose in places where it doesn't belong—just like the good old days."

"Humph. I must be losing my touch. I thought I was being inconspicuous."

"Kind of like a freight train?"

Castillo laughed. "Well. My apologies. I am a little rusty." She looked around. "So whatever happened to your old homeboys?"

"Come again?"

"You know . . ." She looked up, deep in thought. "What were their names? Ah, yes. Gunner and Roach. Where are they? I remember a time when they were practically your shadows."

"Yeah, well." He cast his gaze down. "Unfortunately, they were in a horrible car accident recently. It's been quite an adjustment around here without them."

"Oooh, that's right. I did hear about that."

"Oh?"

"I still have friends down at the station. They had a hell of a time identifying their bodies down at the morgue. A head-on collision is an ugly affair—but with a semi-truck? *Sheesh.* I can only imagine."

Zeke's smile faltered. "Yes. Well. They will be missed."

"Well, of course," Castillo sympathized. "You look like you're *really* taking it hard."

He cocked his head. "What exactly are you insinuating?"

"Insinuating? Oh. Goodness, no. I wouldn't dare."

"You would very much dare," he said, no longer enjoying their game. "Now as much as I would like to continue this conversation, I do have other guests that I need to attend to."

"Yes, of course. I certainly don't want to hold you."

"Not a problem." He turned.

"It's just that . . ."

He stopped, sighed, and then faced her again. "It's just that what?"

"It's just that, you know, there was a video that went viral recently. It was one that captured your . . . shadows engaged in a wild shootout through the seventh district. It appears that they were really determined to take out a woman named Abrianna Parker. Do you know her?"

"No. Should I?" he lied smoothly.

"Well, I have it on good authority that she worked for your girlfriend Tanya Ellison's escort service. I think that's what they're called nowadays."

He laughed. "Your *authority* should check their facts."

"Really? About which part?"

"Ms. Ellison works as a charity event organizer and a highly respected one at that."

"Charity event organizer?" Castillo chuckled. "Man. You give some people a thesaurus . . . But I *will* recheck with my sources. Because they also told me that they'd matched their guns to the shitload of casings outside of Ms. Parker's apartment."

"Huh. That *is* strange. But I don't keep tabs on what my employees or *shadows* do on their days off. Frankly, I was shocked when I saw the video myself."

Castillo's gaze narrowed. "Yeah. I'm sure it was very disappointing."

"Wait. You don't think that *I* had anything to do with it?" he said amused.

"Not at all. Not with you being such a good, upstanding citizen. Not to mention you having such powerful friends—like the people here tonight." She turned and glanced around. "Let's see. There're lobbyists, politicians, defense contractors—and, if I'm not mistaken, a few retired generals."

"You're not mistaken. I collect friends from all walks of life. You never know whose back needs scratched or who can scratch yours. Too bad we never became friends. Who knows, I might have been about to do something to keep you from getting kicked off the force."

"The Teflon Don at work, eh?"

They exchanged plastic smiles.

Zeke broke the silence. "Well. As much as I've enjoyed the conversation . . ."

"You're dirty and I'm going to take you down," she warned.

———◦•◦———

Kadir made the secret knock on the bathroom door.

Madam Nevaeh saw her opportunity and drew a quick breath to scream.

Draya pounced, shoving a chloroformed cloth over the Madam's nose and mouth until she collapsed into her arms.

"Hey!" Abrianna pouted. "I could've handled it."

"Let me guess. You were about to put her through a wall."

Pouty, she shrugged. "Maybe."

"Clear," she called back.

Kadir and Julian rushed inside with a large insulated nylon bag with the Plume's logo printed across it. In less than a minute, they folded Madam Nevaeh into the bag and zipped it up.

"Shouldn't we like . . . I don't know, poke a hole in the bag or something? What if she suffocates?" Draya asked.

Julian reached into his back pocket, removed a jack knife and then slashed into the bag. "Happy?"

Draya shrugged. "Another dead body is the last thing we need."

"Let's go," Kadir said, impatient.

The women grabbed the top part of the bag and the men took the bottom. Together they exited the bathroom just as a bejeweled guest was poised to knock.

"Oh! Excuse me," the woman said, frowning at the large bag and then glancing into the bathroom. But before she could ask them any questions, they were gone.

The four servers crossed through the house with only a few odd looks from the partying guests. In the kitchen, Tivonte's real employees whirled around like human tornadoes, cooking, plating, and rushing food out to the guests.

Tivonte looked up only long enough to give his friends the thumbs up.

———※※———

Zeke continued to be amused by former Lieutenant Castillo. "I'm dirty, huh? Do tell."

Castillo crossed her arms and met his gaze head-on. "You're a drug kingpin who thinks he's smarter than everyone else."

"Guilty. I do think I'm pretty smart."

"I hate men like you," she said, her smile fading. "Preying on society, doling out death to children. How the hell do you sleep at night?"

"Whoa." He stepped back. "You really know how to bring down a party. I've been nothing but polite in letting you stay at my party when everyone knows I abhor party-crashers." Zeke looked up and signaled to one of his men. "You wanna know what I think?"

"I'm dying to know."

"I think that you're still sore that you and that old boyfriend of yours, Captain Holder, have never been able to pin anything on me. Am I right?"

Castillo thought it over. "There might be a *little* truth to that."

"Humph. It's good that you can admit it." Zeke puffed out his chest.

"But you know what they say: persistence pays off." Her smile bloomed again. "We always knew that one day you'd fuck up."

"What are you talking about?"

Blade Carlos reappeared at his side and flashed his badge in Zeke's face. "Zeke Jeffreys, you're under arrest for drug trafficking."

"What?"

"Police! Everybody down!" A brigade of law enforcement in riot gear stormed onto the beautiful back lawn, shocking and alarming the guests.

"What the fuck?" Zeke howled.

Officer Steven O'Day, a.k.a. Blade Carlos snatched Zeke's arms behind his back and slapped handcuffs on him. "You have the right to remain silent. Anything that you say . . ."

Castillo's smile beamed. "Like I was saying, I couldn't miss this night for the world."

"You fucking bitch."

"Yeah, I get that a lot."

———※———

"Hurry. Load her up," Draya ordered, opening the back doors of the caterer's van.

"We are going as fast as we can." Abrianna banged Madam's head on one of the doors.

"Easy," Kadir whispered.

Annoyed, she banged it again.

He frowned.

Abrianna shrugged. "I'm petty."

"Are you two for real?" Draya hissed.

Abrianna climbed up, still holding the front of Madam's body.

"Hey!" a voice barked.

Everyone froze.

"What are you guys doing over there?"

Abrianna, out of view, mouthed to Kadir, "Who is it?"

"Hey, I asked you guys a question."

"Security," Kadir mouthed back.

Horrified, Abrianna glanced around for a weapon.

Draya spun around. "Nothing. We're just . . . grabbing some supplies for the kitchen."

A large lineman-shaped security guy waddled closer to the open van door.

Draya partially closed one of the back doors in a vain attempt to block his line of vision.

"But what the hell is that?" He gestured to the bag and leaned forward.

Panicked, Draya rammed the door into the nosy security guard's face, shocking him. However, she hadn't seen the gun until it went off.

BANG!

Abrianna dropped Madam Nevaeh and screamed, "No!"

Instantly, the four-hundred-plus pound man flew backward and slammed against the back of the house and then dropped like a stone.

Abrianna raced to her friend. "Draya, are you all right?" She gathered her friend into her arms. "Speak to me. Say something."

Draya lifted her shocked gaze to Abrianna. "How the fuck did you do that?"

Julian croaked, "Somebody tell me that I didn't see what I just saw."

Abrianna felt the weight of everyone's eyes on her, especially Kadir's. "I, uh, uh—"

"It came from over there," a man shouted.

"Fuck. We gotta go," Kadir said, leaning down and picking up Draya. "Get in the van," he ordered.

Everyone hauled ass.

Julian climbed behind the wheel as Kadir placed Draya in the back of the van along with Abrianna and Madam Nevaeh.

For a brief moment, Kadir's questioning gaze met Abrianna's, but then he quickly slammed the doors shut—and raced to climb into the passenger seat beside Julian. "Let's go!"

———✦———

"What is it, Dr. Z?" Ned asked his mentor as he turned around, with his hands still high in the air as police swarmed around them.

"Nothing . . . I thought I felt . . ." He shook his head. "No. It couldn't have been Abrianna."

———✦———

The van peeled off as a group of security goons rounded the corner and found their unconscious friend.

Rat-at-tat-tat-tat

Bullets punctured the back of the van, a few of them ricocheted, forcing them to duck or dive for cover.

"What the hell?" Julian shouted, bringing everyone's attention to the line of police cars streaming on to the estate.

"Holy shit," Kadir said, incredulous.

Julian's foot came off the accelerator.

"Don't stop," Kadir shouted.

Julian hesitated, but then slammed his foot back down on the gas.

At the tail end, two police cars swerved and blocked the van's fleeing exit.

"Don't you fucking stop," Kadir ordered again.

Julian tightened his grip on the steering wheel. As they blazed closer, and made it clear that the van wasn't going to stop, the cops scrambled to get out of the way.

But it was too late.

"Hold on!" Julian cried, closing his eyes at sudden impact.

BAM!

Everyone and everything slammed forward.

The two police cars spun like pinwheels in the van's wake.

Draya groaned.

"You guys okay back there?" Kadir asked.

Abrianna, sprawled beneath pans and supplies, pushed herself back up and crawled over to Draya.

Draya rolled onto her back. "What the hell, Jules? Are you trying to kill me?"

"She's fine," Julian said. "If Draya is bitching then she's okay."

"Are they following us?" Abrianna asked.

The guys checked their mirrors. "Not that I can tell," Julian said, relieved.

"Yeah. Well. We better get off this road just in case."

"How is our other passenger?" Kadir asked.

Abrianna turned and moved over to the insulated nylon bag and stopped short. "Uh, guys . . ."

"What?" Everyone asked in sync.

'There's blood," Abrianna announced.

"She was hit?" Kadir asked, coming out of his seat to climb into the back.

Abrianna pulled the bag's zipper down carefully and opened the bag. "Damn."

Blood bloomed across the middle of Madam's white dress, but Abrianna was sure that it was the bullet lodged in the center of Madam's forehead that had killed the woman.

Draya shook her head. "Well, I guess she won't be telling us shit."

52

The Bunker . . .

"Well, if it ain't Bonnie and Clyde," Ghost said, blocking the entrance to his bunker. "Or should I say Clyde and Clyde?" He cocked his head at Abrianna. "Nice disguise."

"Thanks."

Ghost's gaze darted to Julian and Draya. "Damn, if every time I see you, man, your ass don't multiply. What kind of place do you think I'm running here?"

"Really? You're going to do this now? I have an injured woman here. She's been shot."

Ghost straightened. "What? Again?" He glanced at Abrianna.

"Not me this time."

Draya raised her good arm. "It's me."

Ghost's eyes lit with interest. "Well, hello."

Draya frowned.

"You're hitting on an injured woman?" Kadir asked.

"Hell. Is it my fault that women are always getting shot around you?" Ghost stepped back and allowed the small group to come inside.

Hunkered down behind their usual terminals were Ghost's crew. He took a moment to introduce them to Draya.

"Uh, nice to meet you," she said and then looked to Abrianna like *Who is this clown?*

"C'mon," Abrianna said, leading her friend toward the back cot room. "I'll fix you up."

Ghost smiled as he watched them walk away.

Arms crossed, Julian stepped forward to block Ghost's view.

"Oh. My bad." Ghost looked to Kadir. "Just how many people are you planning to tell about this place?"

"Chill. They're cool," Kadir said. "So what happened to you the other night? I thought you'd still be waiting to post bond."

"C'mon, playa. Am I the sort of person to give the cops my real ID?"

"They were putting you in the back of a squad car."

"Just some rookie busting my chops. You know how they do. Of course, I hope you got rid of the van. I had to report it stolen."

"Yeah. We traded that one in for another one and then quickly filled it with bullet holes."

"You know that straight and narrow path you swore you were on isn't looking too damn straight, if you ask me."

"You don't know the half." Kadir looked around and leaned in close so that Ghost's crew wouldn't hear. "What do you know about telekinesis?"

"What?"

"You know . . ." Kadir shrugged. "The ability to move shit with your mind. Have you ever known anyone who can—"

"KADIR!"

Abrianna's shout had the effect of a starter pistol. Kadir and Ghost took off toward the back.

In the cot room, Draya and Abrianna stood in front of the nine-inch TV.

When the guys couldn't see what the immediate emergency was, Kadir asked, "Is everything okay?"

Abrianna shook her head and then pointed to the news broadcast.

Katherine J. Sanders will be sworn in tomorrow as the 18th chief justice of the United States, enabling President Walker to put his stamp on the Supreme Court for decades to come, even as he prepares to name a second nominee to the nine-member court.

Judge Sanders' nomination had been slow walked while the Republican Senate members waited to see whether the new speaker was going to pursue impeachment of the president. But with speaker Reynolds' death, apparently the Senate Majority leader decided to move ahead with the confirmation.

Abrianna stared transfixed at the woman in the corner of the scene. "That's her."

"That's who?" Kadir asked.

She pointed. "That's the other girl from the hotel. That's Kitty!"

"Judge Katherine Sanders?" he thundered. "She's the one you think framed you for the speaker's murder?"

"Yes! I'd know that face anywhere. It's her."

"But why?" Kadir asked, puzzled.

"Didn't you just hear the reporter," Draya asked. "That speaker guy was going to impeach the president. An impeachment meant no confirmation. No Supreme Court."

Ghost slapped a hand across his forehead and whistled. "Holy shit. The same judge that sent you to the clink," he said. "The *new* chief justice of the Supreme Court. Good luck taking her down."

DON'T MISS

THE SCORE by Kiki Swinson

Kiki Swinson, the bestselling author known for "fast, tension-packed" (Library Journal) novels featuring the glamour and grit of Virginia's most notorious streets, shows what happens when a criminal partnership takes a detour that puts its members on the road to jealousy, revenge, and murder . . .

GOING ONCE . . . Identity theft mastermind Lauren Kelly has always had a taste for the finer things. With her lover and accomplice, Matt Connors, by her side, there's nothing she can't buy or steal. But she's not the only one . . .

GOING TWICE . . . When their partner, Yancy, stumbles onto a tycoon's multimillion-dollar bank account, Lauren expects the latest scam will go smoothly—until she discovers Matt and Yancy are planning the ultimate betrayal . . .

SOMEONE'S GOING TO DIE . . . Fortunately, Lauren is one step ahead of Matt. Once she disappears with every last dollar, they'll have no doubt they chose the wrong woman to deceive. But all three of them chose the wrong target . . .

HOT FLASH by Carrie H. Johnson

In this thrilling debut novel from Carrie H. Johnson, one woman with a dangerous job and a volatile past is feeling the heat from all sides . . .

READY, AIM . . . She sweats every detail as a forensic firearms specialist—and as a forty-something single mother. She's got more responsibilities than she can count, more baggage than she wants to claim, and way too many regrets. But Muriel Mabley will do whatever it takes to put Philadelphia's most vicious killer in lockdown for good . . .

BURN . . . Until her troubled younger sister in witness protection receives a terrifying warning—and Muriel's long-time partner, Laughton, reveals he knows more than he should about her and Muriel's shattered past. And when Laughton's ex-wife and her new husband turn up dead, his own secrets will send Muriel down a twisted trail of lethal leads, disappeared witnesses, and the ultimate wrenching betrayal . . .

Available wherever books are sold.

Enjoy the following excerpt from HOT FLASH . . .

Chapter 1

Our bodies arched, both of us reaching for that place of ultimate release we knew was coming. Yes! We screamed at the same time . . . except I kept screaming long after his moment had passed.

You've got to be kidding me, a cramp in my groin? The second time in the three times we had made love. Achieving pretzel positions these days came at a price, but man, how sweet the reward.

"What's the matter, baby? You cramping again?" he asked, looking down at me with genuine concern.

I was pissed, embarrassed, and in pain all at the same time. "Yeah," I answered meekly, grimacing.

"It's okay. It's okay, sugar," he said, sliding off me. He reached out and pulled me into the curvature of his body, leaving the wet spot to its own demise. I settled in. Gently, he massaged my thigh. His hands soothed me. Little by little, the cramp went away. Just as I dozed off, my cell phone rang.

"*Mph, mph, mph,*" I muttered. "Never a moment's peace."

Calvin stirred. "Huh?"

"Nothin', baby, shhhh," I whispered, easing from his grasp and reaching for the phone from the bedside table. As quietly as I could, I answered the phone the same way I always did.

"Muriel Mabley."

"Did I get you at a bad time, partner?" Laughton chuckled. He used the same line whenever he called. He never thought twice about waking me, no matter the hour. I worked to live and lived to work—at least that's been my story for twenty years, the last seventeen as a firearms forensics expert for the Philadelphia Police Department. I had the dubious distinction of being the first woman in the unit and one of two minorities. The other was my partner, Laughton McNair.

At forty-nine, I was beginning to think I was blocking the blessing God intended for me. I felt like I had blown past any hope of a true love in pursuit of a damn suspect.

"You there?" Laughton said, laughing louder.

"Hee hee, hell. I finally find someone and you runnin' my ass ragged, like you don't *even* want it to last. What now?" I said.

"Speak up. I can hardly hear you."

"I said . . ."

"I heard you." More chuckles from Laughton. "You might want to rethink a relationship. Word is we've got another dead wife and again the husband swears he didn't do it. Says she offed herself. That makes three dead wives in three weeks. Hell, must be the season or something in the water."

Not wanting to move much or turn the light on, I let my fingers search blindly through my bag on the nightstand until they landed on paper and a pen. Pulling my hand out of my bag with paper and pen was another story. I knocked over the half-filled champagne glass also on the nightstand. "Damn it!" I was like a freaking circus act, trying to save the paper, keep the bubbly from getting on the bed, stop the glass from breaking, and keep from dropping the phone.

"Sounds like you're fighting a war over there," Laughton said.

"Just give me the address."

"If you can't get away . . ."

"Laughton, just . . ."

"You don't have to yell."

He let a moment of silence pass before he said, "Thirteen ninety-one Berkhoff. I'll meet you there."

"I'm coming," I said and clicked off.

"You okay?" Calvin reached out to recapture me. I let him and fell back into the warmth of his embrace. Then I caught myself, sat up, and clicked the light on—but not without a sigh of protest.

Calvin rose. He rested his head in his palm and flashed that gorgeous smile at me. "Can't blame a guy for trying," he said.

"It's a pity I can't do you any more lovin' right now. I can't sugarcoat it. This is my life," I complained on my way to the bathroom.

"So you keep telling me."

I felt uptight about leaving Calvin in the house alone. My son, Travis, would be home from college in the morning, his first spring break from Lincoln University. He and Calvin had not met. In all the years before this night, I had not brought a man home, except Laughton, and at least a decade had passed since I'd had any form of a romantic relationship. The memory chip filled with that information had almost disintegrated. Then along came Calvin.

When I came out, Calvin was up and dressed. He was five foot ten, two hundred pounds of muscle, the kind of muscle that flexed at his slightest move. Pure lovely. He pulled me close and pressed his wet lips to mine. His breath, mixed with a hint of citrus from his cologne, made every nerve in my body pulsate.

"Next time we'll do my place. You can sing to me while I make you dinner," he whispered. "Soft, slow melodies." He crooned, "You Must Be a Special Lady," as he rocked me back and forth, slow and steady. His gooey caramel voice touched my every nerve ending, head to toe. Calvin is a singer and owns a nightclub, which is how we met. I was at his club with friends and Calvin and I—or rather, Calvin and my alter ego, spurred on by my friends, of course—entertained the crowd with duets all night.

He held me snugly against his chest and buried his face in the hollow of my neck while brushing his fingertips down the length of my body.

"Mmm . . . sounds luscious," was all I could muster.

The interstate was deserted, unusual no matter what time, day or night.

In the darkness, I could easily picture Calvin's face, bright with a satisfied smile. I could still feel his hot breath on my neck, the soft strumming of his fingers on my back. I had it bad. Butterflies reached down to my navel and made me shiver. I felt like I was nineteen again, first love or some such foolishness.

Flashing lights from an oncoming police car brought my thoughts around to what was ahead, a possible suicide. How anyone could think life was so bad that they would kill themselves never settled with me. Life's stuff enters pit territory sometimes, but then tomorrow comes and anything is possible again. Of course, the idea that the husband could be the killer could take one even deeper into pit territory. The man you once loved, who made you scream during lovemaking, now not only wants you gone, moved out, but dead.

When I rounded the corner to Berkhoff Street, the scene was chaotic, like the trappings of a major crime. I pulled curbside and rolled to a stop behind a news truck. After I turned off Bertha, my 2000 Saab gray convertible, she rattled in protest for a few moments before going quiet. As I got out, local news anchor Sheridan Meriwether hustled from the front of the news truck and shoved a microphone in my face before I could shut the car door.

"Back off, Sheridan. You'll know when we know," I told her.

"True, it's a suicide?" Sheridan persisted.

"If you know that, then why the attack? You know we don't give out information in suicides."

"Confirmation. Especially since two other wives have been killed in the past few weeks."

"Won't be for a while. Not tonight anyway."

"Thanks, Muriel." She nodded toward Bertha. "Time you gave the old gray lady a permanent rest, don't you think?"

"Hey, she's dependable."

She chuckled her way back to the front of the news truck. Sheridan was the only newsperson I would give the time of day. We went back two decades, to rookie days when my mom and dad were killed in a car crash. Sheridan and several other newspeople had accompanied the police to inform me. She returned the next day, too, after the buzz had faded. A drunk driver sped through a red light and rammed my parents' car head-on. That was the story the police told the papers. The driver of the other car cooked to a crisp when his car exploded after hitting my parents' car, then a brick wall. My parents were on their way home from an Earth, Wind & Fire concert at the Tower Theater.

Sheridan produced a series on drunk drivers in Philadelphia, how their indiscretions affected families and children on both sides of the equation, which led to a national broadcast. Philadelphia police cracked down on drunk drivers and legislation passed with compulsory loss of licenses. Several other cities and states followed suit.

I showed my badge to the young cop guarding the front door and entered the small foyer. In front of me was a white-carpeted staircase. To the left was the living room. Laughton, his expression stonier than I expected, stood next to the detective questioning who I supposed was the husband. He sat on the couch, leaned forward with his elbows resting on his thighs, his head hanging down. Two girls clad in *Frozen* pajamas huddled next to him on the couch, one on either side.

The detective glanced at me, then back at the man. "Where were you?"

"I just got here, man," the man said. "Went upstairs and found her on the floor."

"And the kids?"

"My daughter spent the night with me. She had a sleepover at my house. This is Jeanne, lives a few blocks over. She got homesick and wouldn't stop crying, so I was bringing them back here. Marcy and I separated, but we're trying to work things out." He choked up, unable to speak any more.

"At three a.m."

"I told you, the child was having a fit. Wanted her mother."

A tank of a woman charged through the front door, "Oh my God. Baby, are you all right?" She pushed past the police officer there and clomped across the room, sending those close to look for cover. The red-striped flannel robe she wore and pink furry slippers, size thirteen at least, made her look like a giant candy cane with feet.

"Wade, what the hell is happenin' here?" She moved in and lifted the girl from the sofa by her arm. Without giving him a chance to answer, she continued, "C'mon, baby. You're coming with me."

An officer stepped sideways and blocked the way. "Ma'am, you can't take her—"

The woman's head snapped around like the devil possessed her, ready to spit out nasty words followed by green fluids. She never stopped stepping.

I expect she would have trampled the officer, but Laughton interceded. "It's all right, Jackson. Let her go," he said.

Jackson sidestepped out of the woman's way before Laughton's words settled.

Laughton nodded his head in my direction. "Body's upstairs."

The house was spotless. White was *the* color: white furniture, white walls, white drapes, white wall-to-wall carpet, white picture frames. The only real color came in the mass of throw pillows that adorned the couch and a wash of plants positioned around the room.

I went upstairs and headed to the right of the landing, into a bedroom where an officer I knew, Mark Hutchinson, was photographing the scene. Body funk permeated the air. I wrinkled my nose.

"Hey, M&M," Hutchinson said.

"That's Muriel to you." I hated when my colleagues took the liberty to call me that. Sometimes I wanted to nail Laughton with a front kick to the groin for starting the nickname.

He shook his head. "Ain't me or the victim. She smells like a violet." He tilted his head back, sniffed, and smiled.

Hutchinson waved his hand in another direction. "I'm about done here."

I stopped at the threshold of the bathroom and perused the scene. Marcy Taylor lay on the bathroom floor. A small hole in her temple still oozed blood. Her right arm was extended over her head, and she had a .22 pistol in that hand. Her fingernails and toenails looked freshly painted. When I bent over her body, the sulfur-like smell of hair relaxer backed me up a bit. Her hair was bone-straight. The white silk gown she wore flowed around her body as though staged. Her cocoa brown complexion looked ashen with a pasty, white film.

"Shame," Laughton said to my back. "She was a beautiful woman." I jerked around to see him standing in the doorway.

"Check this out," I said, pointing to the lay of the nightgown over the floor.

"I already did the scene. We'll talk later," he said.

"Damn it, Laughton. Come here and check this out." But when I turned my head, he was gone.

I finished checking out the scene and went outside for some fresh air. Laughton was on the front lawn talking to an officer. He beelined for his car when he saw me.

"What the hell is wrong with you?" I muttered, jogging to catch up with him. Louder. "Laughton, what the hell—"

He dropped anchor. Caught off guard, I plowed into him. He waited until I peeled myself off him and regained my footing, then said, "Nothing. Wade says they separated a few months ago and were trying to get it together, so he came over for some making up. He used his key to enter and found her dead on the bathroom floor."

"No, he said he was bringing the little girl home because she was homesick."

"Yeah, well, then you heard it all."

He about-faced.

I grabbed his arm and attempted to spin him around. "You act like you know this one or something," I practically screeched at him.

"I do."

I cringed and softened my tone five octaves at least when I managed to speak again. "How?"

"I was married to her . . . a long time ago."

He might as well have backhanded me upside the head. "You never—"

"I have an errand to run. I'll see you back at the lab."

I stared after him long after he got in his car and sped off.

The sun was rising by the time the scene was secured: body and evidence bagged, husband and daughter gone back home. It spewed warm tropical hues over the city. By the time I reached the station, the hues had turned cold metallic gray. I pulled into a parking spot and answered the persistent ring of my cell phone. It was Nareece.

"Hey, sis. My babies got you up this early?" I said, feigning a light mood. My babies were Nareece's eight-year-old twin daughters.

Nareece groaned. "No. Everyone's still sleeping."

"You should be, too."

"Couldn't sleep."

"Oh, so you figured you'd wake me up at this ungodly hour in the morning. Sure, why not? We're talkin' sisterly love here, right?" I said. We chuckled. "I've been up since three anyway, working a case." I waited for her to say something, but she stayed silent. "Reece?" More silence. "C'mon, Reecey, we've been through this so many times. Please don't tell me you're trippin' again."

"A bell goes off in my head every time this date rolls around. I believe I'll die with it going off," Nareece confessed.

"Therapy isn't helping?"

"You mean the shrink? She ain't worth the paper she prints her bills on. I get more from talking to you every day. It's all you, Muriel. What would I do without you?"

"I'd say we've helped each other through, Reecey."

Silence filled the space again. Meanwhile, Laughton pulled his Audi Quattro in next to my Bertha and got out. I knocked on the window to get his attention. He glanced in my direction and moved on with his gangster swagger as though he didn't see me.

"I have to go to work, Reece. I just pulled into the parking lot after being at a scene."

"Okay."

"Reece, you've got a great husband, two beautiful daughters, and a gorgeous home, baby. Concentrate on all that and quit lookin' behind you."

Nareece and John had ten years of marriage. John is Vietnamese. The twins were striking, inheritors of almond-shaped eyes, "good" curly black hair, and amber skin. Rose and Helen, named after our mother and grandmother. John balked at their names because they did not reflect his heritage. But he was mush where Nareece was concerned.

"You're right. I'm good except for two days out of the year, today and on Travis's birthday. And you're probably tired of hearing me."

"I'll listen as long as you need me to. It's you and me, Reecey. Always has been, always will be. I'll call you back later today. I promise."

I clicked off and stayed put for a few minutes, bogged down by the realization of Reece's growing obsession with my son, way more than in past years, which conjured up ugly scenes for me. I prayed for a quick passing, though a hint of guilt pierced my gut. Did I pray for her sake, my sake, or Travis's? What scared me anyway?

Connect with Us

Visit us online at
KensingtonBooks.com
to read more from your favorite authors, see books
by series, view reading group guides, and more.

Join us on social media

for sneak peeks, chances to win books and prize packs,
and to share your thoughts with other readers.

facebook.com/kensingtonpublishing
twitter.com/kensingtonbooks

Tell us what you think!

To share your thoughts, submit a review,
or sign up for our eNewsletters, please visit:
KensingtonBooks.com/TellUs.